LAKE of GLASS

LAKE of GLASS

ARCHIVES OF THE WARDEN

Book One

V. K. DIXON

xenia house press

To my mother.
Thank you for listening to all my random story ideas
for the past twenty-two years,
and for encouraging me to pursue this dream of mine, no matter what.
You will always be my first and best friend.

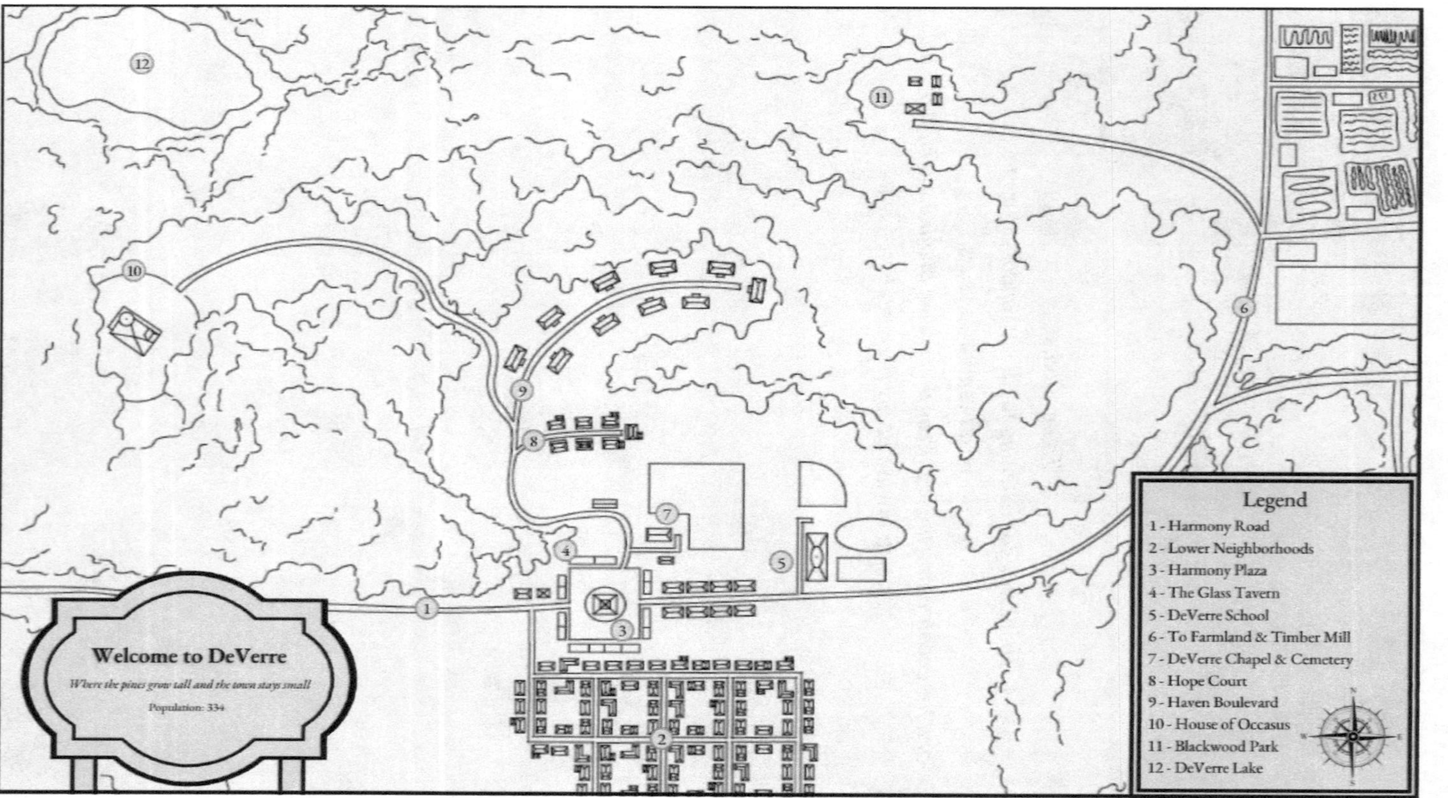

Welcome to DeVerre
Where the pines grow tall and the town stays small
Population: 334
Legend
1 - Harmony Road
2 - Lower Neighborhoods
3 - Harmony Plaza
4 - The Glass Tavern
5 - DeVerre School
6 - To Farmland & Timber Mill
7 - DeVerre Chapel & Cemetery
8 - Hope Court
9 - Haven Boulevard
10 - House of Occasus
11 - Blackwood Park
12 - DeVerre Lake

Table of Contents

CHAPTER ONE

Peter

"We're gonna get ourselves killed."

Peter looked toward his brother sitting in the passenger seat. Spencer's knee bobbed up and down as he fidgeted, arms crossed tightly against his chest.

Reaching over, he gave Spencer's head a shove. "Could you be chill for like five seconds?"

Spencer slapped his hand away, but not before Peter managed to muss some of his shaggy hair. "Watch the road, would you?"

"This is the opportunity of a lifetime, dude!" Peter said, ignoring his brother's scolding tone. "We're gonna be living the dream out here."

Doing his best to flatten his dark hair back into place, Spencer frowned. "So you keep trying to convince me."

"And I wish you'd listen." Peter threw him one last disappointed glance before turning back to the two-lane road. The Jeep's tires skirted around the edge of a pothole. Despite the early morning, the soft yellow sunlight was already getting choked out of view by the encroaching gray clouds overhead.

Tiny drops of rain began to freckle the windshield, and Peter flicked on the wipers. "We've waited for this opportunity since we were kids, Spence," he said, attempting to get his brother excited once more. "We're literally gonna get paid to be authors. Full time. No second jobs. No missing out 'cause we're strapped for cash. No asking Mom to spot us until the next payday. This is it!"

"We're not getting paid to be authors, Pete," Spencer corrected. "We're inheriting a crazy lady's property."

"And the freakin' ton of cash that comes with it too!"

"It doesn't feel right."

Peter sighed and tapped his thumb against the cracked leather steering wheel. Though Spencer had kept his reservations to himself the majority of the trip, the fact that he'd decided to speak up now, when they were less than an hour away from their destination, was frustrating. Spencer's long list of objections seemed to be growing, but Peter had hoped they'd left them behind in Norfolk.

"We never even met her," Spencer continued. "Not once. Mom said *she'd* never met her. So why'd she pick us?"

"Look, we all know that Aunt Diane was . . . a bit off. But I talked with Uncle Matt about her before we left, and he said she wasn't that bad. Just kinda weird."

"She moved across the country to write about ghosts."

Peter rolled his eyes. "We've written about weirder stuff than that."

"Yeah, but she wasn't a fiction writer. She actually believed in ghosts."

"So do you."

"No, I don't."

With an amused grunt, Peter smirked at his brother. "Spence, you've been scared of ghosts since you were two."

Spencer pursed his lips as he slumped back into his seat. Out of the corner of his eye, Peter caught the way his brother's eyes narrowed on him. Their eyes were the most notable difference between them, Peter had always thought. Everyone pegged them as brothers the second they saw them. Dark, wavy hair. Thick, arching brows. Annoyingly pale skin. Trim, narrow frames. Matching crooked smiles.

But despite the similar shape of their deep-set eyes, Spencer had gotten lucky with their dad's genetics, while Peter got stuck with the deep, dark brown eyes from their mom's side of the family. It was those bright blue eyes paired with his quiet and reserved personality that had earned Spencer the attention of every girl since the ninth grade. Now, well over a decade later, the story hadn't changed.

Not that Spencer noticed his good luck, Peter reflected with an inward grimace. Even at twenty-six, Spencer was far too preoccupied with his writing—and too terrified of every woman he met—to see the way they looked at him.

"I have a healthy fear of the unknown, okay?" Spencer grumbled.

"You flinch every time the A/C kicks on."

Spencer turned away without response to watch the hundreds of pine trees whiz by as they continued down the road. Out in the middle of nowheresville-Washington state, there wasn't much else to see. Especially since the morning fog and rain clouds blocked their view of the mountains surrounding them.

Peter shook his head, chuckling at his brother's anxieties. "Listen, I get it," he said. "This whole situation *is* weird. I'm not sure why Diane left everything to us, but . . . well, I'm freakin' happy she did. We're gonna get to do everything we've ever wanted. And who cares if she was a crazy old lady?"

"Her house is gonna be haunted," Spencer muttered, massaging the palm of his hand with his knuckles.

Peter rolled his eyes. "I thought you didn't believe in ghosts."

"I don't."

"Then the house can't be haunted."

Spencer shifted in his seat again. "Fine, maybe it won't be haunted. But I'm still convinced that we're gonna get murdered by whoever killed her."

"There is no murderer, Columbo." Peter smirked. "She died of natural causes at *eighty-three years old*. Other than Great-Aunt Winnie, the rest of that generation of the Collins family are gone. Diane's own husband died like five years ago."

"He was weird too."

"Actually, Uncle Matt said he was pretty cool."

"He was obsessed with unexplained history and supernatural events."

"Who can blame him?" Peter shrugged. "I think it's pretty fascinating stuff myself."

Spencer shook his head. "I still don't like it."

Glancing back at his brother, Peter frowned. He couldn't understand Spencer's seeming inability to get excited about what was happening to them. Ever since he'd gotten that phone call from the lawyer informing them of their great-aunt's death and their impending inheritance, Peter couldn't have been more stoked. Their dreams were on their way to coming true. They would finally get the chance to write a bestselling novel together. He and Spencer had dreamed of becoming famous authors since the respective ages of eight and six. They'd worked hard throughout their childhood, teens, and into adulthood, attempting to earn some semblance of success.

Their efforts earned them scholarships to college and a small, but growing, fan base for their online serial blog. Over the past eight years, they'd written almost two hundred episodes about private investigators, Wenzel and Frankly. Set in 1880s New York, the duo solved numerous crimes and fought off fantastic, supernatural monsters in the process. The serial started out as only a post every few weeks, but over time they gained a large enough following that Spencer made sure to put them on a schedule, releasing a new episode every two weeks for their readers.

Despite their loyal followers, the serial failed to provide the income for Peter to quit his job as a bartender or for Spencer to stop working as a freelance copy editor and part-time barista. The demands of the 'real world' didn't even allow them to do what they really wanted: to write an actual, full-length novel that earned them notoriety and success.

But the inheritance left to them by their Great-Aunt Diane meant they wouldn't have to worry about money anymore. They finally had the exact chance they'd been waiting for.

The only obstacle to this flawless plan? Spencer.

Much to his surprise, Peter's little brother fought tooth and nail against leaving their comfortable, if meager, Virginian existence for the unknown small town of DeVerre, Washington. Spencer didn't like how little detail the lawyer had given them. It worried him that they'd never met Diane. And it freaked him out that they had no guarantee that quitting their jobs and moving across the country would bring them the literary acclaim they sought.

But Peter had refused to let Spencer's fears keep either of them from pursuing their dreams. He wouldn't let his brother miss out on something this incredible. Not when it could change their lives forever.

Looking toward his brother again, Peter worked to keep his voice firm, but understanding. "We have to do this, Spence," he said. "Dad would want us to do this."

Peter watched as a flicker of irritation sparked in Spencer's eyes before he turned back to the trees. But instead of arguing, he pressed his lips together and nodded.

That was the trump card with Spencer, and Peter knew it. Bringing up their dad always got his brother to pony up and act like he had at least a semblance of confidence, even if it was just a show.

Peter didn't like playing on Spencer's loyalty to their dad, but sometimes it was the only way to get him to do anything. He was so scared of making the wrong choice that often he failed to make any choice at all. And while Peter couldn't understand his brother's constant overactive imagination and anxiety, he'd determined a long time ago that if his brother needed someone to level him out and distract him from his worries, then he'd take on the job.

But there were times when Spencer's fear got in the way of his happiness. And Peter had discovered that by bringing their dad into it,

Spencer would do anything to honor his memory.

Tightening his grip on the wheel, Peter tamped down his guilt and pushed forward. "It doesn't have to be forever," he promised. "If we get there and hate it, we can sell the house, cash out our inheritance, and move back to Norfolk. Mom and Ben will be more than happy to have us home, and we'll actually be able to afford living there. But for now, we've gotta at least give this a shot. You know that, right?"

"Yeah," Spencer sighed. "I know."

Silence fell between the brothers as it always did after Peter called upon their father's help. The wipers dragged across the windshield with an occasional *scrape* in the thin drizzle of rain. The sound grated against the classic saxophone and bass of the CD that played in the background. The music always reminded them of their dad. And they never changed it out for that exact reason.

This was his car they drove. The dark green Jeep Cherokee Classic was over twenty years old, having way too many miles and far too many problems for them to drive it across the country. Peter had sold his own beater while Aunt Diane's will was still in probate, knowing it wouldn't do them any good so far northwest. But Spencer had refused to get rid of their dad's Jeep. While it needed constant repairs and got terrible gas mileage—making it a drain on his already tenuous income—it would never leave the family.

And though the engine rattled at random intervals and the doors squealed on their hinges, Peter was glad to have it with them.

They'd crammed everything they could into the back of the Jeep. According to the lawyer, Aunt Diane's home was fully furnished, so they wouldn't have much need for anything but personal effects. Which was fine by Peter. They didn't own much to begin with, and what they did have was a blend of hand-me-downs, online market finds, and roadside discoveries. Beyond that, they'd lived in a tiny, seven-hundred-square-foot apartment back in Norfolk. Though each of them had their own bedroom, it had hardly been enough space for more than a narrow bed and dresser.

Peter was more than happy to sell off or give away what little they had and only box up what they treasured too much to leave behind. He was rather proud of how little they'd ended up bringing with them. He could even see out the rearview mirror, brown boxes and tattered suitcases just peeking into the frame. With all the things they'd let go of, the move felt like a true fresh start. And the views of the Pacific Northwest only added to that sensation.

They'd passed through Spokane almost two hours ago, and civilization felt farther and farther away as they continued north. The lush greenery, giant trees, foggy horizons, and distant mountains flew by the Jeep's windows. Peter thought it was a writer's paradise. Beautiful and dreary and a tad spooky. He had no doubt that their inspiration would reach new heights up here in the top eastern corner of Washington.

Suddenly, Spencer sat up in his seat, knee starting to bounce again as he leaned forward and pointed. "Look."

Following his direction, Peter spotted the antique wooden sign and slowed so they could get a good look at it. The dark slats were grimy at the edges from the damp air. The sign had a green frame and lettering that read:

Welcome to DeVerre
Where the pines grow tall and the town stays small.
Population: 334

"Geez," Peter muttered as they passed the sign. "This place is smaller than I thought."

Spencer scratched along his stubbled jaw, peering ahead to the town awaiting them. Although surrounded by the thick forest, the tiny town of DeVerre, Washington, sat within a widened hollow. A long stretch of road led them past the first buildings. The brothers stared, trying to get a sense of the town that they were shortly to call home. On their left sat a squat, dated gas station with only four pumps. It didn't appear to have the typical convenience store attached, but instead a garage with the sign: Durand's Mechanic Shop & Gas.

Next to it stood the most ironic and archetypical diner Peter was sure the world had ever seen. It sported dingy white walls embellished with '50s mint trim and a bright red neon sign that read 'MacDonald's Burgers & Shakes'. He assumed the inside also housed a jukebox, checkered floors, and waitresses in matching, costume-like uniforms.

To the right they caught a glimpse of what looked to be a large neighborhood, but their path lay straight ahead toward the square. As they neared the roundabout, the rain slowed, and the wipers gave a loud *squeak*. Peter flicked them off absentmindedly as he took in the square. A copper sign on the corner of the sidewalk announced that they'd entered Harmony Plaza, the center of DeVerre. It was as small as expected for a town of three hundred. There were six long buildings along the edges of the square and a large, judicial looking one standing in the center. A tall clock tower rose into the gray sky on the government building.

The roundabout forced them to turn left and work their way around the plaza. They both scanned the long, multi-business buildings around the square.

"Which one is it?" Spencer asked.

Peter eyed the numbers above the doors. "400A."

"These are 700s."

"I see that."

"And that's 100A and B."

"Mm-hm," Peter mumbled, checking out the tavern and police station as Spencer pointed to each one.

They had already wound around half of the circular road when Spencer tipped his chin forward. "There it is."

The long building looked like an *L* that had decided to lay on its back and take a nap. On the far left, a two-story business rose above the rest. The numbers on its brick marked it as their destination. Peter pulled up to parallel park next to it, struggling to keep his eyes off the different building occupants. The bottom of the two-storied end was their stop: the joint law firm, realty office, and brokerage of Descoteaux, Durand, and Descoteaux. The top floor was inhabited by Alarie Accounting while the remaining buildings housed the singular businesses of a bookshop, a coffee shop, and the public library. The fact that they had both a bookshop and a library gave him hope that it might thrill the townsfolk to have a couple of authors as their newest residents.

Peter put the car in park and turned the keys as the clouds began to part. A few rays of sunlight filtered down to them through the windshield. "Hey, look at that," he said, giving Spencer's chest a slap before pointing up at the sky. "I'd say that's a good omen, wouldn't you?"

Though Spencer hesitated, he did wind up grinning. "Yeah, seems like it."

"That's the spirit!" Peter grabbed his phone from the middle console and pocketed his wallet. "Let's go inherit a fortune, all right?"

Spencer chuckled, tugging his denim jacket closer as he stepped into the cold, late morning air after Peter. After locking the car, he tossed the keys across to Spencer and headed for 400A. Though the building carried the hallmarks of age, it was clear that the DeVerrean citizens weren't satisfied to let things fall into disrepair. The brick showed mossy growth and chipping mortar, but the doors and windows appeared new with their shiny black metal frames and fresh glass. Vinyl labels on the door announced the businesses within.

The metal handle was cold and wet against his palm as Peter pulled the door open. He and Spencer stepped inside the modern and pleasant looking office space. Peter glanced around to take in the room. The entry was small, about ten by ten, and a narrow white hall led to four closed doors. Houseplants dotted the room, giving it a welcoming atmosphere. Sitting at the front desk, he saw a young woman about their age with curly blonde hair and lots of freckles.

"Oh," she said, startled at the sight of them. A polite smile came to her lips. "Hi, how can I help you?"

"Hey there," Peter stepped forward, taking the lead when Spencer remained behind him. "I'm Peter Collins and this is my brother, Spencer. We're here to meet with Mrs. Descoteaux."

The girl's blue eyes grew wide at their names. "Oh, yeah!" She nodded, adjusting the collar of her floral-print blouse. "Aunt Nicky told me to expect you. I didn't realize you'd be here so early."

Peter shrugged and grinned. "There wasn't much traffic."

She nodded again. "That's nice."

"Yeah, I always like when it works out that way."

The young woman returned his smile, then her eyes flickered over to Spencer. Peter watched as a soft blush tinged her cheeks and she fussed with her blouse again. "Well, I'm afraid my aunt wasn't expecting you quite so soon, so she's finishing up another appointment. If you'd like to take a seat, she'll be right with you."

"Great, thanks." Peter started to turn around as Spencer headed for the row of chairs next to the door but angled back to her instead. He leaned on the tall desk's counter. She looked up instantly from the note she'd started scribbling.

"Yes?"

"Just—I forgot to ask," he said, keeping his smile as friendly as possible. "What's your name?"

"Oh. Uh, it's Jill."

"Jill," he repeated with a nod. "It's nice to meet you, Jill. Thanks for your help."

"Of course," she said, nose wrinkling with a surprised grin. "It's nice to meet you too."

Peter smiled once more before turning to take the seat next to his brother. He began to shrug out of his leather jacket as Spencer leaned over toward him.

"Do you have to do that?" he whispered.

"Do what?"

Spencer's dark eyebrows dipped low. "Who cares what her name is?

We're here for the reading of a will, not for a girlfriend."

"Dude, chill out," Peter muttered, frowning at him. "I'm just being friendly."

"Why?"

"Because we're gonna be living here. We may as well make some friends."

Though he didn't seem convinced, Spencer sat back in his seat.

Peter looked in Jill's direction, doing his best to appear to be scanning the room rather than checking on her. She finished typing on her computer, then picked up her phone. Peter caught her eyes flitting toward them several times while she tapped on the screen. He assumed she was texting someone by the way her thumbs danced over the screen before she locked it and set it aside.

Jill was pretty in an all-American sort of way. Makeup subtle and outfit cute without looking overthought. But Peter hadn't intended to flirt with her. In fact, he hadn't thought he was. Asking someone's name was common courtesy, wasn't it? And they did need to make friends. Writing was a lonely business. If you didn't have some means of social interaction, you were bound to go mad. Something Peter couldn't let happen if he wanted Spencer to stick with this.

Plus, Peter was somewhat worried that there wouldn't be many people their own age within DeVerre. The average population of small towns was at least two decades older than they were. Their generation didn't often care for small living like this. They wanted fame and fortune and thought the only way to achieve that was in the big city. There was a good chance that the majority of natural-born DeVerreans their age had left the rural town. Especially with how small it turned out to be.

A door clicked open in the hall, catching their attention. Peter and Spencer both sat up straight as two people emerged from the office closest to the entryway. A man and woman shook hands and exchanged the last of their pleasantries before he turned, said goodbye to Jill, eyed the boys with a hint of suspicion, and walked out.

The woman followed him as far as the receptionist's desk. Peter could see a hint of family resemblance between Jill and her aunt with their sharp, pert noses and wide smiles. But the older woman's blonde hair draped over her shoulders in a professional wave rather than with the feminine curls her niece wore.

She smoothed the front of her dark gray suit jacket as she stepped forward and held out her hand as the brothers stood. "Good morning," she said. "I'm Nicole, the lawyer in charge of Diane Larkin's estate. You must be the Collins brothers."

"Yes, ma'am," Peter said, taking a step back after shaking her hand. "I'm Peter, and this is Spencer."

"It's nice to finally meet you in person." Her voice was just as chipper as it had been during their previous conversations over the phone. But something about her smile didn't hold the same warmth Peter had anticipated. "If you're ready, we can go to my office, and we'll go over your great-aunt's will."

Peter grabbed his jacket from the chair as Spencer waited to follow behind the two of them.

The lawyer stepped through the oak doorway of her office and gestured to two seats in front of her massive wooden desk. The white of fluorescent lights overhead mingled with yellow from the pair of lamps on her desk. A couple of fake plants and bright paintings cheered up the windowless room.

Nicole shut the door before taking her seat on the other side. "I hope your trip went well," she said, unbuttoning her jacket as she settled behind the desk. She began shuffling through the mountain of papers strewn across the surface. "How long of a drive was it again?"

"About forty hours, all said and done," Peter answered.

"My goodness!" She let out a polite laugh, adjusting a picture out of the way to sort through another messy stack of papers. "You two didn't drive straight through, did you?"

Peter shook his head, grinning at her even though she kept her eyes trained on her task. "Nah, we took turns and stopped at night," he said, then elbowed his brother. "Spence can't sleep in the car."

"Really?" Nicole tossed them both an absentminded smile before pulling a thick file from the middle of the stack. "Ah, here it is."

Peter glanced at his brother as he felt Spencer scoot forward to sit on the edge of his seat, his eyes trained on the will. He clasped his hands between his knees, the right one beginning to bounce again.

"All right," she said, flipping open the file. "This is a fairly simple process. Diane was thorough, and she made sure that her will could pass through probate with no problem. So I'll read the whole of the will to you to make it official. Then all you'll need to do is sign the documents and deeds accepting her property and assets. If you have any questions, feel free to ask, and I'll do my best to clear up any confusion. Do either of you need anything before we begin? Some water? The bathroom?"

Peter waved his dismissal at the offer, and Spencer shook his head.

"Great, we'll get started." Nicole cleared her throat, turned the top page over, and began to read. "Last Will and Testament of Diane Larkin. I, Diane Larkin, with a place of residence at 1567 Whitehill Way, DeVerre, Washington, 99120, being of sound mind and not acting under duress or undue influence while fully understanding the nature and extent of all my property and of this disposition thereof, do hereby make, publish, and declare this document to be my Last Will and Testament, and hereby revoke any and all other wills, codicils heretofore made by me, Hereinafter known as the 'Testor'. . . ."

As she paused to take a breath, Peter rested his elbow on the cushioned arm of the chair and settled his chin in his hand. His chest buzzed with anticipation, making him want to get up and pace around the room. This was it. After weeks of waiting, here they were, about to inherit a fortune.

Nicole was the one who had called him about their aunt's death. Peter had felt a tinge of discomfort being so excited at the news. But how could he feel anything else? Nicole had said the inheritance was large but that she wasn't able to give him any details until the will was through probate. Now, he was metaphorically on the edge of his seat as Spencer was literally on the edge of his.

"One, Family Identification," Nicole continued. "I am not married. I do not have any children. Two, Exclusions. It is my intention to not specifically exclude any individuals from this Last Will and Testament. Three, Expenses and Taxes."

She took a minute to read about the directive on the third topic before pausing to alert them. "Diane had no debts, so I went ahead and calculated the expenses for her funeral, burial, and taxes under the approval of her Personal Representative."

"Who is . . . ?" Spencer prompted.

Nicole waved her hand in a small arc. "That's number eleven," she said, then returned to reading. "Four, Special Bequests. Aside from my Residual Estate, there shall be the following one individual to receive a special bequest. Cassandra Clement is to receive the current draft of and all my notes for *Secrets of the Lake*. I ask that my great-nephews should also take care of my dear friend. I ask that they should treat her as their own blood, as I did."

Peter and Spencer looked at each other, brows pulled together.

"Who's Cassandra Clement?" Peter asked.

Nicole hesitated, prepared to read on. "Uh. . . ." she gaped at them for a second, resting the will back down on her desk. She motioned to the page. "Like your great-aunt said, Ms. Clement was her friend."

"Huh," Peter pursed his lips as Spencer frowned. "And we're supposed to take care of her?"

"It *was* a request."

"Why isn't she here?" Spencer asked, sounding as confused as Peter felt.

Nicole hesitated again. "Ms. Clement is currently out of town. There was a family emergency, and she returned to Spokane to stay with family for a while. As she is not listed as a beneficiary of the estate, I assured her that she didn't need to be present for this part. She can come to claim her bequest once she returns to town."

"So you already have the draft of her book here?"

"Yes, it's in my safe."

"Mm." Spencer nodded for her to go on.

She scanned both of them as if expecting another question before turning back to the page. "Five, Personal Property. I direct that all of my personal property that has not been directed as specific bequests or a part of my residual estate be distributed to Peter, Spencer, and Cassandra in equity. Whatever one doesn't want, the others may choose to take."

Peter chewed on the inside of his cheek. He didn't like how often this Cassandra lady was showing up in the will. And he wasn't a fan of how Diane expected them to treat her like family. They'd not even known their great-aunt. Now they had to take care of her best friend?

"Six, Digital Assets. I shall have all my digital belongings and accounts be left with a Digital Assets Representative. I direct that Cassandra Clement of 2830 E 6th Ave, Spokane, Washington, 99202, Hereinafter known as the "Digital Asset Representative", to have the power and full control over all my Digital Assets listed in Addendum A."

It took several minutes for Nicole to read through the rest of the digital assets bit, marking Diane's friend as in charge of the distribution and care of her computer, tablet, and phone. Peter wasn't sure why she'd leave an old lady to figure out her tech situation, but he figured if Diane were savvy enough to own a tablet at eighty-three, her friend probably had some understanding as well.

"Seven, Residual Estate," Nicole paused to give them each a meaningful smile. "I devise and bequeath my property, both real and personal wherever situated including any life insurance policies I may have to the following Two Beneficiaries: Peter Collins who is my Great-Nephew and entitled 50% of my Residual Estate. Spencer Collins who is my Great-Nephew and entitled 50% of my Residual Estate.

"Eight, Other Property. If there is any other property not part of the

Residual Estate of Personal Property of this Last Will and Testament all other property should be transferred to Peter Collins and Spencer Collins in equity."

Peter couldn't help but grin as Nicole read on. She went over conditions in case of predeceased beneficiaries, omissions from the will, naming the same Cassandra woman as the personal representative, her discretionary powers as the representative, and many other topics that went over his head. It didn't matter to him that he couldn't understand it all or that her words seemed to repeat over and over again. He was waiting to hear the final closing to the will so they could know just what they were to receive from Diane.

"Sixteen," Nicole read, flipping over another page. "Pet Healthcare Directive."

"Pet?" Peter and Spencer both interrupted her simultaneously.

Nicole glanced at them and nodded. "I would like the following two pets described as: Anguis, the German Wirehaired Pointer, and Nex, the German Wirehaired Pointer, hereinafter known as the "Pets", to be placed with Peter Collins of 125 Main St, Apt. 4, Norfolk, Virginia, 23508, Hereinafter known as the 'Pet Guardian', and shall act as the caretaker of the Pets.

"In the event the above-named Pet Guardian is not able to serve I agree to nominate a Second Pet Guardian known as: Spencer Collins of 125 Main St, Apt. 4, Norfolk, Virginia, 23508."

"She had dogs?" Peter asked.

Spencer tilted his head to the side. "That's kind of cool, I guess."

"We didn't sign up for dogs," he argued. "Why didn't she give them to this Cassandra lady?"

Nicole chuckled. "I think she wanted them to stay in their home."

"Yeah, well—" He let out a huff of irritation. "I didn't know that dogs were a part of the deal."

"Do you dislike dogs?"

"No, they're just . . . I mean they're a lot of work. And what the heck kind of names are Anguis and Nex? You're supposed to name dogs Rover and Spot."

That got a real laugh out of Nicole. "Well, in my limited acquaintance with your great-aunt, she wasn't known for doing what one is 'supposed' to do."

Spencer gestured for her to continue while Peter brooded about why she hadn't mentioned the dogs before now.

"Seventeen, Governing Law. This document shall be governed by the laws of the State of Washington. Eighteen, Special Wishes and Directives." She took one more opportunity to glance at them. "I declare, in addition to the statements in this Last Will and Testament, the following Special Wishes and Directives: There is a caveat to this will."

The brothers sat up straight.

"A caveat?" Peter exclaimed.

Nicole nodded but kept reading. "If, after one year of taking up my estate and the House of Occasus, Peter and Spencer Collins have not shown any proven income or they've failed to take proper care of the home or Anguis and Nex, the entirety of my estate shall move on to Cassandra Clement."

"What?"

"Wait," Spencer held up his hand. "We can lose the inheritance?"

Nicole set the papers down. "Yes, technically."

Spencer looked at Peter in a shock that mirrored what he felt.

"You didn't tell me that," Peter accused, crossing his arms.

Nicole shrugged. "It wasn't my place to. The will was still in probate, and I wasn't allowed to disclose anything more than that you and your brother were listed as the primary beneficiaries."

"So, what?" He kept looking over at Spencer as though his brother could help him understand. "We have to live in the house for a year to prove that we can take care of it and these dogs and make a reliable income?"

"Essentially."

"What if we decide we don't want to live in it?" Spencer asked. "What if we wanted to sell it?"

Nicole shook her head. "That's part of the directive. 'The House of Occasus must not be sold, leased, or otherwise housed by anyone other than my listed beneficiaries, or it shall pass from their possession and onto Cassandra Clement.'"

"The House of Occasus?" Spencer repeated. "That's what she named her home?"

"She and her husband together."

"And we have to live in it for a year or give it to Ms. Clement?"

"Exactly."

"Okay," he muttered, the weight of his following sigh alerting Peter to his brother's mounting concerns. "What if we decided to do that? Give it to her, I mean. Would we lose the monetary inheritance too?"

Nicole raised a dark blonde eyebrow. "Yes."

Running a hand down his face, Peter grimaced. "So, it's live in the house for a year or refuse the inheritance altogether?"

The lawyer opened her mouth to reply, then closed it again. She stared at the page for a minute, flipped back, flipped forward, and shrugged. "Well, I believe it *was* Diane's intent to make it so that the house couldn't pass out of your possession without also losing the inheritance. However, she didn't *specifically* say that. She only said that if you try to sell the house now, you won't inherit. If you wait a year, allow the inheritance to fully kick in, and *then* sell the house—especially if you sold it to Ms. Clement— there's no wording here that would preclude that eventuality."

Peter took a deep breath and turned to Spencer. At least that was more hopeful. They could put up with anything for a year.

"How much is the inheritance?" Spencer's tone still indicated his wariness.

Nicole thumbed through the pages to read the sum. "Straight net worth?"

He nodded.

"Four point three million."

Peter's jaw dropped.

Spencer blinked.

"Holy crap!" Peter exclaimed. "How?"

"It appears that your Great-Uncle William Larkin was quite the investor and managed to save a large sum on his own prior to their marriage," Nicole explained. "Then together they continued their financial success through a similar fashion. And I don't believe either of them were what you'd call 'big spenders.' Through his and her life insurance policies and their management, they were able to offer quite the inheritance."

"No kidding," Peter muttered.

"But we don't get any of that until a year is up and we've met the requirements?" Spencer asked, bringing them back to reality.

Nicole shook her head, a couple blonde strands falling out of place before she tucked them back. "No, no. She locked 90% of the inheritance away until that year passed. But she's allowed access to 10% for living and other expenses to make your time here easier."

"That's four hundred and thirty thousand dollars," Spencer concluded.

"It is."

"Does it cost that much to live here?"

Nicole laughed. "Not at all. The average annual income around here isn't even 10% of *that*."

"So she gave us all that extra to . . . what?" Peter shrugged. "Sweeten the deal? Make us want to stay?"

She didn't have a response.

Running his knuckles over his chin, Spencer stared at the floor. "What happens if we stay for a year, and it's determined we didn't do well enough? What if we don't take good care of the house or we can't make enough money on our own?"

"If you're concerned about money, the threshold is quite short,"

Nicole assured them. "You only have to prove that you have a steady income. She didn't put a number on that."

"But what if we don't?"

Peter heard what Spencer was really asking. "Do we have to pay back whatever we spent?"

"Oh, no. The 10% will be yours regardless of what happens at the end of the year. She put out access to it and didn't put any contingencies on how you spend it. I don't believe Diane was attempting to make this difficult on you. I imagine she just wanted to be sure you took good care of the home, the property, the dogs, and the money she was giving you."

"And you don't think it'll be difficult?" Peter asked. "Taking care of the place or getting a good income?"

"I can't imagine it would be. Worst case you can get a job down at the lumberyard. They always need people there."

Peter slumped in his seat. This wasn't what he'd expected. The money was more, but so were the constraints. And he wasn't sure that Spencer would be willing to give DeVerre a full year. Not if there was a chance they could fail and wind up back where they started.

But they could do it, couldn't they? A year to write and publish a novel. One year to get their blog even more success and widen their audience. Without jobs getting in the way of their work, they could actually focus and get it done. They could make it happen.

"As I've read the will in its entirety," Nicole said, breaking through Peter's thoughts. "We can move on to signing the documents, if you're ready."

Spencer looked up from the floor. "May I ask a question first?"

She gestured for him to go ahead.

"Do you know why Diane named us as her beneficiaries?"

Nicole took a second, her head tipping to the side. "To be perfectly honest," she said, an uncertain tone in her voice, "I didn't know her well. I met her once—when she submitted her will—and we didn't really associate after that. Different circles, you know? She was sort of . . .

secretive. Distant."

"She didn't have friends?" Peter asked, frowning.

"Other than Ms. Clement," Spencer added.

"Right."

The lawyer shook her head. "Not really. I think she spoke with the librarian every so often, but she wasn't the friendly sort. Ms. Clement somehow made friends with her, but I think it was one of those kindred spirit situations. Cassandra isn't known for being the most . . . sociable, either."

"She's not?" Spencer asked, concern lacing his voice.

"Don't worry though," Nicole hurried to say. "She seemed nice enough the few times I met her. Kind of like your aunt. Nice, but. . . ."

"Distant?" Peter offered.

"Yes. Or perhaps . . . independent."

"Cool."

"And you said she's out of town for a family emergency?" Spencer pressed.

Nicole nodded. "I believe she's been gone for a little more than a month. She returned for Diane's funeral, but then went back home to be with her family a while longer. Last I spoke with her—to tell her the will made it through probate—she said that she hoped to return soon."

Peter took a deep breath. He could sense the nerves all over Spencer. His brother had gone back to staring at the carpet, hand over his mouth, shoulders drooping, knee bouncing up and down. His apprehension was understandable. They'd quit their jobs, driven all the way out here, and now there was a chance they might lose the inheritance after all.

But Peter wouldn't let that happen. He'd prove to Spencer that this move was worth the risk. That DeVerre was where they belonged.

It wouldn't be that hard. Between the two of them, writing a novel and building their career *couldn't* be that hard. Could it? They already had a fan base, no matter how small it might be. The blog got well over four hundred views per post already. Which wasn't huge, but it was better than none at all. If those four hundred fans bought a full-length novel, that was a good start.

Yes, they could make this work. There might be the unexpected obstacles like dogs and an old-lady-best-friend to take care of, along with conditions to the terms of the inheritance, but all in all, it was nothing. They could take the year and change their lives. There was no doubt in Peter's mind.

Reaching over to give Spencer's arm an encouraging shove, Peter grinned at his brother before turning back to Nicole. "Where do we sign?"

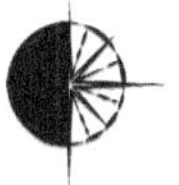

CHAPTER TWO

Spencer

Spencer set the pen back on Nicole's desk as she grabbed the final page to stack with the others.

"Great," she said, a blend of enthusiasm and indifference lining her tone. "That's the last of them. And. . . ." She shut the folder, opened a drawer, and withdrew something shiny. "Here's the keys to Occasus."

Turning to check in with his brother, Spencer's chest grew tight with hesitation. Peter wore his signature grin as their eyes met; right corner of his mouth tipped up in a crooked, boyish smile. People rarely guessed their ages right. Their mom often told them it was a good thing, but Spencer wasn't sure that he agreed. Between their 'youthful' appearance and his own lack of height, he struggled to get people to take him seriously as they often thought he was still in his late teens. It was annoying. And his older brother's impish grin didn't help matters.

Catching Spencer's stare, Peter tipped his head in encouragement toward the keys.

Spencer forced himself to reach out and take them. He felt no more comfortable with the arrangement now that they'd signed the paperwork. "Do you know what Occasus means?"

"I don't. I'm sorry," Nicole said, an apologetic tilt to her words.

As much as Spencer wanted to comment on how creepy the name sounded, he kept it to himself. He knew enough Latin to hear its roots but couldn't pinpoint the meaning.

For the past month, this inheritance was all Peter could talk about. He'd gone on and on about how they were about to 'make it big.' How they'd write hundreds of novels and reach levels of fame like Conan Doyle or Christie or Poe. And while Spencer was under no illusions that there was ever a chance they'd reach that type of success, he didn't want to rain on his brother's parade.

Nor could he pretend that he didn't carry some amount of hope that Peter was right.

It was typical of Peter to have dreams and ideas grander than the world could provide. His dreams often wound up influencing Spencer's, giving him his own delusions of grandeur right along with his brother.

But it wasn't normal for Peter to cling to them with quite so much desperation as he had this.

After Peter had gotten that phone call from Nicole about Diane listing them as her beneficiaries, he'd been like a dog with a bone. He'd talked about it nonstop for the first two days—a rather expected response to any new idea of his. But when the third day came, Spencer thought he'd give it up. That's what he'd always done in the past. Peter's obsessions ran deep but were short-lived.

Yet he'd been as dedicated to their move to DeVerre on the third morning as he had on the first.

Through probate and up until they'd left Norfolk, Peter had been fixated on the move. He'd sold everything but his clothes, books, and notes. He'd quit his job in advance so that he could focus on packing. He'd even written his next episode for the blog early rather than waiting until the last minute to hand it to Spencer for editing.

And while there were thousands of things about this move that could go wrong, Spencer knew as he picked up the keys from Nicole's desk that it was too late to turn back now. They were here in Washington state; they'd quit their jobs, vacated their apartment, forfeited their security deposit, downsized to one car, and just signed the paperwork that made them property owners.

To his surprise, the thought sent a strange jolt of anticipation through Spencer.

He wasn't sure whether it was fear or excitement that suddenly caused his hands to tingle around the keys to their home. He'd never owned a house. The weight of its responsibility was daunting and thrilling all at once.

Nicole led them back to the reception area. They stood side by side, looking out the large front windows as she gave them directions to the House of Occasus. "Other than the farms out toward the mill, your property is the most secluded in town," she explained.

Spencer felt his nerves spike. "Secluded?" he asked. "Like, it's isolated?"

"I wouldn't say isolated, exactly. You can get there in less than ten minutes. But unlike the rest of the homes in DeVerre, you can't see it from the main road."

"Sounds perfect for a couple of writers like us," Peter said, hand clapping on Spencer's shoulder with a *thump*. "It'll feel like a writing retreat or something."

"We've never been on a writing retreat," Spencer reminded him.

He shrugged. "We can pretend that's what this is."

"So you're both writers like Diane, then?" Nicole asked. Her niece, Jill, looked up as they all stood in the entry.

Peter nodded. "We sure are. But we write fiction."

"I thought Diane wrote about ghosts?"

"She did."

Nicole passed a smile to Jill. "Sounds like fiction to me."

"It does, doesn't it?" Spencer muttered.

"Well, like I said before," Nicole continued with that same polite laugh as earlier. "I didn't know Diane all that well, but she always did strike me as quite the character."

"That's what we've heard," Peter said, his grin ten times more genuine than the lawyer's or her niece's.

Observing the group before him, Spencer couldn't help the concern that leeched into his thoughts as he scanned the first DeVerreans they'd met. The women were nice enough, but there was something about the tone in their voices and the withholding look in their eyes that gave him pause. Were they as disingenuous as they appeared, or were they just uncomfortable with outsiders?

Reaching out to shake their hands again, Nicole gave them each a professional nod. "I won't keep you any longer. I imagine these last few days have been quite exhausting. Enjoy settling into your new home, and welcome to DeVerre."

"Thanks," Peter said, slipping his dark brown jacket back over his shoulders, "for the welcome and for all your work on our great-aunt's estate. You've been super easy to work with this whole time, and we appreciate all your help."

Nicole didn't seem to know how to take his effusive gratitude but nodded anyway as she smiled and shook Spencer's hand.

"Thanks," he mumbled, his quiet tone a damper to balance out his brother's overenthusiastic personality.

As they moved to the door, Peter waved to Jill. "It was good to meet you," he called.

"You too," Jill said again.

"That pink's a nice color on you, by the way," he added. "See ya later."

Spencer fought the grimace that came to his face as he saw Jill flinch. Like most women, she seemed unsure of what Peter meant by the compliment. He wanted to warn her that its aim wasn't flirtatious. There was little chance Peter even realized it came across that way. That was the problem with his brother. He had no notion of where the line between being nice and making a move existed. He couldn't even see how they often blended into one another. But instead of trying to assure the stranger that his brother was just an overly kind human being, he pushed through the door behind him.

Spencer checked to see if Peter gave any indication that he'd noticed Jill's reaction but found him scanning the square as if nothing had happened. They both shivered as a cold breeze cut through, moving to pull their jackets tighter.

"Dude, it's freakin' cold up here," Peter said, pushing a hand through his dark hair. Portions of it stood on end from the tousle and the wind.

Spencer nodded, shoving a hand into his pocket as he headed for the driver's side of the Jeep. "Yeah, I'm not any more used to it than you."

"So what do you think?" Peter asked, waiting for him to unlock the car. "Can we handle the cold for a crapload of money and a house?"

Spencer took his time climbing into the Jeep to consider the question. The difference between a Virginian and a Washingtonian October might have been startling, but more was bothering him than the cold. There was so much at stake with their move.

Yes, they finally had the chance to become full-time authors. And that was fantastic! They'd dreamed of it and talked about it for longer than he could remember. But this wasn't how he'd pictured it going.

In order to accept this version of their dream, they'd had to abandon everything. Their mom and stepdad. Their aunts and uncles. Their cousins. Their friends. Their secure, if annoying, jobs. Their tiny but comfortable apartment.

They'd lived in Norfolk their whole lives. They knew it like the back of their hands. The roads, the restaurants, the stores, the movie theater, the book shops—the exact path everywhere they needed to go. They knew it. Absolutely and completely. It was dull and difficult. It was hard to get ahead, and it didn't support their dream. But it was safe. It was known.

Spencer had never been a risk taker. Not even as a kid. He liked to know his odds and decide whether taking the leap was worth it; he rarely thought it was.

And out here in DeVerre, Washington, the weather was the least of their worries.

"It won't be cold all year," he said, turning on the Jeep. It revved up after a couple of sputters. "But what about the rest of it? What about that Cassandra lady?"

"What about her?" Peter asked, brow raised. "She was Diane's best friend or whatever. I imagine she'll want to honor her wishes and see us succeed here."

"Diane asked us to take care of her."

"Yeah. . . ." He sighed. "Yeah, that does weird me out a bit. Do you think she's ill or something?"

Spencer scoffed as he pulled onto the roundabout. "I doubt it. If she could travel from Spokane for the funeral and then back for whatever emergency her family has going on, she's probably pretty capable for an old lady."

"Why would we need to take care of her then?"

"Maybe it's more of a financial thing. Like, make sure she's okay and stuff?"

"Yeah, probably."

"I'm not sure why Diane didn't just leave the place to her though," Spencer continued, taking the left onto Trinity Lane and up toward the north side of town. They passed a whitewashed chapel on their right while the single-engine fire station lay dead ahead. "If she likes her well enough to leave it to her if we don't want it, why not give it to her in the first place? It isn't like Diane knew us."

"Maybe she wanted to help out some fellow writers?" Peter offered.

"Did she know we're writers?"

"I don't know."

Spencer sighed, settling back into the leather seat as he turned the

Jeep with the sloping curve in the road. "What if we hate it here, Pete? We've never lived somewhere this small or this far from home. And we don't know *anyone*. It's about to be the holidays. We can probably afford to go home now, but we've got the house and the dogs to think about. *And Ms. Clement.*"

With a loud, amused huff, Peter punched his arm. "Are you seriously using Thanksgiving and Christmas as an excuse not to take *four hundred and thirty thousand dollars*? At a minimum!"

"It's a year," Spencer reminded him as they passed two neighborhoods before veering to the left onto Whitehill Way. The road wound ahead of them, enclosed by trees. "What are we gonna do in the middle of nowhere for a year?"

"Write a freakin' book!"

He rolled his eyes. "And what if it doesn't make us any money? What if at the end of the year, we're no better off than before?"

"That's impossible," Peter argued. "Look, no matter what happens, we're better off at the end of the year. We take the next twelve months to turn *Wenzel & Frankly* from an online serial into a full-length novel. If we've not made a dime by the end, who cares? Worst case, we spent the year writing a crapton, and then we leave."

Spencer frowned. He felt his pessimism getting the better of him. "Actually, worst case, we get murdered like Diane."

Next to him, Peter pressed a hand to his forehead and muttered a sarcastic prayer. Then he tossed both hands into the air. "How many times do I have to tell you? The lady died in her sleep! She was freakin' old. It was her time."

Under normal circumstances, Spencer would have responded to his brother's less delicate comments with reproach. But as he guided the Jeep around the bend, the sight that opened up before him stopped all his thoughts.

Half a mile up the road, the House of Occasus loomed ahead of them. A wrought iron gate and brick fence lined the property, disappearing into the trees. Patches of grass had already turned brown in the autumn air and a thin smattering of trees dotted the yard. Even at the peak of the day, the clouds darted to block the sun, keeping the sky gray while thin beams of light passed through them.

If the gloomy scenery wasn't evocative enough, the house itself was the stuff of nightmares.

Spencer's stomach dropped as his mind raced through every image of spooky old houses from films, paintings, and his own imagination to compare with this mansion.

Occasus was the epitome of imposing and haunted. A blend of red brick and gray siding adorned the façade. Dozens of windows covered all sides of the three-storied house. A large porch wrapped around the front and along the rounded right side. Two brick chimneys rose high above the turret-like roof to the far right. The black shingles on the roof looked to be in good repair from the distance, as did the rest of the house, but even in the middle of the day it looked as dark as it was empty.

"Whoa," Peter gasped, eyes locked dead ahead. "That's . . . whoa."

"Yeah."

"I don't . . . that's big."

"Yeah."

"It's just two of us."

"Yeah."

Peter turned to him, a small, worried frown tugging his brows together. "You good?"

Taking a deep breath as they pulled through the open gate, Spencer hesitated. Was he good? He doubted it.

"It's just a house," he muttered, doing his best to remember that he was an adult and houses shouldn't scare him. No matter how spooky their exterior. "I'm fine."

But Spencer didn't feel fine. Not even as he pulled up to the edge of the driveway and put the car in park. His stomach rolled with anxiety, thinking about what might lurk behind those dark curtains and past that black door.

Ominous.

That's how he'd describe the house. Ominous and foreboding. Like it was warning you not to enter. As though it were harboring secrets as dark as night and mysteries as complex as *Baskerville.*

In the instant that Spencer thought about the literary Hounds, barking erupted from inside the house. Both brothers jumped at the low, rolling barks that held protective and territorial growls within them.

Nicole had told them that some people from the church had volunteered over the last month and a half to take care of the dogs while the will passed through probate. She mentioned that they were well trained and gentle, but their intent was to be guard dogs from the outset. With a swell of worry, Spencer wondered how they'd manage to get the dogs to trust them.

"Dude," Peter frowned, glaring at the front door. "Dogs weren't supposed to be part of the deal."

"It'll be fine," Spencer said as he unbuckled his seatbelt and opened the door. "They'll just have to get used to us."

"Get used to *us*?" Peter scoffed. "We'll have to get used to *them*! We've never had so much as a goldfish, let alone dogs."

"No, but we always begged Mom for them when we were kids."

Though Peter continued to grumble, Spencer took cautious steps up to the porch. Its dark wood bore the marks of age and weathering. A swing hung in front of the far-left window while a couple of chairs and a side table rested to the right. Three small, rectangular windows on the door provided a peek into the house for anyone taller than Spencer.

Peter hurried to stand at Spencer's side as they approached the door. "You've got the keys, right?"

He jingled the key ring and offered them to his brother.

With a shrug and a nervous smirk, Peter gestured to the door. "Feel free to face your fears, bro."

Spencer clenched his jaw at the jab but pushed ahead and unlocked the door. Whether Peter himself was hesitant to enter the house or not, he had a point. If they were going to live in Occasus, Spencer needed to get past his overactive imagination.

The barking halted as Spencer let the door swing open. Peter took a step back, but Spencer held his ground as the dogs ran to the threshold, their warning growls resumed. He had begged their mom for dogs ever since he could remember, and he'd studied them endlessly to try to prove to her that he could take care of one. Then the brothers had moved into their apartment and couldn't afford the time or money required for a pet. None of that research ended up working in his favor. Until now.

Forcing himself to allow the dogs to appraise him, he stood stock still and unflinching. Spencer did his best not to stare as he tried to appear unthreatening. He'd never seen or heard of German Wirehaired Pointers before Nicole read the will, so he'd not known what to expect. But despite their cautious barking, he thought they were rather cute.

Somewhat terrier-like in appearance with their wiry hair and trim build, the pointers stood almost to his mid-thigh. Their sharp, alert eyes glowed amber, even in the dim light. Though their builds and coloring were identical, there were easy markers to distinguish one from the other. While the dog on the left had a roan coat of reddish-brown and white, the right's held spots with larger patches of the same colors and a blaze of white between its bushy brows.

The dogs' barking dwindled, and Spencer crouched down, holding out his hand to offer his friendship. Both dogs edged toward his hand, brown noses sniffing the air around his knuckles. "That's it," he whispered to them. "We're here to take care of you."

The roan-coated dog stepped through the doorway and licked Spencer's hand. He chuckled, reaching to pet its head. Eagerly, the other dog pressed in for his own attention.

"Nice," Peter said, stepping forward to pet the dogs too. "How's it going, buds?"

But both dogs recoiled back as Peter neared, growling and barking at him once more.

Peter jumped back, hands held in the air.

"Hey, hey." Spencer reached toward the dogs to calm them. "Cut it out. He's cool."

The dogs stopped barking, but eyed Peter as though unconvinced.

Spencer turned to smirk back at his brother. "I guess you make them nervous."

"Yeah, well they make *me* nervous."

"They're not going to hurt you."

"I dunno." Peter narrowed his eyes at the dogs. "They're looking at me like I'm lunch."

Spencer chuckled and reached for the dogs again. "Come 'ere," he whispered. He patted each of their heads, scratching behind their ears as he checked their collars. The one with the roan coat was Nex, and the one with the blaze was Anguis.

"Nice to meet you gents," Spencer addressed them formally.

They only blinked and nudged his hands in response.

Rising, Spencer felt his stomach soothe. Even if Occasus was the creepiest house he'd ever seen in person, at least the dogs that protected it were sweet. Maybe he didn't have to be so afraid of what lay inside after all.

When Spencer walked into the house, the dogs trotted down the entry hall.

"Not sure I feel welcome here," Peter muttered. He shut the door with a *thud* after he snuck in behind them.

"They'll get used to you soon."

"I hope so."

Staring at the house before them, Spencer took a deep breath. It was amazing. And just as daunting as the exterior. Everything looked original and vintage despite its immaculate condition. The walls were a warm cream and the trim deep walnut. The floors were even darker than the trim, the stairs made of the same, high polished hardwood. A thick rug covered the center of the entry, and a complementary runner hugged the steps.

To their left in the foyer, a coat closet awaited their jackets. The staircase beside it led to the second story. The dogs padded toward another room to the right, so Spencer gestured toward it, and Peter took the lead. They walked into what appeared to be the living room, two antique couches with red damask fabric flanking the fireplace in the corner. The room rounded off in the corner, and Spencer knew that's where the turret outside got its shape. A pair of wingback chairs sat within its circular protrusion.

Though they could have taken an hour or so studying every inch of each room, the Collins brothers moved through Occasus quickly, drifting from one room to the next. There was too much to take in to linger the first time. Not with how many books and paintings, busts and placards, photos and novelties there were in every nook and cranny.

When Nicole had told them the house was fully furnished, she'd made what was possibly the biggest understatement of the century. Intricate and detailed pieces covered every inch of the space, catching the eye everywhere they looked. And yet, all of it was tasteful and placed in such a way to make the house feel whole and curated.

After their short tour of the living room, they walked through a pair of open French doors into what Spencer assumed had been Diane's office. A large partners-style desk in lacquered mahogany sat at the back of the room next to the window. Books and papers covered its glossy surface. A second fireplace sat in the middle of the far wall with a black marble surround and hearth. A shiver ran down Spencer's spine when he caught a glimpse of a decorative skull resting on a book within the built-ins.

Through the office, they continued to the dining room. There, a bay window butted out into the yard with its floor-to-ceiling frames. A massive table filled the space. An unexpected sight, considering Nicole's appraisal of Diane's 'distant' personality. Spencer doubted their great-aunt had been one to host dinner parties.

They moved through the open door at the back of the dining room and into the kitchen. Another staircase lay to their right. The laundry stood in a rather large room to the left. It was clear that Diane and her husband had updated the kitchen within the past decade. It was beautiful, massive, and as thoroughly decorated as the rest of the house. A large walnut and black granite island sat in the middle of the room, a vase of long-dead wildflowers in the center.

Spencer made a note to remove the flowers as the brothers proceeded upstairs. The second story turned out to be a far less eventful exploration despite the same opulent décor. It housed four bedrooms and two bathrooms. The same cream walls and walnut trim filled each space. Two equally sized rooms sat across the hall from one another. Each room was larger than the size of their two apartment bedrooms put together. Though sheets covered most of the furnishings to keep the dust from settling in, Spencer caught glimpses of beds, dressers, and bookshelves in the guest rooms. A smaller room sat at the back of the second story, right next to the shared bathroom.

At the front of the house was the master suite. It was by far the grandest room they'd seen yet.

"Dibs!" Peter shouted, pushing into the room ahead of Spencer.

Spencer frowned, following him through to peer into the giant bathroom. "What are you, fifteen or something? I didn't even get to see it."

"Sucks to suck," Peter said. They stood together, taking in the luxurious white and gold fixtures of the bathroom. "I won by the rules of dibs."

"You do remember that we had a deal coming out here, right?" Spencer reminded him. "I get first choice on the rooms."

Peter pursed his lips. "Yeah . . . I—I did say that, technically."

"So I want this room."

He held his ground as the brothers stared each other down. Their stance mimicked one another, crossed arms and raised brows, daring the other to back down first. Peter's brown eyes darted around the room, and Spencer knew he was searching for some way to win. He watched him look from the fireplace in the corner to the round wall of windows and down to the bed nestled within them.

A slow grin spread over Peter's lips. "You sure?"

Spencer narrowed his gaze. "Yeah. . . ."

"All right. I'm proud of you."

"Why?"

Peter shrugged. "I didn't expect you to be comfortable sleeping in a dead lady's bed."

Spencer froze.

Tilting his head, Peter stared at the bed as if seeing it for the first time. "On second thought," he said, edging toward the door, "you can have it."

"No thanks." Spencer rushed to follow him. "I'm not interested."

They shut the door and walked to the two rooms in the middle of the second floor.

"I'll take this one." Spencer pointed to the one on the left.

"I'm good with that one," Peter said, gesturing to the right.

"Cool."

"Cool."

Spencer tried to shake off the thoughts of every ghost story that took place in ancient houses like this. They each took one nervous glance at Diane's door as they turned to the staircase at the front of the house. A third flight led to the final floor. They rushed up the steps to forget the creepy fact that they'd fought over the one room in this house that was beyond a shadow of a doubt haunted.

The third floor was a disappointment. Its narrow hallway only held two doors: one that led to the attic and locked one at the far end. Spencer slid the keys back out of his pocket to try it but discovered that the lock was one of the old-fashioned, skeleton types. Peter said he'd check the office, certain he'd find the key in there.

"Could be in Diane's room?" Spencer suggested.

Peter frowned. "If it is," his voice dipped low as he eyed the locked door. "This room will have to stay a mystery."

Spencer smirked, and they hurried back to the first floor.

Once they settled on the couches in the living space, Nex rested at Spencer's feet while Anguis lounged by the fireplace.

"So I was thinking about it," Peter said, eyes scanning the whole room before settling back onto Spencer. "We need a game plan."

"I agree."

"We know we have a year to get this figured out," Peter continued. "So we know how to plan. We need something simple and straightforward to keep us focused."

"For sure."

"Like we've said a million times before, *Wenzel & Frankly* is ready to be a series. The blog has more than enough material for a novel, and we've got so many more ideas for it. And we've got an audience already primed. It's the perfect project."

"Exactly."

"So that's our goal, right?"

"Write the first novel of *Wenzel & Frankly*. Right," Spencer confirmed.

"Everything leading up to it has been a precursor, a foundation, a framework."

"Yeah."

"Now we tell the real story."

"Right," Spencer paused. "But how?"

Peter scratched his head. "I guess we have to line up the serial to introduce the plot for the novel."

"What's the plot for the novel?"

"The same plot we've always talked about."

Spencer frowned. "We've had ideas, Pete. We've never sat down and plotted the thing."

"So? We've never plotted the stuff for the blog."

"A novel is different from a never-ending sequence of updates on a blog," he argued, feeling overwhelmed at the prospect of writing a full novel for the first time. "We've got to take this seriously if we want it to be a success."

"You're right," Peter agreed with a heavy sigh. "You're right."

Spencer nodded.

"So how do we plot it?"

He blinked, then shrugged. "I dunno."

"Guess we'd better figure that out."

Spencer chewed on the inside of his cheek. "I guess so."

The two of them stared around the living room, taking in the immenseness of everything they now owned. All their minimal belongings were still in the Jeep. They needed to bring them in and get themselves settled. But Spencer couldn't help feeling like he was encroaching on someone else's space here in the House of Occasus.

It didn't matter that Diane had left them the house; everything inside was still hers. The dogs, the rooms, the furniture, the décor—everything. They were mere intruders.

"Don't worry," Peter said, drawing his attention back to him. He gave him an encouraging smile. The kind that told Spencer that his brother thought he was on the verge of panic.

It didn't matter that he was wrong. Spencer returned the smile, hoping Peter would feel the gratitude contained within it. Ever since their dad had died when they were kids, Peter had stepped up to take on the role of his protector. It wasn't the same. It couldn't be. But he felt how much his brother loved him all the same.

Spencer wasn't as fragile as his brother liked to pretend. Yes, things frightened him. Sure, he often got freaked out over nothing. But he knew it was all ridiculous. He knew none of his own fears were logical. He just couldn't keep his brain from going haywire when it latched onto something that spooked him.

But he wouldn't take away the chance for his brother to feel needed.

"We're gonna make this work, Spence," Peter promised.

"You think so?" Spencer asked, massaging the palm of his hand.

"No, I know so. And I know you're the real writer between us. I've always been the idea man. I'll do my part, obviously, but I don't want you to worry about anything. You focus on the writing, and I'll take care of everything else."

Just like it had before, Spencer's chest grew tight with hope. Their dreams might actually be possible. Being authors was a shared dream for him and his brother, but they each had their own definitions of success.

For Peter, it meant renown and proof that he'd made it. It was a marker that promised he was capable, both as a writer and as a brother, son, and man. It was the validation of his worth.

For Spencer, it was wholly different. He didn't care about the renown. He didn't need the validation. He wanted the escape.

Writing was his one break from reality. It was his safe haven. The one place he *could* control his world. The solitary space in which fear couldn't overtake him and he was in charge of his own imagination.

And with Peter's offer came the chance to ignore reality and just write. He could forget obligation and responsibility and every weight that kept him tethered to the real world and focus on the one thing that made him feel truly alive.

"Really?" Spencer asked, sure it was too good to be true.

Peter nodded, then glanced at the dogs. "Well," he smirked. "Almost everything."

A light chuckle escaped Spencer. Relief flooded him as he realized that Peter was right. This move to DeVerre wasn't quite the risk he'd thought. It was going to be everything they had always wanted.

"They'll warm up to you," he promised, gesturing to the dogs.

Peter pursed his lips, glaring at Nex dubiously. "I doubt it."

CHAPTER THREE

Peter

Peter yawned as he cracked open the fridge. Staring lazily at its sparse drawers and shelves, he rubbed a hand over his sleepy eyes. He wasn't much for mornings in general, but even less so after their late night.

The brothers had unloaded the Jeep and unpacked their most important belongings. Then Peter took the time to search the office for the key to the mysterious locked room on the third floor. He'd given up after an unproductive hour.

Upon discovering that the kitchen was completely devoid of anything edible, they'd gone out to pick up dinner from Speedy's Pizza on the corner of the square in town. Though neither of them was much for cooking, Peter shared Spencer's dislike of leaving the house for a meal. But as even the pizza place didn't deliver, Peter thought their odds of anywhere else in town bringing them meals was unlikely.

They'd devoured the pizza before going up to finish unpacking and prepping their new bedrooms. It took them hours to clear the furniture of the white sheets, remove the creepiest portraits from the walls, and fill the closets and dressers with their clothes. Peter thought the décor in Occasus mimicked the rather Dickensian style of the exterior. It cast an eerie presence to certain knickknacks within the rooms, so they'd agreed to remove those as well.

Through the evening, they had worked both together and separately in their rooms, passing between the creaky hallway whenever they had questions or needed help. Neither of them had enough confidence to totally redecorate or make the rooms their own, but after several hours of work, the bedrooms were more homey than before and they were too exhausted to care anymore.

Peter had forced himself to wake early so that he could make good on his promise to Spencer. He intended to run some errands, clean up the house, and get them settled. But he figured that while he was out, he might as well indulge his curiosity and do some exploring too.

For now, he puttered around the kitchen, groggy as he tried to pull together a grocery list. There wasn't much in the pantry, even with its massive size, and he wound up tossing most of it, knowing they'd never touch it themselves. The cabinets held pots and pans, herbs and spices, dishware and glasses. He scanned the freezer—which was empty—and was still staring into the fridge a minute later.

A high-pitched *ding, ding, ding* from the fridge made him jump, and Peter tried to shake himself from his drowsy stupor. He reached in and grabbed a stray carton of orange juice, letting the door swing shut. He was in the middle of scrunching his nose at the acidic smell when Spencer ambled down the stairs with a sluggish gait.

"Morning."

"Morning."

Spencer yawned and rubbed the back of his head as he wandered over to the counter. He picked up one of the ceramic mugs, tipping it toward Peter in a salute. "Thanks for making coffee."

Finishing out the yawn that Spencer's had triggered, Peter shook his head. "I didn't make coffee."

"Dude?" Spencer lifted the full coffee pot to show him the evidence.

Peter stared at the dark brown liquid in confusion. It waved with a gentle slosh as Spencer began to pour himself a cup. He scratched his forehead, trying to remember what he'd done in his morning daze. "Hm, weird," he muttered, then hefted a sigh. "Guess I was more tired than I thought. Pour me one too, would ya?"

After Spencer set a mug next to the fridge, he went to take a seat at the island. "I'm surprised you're up this morning . . . I mean, this early."

Peter dug through the fridge, pulling old groceries out with impunity. When it was finally empty, he kicked the fridge's door shut with his foot and dumped the lot of it in the trash. Then he took the bar stool next to Spencer. "Same. But I was thinking of heading into town to check it out. Maybe meet a couple people and get a feel for the place. Care to join?"

"Actually, I was gonna do some research and get started on an outline for the book," Spencer replied, running a thumb along the rim of his mug. "Get all our ideas organized, you know?"

"Yeah, that's smart. You figure out the Wi-Fi last night?"

"Yeah, I just had to push the button, and it hooked right up."

"Great."

Peter hesitated. He wondered if he should check to be sure that Spencer was all right to stay in the house by himself. Often his brother didn't like being alone in unknown places, and with the general vibe of Occasus, he doubted that Spencer could control his imagination long without company. He considered offering to stay but figured that acknowledging Spencer's irrational fears would only remind him of them.

Peter was still musing when a *thunk* drew their eyes to the back door where the dogs had just slipped in through a pet door. Their coppery fur was damp from the early morning rain. They both hurried toward Spencer, completely ignoring Peter, and took a seat at his side.

He gave them each a pat on the head before returning to his coffee.

"You think they're hungry?" Peter asked, eyeing them warily.

Spencer shrugged. "I'm not sure what their routine is, but I'd guess so."

"Mm, mkay." He hopped off his stool and headed for the pantry. "Looks like it's raining again. You mind if I take the Jeep?" He filled the dog bowls with the kibble he'd found earlier.

"Go for it."

"Cool, thanks."

"Thanks for taking care of the shopping."

"I told you," Peter said, setting the bowls back into place. "I'll take care of the details while you take care of the story. When you need me for ideas or writing, get me. I'll make sure this place is running smoothly in the meantime."

Spencer gave him an appreciative smile, resting his hands on the mug.

Giving the dogs a wide berth as he moved through the kitchen, Peter finished off his shopping list and coffee before heading up to grab his leather jacket and the keys.

The drive back to downtown DeVerre was scenic and easy even in the rain. As it was a Saturday, he expected to find several people out and about, enjoying the weekend. But he found even less activity in the square than the previous day.

Parking in the same spot as the day before, Peter decided he'd take his time and get to know the town. He stopped into the bookshop first, hoping to meet fellow bibliophiles. The shop was tiny, but charming. Hundreds of books with varying levels of interest to him lined the shelves. There was a rather large nonfiction section which he had no interest in, but over half the shop was fiction, so he approved of that. He met the owners, Frank and Eloise Chastain, who welcomed him to DeVerre with enthusiasm. They were a reasonable amount older than him and Spencer, which was rather disappointing. But they were both easygoing and neighborly, which gave Peter hope that DeVerre would provide more of a social life than he'd anticipated.

"We heard you were a writer," Frank said, his brown eyes shining with interest. His bright smile contrasted against his dark skin, making him look twice as happy. "Maybe we could sell your stuff here."

Peter chuckled, not wanting to betray how much he hoped that would happen. "Yeah, that'd be cool."

"You got anything out right now?"

"Nah, unfortunately all we've got is our online serial at the moment."

Eloise grinned, her blonde braid and freckled nose reminding him of Jill despite the notable age gap. "Oh, really? What's it about?"

"Uh, well, it's about these two PIs, Wenzel and Frankly," he explained, settling into his spiel. "It's set in the late 1800s in New York City. Wenzel's from London, recently moved to the States, when he hears that some strange stuff is going on in the city. He teams up with his new pal, Frankly, and they save the city from monsters."

The couple shared a grin.

"That sounds fantastic," Frank said, ringing up the book Peter had picked. "I'd love to read it."

"Thanks, yeah, we like it. And here. . . ." Peter dug into his wallet to pull out two cards. "One to pay and one for you to check it out. I know business cards are kinda old-fashioned, but it's the easiest way to get people to the site."

"That's great. We'll be sure to give it a read," he promised.

Peter hoped he was telling the truth.

After tossing his purchase into the Jeep, he swung by the café next door. The shop was named Coffee & Croissants, so he picked up one of both. He met one of the owners, Joel Dumont, who ran the shop with his wife and sister-in-law. He was nice, though not as friendly as the Chastains. But the pastry was good and the coffee strong, so Peter had no complaints.

When he stopped to see the library, it surprised him to find it closed. Unlike other public libraries he'd visited, the sign on the door announced that DeVerre's was only open Monday through Friday from 8 a.m. to 5 p.m. So he settled for a peek inside the dark room. He couldn't see much beyond the massive bookshelves, but it was enough for him to feel satisfied by its size.

Peter took his time wandering the square, familiarizing himself with the shops and businesses of DeVerre. He walked past Guillaume Electric & Appliance Care, then Guillaume Plumbing. There was a barber and a pawn and thrift shop next. He bypassed DeVerre Police Station and The Glass Tavern, having no use for one and planning to return to the other. The pizza place sat beside the gym, Summit Fitness, which he knew Spencer planned on visiting after noticing it the previous night. On the far side of the square he could see the hair and nail salon as well as the dry cleaner and tailor.

Without interest in any of those businesses for himself, Peter decided to continue his walk down Harmony Road to see what else the town had to offer. It proved to be hardly any more exciting. Two doctors' offices—a dentistry and a family counselor—shared one building and across the way was the town clinic. The veterinarian shared space with the pet shop and groomer. There was a hardware store, a general store, and a grocery store all farther down the road. At the end, he saw what looked to be a higher scale restaurant and, finally, a bowling alley.

By the time Peter looped back around to the square, he'd long finished his coffee and croissant. He glanced at his watch and shrugged. Even with his 'early' start on the day, it seemed he'd be heading for a late lunch.

Peter hurried across the square, over the grass lawn of the government building, and toward The Glass Tavern. The outside reminded him of a traditional Irish pub. The green and gold lettering on the windows announced some of their fares including burgers, sandwiches, and fries. The awning and door bore that same Kelly green and gold trim.

A bell chimed as he pushed through the door. Peter scanned the room, noting its size in comparison to the other shops he'd entered. It was about twice as large, only partitioned by the occasional beam. Booths with dark brown leather lined the walls while tables and chairs smattered the rest of the hardwood floor. On the far side of the room, the bar glowed in the dim lighting. Its mirrored shelving reflected the light through various bottles of liquors and mixers. Having worked as a bartender for the past seven years, he had no trouble visualizing the other side of that dark wood bar.

The hostess stand was as empty as the room, but the bartender lifted a hand in greeting. Peter walked straight over to take the seat right in front of the young woman.

"Hey there," he said, smiling as he settled his jacket on the back of the stool.

"Hi," she replied, returning the smile.

Though Peter hadn't met many DeVerre residents yet, she didn't look like any of the women he'd seen so far. While he'd concluded earlier that Frank from the bookshop was biracial, this young woman's deep skin tone was of a richer brown. It reminded him of sepia photographs, warm and almost bronzed. Her work uniform was simple, but somehow her willowy frame and taller-than-average height made it appear far more sophisticated than it should. She had a reserved smile, but it was different from the people at the coffee shop or Nicole and Jill's. He could feel the authenticity behind the grin as her eyes squinted with the action.

"What can I get you?" Her voice was gentle, though deeper than he'd expected.

Resting his arms on the bar top, Peter took another glance at his watch. "Is it too early to drink?"

She smirked. "I'm here, aren't I?"

"Good point!" He chuckled. "I came for lunch, but it doesn't look like you've got much going on, so I figured I could help make your day more interesting."

"I'd appreciate that." She pulled a pad out of the black apron around her waist and gestured to the empty room. "With our current high volume of customers, I've got the lucky job of being both waitress and bartender, so feel free to give me your order."

Peter considered asking for a menu before deciding against it. "What do you recommend?"

"Can't go wrong with a Reuben and fries."

"You know. . . ." He grinned. "Sandwiches are my favorite! Literally any sandwich, and I'm happy."

Her smile grew as she tipped her head to the side as if unsure if he were telling the truth. "You want that, then?"

"Yes, please."

"All right, I'll put this in real fast." She scribbled on the pad as she turned toward the kitchen door.

Peter took the opportunity to get a quick glance at her name tag— *Anna*, it read—and clasped his hands together as he waited for her to return. When she reappeared, she hovered near the back of the bar by the shelves.

"So what's your drink?" Anna asked.

Peter quirked his brow. "Who says I have a particular drink?"

She shrugged, the motion causing the rolled sleeves of her white button up to slip down her forearm. She tugged it back up as she leaned against the counter behind her. "Something tells me that you're the sort of person who plays favorites."

Peter laughed and nodded. "Busted."

"So what is it?"

"It's my own thing."

Her thick eyebrows pulled together. "Your own thing?"

Peter gestured to the bar, then between the two of them. "We share a common interest."

"Bartending is my job," Anna said. "I wouldn't call it an interest."

"It was my job too, until a couple weeks ago."

"Really?"

"Yep."

"And you created your own drink?"

"I did."

"That makes you pretty high maintenance, you know?"

"So I'm told."

"Didn't you hate it when people ordered 'their own' creations?"

Peter pursed his lips and shrugged. "No. It made work more fun."

"That's fair, I guess."

"Do you want to know what it is? My drink?" he asked. "Or is that too obnoxious of me?"

Anna laughed, pushing off the back of the bar. "It *is* obnoxious, but it's also not boring. Go for it."

Rubbing his hands together, Peter leaned forward and pointed to each ingredient as he explained. "All right, so we start with a cube of ice to keep it chilled, of course, then you toss in a double shot of rye whiskey. Preferably Bulleit, which I see right over there. Then you add a splash of Angostura bitters, fill it to the top with some ginger beer, peel off a nice bit of lemon, twist it over the drink to get that goodness in there, et voila— you've got my drink."

As she listened to his instructions, Anna set to work. She splashed in the bitters as he finished up. "Yeah," she muttered, a hint of laughter in her tone. "I was right."

"About?"

"You. You *are* high maintenance."

Peter grinned.

Anna peeled the lemon, twisted it over the drink, and set it before him. "Et voila," she said with an annoyed smirk. "You've got your drink."

"Thank you." He took a sip. "It's perfect."

"It's easy."

"Which makes it a great drink."

"It's basically a mule."

"But it's not."

Anna sighed and leaned against the back of the bar again. "What do you call it?"

He smirked. "I call it the 'Pete Collins.' Kinda like a Tom Collins, but my name instead."

"That's nothing like a Tom Collins."

"But my name *is* Peter Collins, and it's my drink, so may as well play off a good name, right?"

She shook her head as she laughed at him. "So you're the older brother?"

Her sudden shift in topic forced Peter to reorder his thoughts. "Yeah, how'd you know?"

"News travels fast in small towns." She tucked a curling wisp of hair behind her ear.

"I take it you heard we got in yesterday?"

Anna nodded. "My boss and Nicole are distant cousins. We found out last night."

"Is everyone in this town related to each other?"

"No, but most of them are."

"Are you related to anyone?"

"Yeah."

"Who?"

"Too many to name right now."

A bell rang in the kitchen, and Anna went to retrieve his lunch from the pass through window. Once she'd set it in front of him, he picked up the conversation with another question. "Have you lived here your whole life?"

"Yep. Most of us have."

"Really?"

She nodded.

"I guess in a town of three hundred you wouldn't have many people coming in and out."

"Not at all," Anna confirmed. "When you're born in DeVerre, you live in DeVerre. Even those who do leave, come back. And as we aren't the most welcoming town in the States, we don't have many people trying to move here to join us."

"Well, now you've got me and Spence."

"Seems we do."

Peter set the sandwich back on his plate as a thought struck him. "Diane wasn't native here either."

"Nope."

"Hm, that's funny. I guess she roped some of her own relatives into coming here."

Anna drifted toward him, coming to lean a respectful distance away on the counter. "Did you know her well?"

"Diane?"

"Yeah."

Peter scoffed. "No, we never even met her."

"Really?"

"Really."

"Why'd she leave you the house, then?"

"Wish I knew."

Anna picked at a gash in the wood. "You're planning to stay, though?"

"That's the plan."

She nodded but didn't reply.

Sensing a deeper motivation behind her question, Peter wiped his hands on his napkin. "Shouldn't we?"

Anna met his eyes, hers wide in surprise. "I don't know."

Taking in the way she'd pulled back and begun to play with the pendant on her necklace, Peter measured her nervousness. It seemed all the people in the town were more hesitant than welcoming. He couldn't decide if they were hiding something or if the curiosity of a newcomer actually threw the people of DeVerre for a loop.

Pulling up the sleeves on his Henley, Peter tried to appear as unassuming as possible. "Is it that uncommon for people to move here?"

Anna nodded again, some of the curly wisps of her hair dancing around her face. There was something about the way her face softened in her uncertainty that made her look younger than he'd first guessed. Maybe mid-twenties? No older than Spencer, certainly. But now he wondered if she might be even younger than that.

"In that case, it seems strange that Diane moved here at all. Our family always said it was for her writing and Uncle Liam's research, but . . . I mean, what research was he doing out here?" He hoped she would take the bait.

"Research?" Anna bit her bottom lip in thought. "I knew she was a writer. Her book is in the library, and I think she was working on another one. But I didn't know that her husband was researching anything. What did he study?"

"History, I think." Peter felt a sense of disappointment. Did Anna really not know anything about his great-aunt and uncle? "Never met him either, so everything I've heard is secondhand."

"And they left the house to *you*?"

"Trust me, I'm as weirded out as anyone."

She seemed to believe him.

Anna fussed with a few glasses behind the counter. "What kind of history did your uncle study?"

"Honestly, I don't have a clue. Did you ever meet him?"

"William Larkin? Yeah. We saw each other at church and around town every so often."

"Then you probably know more about him than me or Spencer."

"Mm."

Peter continued to eat his sandwich as Anna cleaned up behind the bar. She never went far but allowed him to finish up his meal without interference. It wasn't until he set his empty cup back down that she spoke again.

"I had a thought," she said.

"Oh yeah?" he replied, resting his arms on the counter. "Whatcha got for me?"

With a shy smile, Anna came closer. "I think . . . well, I may know someone who can help you find some answers. About Diane and Liam."

"Oh yeah?" Peter leaned in with instant interest.

"Yeah. My sister, Ava." She gestured toward the door. "She's the librarian. If Liam was doing research, it's likely he went there. She may not be able to answer all your questions, but . . . Ava knows a lot about this town that no one else does. If you have any questions, go to her."

"Your sister?"

She nodded.

"All right, thanks." Peter dug his wallet out of his pocket. "How much do I owe ya?"

She gave him the total, and he settled the cash plus an extra twenty on the bar top.

"Appreciate the drink, the meal, and the company, Anna," he said.

She frowned at the use of her name, then sucked in an understanding breath and gestured to her name tag.

He lifted his chin in acknowledgment.

"Right." She chuckled. "It was interesting to meet you, Peter. Or do you prefer Pete?"

"Whatever suits your fancy."

She crossed her arms and smirked. "Good to meet you, *Peter*."

"Same to you, *Anna*."

She raised a hand in a half-hearted wave as he turned to go.

But he didn't get halfway around before another thought stopped him. "Hey, uh," he said, snapping his fingers and pointing back to her. "One last question. Do you know Cassandra, uh . . . oh shoot, what was her last name?"

"Clement?"

"Yeah! Clement! Cassandra Clement."

Anna gave a slow nod. "Yeah, I know her."

"You do?"

"Like I said, it's a small town. Everyone knows everyone. Literally."

"Oh cool." Peter played with the zipper on his jacket. "So . . . is she, like . . . nice? Our aunt asked us to take care of the lady and . . . I dunno, are we gonna have to put her up and feed her and stuff?"

Anna's eyes narrowed in confusion.

"I mean, I just don't really know what to expect," he hurried to explain. "Like, did she live with Diane or something?"

Understanding seemed to dawn on her. "Oh, no, I mean she has a place here in town. Or, well," she corrected, "she lives with some family. Her mom's cousin, I think."

"Cool, cool." Peter nodded. "Yeah, good to know. Just—Spence and I weren't sure if we needed to prep ourselves or whatever. Old people can be weird to live with."

An amused grin spread over Anna's face as she played with her necklace again. "Right."

"Right, well. . . ." Peter backed up and sighed. "Thanks again, for everything. My compliments to the chef. And to the bartender."

She dipped her head politely.

"You did good on the drink," he reassured her.

"Glad to hear it."

"I'll be sure to bring Spence with me next time so you can meet him."

He watched her subtle hesitation before she grinned and replied. "That sounds fun. Especially if he's as obnoxious as you."

Peter laughed. "Nowhere near," he said, then pushed out the door and into the rain of DeVerre.

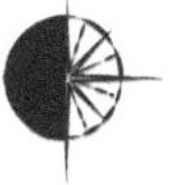

CHAPTER FOUR

Spencer

Old houses were the bane of Spencer's existence. He hated how they creaked as they settled. The way the shadows clung to the darkest halls and corners. How they collected cobwebs and dust like a blanket of the past. And most of all, he hated the way the wind howled outside the windows at night like a siren of coming specters.

He had forced himself to spend their first day at the House of Occasus focusing exclusively on work. He'd had a final edit to do before uploading the next episode of *Wenzel & Frankly* to the blog, then he spent the rest of his time researching all that he could to help them write their first novel. They each had a few snippets they'd written for the book in the past, but nothing had ever been finalized. So far, the serial had received all their attention as it was the only thing that showed promise.

The distraction of work helped to ease his jumpiness. Often, he forgot where he was during the day. Though he would have liked to set himself up in the office to work at that magnificent desk—the exact sort of desk he imagined every *real* author wrote at—he didn't feel comfortable moving

Diane's stuff. So he set up in the dining room at the large table instead. The chairs were moderately comfortable, and the bay windows provided a beautiful view of the pines on the property. Every so often, he'd look up to see Anguis and Nex running across the lawn or playing in the rain. And, in the light of day, he felt no real discomfort within Occasus.

He'd kept his head down, gathered multiple methods of plotting, organized all their present work, and mocked up a couple of outlines to show Peter. He felt rather accomplished by the time the sun set on their second day at Occasus.

But his calm didn't last.

As soon as he went up to his room to sleep, Spencer felt his throat tighten and his heartbeat start to pick up.

There was no reason for him to be afraid. It didn't matter that the room of a dead woman was only a handful of steps down the hall. Ghosts weren't real. He'd spent the entire day in the house, and it had given him all the proof he needed to know it was as normal as any other. It wasn't haunted.

Yet, he couldn't help but suddenly see his four-poster bed as menacing, the way it towered near the low ceiling. He didn't like the way the heating system *thunked* when it kicked on and began to set the curtains swaying. And he failed to prevent his imagination from summoning forth a fear that the antique mirror might reflect something other than his face when he looked into it.

The feeling that something was watching him had lurked at the back of his mind since they'd moved into the house. He knew it was ridiculous. But on more than one occasion during the day, when he'd paused to consider a thought or leaned back to stretch in his chair, he could have sworn he caught a glimpse of a shadow in his periphery. He hadn't told Peter anything about his paranoia, knowing his brother would only make fun of him for it.

Spencer sighed, the sound cutting through the quiet of the room. He ran a hand over the back of his neck. He knew he was being stupid. Every single thing in the House of Occasus was as mundane as the rest of the world. But that didn't stop his mind from sparking with billions of ideas of what mysteries might hide in those shadows that lingered at the corner of his eyes.

That was the real problem for Spencer. Everyone thought he was overly anxious and paranoid all the time. But they didn't understand. It wasn't that he was actually afraid; he just couldn't stop his thoughts from wandering.

No matter how logical Spencer tried to be, his imagination inevitably perked up and gave him something to think about that sent chills down his spine. And this creaky old house was a wellspring of material to send his mind reeling.

He tossed the four-poster bed a dubious glare. It was no use trying to sleep when his mind was already riled up. He knew himself well enough to know he wouldn't get a wink of sleep if he tried to manage it on his own.

Spencer hurried downstairs to find Peter in the living room. His brother sat on the couch, reading the outlines that Spencer had developed.

"Hey," Peter said, barely glancing up from the pages. "I've made some notes."

"Sounds good," Spencer muttered, not interested in getting caught up in conversation. "You see the dogs recently?"

Peter gestured toward the office.

Reluctant to enter the dark room, Spencer gave a low whistle. The jingle of their tags preceded their arrival. "Come on," he said to them with a flick of his wrist. They followed immediately. "Night."

"G'night," Peter replied, distracted as he chewed on the back of a pen.

Up the stairs and back to his room, Spencer ushered the dogs in, shut the door, and motioned to the bed. Anguis and Nex stared at him and sat.

Frowning, Spencer pointed to the bed. "Up," he ordered.

They blinked in unison.

He got on the bed thinking that it might be their training to let the human have priority. "C'mon," he said, patting the blankets.

Anguis lay down.

"I thought you two liked me?"

Nex yawned.

"Fine," he grumbled, working his way under the covers. "But you're stuck in here with me, so you can either stay on the hard floor or you can sleep on the soft bed. Your choice."

Anguis closed his eyes.

Nex padded to the side of the bed.

Spencer watched.

Nex turned in two circles, then lay down on the rug.

"Fine. Be that way." Spencer grabbed his book and plopped against the pillows. He read for a little over an hour before he felt that he'd exhausted his mind enough to sleep without too much trouble. After he turned out the light, the shadows still haunted him, but he managed to fall asleep knowing that the dogs would alert him if anything was amiss.

And they slept in the room with him from then on, making the lingering premonition of being watched by some ghost drift into the void.

~

The Monday morning after their arrival, Spencer was back at his spot at the dining room table and deep in thought as he attempted to restructure the story according to Peter's notes. They had dozens of plot holes already, and he had no clue how they'd patch them up. Yet Peter kept adding ideas to the stack.

He ran his hands through his hair. Peter's disorganized method of plotting frustrated him to no end, but he had to admit that some of his brother's ideas were brilliant. After all, it was Peter's genius that took Spencer's menial character-based story and developed it into an epic monsters-and-mystery hit online. They wouldn't be anywhere without his hairbrained suggestions.

Just before lunch, Peter finally arrived downstairs via the kitchen, cup of coffee in hand. He was fully dressed, from his ever-messy hair and leather jacket, all the way down to his dark boots. "Sup?" He took the seat at the head of the table on Spencer's left.

"Hey," Spencer replied, motioning to the outlines. "Trying to figure out if this is too convoluted. Do you think that we can legitimately get the doc to the sewers without it seeming coincidental?"

"So what if it's a coincidence?" Peter asked. "Coincidences happen all the time."

"Nothing is a coincidence."

"That's absolutely ridiculous." His brother's left eyebrow tipped up as he smirked. "You're telling me that nothing in this world is coincidence?"

"How could it be?"

"How *couldn't* it be? There's so much freakin' stuff in it. This table being in this house is coincidence. The manufacturer of that shirt you've got on coincidentally picked navy, and you coincidentally needed a navy shirt. The trees out there coincidentally grew in the right spot not to get cut down when they built this house."

Spencer capped his pen and leveled a glare at his brother. "I know you don't believe that."

"Sure I do."

"Then you don't believe in God."

Peter scoffed. "Don't be stupid. You know I do."

"If everything happens by coincidence, then what role does God have?"

"Okay, now you're not playing fair. I just woke up. I can't have a theological debate this early in the morning."

"It's ten forty."

"Yeah, but you've been up for what? Six hours?"

"Three."

"Your brain's way ahead of mine. I need at least another hour to get going. Speaking of going. . . ." Peter took a long swig of his coffee. "We need to head out."

"What, do we have an appointment or something?"

"Something."

Spencer sighed. "Where do we have to go?"

"I already told you on Saturday. Anna said her sister could tell us about Diane and Liam. The library opened at eight. We've given her time to get settled in; now we should go visit."

"Two hours is more than enough time to settle in."

"What's your point?"

Shutting his laptop, Spencer bit his tongue around the retort that came to mind. "Nothing. I'll go get my stuff."

They were out the door in minutes, but the Jeep refused to start after only a day of disuse, so they decided they'd have to walk into town.

"Good thing it's sunny today."

"Don't say that," Spencer warned.

"Why not?"

"You'll jinx it."

Peter gave a snort of a laugh. "Right. In that case. . . ." He looked up at the clear sky. "Good thing it's rainy today."

Spencer had to admit, the walk was rather pleasant. Though there was a chill in the air, with their jackets and the sunshine, the coolness felt nice. And, if nothing else, DeVerre was beautiful. Like a landscape from a fantasy novel or movie with its evergreen forest and natural soundtrack. As far out and isolated as it was, the hum of the urban world didn't seem to exist. The quiet permeated everything, only the occasional scuttle of an animal or twitter of a bird daring to interrupt the calm. The branches of the pines rustled. Their footsteps sounded in gentle *thumps* against the hard earth. But otherwise, it was silent.

What took about six minutes to drive, took them almost half an hour to walk. And while neither of them was in what one might consider the peak of fitness, Spencer at least made a point to counteract the sedentary lifestyle of a writer by going to the gym. The brisk walk felt nice after the long week of being stuck in a car and settling into the house.

Peter let out a heavy breath as they finally stepped up onto the sidewalk. "I'm never doing that again," he grumbled, shedding his jacket.

Spencer eyed him. "You need to work out more."

"Do I look like I need to lose weight?" he demanded, gesturing to his lanky frame.

"You wouldn't be winded if you took care of yourself."

"You need to stop acting like *you're* the big brother."

"Then stop being an idiot."

Peter gave his shoulder a shove and pulled open the library door.

Spencer stopped inside the entryway, gazing around in fascination. It was unlike any public library he had ever visited. There were the usual bookshelves and books, of course, but that was all that he could recognize. A sign at the front desk read: *For Service, Head to Back.*

The stuffed bookcases rose to six feet, a maze through the whole building. An overflow of books covered the tops of the shelves along with dozens of plants —vining, bushy, and flowering alike. Where the walls weren't covered by the shelves, they could see the paneling of more wood that wrapped up onto the ceiling. The dark brown tiled floors peeked out from under a smattering of old Turkish rugs in reds, blues, and yellows. The smell of floral tea and spices cut through the typical mustiness of pages and ink.

This wasn't a library, Spencer thought, but the den of some folkloric sage.

He followed Peter toward the back of the building, through the dozens of shelves. When they rounded the final bookshelf, they found the librarian seated at a long table. Though Spencer didn't think sitting was the correct definition. She was more lounging, feet propped on the table, crossed at the ankles as she leaned back in her chair. The woman didn't appear to notice them as her eyes continued to scan the paperback novel in her hands. She wore a pair of brown loafers like any librarian might, but once again, the stereotypes failed. Her long black hair hung to the middle of her back in dozens of thin braids. She wore a white tee tucked into ripped denim, a baggy green and yellow plaid button up layered overtop.

"Anna said you'd come by," she said, her dark eyes drifting up to them as they came to a stop. She slipped a finger between the pages to act as a bookmark. "I expected to meet you yesterday."

Spencer looked at Peter, deferring to him as he was the one who'd met her sister.

On the spot, Peter floundered. "Uh. . . ." He scratched the back of his head. "You were open on Sunday?"

A thin smile crossed the woman's lips. "No," she said. "I meant at church."

"Oh."

She eyed them as if suspicious of them after that answer. "Are you opposed to church?"

"No," Spencer was quick to assure her.

"Are you religious?"

He hesitated. "I mean, kinda."

"We prefer to call it 'relational.'" Peter clarified.

"But you're Christians?" she pursued.

"Yeah." Peter said as Spencer nodded.

"Yet you didn't come to church?"

The brothers exchanged a look, not expecting their failure to attend to have garnered so much reproach. They'd thought about going. They attended church practically every Sunday back in Norfolk. They'd even had a conversation about going to the church in DeVerre. But with so much to unpack, they decided it'd be all right to skip the service for a week.

"It's fine," she said, kicking her feet off the table and sitting up straight. "But let me advise you: if you want the people of DeVerre to think you're all right, you need to show up at church."

Spencer pointed over his shoulder with his thumb. "We were busy setting up the house."

"And I don't blame you for wanting to get stuff done," she admitted, though it sort of sounded like she was blaming them. "I'm just trying to help you out. DeVerre Chapel has a 98% attendance rate. You *not* showing up tells the rest of the town that you don't care about making connections or about their faith. And while the other 2% of DeVerreans already hate the majority of the populace and don't care if they're shunned, I imagine that's not the foot you were hoping to start out on."

The brothers stared at her. They hadn't gotten a scolding in over a decade. It felt like being a teen again.

"I'm Ava, by the way," she said, tossing the book to the side and resting her arms on the table. "How can I help you?"

The brothers' stunned silence caused them to lag for a moment more, then Peter stepped forward. "I'm Peter," he said, then pointed to Spencer with the typical flourish of his wrist. "He's Spencer."

"I know."

"Cool."

"Did Diane attend the church?" Spencer asked, hoping it would be a good segue. He wasn't sure why, but the woman made him nervous. It was as if her dark brown eyes were cutting through every presentation and word to find the truth.

"Right, that is why you're here, isn't it?" Ava sighed. "Look, I'll tell you what I told Anna the other night: I spoke to Diane and her husband from time to time, but I didn't really know either of them."

"You didn't?"

"No," she said. "No one did."

Spencer watched Peter's frown cycle through the same surprise and disappointment he felt. "So you can't tell us anything about them?"

Ava shrugged. "Of course I can. I may not have known either of them well personally, but I know more about this town and the people in it by reading and listening than anyone else. More than I should."

There was another tick of silence.

Spencer began massaging the palm of his hand. "So . . . what can you tell us?"

"What do you want to know?"

He glanced toward Peter, and the brothers shared a look of concern. What should they ask? They hadn't discussed this. Anna said her sister would have answers, but they hadn't thought about what questions to ask to obtain those answers.

Spencer asked the first one that came to mind. "Do you know why they moved here?"

"Research," she said without hesitation. "Diane, for her book. William, for his studies. I believe he was writing an essay."

"About what?"

"Which one? Her book or his essay?"

"Both," Peter said.

Ava tucked a few braids behind her ear, a row of tiny gold hoops reflecting in the light. "She wrote about ghosts—their presence, their sightings, and the like within the northeastern side of Washington. And he was studying theology and unexplained encounters. Angels and demons and such."

A shiver ran down Spencer's spine. He couldn't help glancing over his shoulder to check the rows of books behind him as that nagging feeling of being watched reared its ugly head again. He knew it was pointless. There was no one in the library but Peter, Ava, and him. Yet his hands went numb at the thought of their great-aunt and uncle's work.

Ghosts? Angels? Demons? And such? What was 'such'?

"And they got most of their research here?" Peter asked as Spencer remained mute.

"They did."

Peter scratched at the thin stubble along his jawline as he glanced at Spencer. "Is DeVerre known for ghosts?"

Ava shook her head. "Not particularly."

"So why choose DeVerre?"

"It's somewhat central to the area of her interest. And we are a religious town. It fit both of their pursuits, I suppose."

Another beat of silence.

A light chuckle escaped Peter. "So we don't need to worry about haunted houses in DeVerre, right?"

Ava pressed her lips together in an amused grin. "No."

"Cool."

"Any other questions?" she asked.

"Yeah," Peter said, leaning against a bookshelf.

Ava frowned at him.

He stood back up. "Do you know why she left Occasus to us?"

"No," she shook her head. "Diane didn't consider me a close enough confidant for that. Came to me for research alone."

"Research on ghosts."

"And on the area." She sucked in a deep breath as she studied their faces. "If you have personal questions like this you should save them for her friend, Cassandra. She'll be the only one who knows the answers."

Spencer tipped his head, surprised. "Only her?"

"She was Diane's sole friend. Half the town was weirded out by your great-aunt and the other half straight up didn't want her here. They thought she was pretentious."

"Why?"

"She *was* pretentious."

"Checks out," Peter muttered.

"She came in, bought up the old Varon estate, changed its name, and started digging into people's pasts. All for research on her book. People don't like that. And with you two being her outsider nephews, you're bound to get the same heat as her. If not more."

Peter frowned and crossed his arms. "So we need to show we have no interest in disrupting their town by, what? Going to church?"

"That would be a start."

"All right," Spencer said, hoping he sounded agreeable enough. "We can do that."

"Do you think that'll be enough to make people trust us?" Peter asked.

"For now," she said.

"And do you have any idea when this Cassandra lady will be back?"

Ava narrowed her eyes. "She had a family emergency."

"Which was?"

"Her mother's in a coma."

"Oh." Peter grimaced. "Sorry."

"Don't apologize to me," Ava said with a shrug. "She and I aren't close."

Spencer supposed they wouldn't be. If Diane was offensive enough to only manage making one friend in DeVerre, that woman and Ava would likely have far less in common than their age difference alone.

"Do you know what happened?" Spencer ventured.

"Not really," she said, confirming his suspicion. "What I've gathered is that her mother was involved in a vehicular accident about two months ago. She hit her head hard enough to put her under, and she's not woken up since. I think Cassandra will be there until they hear one way or another about the prognosis."

"That sucks," Peter said.

Spencer nodded. "Should we do something?"

"Like what?" Ava asked. "You've clearly never met her. What could strangers do to help in a waiting game like that?"

"I dunno," he shrugged. "I just feel like . . . I don't know. Diane asked that we take care of her, and I feel like we should do something."

Ava eyed him for a couple extra seconds. "You're the sweet one, aren't you?"

"What?"

Peter chuckled.

"And you," she said, pointing to him. "You're the annoying one."

"So your sister said."

"Sarcasm doesn't go well here," she warned.

Peter shrugged. "It's about all I got."

Quickly, Spencer set a hand on his brother's arm to stop any further retorts. "Thanks for all your help," he said, giving a final scan to the room. "I just have one last question."

"Go for it."

"You got anything about 1880s New York City in here?"

Ava spent the next thirty minutes walking them through the library to help them pick out books that would aid in the research for their novel. She got them historical references, guides to the language of the era, a handbook on mythological creatures that might inspire the beasts their protagonists fought, and a few books on writing that she thought would help them prepare better.

She turned into a different person when talking about books. Far less intimidating and much more interested in conversation. She actually gave them a genuine smile and a laugh a handful of times while they perused the shelves together. The original confidence, assertiveness, and intelligence was no less tempered by this dichotomy of friendliness and enthusiasm. It was interesting. And he would have thought it was attractive if it weren't for the pair of gold bands he caught sight of on her left ring finger, one plain and the other what appeared to be an antique emerald.

The walk home was far more exhausting with the weight of the books in their arms. Peter complained most of the way—in between his pondering of their conversation. They discussed what they'd learned about Diane and William Larkin's research. Spencer didn't like the suggestion that they had chosen DeVerre for its proximity to supernatural activity, but he tried to forget about it. And he could hear the way Peter worked hard to dance around the subject as he spoke. Whether due to his own discomfort or to ease Spencer's, he couldn't tell.

They ate a late lunch when they got back to Occasus before taking time to read through the library books. Peter took the one on mythological creatures—the original idea of adding the beasts to their story being his—and Spencer looked through another for ideas on plotting out the story. He wanted to be sure that once they got writing, nothing could stop them.

After a couple hours of reading, Spencer decided he'd been stationary for long enough. Whenever he needed to work through problems in writing, he felt the need to get up and move. It inevitably got his thoughts turning in the right direction and almost always ended with an epiphany.

"I'm gonna take a walk," he told Peter as he stood and stretched, then called for the dogs.

"You got some ideas?" his brother asked.

"Yeah."

"Cool. Well, I'll be here coming up with some baddies to fight."

"Have fun."

"You too."

The dogs pattered after Spencer, ready to rush through the trees. Though there were thick clouds blocking most of the light, the rain remained at bay. He wondered if he would like the constant rain of the Pacific Northwest. Often in Norfolk, he enjoyed the rainy days. They made him feel productive and focused. Like the world wanted him to get his writing done and forced him to stay inside to do just that.

But Washington was famous for constant rain. He wasn't sure how he'd cope with that, living in a house as dark and dreary as Occasus and a town as strange as DeVerre.

Forcing himself to turn his thoughts back to the book, Spencer tried to puzzle out what the plot of their novel would be. That was the problem, he discovered. With their serial, it hadn't been an issue. Having enough story to fill a single post was never difficult. But having enough for a full-length book? That was overwhelming.

Their story had a general theme and direction, but each time they published anything on their blog, it was more of an episode than a complete story. They'd been working toward some general and some major arcs for a while, but nothing definitive. Now that they were finally getting to write a thought-out plot line for *Wenzel & Frankly*, he wasn't sure they had enough to carry them through.

Not when they didn't have an end goal in mind yet.

They needed a direction for their characters. A purpose to their story. Something that would change Wenzel and Frankly's lives.

A *snap* cut through the trees, tearing Spencer from his ruminations.

Spencer scanned the forest around him, his heart kicking into overdrive as he froze in place. He couldn't see any sign of movement but felt the hairs on his neck and arms rise. The shadows of the afternoon seemed longer than usual against the darkening gray of the sky.

Spencer took a step back, unsure if his mind was playing tricks on him again or if someone really was watching him.

The crunching of earth under foot came from the same direction of the snap. A shaded figure appeared through the trees several yards away. Spencer's muscles relaxed as he realized it was moving away from him and farther into the woods.

Taking another step backwards, Spencer narrowed his eyes. The man was too far away for him to see much more detail than that he was, in fact, a man, with light hair and a dark jacket and slacks.

Nex lifted his nose, sniffing the air.

Before Spencer could stop the dog, Nex's amber eyes caught sight of the man, and he let out a rumbling bark.

The man stopped and turned toward them.

Spencer thought to hide but knew he couldn't move fast enough.

Taking in the sight of the dogs and Spencer, the man raised a hand in a wave.

Not sure what else to do, Spencer returned it.

The faint shadow of a polite smile crossed the man's face before he turned and walked away.

Spencer stared into the forest after him.

It shouldn't bother him. He knew it was fine. It was a citizen of DeVerre out for a walk in the woods just like him. Someone probably looking to work out their own thoughts as well.

Yet Spencer couldn't stop his mind from developing other, less plausible reasons for someone to come out into the woods. He couldn't stop thinking that this man was up to some nefarious business. That he was out here to accomplish some clandestine behavior, and Spencer had caught him in the act.

Turning away, Spencer rubbed his hands over his hair. He had to get home and back to Peter. Back to someone who could talk him out of the things his imagination whispered to him. Back to his writing. Back to sanity.

CHAPTER FIVE

Peter

After the past few days of settling in, doing their basic research, and compiling their thoughts, Peter met Spencer at the dining room table to have their first official brainstorming session for the novel. The misty morning rain spotted the windows, casting a gray hue over the room. Peter turned on both lamps on the sideboard as well as the golden chandelier to get the dining room bright enough for their work.

Spencer opened his laptop as Peter dropped into the chair at the head of the table. While his brother got his digital notes up and running, he flipped open his notebook and clicked his pen. "Okay," he said, giving his voice an officious edge. "The meeting can start. What's first on the agenda?"

"Well," Spencer replied, clicking the trackpad, his eyes glued to the screen. "First off, I think we need to decide what our plan is."

Peter huffed. "Obviously. That's the point of this. We have our ideas, and now we've gotta turn them into a novel."

"No, that's not what I mean."

"What *do* you mean?"

"I mean we have to know what our goal is. It's fine to write a book in a year, but if we don't get it published, it won't matter. Writers don't get paid until after they've done the work."

Though Peter saw the merit in his reasoning, he wasn't sure how it applied. "What's your point?"

"If we don't make money on this, it won't matter if we want to stay in DeVerre or not," his brother explained. "Diane's will made it clear: We've got to have proven income in our names to keep the house and earn the rest of the inheritance."

Peter pressed his lips together, unhappy with the direction of the conversation, as Spencer continued.

"Four hundred thirty thousand is a good amount of money. We could probably make it . . . I dunno, three or four years if we're smart. But it won't last forever."

"All right, I see your point." Peter sighed, his earlier enthusiasm to discuss his ideas waning. "You're the one who's done all the research. Do you think we can get this published and turn a profit before a year is out?"

"Well. . . ." Spencer hesitated, scratching his stubbled jaw. Neither of them had thick enough facial hair to grow out full beards, but that didn't stop them from trying every so often. "It depends. Do we want to get picked up by a publishing house or are we doing this ourselves?"

Peter scowled. "You know how I feel about book deals."

"Yeah, but how do you feel about advances?" Spencer countered.

Peter crossed his arms to defend against the incoming logical argument.

Spencer leaned forward as he pleaded his case. With his brows pulled together and his mouth downturned, his brother at least had the decency to appear reluctant at his proposition. "If we get a deal with a publisher," he said. "They'll give us an advance which is viable income that we can prove immediately. If we do it all ourselves, we'll have to wait for the cash to come in through sales. And that could take years—multiple of them, not just one."

"Yeah, but we've talked about this, Spence," he reminded him. "Publishing houses make you sign over the rights to your work, and if we do that, we lose control of the story. A publisher will get all say—they might even tell us what to write if they don't like our plans. And what if they decide it's not selling well enough? They can pull the plug on us and then what?"

"You're right," Spencer shrugged. "And you know I don't love that idea either. But . . . well, I mean, we may end up having to get jobs, Pete."

"What?"

"Writing the book is great, but we won't see a dime from it until it's out there in the world." He gave the table a calm thump with his hand for emphasis. "And even then, our fan base isn't large enough to support us financially yet. Not that fast, at least. It will take the whole year to get the book ready for publication, and we won't have time to wait for the proof of steady income to stream in."

"She never said anything about *steady* income."

"She said '*proven* income.' One singular paycheck isn't proof. We have to *prove* we have money coming in on a regular basis to take care of the estate."

Peter sighed and ran a hand over his face. This was the part of being the big brother he always hated. The details and facts of the world were irritating. This was supposed to be their big break. The chance to live their dreams. And now they faced the same problems they'd had in Norfolk— just on a delay.

"We have to figure out a backup plan if we aren't willing to pursue traditional publishing." Spencer's tone was resolved.

Unable to stop the disappointed frown that pulled the corners of his mouth down, Peter eyed his brother. He could see by the adamant expression on Spencer's face that he needed answers. Uncertainty never meant much to Peter. He found himself liking it most of the time. Enjoying the novelty and excitement of the unknown. Anything could happen, and it was fantastic.

But Spencer was the opposite. He needed the security of knowing what they would do if all their grand plans came crashing down around them. If their risk in moving across the country turned out to be a huge mistake.

Peter opened his mouth to reassure him they'd figure it out, but a loud series of *thuds* from the other room made them both jump.

Jerking around to see what caused the commotion, Peter couldn't find the source. There was no movement in the office, the hall, or the kitchen. The dogs still lounged at Spencer's feet, though both had lifted their heads at the sound. Anguis let out a snort and settled his head back on his paws.

"What was that?" Spencer asked, his voice tense as his eyes darted around the room.

Determined to resolve the issue and calm his brother down, Peter rose to inspect the office. "I dunno."

Crossing the threshold into the office while Spencer inched along behind him, Peter scanned the room. He saw the culprit in a matter of seconds. "Well, Dr. Watson," he said, putting on an admittedly awful British accent. He gestured to the four books now strewn on the floor next to the credenza in the corner. "It seems we've got ourselves a case of toppled books."

The look on Spencer's face said he wasn't amused. In fact, Peter thought he looked downright panicked.

Peter sighed. "C'mon, man," he said, crouching down to pick up the mess. "You can't let a rickety stack of books freak you out like that. They just fell over."

"Yeah, but how?"

Peter could hear the thread of hostility in his voice, amplifying his own irritation. "Dude, they were probably just stacked poorly. The weight distribution was off, time did its work, and they fell. Science, man."

Spencer raised his brow. "Science? Really?"

"Yeah."

"We've been here for six days now and neither of us has touched this office or those books. We hardly step in here. You think a stack of books just *happened* to topple over?"

"I told you the other day, coincidences happen all the time."

"Things don't move on their own."

Though Peter was used to Spencer's fears, he couldn't help thinking that this response seemed like an overreaction, even for him.

"You're like those crazy superstitious people who look for bad stuff to happen to them." Peter gestured to the house. "You think this place is haunted so you're looking for evidence that it is. Stop looking, man. It's a normal house."

Heaving a sigh, Spencer turned back to the dining room. "I hate this place." Peter heard him mutter as he dropped back down in front his laptop. Nex rolled over and onto his feet. "All right, so we're gonna publish the book ourselves and just hope we make enough? That's what we've decided?"

Though Peter wanted to push the issue and get Spencer to see his point, he forced himself to let it go. When something scared Spencer the best way to fix it was to distract him from the issue. If he needed to escape his fears about the house through their book, Peter wouldn't stop him.

"I think," Peter replied, taking his seat again, "you're thinking too far ahead. Let's focus on writing, and we can figure out the publishing thing when we're ready to publish it."

Though he hesitated, Spencer gave him a firm nod of acceptance.

"Great. Now. . . ." He grabbed his notebook. "Let's get to work."

They spent the next several hours discussing their first novel. Spencer was better with the practical side of pulling together the pieces while Peter could spit out idea after idea and break them out of any block. It's how they'd come up with the idea for *Wenzel & Frankly* in the first place. Back in college, Spencer had wanted to write a noir-style, historical fiction about an ex-doctor turned inspector but couldn't manage to get past the character creation. He had designed Doctor Frankly to the T. If anyone asked, Spencer could tell them everything about Frankly. From his birthplace to his alma mater. His mother's name to the name of his boss. His address in NYC to his favorite local pub. He even had a list of what clothing he owned.

Peter couldn't tell anyone half those things about Wenzel. He knew he was born and raised in Waterloo, London. He knew that he was a PI who left Europe when he discovered the monsters within New York City. He knew he wore a top hat and carried a cane (that was secretly a sword). But he didn't care to memorize much else. That was Spencer's job.

And it was Peter's job to provide an explosion of ideas for Spencer to sift down to the appropriate scale.

So that's what Peter did.

Their book had to be grand. It had to be epic. Something that would amaze all their online fans and newcomers alike. Something that the critics would rave at. It had to be different and unique and incredible. So he spilled out every idea that he'd scribbled down in his notebook. Even the ones that he didn't think were that great himself.

It was too much.

"I don't know," Spencer said, after several hours of trying to sort through the aftermath. "It's a cool idea, but I feel like destroying an entire third of Central Park is gonna be a problem that we don't want to have to solve."

"But imagine the fight!"

"Yeah, but what's the point?"

"It's legit!"

"It doesn't move the story forward at all. Neither Wenzel nor Frankly want people to find out about these monsters. They would do everything in their power to keep it from getting out in the open."

"Yeah, yeah, you're right." Peter sighed as his stomach rumbled. "Could they at least have a cool chase scene in the park or something?"

"Yeah," Spencer nodded, a slow smile coming to his lips. He gave him a small chuckle, and the nod became more enthusiastic. "Mkay, yeah, I could see that."

"Cool." Peter sat up and shut his notebook. "You hungry?"

Spencer nodded. "Yeah, I could eat."

"Good, let's go to the tavern."

"Mm." His brother pursed his lips, still scrolling on his laptop. "I don't feel like going out."

"C'mon, I promised Anna that I'd bring you by days ago."

Peter watched a grimace cross his face. "Why?"

"What do you mean, '*why*'? We need to make friends, dude."

Spencer scoffed. "I don't trust you."

"Why not?"

"You've tried to set me up before, and I'm not interested in that again."

He huffed as he pushed the chair back in place. "Would you relax? I have zero interest in setting you up with Anna."

Spencer's eyes narrowed. "Because you took an interest in her yourself?"

"Don't be an idiot." Peter smirked. "Sure, she's cute, but I think she's too young for me anyway."

"Seriously? There's no way Ava's younger than us."

"So what?"

"So her sister can't be *that* much younger. Not too young for you to take an interest in at least."

"Oh my God, do you *mind*?" Peter threw his arms out to the side, exasperation pushing him into his more dramatic nature. "I'm just trying to get us a semblance of a social life here. I'm no more interested in a girlfriend than you are at the moment."

They both knew that wasn't wholly true.

Peter had always been more interested in finding a girlfriend, if only because the thought of getting involved with anyone terrified Spencer while Peter actually wished that he had the chance. But that wasn't the point.

"Can we please just go? I'd like to make some friends while we're living here."

Spencer shut the laptop. "Fine," he said, taking his time to rise and clean up his things.

When they got down to the center of town, the sun had disappeared behind the trees, coloring the sky a deep rust. There were only a few cars parked around the entire square, but The Glass Tavern was busier than it had been during Peter's first visit. Not that that was difficult to top. Instead of being empty, there were small parties at three of the tables. One held a couple, another a family of four, and the last a trio of men.

The bell chimed a second time as the door shut behind them, and Peter scanned the room. He spotted Anna at the bar again and bypassed the empty hostess stand as he led Spencer toward her. She saw him coming and tipped her chin up in greeting.

When the brothers sat down, Anna grinned as she continued to work on her orders. "Hello again," she said, her gold necklace catching in the light. "How'd you know I'd be working tonight?"

Peter shrugged. "I didn't. I just hoped you would be."

"Seems you have good luck." Her eyes flickered over to his right where Spencer sat.

"Oh, yeah," Peter gestured toward him. "This is my brother, Spence."

"Nice to meet you, Spence." Anna paused in her work to offer a hand.

"Spencer," he muttered as they shook hands, his lips pressed together in a thin smile.

She gave him a knowing nod. "*Spencer*." She returned to her work, peeling a lemon as she continued to chat. "You two here for dinner or just drinks?"

"Both, preferably," Peter replied.

"Good." Anna set a drink in front of him.

His drink.

"Thanks," Peter exclaimed, picking up the glass and tipping it toward her.

"No problem." She turned to Spencer. "Do you have your own concoction too?"

Spencer eyed the tumbler, then turned back to her. "Ah, no. I'm the boring one."

"Really?"

"Yeah. I'll have water, thanks."

"Okay." She grabbed a pint glass and pitcher. "Well, I'm pulling double duty again, so I've got to go check on these tables and drop off some drinks. Here's a couple of menus in the meantime. I'll be back in a second to get your orders, all right?"

"Sounds good." Peter said, passing her a grin before she walked around the corner.

Spencer slugged his arm. "You freakin' liar."

"First of all, *ow*!" Peter rubbed his arm. "Second, what are you talking about?"

"You *are* interested in her."

"I am not!" Peter promised. "You're only saying that because she's pretty and made my drink for me. Perfectly, I might add. But that doesn't mean I'm interested."

Spencer scoffed, shaking his head as he lifted his cup of ice water.

"I swear!"

"I don't believe you."

Out of the corner of his eye, Peter caught Anna on her way back over. "Seriously," he whispered, determined to get his brother to listen before he ended up making it awkward. "I'm *not* interested. And it would be nice if you wouldn't screw up our first friendship here by suggesting that I am."

"Fine," Spencer muttered, though he didn't sound convinced.

Anna returned, tucking a wisp of curly hair behind her ear. She'd pinned it in a bun again, but it was obvious her hair didn't care to listen to the dress code of her workplace. "Do you guys have any questions about the menu?"

Peter shook his head. "I know what I want."

"A sandwich?" she guessed.

He chuckled and nodded. "You pay a lot of attention to people, don't you?"

"Not especially so," she replied. "You're just more open than most people."

"You mean he doesn't shut up," Spencer joked, eyeing her with a small smile. "I'll have the bacon cheeseburger."

"Fries okay?"

"Yeah."

Anna turned back to Peter. "How about you?"

"I'll have the Italian with the potato salad."

"Bold choice," she teased, taking up the menus. "Be right back."

Once the kitchen doors swung shut behind her, Spencer scoffed again. Peter turned back in time to see him running a hand over his huge smile.

"Can you not?" He elbowed his brother in the side.

"Sorry," Spencer muttered.

Peter sighed and glared at the bottles at the back of the bar. It didn't matter what his intentions were, Spencer was right. He did have an interest in Anna. She was nice and personable and darn cute too. He liked the way she so evidently tried to pull herself together and yet her unruly curls wouldn't allow for it. But he hadn't lied when he said he wanted to make friends more than he wanted a girlfriend. Especially since they had their novel to keep them busy.

Neither of them had had much luck with women so far in life. For Spencer, it was always because he was too lost in his own world and too distrusting to let anyone in—let alone a woman. Romance scared the poor guy just like everything else did. His relationships never even got off the ground, let alone got serious.

But for Peter, his bad luck was because he invested too much, too quickly. He ended up scaring every woman away from a serious relationship. It didn't matter that he tried to be the best boyfriend a girl could ask for; they inevitably told him the relationship wouldn't work.

That they just weren't the right fit, but they'd really like to remain friends with him.

There had been a couple of times that each of them had managed to make a relationship last beyond the first few dates. But that had been early in college, and it'd been years since either of them tried to give it a go with any woman.

Peter was beginning to think they'd end up the two bachelor brothers who wrote epic novels. He couldn't say the idea was totally unappealing. He and Spencer were used to living together. They got along splendidly, and life was easy. But somehow it made him feel perplexingly lonely, imagining that life for himself.

"So," Anna said, breaking into his thoughts as she returned to clean up the back of the bar. "Ava mentioned that you swung by the library."

Both Peter and Spencer perked up at the conversation starter.

"Yeah," Peter confirmed. "Your sister's weird."

Spencer nudged him. "She seems cool."

Anna chuckled. "She's the best." She raised her brow at Peter. "Though some people don't take to her candor."

"Hey—" He raised his hands in surrender. "I have no issue with candor. I just wasn't expecting a lecture."

"Right." She sighed. "She mentioned she told you to come to church."

"And not to use sarcasm."

"She was right." Her slim shoulders lifted in a shrug. "If you want people here to like you, you need to show up and prove that they can trust you."

Spencer rested his arms on the bar top. "I still don't get why moving here makes us untrustworthy."

"You're an outsider." She said it as if it was an obvious flaw.

Peter met Spencer's confused gaze with an amused frown.

"That doesn't make us inherently untrustworthy," his brother insisted.

"It does to the people of DeVerre."

Peter raised his brow. "You and your sister included in that?"

Anna's lips tipped up in the corner. "Yeah."

"Hm." He clicked his tongue on the roof of his mouth. "That's disappointing."

A bell dinged in the back, and she disappeared for a second to retrieve their meals.

"Can I ask you something?" Peter asked as she set the plate down.

She hesitated but nodded. "Sure."

"Your sister. . . ." He grinned before he took a bite of the sandwich. "She seems a bit young and cool to be a librarian."

Anna laughed. "She does, doesn't she?"

"Not sure I've ever met a librarian who wasn't over fifty."

Another, even richer laugh brightened her whole face, dark brown eyes nearly closing as she set a hand to her mouth. "Yeah, well she's a good two decades shy of that."

Peter couldn't help the warmth that spread through his chest at making her laugh that much. "How'd she get the gig?"

She shrugged. "It's sort of the family business."

"Huh?"

Anna bit her bottom lip as if trying to decide if she should share. "My mother's family—the Rayne family—helped found DeVerre. They were the first to run the library, and the role sort of gets passed down. Our mom ran it, and now Ava runs it."

"Will it ever get passed to you?" Spencer asked.

She let out a thin chuckle. "No. I'm not . . . that's not really my thing."

"What is your thing?" Peter asked.

Leaning against the back of the bar, Anna hesitated again as she played with her necklace. "I'm, uh . . . I'm sort of an artist."

Peter felt his eyes go wide.

"Sort of?" Spencer prompted.

"I mean, it's nothing serious," she explained. "Just a hobby."

"That's cool."

"Can we see your stuff?" Peter edged forward in his seat as though she had the work hiding behind the bar with her.

"Uh. . . ." Anna floundered as her eyes flickered to the far-right corner.

Peter could see a spiral-bound notebook sitting on the counter. "Is that it?"

"Yeah." The sudden way her voice went flat alerted him that he'd struck a nerve.

Peter softened his own tone, easing off his curiosity. "Well, if you ever care to show off—" He gestured to Spencer and himself. "We'd be more than happy to see your work. But no pressure."

Anna nodded but didn't make any offer to get her sketchbook or show them anything.

"What kind of art do you do?" Spencer prompted, a lightness to his own question. "Painting? Sculpting?"

"Um, I mostly sketch—" She shrugged. "But painting is my favorite."

"That's awesome. I've always wished that I could draw."

"It just takes practice."

He grinned. "Well, you need time to practice."

"And we're rather short on time these days," Peter nudged his brother's arm. "Being up in that big house with nothing to do but write."

"Writing takes a lot of work," Spencer reminded him.

"And you've got to take breaks occasionally."

To Peter's surprise, Spencer didn't fight him but turned back to his burger.

"If you're looking for a break," Anna said, drawing closer to their seats at the bar, "*and* a chance to make a good impression on the town, I have a suggestion for you."

"Oh, yeah?" Peter nodded. "We're all ears."

She motioned toward the door. "Friday nights, there's a softball game. We're nearing the end of the season with winter coming up, but there are a few more games left."

Anna must have seen the disinterest in both their faces as she hurried to explain. "It's a big deal here. The school isn't large enough for organized sports on its own, so it's a town-wide league. Everyone sixteen and up can join. It's a major event every Friday. It'll impress people if you make the effort to show up."

Peter turned, brows raised, to look at Spencer.

Spencer shrugged and nodded.

"Will you be there?" Peter looked back at Anna.

She smiled. "Yeah."

"All right." He grinned. "Guess we will, too."

~

"Again with that jacket?" Peter glanced up as Spencer hurried down the stairs on Friday night.

"What?" Spencer said, pulling at the worn denim. "It's comfortable."

"It's like you're headed off to the ranch to herd some cattle or something." Peter walked over to give the frayed collar a flick. "You look ridiculous. I'm embarrassed to be seen with you."

Spencer gave him a bored once over. "Says the guy dressed like Tom Cruise in *Top Gun.*"

"Hey!" Peter raised a finger in defense. "It's a classic look."

"Sure it is. Can we go now?"

The Jeep took a handful of tries to get started, but they made it through town and past the rest of the businesses before turning left onto Starling Street. The softball field sat behind the school along with a track field and playground. As they pulled into the parking lot, they saw that Anna was right. There were more cars here than Peter had seen at any point in DeVerre, and hundreds of people milled about near the ball field.

"Dang." Peter gasped, staring at all the people. "This town really doesn't have anything better to do on a Friday night than go to a softball game, do they?"

"It's a small town. What do you expect?"

"I dunno. But this weirds me out."

"Me too."

Peter grunted and unbuckled his seatbelt. "Ready to get stared at all night?"

"No."

"Good." He opened the door. "Let's go."

Joining the crowd as they walked up the path and the short distance toward the field, Peter scanned the faces. He saw the Chastains on the far side of the ballfield and caught a glimpse of the coffee shop owner, Joel, as well. A group of younger women hung around the dugout, chatting with the players. Peter spotted the law office receptionist, Jill, amongst them. A team in blue played as the 'home' team and a team in green represented 'away.' Some of the players were running drills while others stretched. The pitchers for both teams were warming up with the catchers along the sides.

The DeVerrean population clustered around the field's fence. It was easy to see that many of them shared similar features. Angular and refined, most of them had sleek oval shapes as their facial structure. But then Peter saw others that looked more like Anna and Ava with a more heart-shaped face. Their hair ranged in color, about a fifty-fifty split of light and dark. Many were pale skinned like Peter and Spencer, but he observed a fair amount of diversity as well. Not only those of Anna's clearly multiethnic background, but also a few of distinctive Asian and African descent.

It was an eclectic and intriguing group of people. Most of them were dressed in similar fashion. Simple, but pulled together. Casual, but not sloppy. It seemed that there was a reverence for this event that wouldn't allow for something as schlumpy as baggy jeans and tees.

As Peter led the way up the center of the path where it curved toward the 'away' team's side, they spotted Anna near the concessions stand. Out of work, she'd dressed differently, and her hair hung loosely down her back. It looked like a cloud, full and curling around her face. Used to seeing her in a white button up, the bright blue sweater she wore didn't match the reserved appearance Peter had come to expect from her.

Peter would have immediately complimented her on the way the sweater suited her if it weren't for the lady at her side. He and Spencer slowed their pace, realizing that she was occupied, but she waved them over with a smile as soon as she saw them.

"I'll have to check to be sure I'm off work," she was saying as they approached. "But I'd love to join you."

"Wonderful," the lady said, her voice smooth and refined. "I'll count you as coming unless you tell me otherwise."

"Thank you," Anna replied, then motioned toward the brothers.

The woman turned, her bright blue eyes taking in the two of them. Of all the people at the game, she was the most overdressed. She wore a light pink blouse tucked into pleated khaki slacks and a string of pearls around her neck. Her cropped blonde hair hovered above her shoulders, not a strand out of place. With the thick heel on her boots, she managed to tower over Anna's already taller-than-average height for a woman.

"Hello," she said as they approached. Her smile was curious, but polite.

"Hey," Peter gave her his best friendly grin.

"Hello," Spencer said, his own smile managing to meet the social demand.

Anna stepped forward. "Peter, Spencer, this is Mrs. Giana Frossard. Gia, this is Peter and Spencer Collins."

"Ah, yes," Gia Frossard said, still taking them in. "Diane's nephews."

"Great-nephews," Peter corrected.

"Right." She gave a chuckle that sounded fake to Peter. "You've been in town a week now, is that correct?"

"Yep, we got here last Friday."

"I hope you've been settling in all right."

"Just fine, thanks. DeVerre's a pretty nice place."

Gia raised a brow as she appraised him. She seemed pleased with the compliment. "Yes, it is, isn't it? I take it you're staying then?"

Peter shrugged. "Seems like it."

"Hm." She turned back to Anna. "You, uh, know them well already, I take it?"

Anna grinned and gave both brothers a glance. "I don't know about *well*." She shrugged. "But I'm considering making them friends."

"Appreciate it," Peter tipped his chin up toward her.

He felt Gia sizing them up as her eyes continue to scan at them. "Well, if you can earn Anna's friendship, it's one of the best endorsements you can get in our little town." She turned away from them to smile at Anna. She reached to brush a curl over the younger woman's shoulder, then patted her arm. "Have a fun evening, dear. I'll see you next week for the committee."

The three of them let Gia get out of earshot before turning back to each other.

"Committee, eh?" Peter asked. "You part of a club, Annie?"

She narrowed her eyes at the nickname but didn't correct him. "No, nothing like that. The Frossards are throwing a Halloween party at the end of the month, and Gia asked me to help plan it."

"She needs a committee to plan her party?" Spencer asked.

Anna shrugged. "It is for the whole town."

"The *whole* town?" Peter was surprised. "In her house?"

"Well, it's sort of a neighborhood thing," she explained. "The Frossards live on Haven Boulevard—"

"Wait," he interrupted. "Isn't that the one with all the fancy houses?"

"You're one to talk." She raised her brow. "Occasus is just as big as any of those houses."

"And, like, a hundred years older."

She grinned. "Anyway. . . ." she motioned in the direction the woman had gone. "Gia heads up the planning committee for the Halloween party. Haven Boulevard hosts by having a bit of a block party."

"Do you live on Haven?"

"No."

"So why'd she ask you?"

Peter watched a faint blush come to Anna's temples. "Oh, uh. . . ." She shrugged. "Well, I'm sort of best friends with her son."

"Ah." Peter did his best to tamper his grin as he gave Spencer a knowing look.

Best friend? More likely, boyfriend.

He should have known from the start; she was too pretty and sweet to be single.

Spencer returned the grin, scratching his jaw. "Is that why she said earning your friendship is an endorsement?"

"I guess." She started tugging on the curls that had drifted back over her shoulder. "It's sort of a big deal—being friends with the Frossards. Gia's husband, Alex, is the town doctor, and everyone sort of looks up to them."

"Wow." Peter smirked. "I didn't realize we were hanging out with the cool kid in town."

Anna's blush deepened as she dipped her head down and rolled her eyes. "I'm hardly the cool kid." She edged toward the ball field. "Looks like the game's about to start. We should find a seat."

They turned to follow, but Peter scoffed at the mass of people settling in for the game. "Where are we gonna sit? The whole of DeVerre is here."

"That's what happens when you wait until the last second to get a seat." Anna reached over and grabbed the edge of Peter's jacket sleeve. "Come on, we can sit over here."

She led them to the patch of green by the home team's dugout, on the far side from most of the bleachers. There was a single bench, already taken up by a few teens too young to join the game, but she dropped on the grass a handful of feet away. Peter and Spencer plopped next to her with far less grace than she'd shown.

"Man," Peter muttered. "I feel like I'm in high school again."

Spencer grunted. "Don't remind me."

Anna grinned as the teams took the field. "You didn't like high school?"

"No," the brothers said in unison.

She laughed. "What?"

Peter huffed. "Who did?"

"I did."

"Really?" He drew up his knees to rest his arms there. "Lucky you."

"Play ball!" The umpire called the start of the game, and the pitcher threw the first strike.

Anna took the time to explain the league to the brothers. There were four teams: the Angels, the Farmers, the Jacks, and the Ravens. Tonight's teams were the Angels in royal blue and the Jacks in pine green. They had the biggest rivalry in the town as Dr. Frossard and Reverend Chapelle were on the Angels while the town marshal, Thomas Garnier, was on the Jacks.

"The Chapelles, Garniers, and Frossards all go back to the start of DeVerre," she explained.

"Like your family?" Peter asked.

"Yeah, but it's a bit different with them. See, DeVerre was founded by Matthias Varon along with his cousin, Frederic Chapelle, and their best friend, Horace Garnier. Matthias became the mayor, Frederic the reverend, and Horace the marshal."

"Where do the Frossards come in?" Spencer asked.

"Well Leopold Frossard was the town doctor back then and helped to get the town up and running. While he wasn't as close with the three of them at the start, he quickly became a strong part of DeVerre's community. Over time, the four families became the core of everything in DeVerre. The rivalry is all in good fun. Thomas and Samuel—the reverend—are still super close and, as he's almost ten years older than them, Alex is a sort of mentor and confidant for them both."

"So it's a good-natured rivalry?" Peter surmised.

"Exactly."

"That's nice," Spencer said, eyes glued to the game.

Peter frowned as he scanned the field. "Eh. Sounds boring to me."

Anna laughed as she shook her head.

Throughout the game, she continued to point out the most important members of DeVerre. They spotted Dr. Frossard when he went up to bat. He looked exactly like Peter would have expected after meeting his wife. Tall, well-built, and blond. Like Barbie's boyfriend, Ken, but in his early fifties.

Pitching for the Jacks, Marshal Garnier stood in great contrast to the doctor. He had a dark tan and a bit of black hair peeked out from under his ball cap. His slight frame made Peter guess that he stood closer to him in height than the doc.

There were several others, but they all sort of blurred together for Peter after a while. You could only take in so many people who looked so similar before you forgot who was who.

After almost an hour of gameplay, everything came to a halt as a town patrol car pulled up to the field. As one, the crowd craned their necks to peer at the flashing lights. A young man dressed in uniform jumped out and ran onto the field. He looked so young that Peter didn't think he could be far into his twenties.

Anna sat up straighter, as did most of the other spectators. Peter glanced back at her, noting the way her eyes followed the officer. There was a rising tension crackling in the air as the umpire raised his arms, calling time out.

The Jacks were up to bat, so the marshal was in the dugout when his deputy came to get him.

"What's happening?" Spencer asked, learning toward Anna.

"I don't know," she whispered. "But it's gotta be bad for Hunter to interrupt the game."

A low hum began in the crowd as the marshal hurried to gather his things and follow his deputy. He called his excuses to the ump and the teams, telling the Jacks to sub someone in for him. Seeing that the two cops were coming their way, Peter hopped up.

"What are you doing?" Spencer hissed as Anna stared at him.

"Don't worry," he said, waving them off. "I'll be right back."

Before they could stop him, Peter hurried toward the parking lot. He pulled out his phone and held it up to his ear as though he were on a call. He paced along the sidewalk, watching as the marshal and deputy got closer.

"You're sure?" the marshal asked, hefting his bag farther onto his shoulder.

The deputy—Hunter, Anna had called him—gave an apologetic look. "I'm sorry, sir, but yes, I'm absolutely sure. It's Jess."

"Damn," the marshal muttered. "It's gonna devastate David. Be sure none of this gets out until I tell him, all right? I gotta take care of my family first."

The deputy was silent as he nodded.

Peter turned to pace in the other direction and rubbed his hand along the back of his neck as he pretended to listen to someone. He occasionally mumbled things like "uh-huh," "yeah," and "okay" so he wouldn't appear suspicious.

The men arrived at the cop car.

"You're positive it's the same as before?" Marshal Garnier asked.

"Yes, sir," Hunter replied. "Same COD and wound pattern."

The marshal continued to talk, but Peter didn't hear what he said as the men hurried to get into the car. It wouldn't have mattered if they'd stayed outside. He wasn't sure he'd be able to listen to anything after that bombshell anyway.

COD.

Cause of Death.

Peter almost dropped his phone.

Someone was dead?

The cop car pulled away as Peter turned back to the ball field. Though the players went back to the game, it was obvious that the crowd wasn't paying the same attention. Even Spencer and Anna were looking over at him still standing on the edge of the parking lot.

Someone was dead.

Peter's stomach dropped as he watched his brother from the distance. There was no way he could keep this from Spencer. Not for long, at least.

In this small town where everyone told everyone everything, the news would be buzzing by morning. And especially if the victim was a family member of the marshal's. . . .

Same wound pattern, the deputy had reported.

This wasn't just some random death, Peter realized. It was murder.

A repeat murder. Maybe only the second, but maybe the third or fourth.

If there was a murderer on the loose, there wasn't a snowball's chance in hell that Spencer would stick around.

Peter's stomach dropped. He suddenly felt like Wenzel. As though the world was going mad around him and he was desperate to save it. To be of some help.

But he wasn't Wenzel. He wasn't a private detective, and he didn't have special abilities to stop bad guys.

He couldn't help, and he couldn't stop Spencer from leaving town tomorrow.

Their chance at living their dream was over.

Peter turned and looked down the road as the cop car disappeared. The fragment of an idea formed in his mind.

There was only one way he could get Spencer to give DeVerre a chance now. Only one way to hold onto that inheritance from Diane.

A small-town cop couldn't be accustomed to tracking a murderer, let alone a repeat murderer. And if it was a family member, it would be an especially hard case for him.

For the past several years, he and Spencer had studied murder for their stories. If anyone might have some insight, it would be them. It was farfetched, he knew, but maybe they *could* help?

Maybe it would even earn them some favor with the town.

And if nothing else, maybe getting this murderer off the streets could keep Spencer in DeVerre a little longer.

CHAPTER SIX

Peter

"Did you move my book?" Spencer asked the second he entered the kitchen the next morning.

Peter squinted against the early light as he sipped his coffee. "What are you talking about?" he mumbled, noticing his brother's irritated tone.

"I was reading my book last night, and this morning it was across the room on the dresser." The shake in Spencer's voice was subtle, but noticeably present.

Peter smirked, amused by his brother's constant paranoia. "You sure you didn't put it there yourself, Poirot?"

"I was reading it in bed," Spencer countered. "I put it on the nightstand before I went to sleep."

"Maybe you took a little stroll in your sleep last night." Peter took another casual sip. "Or maybe you moved it this morning while you were still half asleep."

Spencer crossed his arms, clearly not amused with his brother's lack of concern.

Ignoring him, Peter jumped up from his seat, too focused to get sidetracked by Spencer's overactive imagination. "Forget about that," he said, pouring fresh coffee into a travel mug. "I've been up for hours waiting on you."

"What *are* you doing up so early?" Spencer asked, a nervous glint in his eyes.

"The police station opens at eight. I wanna get there first thing."

Spencer stared at him, ignoring the proffered coffee mug. "You can't be serious."

"Why not? I told you last night, I think we could be a real help."

He watched his brother's chest rise and fall in a giant, exasperated sigh. "We aren't gonna chase a murderer. We're in enough danger as it is. What if the other victim they mentioned was Diane? What if we're next?"

"You don't have any long-term memory, do you?" Peter set the mug on the counter, then clasped both of Spencer's annoyingly muscular shoulders in his hands. "*Diane died in her sleep!* Try to remember that this time, would you?"

Spencer took up the coffee as Peter backed away, continuing his argument. "And even if you were right—which you very much are not—why would the murderer choose to kill the marshal's family member next instead of us?"

"Maybe she was in the wrong place at the wrong time."

"And maybe you need proof to let this whole theory go." Peter grinned. "Which is exactly what I'm gonna get you by solving this mystery."

Spencer sighed, reaching for his denim jacket. "You're gonna make us look like idiots."

"I prefer the term 'geniuses.'"

"Let's get this over with, okay?" Spencer grabbed the keys from the island. Anguis and Nex lifted their heads at the jingling. "Stay here, guys. We'll be back soon."

"See ya, pups." Peter went to pat Nex on the head as he walked past.

A low growl sent his hand flying back as the dog recoiled from him.

Peter hurried after Spencer. "They hate me." He grabbed his own jacket from the rack.

"You've got to give it time."

"They didn't need time with you."

Spencer shrugged as he locked the door behind him.

Peter crossed his arms, glaring at the parting curtains. Anguis pushed his head through the fabric, watching them on the porch. "I want it too much, that's what it is. They can sense it."

"You're thinking of cats." Spencer headed for the Jeep.

They got down to the station at 8:04 a.m.

It was exactly what Peter imagined of a small-town police station. Drop ceilings, cream walls, brown tiled floors, two large desks out front, and one cubicle-like office in the back.

"Good morning," a woman said from the front desk. She appeared to be somewhere near their mother's age, her dark hair pulled into a low bun that showed the gray at her temples. "How can I help you boys out this morning?"

"Morning," Peter said, taking the lead as usual. "Love those glasses. They really complement your eyes."

"Oh. . . ." She furrowed her brow at first, then smiled. "Thank you."

"I'm Peter. This is my brother, Spencer."

His brother gave a wave.

She waved back with a polite smile.

"We were wondering if we could meet with the marshal."

The woman glanced back toward the office. "Tom and I only got in a few minutes ago, but he's got to go back out in a moment. May I tell him what this is in reference to?"

"Sure." Peter drew his shoulders back to be sure he appeared as confident as possible. "We'd like to discuss the *incident* from last night with him."

She tugged on the sleeve of her black sweater. "You mean Jess's death?"

"Uh." Caught off guard her forthcoming nature, Peter hesitated. "Yeah."

With a nod, she rose. "Let me check if he's got a second to speak with you."

She was gone for less than a minute. Peter scanned the office another time, and Spencer sighed, muttering that this was a dumb idea.

"Tom will see you," the woman—Marshal Garnier's wife, he guessed—said on her return.

"Thanks." Peter moved for the door with Spencer close at his side.

Mrs. Garnier shut the door behind them as the marshal stood. "Morning, boys," he said, holding out his hand to shake each of theirs. His own dark hair bore the peppering of a few grays, but he looked like a fit officer of the law. Trim, but well built. Short, but broad. Professional, but rugged. "What can I do for you?"

Taking the seats the marshal gestured to, Peter glanced at Spencer. "Uh, well," he fumbled, feeling his confidence slipping now that it was time to offer up their expertise. "It's more about what we can do for you."

The marshal narrowed his dark brown eyes. "I'm sorry? I don't understand."

Spencer clasped his hands in front of him and stared at the floor.

"It's just. . . ." Peter cleared his throat and tried again. He grinned at the marshal. "Do you know much about us, sir?"

"'Fraid I don't, son."

"Well, we're writers. Mystery writers."

A bewildered expression pulled the marshal's brows together. "Excuse me?"

"We're well versed in solving crime, you see. It's what we do. Or rather. . . ." Peter chuckled. "We sort of create the crime to solve in our stories. But that's really my point here. We know how to solve mysteries."

The marshal sat back in his chair. "Am I understanding you correctly, son? Are you . . . offering to help us solve this investigation?"

"Yes, sir." Peter hoped the marshal would understand how seriously he was taking his own words. "We may be new to DeVerre, but it's our home too now, and we'd like to help keep it safe. And what better way than by catching the murderer?"

Several seconds ticked by as the marshal eyed him. He glanced at Spencer once but seemed to decide his detachment in the conversation excluded him from inspection. There was an indistinguishable look on his face as he studied Peter. His lips turned down in a slight frown, but whether that was from disappointment, concern, or focus, he couldn't tell.

Finally, the marshal ran his fingers along his thick mustache. "Did you see something, son?"

Peter faltered again, confused by the question. "What?"

"Did you witness the crime?"

"Oh, no, I just—we can help with the investi—"

"I appreciate the sentiment, boys, I really do," the marshal said, cutting him off. His voice turned condescending. "But this is a straightforward case. And we already know who our 'murderer' is."

"You do?"

He gave him a superior sort of nod.

"And?"

"It's a wolf."

Spencer looked up finally, his mouth ajar.

Peter stared back at the marshal in shock. "What?"

"This is the second wolf attack this year. We had a farmer die about a month ago in the exact same fashion. Nothing sinister, just a damn nuisance."

Peter didn't know why, but his stomach dropped in disappointment even as Spencer let out a relieved sigh.

"Now if you boys care to be of help," the marshal continued, "we've got hunting parties set up for the whole week to find the animal. However, as you two are city boys, I'd imagine a hunt isn't your forte."

"We'd be happy to help anyway, sir," Spencer said, though Peter knew it was out of obligation to do the right thing more than a genuine desire to be part of the hunt.

The marshal turned his skeptical gaze on him. "You know how to shoot a rifle, kid?"

"Uh, I mean, in theory."

"Best stay home then. Appreciate the willingness, though." He gave them each a dismissive nod and stood again. "Have a good day, boys."

Spencer jumped up, ready to go, but Peter took his time rising. He didn't like the way the man had showed so much disregard for them and their offer. Sure, authors weren't trained detectives, but they weren't stupid. The two of them had done tons of study on all forms of crime over the past several years. They probably knew more than the deputy and the marshal put together, thanks to their research. It might not be street smarts, but they had extensive knowledge on crime and procedure.

Yet Marshal Garnier was looking at them as though they were upstart kids looking to goof off. He didn't even think they could be helpful in tracking down a wolf.

Frustration getting the better of him, Peter turned back to the marshal as Spencer opened the office door. "Can I be honest, man?" He didn't wait for a response from the surprised cop. "I'm twenty-eight. It's weird enough for you to call us 'son' like we're your kids when we literally just met. But you don't have to insult us by calling us 'boys.'"

The marshal furrowed his brow as he scanned him, as if taking him in anew. "I wouldn't have thought you a day over twenty-four."

Peter shoved his thumb toward Spencer. "And how old do you think he is? Twelve?"

He shrugged. "About twenty-four."

"We're not twins, man."

"Look, *son*." The marshal's tone was hard and unyielding. "I don't care how old you are. We don't need your help. Now, I've got work to do, so you can see yourselves out."

Fuming, Peter pushed his way out of the office and past Spencer. He didn't wait on his brother as he heard him apologizing to the marshal and his wife. Nor did he stop after he'd followed him out to the street.

Peter took a right out of the police station and marched straight into The Glass Tavern. The bell of the restaurant chimed overhead as he shoved open the door. He didn't slow down until he plopped onto the barstool directly in front of Anna. "I need a drink."

"What's going on?" She glanced at Spencer as he caught up and took the seat next to Peter.

Peter huffed. "The marshal's a dick."

Spencer shook his head. "He had a point, you know?" He sounded annoyed as well, but not at the cop. At Peter. "We *aren't* detectives, Pete. We write about them. What could we actually do in *any* case? And this one's already closed!"

"It's not about that," Peter argued, feeling his humiliation rising. He needed to defend himself. To prove his reasons were justifiable and it was the cop who was in the wrong. "He acted like we were stupid for even offering to help. Like we were too incompetent to be of any good."

"And what good would we be?" Spencer countered. "You really want to hunt a wolf?"

"I *want* to be of use."

Spencer turned away with a heavy scoff. Silence fell between the brothers.

Anna stared at them both as she set coffees on the counter in front of them. They were all quiet for a few beats. Peter took a sip from his mug.

"You know," Anna muttered, "I know I wasn't there, so I don't really understand, but . . . I think it's nice. That you care."

"Thanks," Peter replied, the pressure in his chest releasing a bit with the knowledge that *someone* was on his side.

"But. . . ."

"Oh, come on." He tossed his hands in the air at the immediate let down.

Anna fixed him with a firm glare. "DeVerre isn't a trusting place, all right? And you're trying to step up too fast."

They both stared at her, not accustomed to her use of so strong a tone.

"Everyone is going to be suspicious of you two for a long time, okay? And the best way for you to get rid of that suspicion is to lay low and behave like everyone else. Come to the games on Fridays. Show up at church on Sundays. Be at every event you get an invite to. Live your life, and let people decide for themselves when they want you in theirs. Otherwise, you're going to scare them off."

The brothers were silent as they took in her advice. It was sound, Peter supposed. No one here knew them. A week wasn't long enough to make lasting friendships that were built on trust. It didn't matter his intentions. The marshal would never entrust any case to a stranger like him. Who would?

Peter sighed, running a hand through his hair. They'd shown up in DeVerre a week ago, and he was trying to pretend like they'd been there for years. Why? Because he needed this to work.

If they failed, they'd have to go back to reality. And for Peter, that reality was getting more and more grim by the year.

He was nearing thirty, and they still hadn't managed to get their writing up and running. He'd put his whole life on hold for their potential career. Girls never stuck around because he wasn't 'ready.' He didn't have a steady income because he'd focused on building his creative career rather than a stable one. He couldn't afford a real home or a reliable car, let alone a wife and kids.

If they failed here, Peter would have to make a decision. Life as a struggling— and likely failing—artist or life with a family at the steep price of settling for a normal job.

Taking another swig of his coffee, Peter glanced up at Anna. She'd said that DeVerre wasn't a trusting place. That it would take a long time of continued evidence of their trustworthiness to get people to accept them. That if they tried to force their way in, they'd scare people off.

He frowned, the realization dawning on him as she stared back, arms crossed tightly over her chest. "You don't trust us either, do you?"

Anna lifted her left shoulder in a shrug. "Not yet."

So there it was. They were alone in DeVerre with only each other to rely on. No one was on their side, no one cared if they stayed, no one would help them figure this whole new life of theirs out.

"I want to, though," Anna said, cutting through his self-pity. Peter heard a soft, hopeful tilt to her voice. "So please, prove me right."

Peter grinned, happy to find that they weren't totally on their own. "We'll do our best."

They stuck around with Anna for the next hour as they finished their coffees. "I've got the night off, by the way," she said as they gathered their things to go. "I'm supposed to meet with some friends at Pinewood Pins if you want to come."

"You sure they'll be all right with us joining?" Spencer asked.

Peter slugged his arm. "I do believe she told us to accept *every* invitation we receive." He turned back to Anna. "We'll be there."

A heavy mist fell, drenching everything as they stepped outside of the tavern. They hurried to the Jeep and followed the circle back toward Occasus. The CD of Sting's greatest hits was playing again, reminding Peter of their dad. He glanced over at Spencer, silent as he drove them home.

They both favored their dad in practically every way. One of the only ways in which Peter was similar to his brother. They'd gotten their dad's looks and shared a love for writing.

But after their dad had died fourteen years ago, grief was another thing they shared.

David Collins had been the perfect dad. Funny, caring, smart, and strong. He'd given Peter and Spencer everything they had needed as kids. He'd made Spencer feel safe and Peter feel important. It was his love for mystery TV shows that had gotten them into the genre themselves. Of course, he had watched shows like *Matlock* and *Magnum, P.I.* while they wrote historical fiction that centered around monsters and magic. But it was their dad who had instilled the love of mystery deep within them.

He was the reason they had never given up on their dream to make writing a real career. The only reason that tough times, loneliness, and disappointment hadn't stopped either of them. The reason that Spencer had faced his fears by coming out here. The reason that Peter refused to let their only chance go.

"Hey," Peter said, giving his brother's arm a gentle punch.

Spencer glanced over at him.

"I'm sorry," Peter continued with an apologetic grin. "You were right. It was a stupid idea going to the marshal."

A slow smirk spread over Spencer's lips. "Yeah. It was."

Seeing that the apology had been received, Peter took the chance to bring some levity back to their day. "I still think we could have solved it though."

Spencer laughed. "*Murder, She Wrote* always was your favorite show."

"*My* favorite?" Peter scoffed. "Do I need to remind you that it was *you* who told everyone that he wanted to grow up to be Jessica Fletcher?"

"I said I wanted to be *like* her."

"Whatever you say, J.B. We're in our own Cabot Cove now."

"God, I hope not! Pretty soon it'd just be you, me, and the doc."

"Sounds terrible."

Without warning, the engine of the Jeep revved to an unnatural whine as the incline rose the smallest grade. "Uh-oh." Spencer gave the dash a worried pat. "C'mon, bud, we're almost there."

Peter sighed. "Seriously? I can literally see the house from here."

Two sputters, one cough, a final rev, and the engine died.

Spencer glanced at him.

"What happened?"

"I don't know." Spencer put the car in neutral. "Come on, we'll have to push him the rest of the way."

"Push him?"

"He's done this before." He opened his door. "He just needs a break."

"Dude, you gotta get this thing fixed." Peter unbuckled his seatbelt to join his brother in the misty rain. "We've got an insane amount of cash in our bank account now. We can afford for you to take a bit of it for this old guy."

Spencer didn't respond, frozen as he stared past Peter's window, blue eyes wide.

Peter turned around in his seat to follow his gaze. He searched the pines around the road. Green and brown were all that he could see at first. Then the movement caught his attention.

A man was walking through the forest, trudging through the rain as though it weren't a bother. He wore a dark green jacket and a pair of casual trousers that looked too nice for a hike, but the man was too far away for Peter to catch any more details.

"Tell me you see him too," Spencer muttered.

"Yeah," Peter confirmed, more concerned by the shake in Spencer's voice than the stranger. "Yeah, I see him."

"This is the third time I've caught him wandering the woods around here in the past week."

"Really? Hm, that's . . . I mean, he's just out for a walk."

"He weirds me out."

"Everything weirds you out."

Spencer's eyes didn't deviate from the man's path. "You think he's up to something?"

"What? No way." Peter glanced over his shoulder again.

It *was* a rather strange place to go for a walk. There was nothing out this way but Occasus. They'd learned that the Blackwood Park had walking trails from Anna, but that was up to the northeast of DeVerre, and this was in the opposite direction. If the guy wanted to go on a pleasant stroll, why not head up there? Or even go downtown?

Peter frowned. "Hm." He watched the man disappear, feeling a bit foolish for falling into Spencer's paranoia. "Maybe."

CHAPTER SEVEN

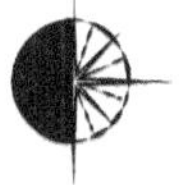

Spencer

After their conversation with Anna on that morning, Spencer had a lot of time to think. He attempted to fix up the Jeep to no avail, tossed a tennis ball for the dogs, and finally reverted to sitting at the dining room table, staring blankly at his laptop for the rest of the afternoon.

Peter's sudden desire to solve the case and his resulting freak-out woke Spencer to a realization about his older brother that he hated. It didn't matter how confident a front Peter put on for the world, he was just as scared as Spencer. But unlike Spencer, his fear didn't revolve around all the impossible things that his imagination concocted. No, Peter's fears all centered around his fear of failing. That he would never be enough. That he would always be lacking. And his stupid plan that morning could only have been driven by his desperation to make DeVerre work. To make their dreams work.

Since they'd been kids, there had always existed an understanding between the two of them. Peter would take care of Spencer and Spencer would take care of Peter. No matter what.

After the tragedy of their dad's unexpected death, it was the promise they'd made to each other. Neither of them would ever be alone. They'd always have each other. They could always rely on each other.

Their mom was great through it all, but she was grieving herself. It was a mutual agreement between the boys not to put pressure on her. Together they would help her, and alone they would help each other. She'd have hated their decision if they'd ever told her. But thankfully they never had to divulge their pact. After waiting a long six years, their mom started dating again. But only after the two of them forced the issue. They wanted to leave home and weren't happy with the idea of her being alone for the rest of her life. She married Ben Powell, a friend of their Uncle Matt, a year later, and the boys finally felt their job of taking care of their mom was complete.

Now that they'd moved to DeVerre, it really was just the two of them. And Spencer needed to hold up his end of the deal. He needed to take care of his brother. To make sure that DeVerre worked for him. To make sure that Peter finally found the success that he so desperately wanted.

All his thinking led Spencer to one conclusion. He had to give the town a fair shot for Peter's sake.

And if he was going to do that, he needed to start acting like this was their home.

So Spencer made sure to get them out the door and to the bowling alley on time. Peter said they needed a social life, so a social life they would have. Among Anna's friends were older brother, Aaron, and his girlfriend, Haley, who also worked at the tavern. Aaron was far quieter than either of his sisters. But Haley was more talkative than both of them, though she was less annoying than Spencer expected upon first meeting her. It was more like she struggled to contain her excitement to talk *with* them rather than her desire to talk *at* them.

It was an odd dynamic to watch, the reserved Aaron and bubbly Haley. Aaron focused on the game, keeping score, and taking his turns while she was busy socializing. But he'd always set a gentle hand on her arm when it was her turn and give her a high five whether she did well or not. Spencer found himself enjoying the couple's company.

Anna's other friends were nowhere near as interesting, though they were all nice people too. There was a married couple—Cory and Reagan—and a young, brunette woman named Danielle. It turned out that while most of them worked together at the tavern, they were all in the same Bible study group along with another couple who'd had to miss the bowling night. No one in the group seemed particularly interested in Peter or Spencer, so he didn't mind when they all left first. Only the siblings and Haley remained with the brothers.

When he found out that Spencer hadn't been able to get the Jeep back up and running that day, Aaron raised his chin toward him. "You don't have a car tonight?" he asked.

"Uh, no." Spencer passed him a disappointed grin. "It's kind of old, and it isn't the first time it's died on me."

"Ah, I see." Aaron pushed his wire rimmed glasses up his nose. "You think you could get it running long enough to bring it by the shop on Monday?"

"The shop—you mean the mechanic shop?"

"Yeah."

Spencer scratched the back of his head. "To be honest, I'm not sure. I don't have a clue what's going on with it."

Aaron pursed his lips in thought. "Well, how about this? I'll come by and see if I can get it running. Then I'll bring it to the shop, and we can make sure the problem doesn't happen again."

"You're a mechanic?" Peter asked, a hint of awe in his voice.

"Yeah," Aaron confirmed like it should be obvious.

"He's a really good mechanic," Haley said, slipping her arm through his and smiling up at him.

He gave her a soft smile. "We're closed on Sundays, but I could come pick it up tomorrow if that's better for you?"

"Yeah." Spencer felt relief welling up within him, allowing his shoulders to relax. He'd begun to fear that he'd have to give up the Jeep. "That would be awesome. And whatever's better for you works for us."

"Cool. How about I come by after church? I can have Haley drive me up, and then I'll take your Jeep back."

Haley nodded, her curly blonde hair bouncing around her face. "I'd be happy to!"

"Great! Thanks," Spencer said.

Peter clamped a hand on Spencer's shoulder and leaned toward Aaron. "You're a freakin' godsend, man," he insisted. "You're probably my new favorite person."

Aaron turned to Anna as if confused by Peter's enthusiasm. "Uh, yeah," he said, shifting from foot to foot. "No problem."

Though it was out of their way, Haley offered to take the brothers home before she dropped Anna off. Aaron had ridden his motorcycle— which, to Spencer's chagrin, made Peter insist he needed one of his own—so he said goodbye to them at the bowling alley.

When they walked into Occasus as Haley and Anna pulled back through the gates, Spencer felt that the whole evening had been a success. Peter was grinning from ear to ear, talking nonstop about all the ideas he'd had for the book during the day. It was like the meeting with the marshal had been erased from his brother's memory and he was back to his old self.

Scratching behind the dogs' ears when they both came to greet him, Spencer smiled. For the first time in days, he felt calm within Occasus. And a sprig of hope began to grow in him, thinking that perhaps things within DeVerre might not be so bad after all.

~

The following morning they had to leave early so they could make it to the church on time. Spencer was thankful that there wasn't rain, but taking a walk so soon after waking up wasn't his preferred way to spend a

Sunday. Still, he pushed both himself and Peter through their sluggish moods to ensure they wouldn't be late.

Like the rest of the town, DeVerre Chapel checked off several boxes in the small-town playbook. Its white, wooden slats were chipping from age, and the steep pitch of the roof met together in a triangle. A weathered cross hung over the door beneath the soffit. A long line of churchgoers were ambling into the chapel when the brothers arrived.

As Spencer walked into the chapel for the first time, he took his time to study all the details. The interior was a curious blend of modern and traditional. The lights overhead were modest and contemporary. The structure was simple with a small, closed-in booth to the right of the door for the soundboard and PowerPoint and what Spencer guessed to be the office behind a closed door to the left. The sanctuary was large and clean and took up most of the building. Dark wood covered the floor contrasting the stark white walls. Wooden pews filled the room, spaced to line up with the gothic, arch-framed windows. The stage at the front and the pulpit itself bore a more traditional design, but everything else looked updated and fresh. A row of electric musical instruments were settled at the back of the stage. There were modern conveniences apparent all throughout the church.

Spencer was pleased to find it didn't feel nearly as creepy as he would have expected from a town such as DeVerre.

However, it didn't take him long to feel the distinctive atmosphere of sorrow in the air. The congregation all spoke in hushed whispers about the failed wolf hunt of the previous night as they took their seats. Peter and Spencer sat at the back of the building. No one spoke to them, but it wasn't much of a surprise. No one knew them.

Reverend Chapelle got up and began the service with a moment of silence for the marshal's cousin's daughter, Jessica Calderon. She had been young—only a couple of years older than Peter—and she'd left behind a husband and two little girls. Spencer felt terrible for the family. And looking around the congregation, he felt sorry for the people of

DeVerre. From the looks of things, it genuinely seemed that everyone in the church was sharing in the grief of her loss. He caught a glimpse of Anna and Ava toward the front on the far left, but the crowd blocked most of his view of the women.

After a short time of worship, the reverend taught a good sermon. It referenced the beauty of grief as it was a depiction of how much we love our lost family and friends. But his words reminded Spencer too much of their dad, and he wound up writing notes for *Wenzel & Frankly* the majority of the service to block out the reverend's voice. He only put away his notes as the reverend concluded his sermon with a prayer.

"Draw us to the heart of your Son," he prayed, head bowed. "Inspire us by your Holy Spirit, and teach us to see the unseen. Amen."

All in all, Spencer found it to be like any other service he had gone to in Norfolk. He wasn't sure what exactly he'd anticipated, but with DeVerre's distrusting and standoffish population, it surprised him how normal it all seemed. How mundane.

Aaron and Haley found them after the service, and they rode back to Occasus with them. It took Aaron the better part of an hour to get the Jeep running, but soon he was back on his way to town. From there, the brothers spent their evening developing the start for their novel.

The night brought more rain with it as they settled into the living room, stretching out on the couches as they read. With the gentle tap of raindrops on the windowpanes and the waning evening light, the house felt peaceful and serene. Nex had curled up on the floor, and Spencer let his hand dangle to brush the dog's wiry fur every few pages.

Spencer smiled as he glanced over at his brother, his dark eyes narrowed on his own book. It was odd, but after his initial and admittedly irrational fears during their early days at the House of Occasus, Spencer realized that somehow he'd become comfortable within its mysterious and gloomy halls. It was beginning to feel like home.

The next day, Spencer got up early and headed straight for Diane's office. The dogs watched as he started by taking inventory of the books that were stacked haphazardly throughout the room. There were holes in the shelves where some of them clearly belonged, so once he assessed the way Diane had organized her books, he began the slow process of putting them all back into place.

"What are you doing?" Peter walked in with a fresh cup of coffee in his hand. The right side of his hair still stood on end from sleep, and there was a definitive half-awake glint to his eyes as he yawned.

Spencer finished straightening a row of books as Peter dropped into the desk chair. "Cleaning up. If we're gonna live here, we're gonna have to make it less creepy." He grabbed the spooky skull from the shelf. "Starting with this thing."

Watching as he tossed the skull into a box, Peter nodded. "Mkay, I can get behind that. Are you just planning to clean up in here or are you gonna do some rearranging too?"

Spencer moved to the next stack of books. "Yeah, I thought we could move the desk away from the window and into the middle of the room."

"Why?"

"'Cause we should get a second one and put them up against one another. Then we can both be working at the same time."

Peter grimaced. "I don't wanna stare at your stupid face while I'm writing, weirdo."

"Then don't."

"What if I want to look out the window?"

"Then look out the window."

His older brother kicked off the desk, sending the chair spinning as he smirked. "I can't if your fat head is in the way."

As payback, Spencer whacked his head with a book mid-spin.

"Ow!"

"If you don't like my idea, that's fine. But you'll be the one working at the dining room table."

Peter continued to rub the back of his head. "No, I'll work in the living room. I don't need a desk anyways."

"I still want to move the desk."

"Why?"

"It's distracting," Spencer explained, "sitting at the window."

"Hmph, well fine. We'll move *your* desk, and you can have the fancy office all to yourself."

Despite his teasing, they spent the next several hours cleaning the office. It took them through lunch and into the evening, reorganizing the books, sifting through papers, and removing the knickknacks that Spencer disapproved of most.

It was the desk that took the majority of their time as they kept finding things that halted their progress. The first distraction was the picture frame they found hidden among all the papers. It was a two-sided frame, but both photos were of the same couple. One taken on their wedding day and the other in front of Occasus later in life.

Peter and Spencer stared at the photos of their Great-Aunt Diane and Great-Uncle William Larkin. She looked a lot like their Grandpa Phillip, with her heavily hooded eyes and thin-lipped, crooked smile. She had dark hair in the first picture and bright silver hair in the second. And at her side in both stood a dashing man with the most impressive mustache Spencer had ever seen. He looked dapper and charming. His eyes twinkled even in the photograph. And he smiled with a palpable sense of joy.

Feeling that the photographs deserved a place of honor, Spencer moved the frame to the fireplace mantle in the office. The couple might have been unusual, and he may not have understood why Diane had left the brothers her home, but he thought it would please her to see them making it their own while still honoring her memory.

As they shuffled through the drawers and packed away all Diane's things with care, they also ran into dozens of notes for her first book. Spencer had no interest in reading about ghosts, so he handed all the papers to Peter who squirreled them away to the living room for later inspection. They discovered a box in the bottom left drawer labeled 'Liam.' Though he felt guilty for peeking in at first, Spencer soon discovered it was only more research, but this time for their uncle's essay. Peter took that too.

Though they worked late, there was still a ton to do the next day. Once Spencer finally got the office set up to his liking, they took the boxes of Diane's things up to the attic. When they found that there was little in the attic but a few other boxes marked as winter clothes and holiday supplies, they decided to tackle the rest of the house. Together they moved out all the creepy or old-lady type decorations and only kept what felt natural. At the end of the night, the rooms were far more comfortable as a result, and it was far easier for Spencer to forget they were living in what he considered a haunted house as he fell asleep each ensuing night.

As their second week in the house progressed, the brothers worked hard on the book as well as the blog. With a start to the novel finally underway, they had a direction for the next few episodes of their serial. And as they were approaching their next bi-weekly upload, Spencer got busy developing the next chapter of the story as it was to be set in Frankly's point of view.

He was happy, his mind busy and content to work on the projects he'd set up for himself. Besides keeping up with his busy schedule, Spencer made a point to get down to the gym each day for the noon class. Ever since he and Peter had been kids, he had gotten used to having some sort of sport or exercise in his life. Their mom had put them in karate at an early age, and while Peter had no interest in it for himself, Spencer had thrived. He stuck with the lessons all through high school, earning his black belt. It gave him a sense of self-assurance that, if for any reason he should need to, he *could* defend himself. And as his imagination regularly convinced him that he *would* need to, it made him feel a fraction safer.

When he got into college, he transitioned to going to the gym on a regular basis. The physical activity always made it easier for him to sit still and write afterward. Walks were nice, but they had never given him the same results. Now that he was renewing his routine in DeVerre, he was already seeing the benefit after just the first couple days. He was more focused and clearer-headed and the words flowed out with ease each time he sat down to write.

To his delight, Aaron eventually got the Jeep fixed up, though most of the week was spent waiting on the parts. But he called Spencer on Friday to let him know it was ready. It was a hefty sum for all the labor that had gone into it, but Aaron promised that it was worth it as he handed him the keys. "The ol' girl won't be giving you trouble anytime soon."

"Thanks," Spencer said, just happy to have the Jeep back.

"We're about to head to the game," Peter spoke up from Spencer's side. "Care to join?"

"No thanks." Aaron ran a hand over his buzzed black hair. "I'm not much for social gatherings. I prefer cars to people."

Spencer smiled and nodded. "I understand that."

Peter smirked, tossing a thumb in his brother's direction. "And I understand because he's like that, but with books."

Hopping back into the Jeep, Spencer smoothed his hands over the leather wheel. It felt good to be back in the driver's seat. Like coming home. He turned the key in the ignition, and it purred to life.

"Now *that*—" a wide grin spread across his brother's face. "Is more like it!"

They headed to the game to find most of the town already there. The Ravens were playing the Farmers, marking the field with their black and yellow tees. It took the brothers about fifteen minutes of searching to realize that Anna wasn't there. They did find Haley, however, who waved them over to join her in the stands. "She's working," she explained. "There's rarely any customers on game night, but someone's gotta run the place."

Haley introduced them to a few more people, and as the game went on, it began to feel like they were actually a part of DeVerre. Peter joined in on the cheers and conversation while Spencer spent most of his time observing the people around them. Perhaps it was Haley's and Peter's more outgoing natures that put the others at ease, but with the overall friendliness and high spirits amongst the bleachers, Spencer felt that the townspeople were beginning to warm up to the idea of the brothers living there. One week would never be enough to totally break through the barrier of mistrust in the town, but he hoped it was a good start.

"Why don't we swing by the tavern?" Peter asked after the game. "We don't want Annie missing out on all the fun."

"All right," Spencer agreed, satisfied as the Jeep started up without hesitation once more.

The moment they sat down, Anna set a water in front of Spencer and got to working on Peter's cocktail. "You two must have been busy," she said. "I haven't seen you all week."

"Well, we've been fixing up Occasus," Peter explained quickly. "You wouldn't recognize the place."

Anna grinned. "Especially since I've never been there."

"You haven't?" Peter's eyes grew wide. "Oh, man, you gotta come over sometime. It's a cool house."

"Sure, that sounds fun."

"If you think they'd enjoy it," Spencer added, "Aaron and Haley could join. We could have a game night or something."

Anna's smile spread as she handed Peter his drink. "Yeah! I think they'd like that a lot."

"Great!" Peter said, giving her arm a tap before she pulled away. "You working tomorrow?"

"Yes, but I have Sunday night off."

"Perfect, let's do it Sunday then." He lifted his glass for a sip. Then he snapped his fingers and pointed at her. "Oh, yeah, and then I can show you the stuff we found!"

Anna laughed at his obvious enthusiasm. "What did you find?"

"Diane's research for her first book. And Liam's stuff too. Though his stuff was hard to understand. It's, like, super complicated theological and historical documents. A bit too involved for light reading." Peter leaned in toward her conspiratorially. "But Diane's stuff . . . man, it's crazy. There's all kinds of weird ghostly things in it."

"And you wondered why I didn't want to read it," Spencer shuddered, then gestured toward the taps. "Hey, you got a wheat over there?"

Anna raised her brow. "You want a beer?"

He shrugged. "I drink one every now and then."

"He's a simple sort of man," Peter declared, settling a hand on his shoulder. "But thankfully, when he drinks, he drinks the good stuff."

"Well, we don't have much in the way of 'good stuff,'" she replied with an amused, but apologetic tilt to her voice. "But we do have a couple of craft brews on tap from Spokane. No wheat, though. Just an IPA and an amber ale."

"That's fine," Spencer brushed Peter's hand off his shoulder. "I'll take the amber."

As she poured the beer, Peter rested his arms on the counter. "How about you, Ann? You interested in Diane's research?"

"Uh . . . I don't know," she said, passing him a hesitant grin. "I'm not much for ghost stories."

Spencer thanked her for the drink as she set it down. "They freak you out too?"

"Most of the time."

Peter sighed. "Why am I surrounded by scaredy cats? *There's nothing to be afraid of.*" He emphasized each word. "It's all hearsay and silly folklore."

"So you don't believe in ghosts?" Anna asked.

"Not a chance!"

Spencer nodded in agreement, though the very conversation was starting to make his brain come up with all sorts of counterarguments and imaginations that said otherwise.

"Do you?" Peter tossed the question back to her.

Anna hesitated with a small shrug. "I dunno. I mean, I know there are a lot of things out there that we can't explain. And people have a lot of convincing stories. But . . . I guess it doesn't make sense to me. Believing in God the way I do. If there are ghosts . . . well, why?"

"That's a good question." Peter brooded, then his lips tipped up in a mischievous smile. "One that Diane's research might have the answer to."

She laughed and leaned against the back counter. "Well, maybe I'll give it a look in that case. Who knows, maybe Diane and Liam were onto something with their ghosts and theological research."

"They certainly had some goofy ideas if my reading has been any indication," Peter said with a chuckle.

"They always were a funny couple," Anna agreed. "I kinda thought they were cute though. He was always so sweet to her, and it was obvious that she adored him. They would even talk to each other in Latin sometimes."

"Yeah." Peter scoffed. "'Cute' is the *exact* word I'd use to describe that."

Anna's frown couldn't hide her amusement.

"Did you ever happen to hear what she was working on for her second book?" Spencer asked, hoping to get some more understanding of their great-aunt.

She shook her head. "I imagined you guys would have found that somewhere in the house too."

"Nah," Peter brushed his hand through the air. "She left her draft and research to that Cassandra lady. I guess the lawyer, Nicole, is holding it for her until she gets back."

"But her first book *was* about ghosts, right?" Spencer asked. "I'd imagine the second was about the same thing."

Anna tipped her head to the side in thought. "Yeah, that would make sense. But the little I knew of Diane, she was enough of a character to write something even stranger than that." She shrugged. "I did like her though. I was sad to hear that she died."

"You were?"

"Yeah, I mean, she was odd and all, but she was nice. And I always felt like . . . like she knew that she was different. In a good way. Like, she knew, and it made her happy. Like she felt set apart and special.”

Spencer chewed on the inside of his cheek as Peter stared at her, silent.

Anna grinned at them. “She left good tips too.”

Peter grunted out a laugh. “Well, that’s just ’cause you’re the best bartender-slash-waitress the world has ever seen.” He gestured to his glass before he hopped up from his stool. “Make me another, will you? I’ll be right back.”

Spencer watched as his brother turned the corner to the restrooms and Anna started making his signature cocktail. He turned back to study her process. She had the drink memorized already, and she’d even begun skewering the lemon peel with a toothpick to set on the edge and make it prettier.

“Your brother’s a funny one.” The young woman spoke suddenly, humor in her voice.

“Yeah, he is,” Spencer agreed, wondering if she truly grasped Peter’s personality or if she found him amusing alone. So often that was the case with his brother. People liked him, but they didn’t value him the way he valued them.

Spencer thought he ought to make sure she understood. “He likes you a lot though.”

Anna froze and looked up to stare at him.

Realizing how his words had likely come across, Spencer hastened to correct it. “Uh, no, sorry—uh, not—not like . . . *that*,” he said, then thought he might have ruined Peter’s chances if he *did* like her like *that*. “Well, I mean, maybe like *that*—I—I don’t know, he hasn’t said that or anything, but. . . .”

She just watched him, mouth ajar.

Spencer grimaced and worked to fix the mess he’d made. “What I mean is that he likes you as a friend. Like, he thinks you’re cool.”

There was a heartbeat of silence before Anna finally smiled. “Right.” She nodded. “I like him as a friend too.”

"Good. Yeah, 'cause . . . well, the point I'm trying to make is that Pete is a pretty dedicated person."

"Dedicated?"

"Yeah, he's . . . he's loyal to a fault. And it's gotten him into trouble before so . . . I just thought I should let you know because I know he comes across as goofy and sarcastic, but . . . he's really very serious when it comes to the people he cares about—family, friends, or whoever they happen to be. He kind of goes all in and . . . well it's been known to scare people off. And I thought you should know that he's going to take your friendship seriously. Probably more than you expect."

Anna was quiet as she took in his words. She glanced toward where Peter had disappeared. Then she turned back to Spencer, and he could see by the softness in her expression and her dark brown eyes that she understood. Really, truly understood.

"I respect that," she said. "I really do. And . . . I know what that's like. My family—they're everything to me. My parents, even though they've moved. My sister and her husband. My brother. Even Haley. I love them all. And my friends are no less important to me."

She paused and set the fresh cocktail on the bar top before meeting his eyes again. "I know that I've only known you two for a short time, but. . . ." She shrugged. "I'm impressed. By you both. I know that DeVerre is . . . crazy and weird and in the middle of nowhere, but . . . I'm glad you guys came. And I really hope you stay."

Thankful to know that she could appreciate his brother for who he was—whatever Peter or Anna's interest in each other—Spencer felt satisfied with the outcome. "Me too," he said, suddenly realizing that it was true.

As strange as it all was, DeVerre was growing on him. And he thought that no matter the curious interests of their great-aunt and uncle, no matter the rabid wolf in the area, no matter how dark the nights got, they could make their home here.

CHAPTER EIGHT

Peter

Life was going well. Better than Peter had anticipated.

It was odd the way Spencer was settling into their new life in DeVerre. As though he'd had no qualms from the moment they'd gotten the news of their inheritance. He'd buckled down, gotten to work on the serial, and figured out a solid start to the novel that Peter couldn't fault. His brother had already settled into a routine of writing, working out, writing some more, taking the dogs on long walks, reading a ton, and, when the nights called for it, socializing with their new friends. He was impressed with the change in Spencer. And he couldn't deny the results. Spencer had already begun to work on the first chapter of the novel, and all Peter could do was wait.

Yes, life was going well.

And he was bored out of his mind.

After reading through Diane and Liam's research, rearranging his room for the second time, and giving up on another search for the key to the locked room upstairs, Peter finally complained about his boredom to Spencer.

"You could get working on Wenzel's episode for the blog," was Spencer's ever-practical suggestion.

Peter brushed that off. "It's not due for another week."

"There's nothing wrong with getting work done early."

"You know I do my best work under pressure."

Spencer shrugged and went back to writing.

Tired of waiting around the house for something to do, Peter decided to find some form of entertainment. He gathered up the library books they no longer needed, got the keys off the island, failed in his attempt to pat Anguis on the head, and went to DeVerre's town square. If he couldn't do anything to help Spencer or get their book going, he might as well learn something interesting about their new home. And he couldn't forget the way Ava had mentioned knowing everything about the town and its residents.

"What are you doing here?" Ava peered at him from over her novel.

The floral scent of her tea permeated the air as Peter approached the desk and dropped the books he was carrying on the surface. "Just returning these." He scanned the room. "This place is cool, by the way. Did you decorate it all yourself?"

Tipping her head to the side to study him, Ava narrowed her gaze. He got the unmistakable feeling that she knew there was more to his visit. "My mother did. I've made my own additions, but most of it was her."

"It's cool."

"You said that already."

"Well, it's *really* cool."

She shut the novel, tossed it on the desk, and leaned forward. "What do you want, Pete?"

"May I?" He pointed to the chair across from her.

Ava hesitated, then nodded.

Peter sat down. "I want to know about DeVerre."

She huffed. "That's a large topic. How much do you want to know?"

"Everything that you know."

"You don't have the time or attention span for everything I know."

"Try me."

Crossing her arms, she leaned back in her chair. The hum of classical music played in the background as she stared at him.

He stared back.

She was rather pretty, he thought. A lot like Anna. Warm brown skin, black-brown hair, strong brow, sharp features. But much closer to Peter in age and far less friendly than her younger sister.

"Okay, fine," she said, pulling her feet up into the chair with her. "Matthias Varon founded DeVerre in 1884 along with one hundred sixty-two other settlers. They built the town here in the Blackwood Forest and bought up all the surrounding land for the lumber mill. Since then, DeVerre's main exports have been lumber, produce, and livestock."

"So you're telling me that a town of one hundred is only three hundred after more than a century?"

Ava grinned. "DeVerre isn't much of a hot spot. We don't have tourism nor any appeal to draw in new residents. No one knows about us, and we like it that way."

"Mm," Peter ran a hand along his scratchy jaw. He wondered if he should've shaved before coming. It would've helped him to look more serious. "Doesn't seem like that would do much to help avoid inbreeding."

She rolled her eyes. "We're small, but we're not bumpkins. No one here has any interest in kissing cousins."

"But everyone *is* related?"

"Just about."

"So how do you find people to marry?"

A wry tilt spread over her lips. "Some of us go off to college and pick up our spouses there. Others travel for work and meet people."

"You're married, right?"

She nodded.

"That's what Spence said. How'd you meet your husband?"

"College."

"And he didn't mind moving back here?"

"Not at all. It fascinated him."

"That's cool." He pressed his lips together and leaned against the table. "So why haven't we met any Varons yet? Anna told us they were the main family back in the day. They die out or something?"

Ava tugged on the thin gold chain she wore. "That's exactly what they did."

"Really?"

"Back in the '40s, Matthias's great-grandson, Michael, murdered his own father, Matthew, and then committed suicide. As the last remaining Varon, the line ended with him."

Peter gaped at her in shock. "What?"

"Michael Varon was unstable. The police records say that Lloyd Frossard, the primary doctor at the time, was already treating him for psychosis. Apparently, he had been seeing apparitions and thought that they were trying to kill him. As Lloyd wasn't a psychologist, he couldn't diagnose him correctly, but it's presumed that Michael was a paranoid schizophrenic."

"Oh boy." Peter sighed. He wouldn't be sharing that bit of the story with Spencer any time soon. He didn't want to disrupt the state of calm that had come over his brother lately.

"Yeah," Ava gave him a morbid smirk. "DeVerre has its own sordid past just like all other towns."

"But . . . that bad behavior hasn't continued, right?"

She shrugged. "Not enough to matter."

He didn't like that answer.

"DeVerre isn't the perfect town, but it is a good town. You don't need to worry about any deranged psychotics walking the streets."

Peter felt a sudden influx of what he assumed Spencer felt at all times. First they learned that a killer wolf roamed the area, and now this? A chill spread over him realizing that they lived in the former home of an insane murderer.

A tension crept in at the base of Peter's neck, and he had to work to keep his voice calm. "So you'd say it's rather safe?"

"As safe as a place in the middle of nowhere can be. But Tom does a good job as marshal, and the rest of the leadership does well enough at not being idiots."

He wanted more confirmation than that. "Who is in leadership? I haven't heard anyone talk about the mayor or city council or whatever it is you have here."

"It depends on who you ask," the librarian replied, her eyebrows arching over a sudden mischievous glint in her eyes. "But *technically* Fred Guillaume is our mayor. He's not the brightest bulb in the box, but he actually cares about the town, so he does a decent job. As far as who's *really* in charge, that's an ever-raging battle between the Frossards, Chapelles, and Garniers. The Guillaumes might have obtained the official title of mayor after the Varons died off, but they've never truly controlled anything."

"Wait," Peter held up a hand to halt her. He felt like the family tree of DeVerre was swimming around in his head. "You're telling me that the same family has gotten the office of mayor every time?"

"Yep."

"How?"

"The same way that the Garniers have always been our law and order, the Frossards our doctors, and the Chapelles our reverends. Same reason I'm the librarian. We don't like change here in DeVerre. If the Varons were still alive, they would be head of the government instead of the Guillaumes, no doubt in my mind."

"That seems sketchy."

"Because it's easy for corruption to seep in?"

"Yeah."

Ava shrugged. "I won't lie, there's plenty of that going on. Like I said, the Guillaumes don't control anything despite being the mayoral family and the ones who comprise the majority of the labor force in the town. They're run by whoever happens to have the ear of the mayor at the moment. But the good news is, none of it matters."

"How can corruption not matter?"

"Because it's all just nepotism and favors. Petty arguments, gossip, backstabbing, and rivalries. They don't hurt the people of DeVerre. And isn't that all that matters? They can play their stupid games, keep their foolish secrets, and enjoy the drama of their lives so long as it doesn't affect the citizens. Besides, all their scheming comes down to is a popularity contest. The people of DeVerre are really just kids who never left high school."

"But what do they stand to gain from it?" Peter asked, incredulous. It was hard for him to believe that such blatant shadiness didn't also come with a dark side. "If it's all pettiness and a popularity contest, then what's the point?"

Ava seemed unfazed by his pressing. "Power." She shrugged. "Whatever little amount of power that exists here in DeVerre."

"And that doesn't bother you?"

"Of course it does." She wrapped her thick yellow cardigan closer around her. "But there's nothing I can do to make the people of this town grow up. Trust me, I've tried."

"Did Diane do that too? Attempt to change the corruption and make them grow up?"

"In her own way, I suppose so."

"Is that why people didn't like her?"

"Pretty much."

"Hm." Peter stared at the bookshelves behind Ava's left shoulder. This news about their new home bothered him. Not only because it was odd and troublesome and Spencer would take it as confirmation that these people were secretly crazy. But it bothered Peter because there was something wrong, and he couldn't fix it. He liked fixing things. It made him feel useful—like less of a waste of space than usual.

Every instinct in him screamed to do something and change it. To go find all these people, sit them down, and get to the bottom of their stupid power struggle. He wanted to be part of this town—to matter to it as much as it mattered to him—and that meant getting involved. But he'd already tried that with the marshal, and it had ended poorly.

Anna had advised them to lay low until DeVerre trusted them. But how long would that take?

"Do you. . . ." Peter pushed a hand through his hair and sighed, working to tame his frustration. "Do you think it can change? Ever?"

"Maybe."

"Depending on?"

"The right people stepping up to change it."

Peter nodded.

"It isn't you."

"What?"

"I know what you're thinking." Ava leaned toward him. "But it's not going to be you or your brother. You're outsiders, and it will have to be a natural born DeVerrean who says enough is enough. No matter how much trust you earn, it will never be as much as someone who's lived here their whole life."

"Oh, yeah, no." He scratched the back of his head, attempting to laugh off the way she'd seen through him. "That's . . . that's not what I was thinking."

The knowing grin on Ava's face said she didn't buy his lie. She crossed her arms as she eyed him. "You two are doing well, though. Socializing and showing up. Anna's kept me up to date."

Peter felt himself perk up at that. "Really? Cool, yeah, that's good to hear."

"And Aaron likes you both too, so that speaks volumes. Obviously, they're my siblings, so I value their opinion, but it bodes well. Anna is close to the Frossards, and if they approve, the town approves."

"Yeah, she mentioned her relationship with them. I don't think that Gia-lady cared much for us though."

"Gia doesn't care for most people."

"Seems like she's that type."

Ava poured herself another cup of tea. "And what about you two?" she asked. "Are you liking it here so far?"

"Oh, yeah. Yeah, I think so."

"You *think* so?"

Peter nodded as he shrugged. "I mean . . . I dunno, it's weird. It's small and quiet and way different from Norfolk, but it's cool 'cause of that stuff. But. . . ."

"But?"

"I'm just not used to it," he said. "How quiet it is. How there's nothing to do. And I guess . . . I dunno, I'm waiting for the other shoe to drop."

Ava raised her chin, some of her braids falling over her shoulder. "What do you mean?"

"I didn't think we'd make it this far, to be honest. I thought Spence would make us pack up after the first week, but . . . he seems to like it. And I'm just . . . I'm worried that he's putting on a front for me."

"Why would he do that?"

"We sort of have a pact to take care of each other. And he knows how much I want this to work."

"And you think he'll go back on your promise to each other because he doesn't like it here?"

"Yeah. I mean. . . ." He let out a laugh that sounded more like a scoff. "This place is Spencer's actual worst nightmare come true. We're living in the house of a dead old lady who studied ghosts. And now, it turns out that the house belonged to the extinct founding family of the town, one of whom happened to be a psycho murderer. That, paired with the fact that this town is filled with distrusting citizens, governmental corruption, and a freakin' killer wolf on the loose, is a horror story waiting to happen."

Peter shook his head, bemused. "The only thing that could make it worse is if there actually *were* ghosts in the area."

Ava smirked. "You'd better hope he doesn't find out about the lake then."

"What?"

"DeVerre Lake," she said. "The town's namesake. It's really beautiful actually. You should check it out."

He cocked his head. "But you just said Spencer shouldn't find out about it."

"Yeah, well, I just mean he shouldn't find out what people say about it."

"What do they say?"

"That it's haunted." She said the words nonchalantly, like she wasn't dropping a bombshell in his lap. "You know, ghost sightings and the like. But it's all rumors. Stuff for the teens to gossip about and mothers to warn their children away from."

Peter ran a hand over the front of his face, sure that this was the end of it all. "Ah, man. Spence'll freak out."

"Don't tell him," Ava advised. "But take him there and show him that it's normal before he hears about it. Otherwise, your odds of staying will drop exponentially."

"You think?"

She nodded. "Occasus was built on the closest spot to the lake in town. Even going through the park is a farther walk."

"Really?"

"You guys could make it in about thirty or so minutes if you wanted." She did some calculations in her head, then nodded. "You're technically closer to it than town. It's just a more challenging hike through the woods."

"That's not good."

"It isn't haunted," Ava insisted. "And the sooner you get him there to prove it to him, the less you'll have to worry when he hears those stupid stories."

Peter considered her words. While she didn't know his brother well, the advice was sound. If Spencer heard the stories before ever seeing the lake, it would give that overactive imagination of his time to stew and create a million possible ways those rumored ghosts could murder them. And the fact that they lived so close to a lake that was supposed to be haunted would make it an inevitable reality in his mind.

But if he could get Spencer out there before he had any sort of ghostly association with the place, Peter could help channel his imagination in a better way. He could be sure to shoot down every frightful thought and build up all the pragmatic ones.

It was just a lake, and Spencer needed to see it that way.

Pushing himself out of the chair, Peter managed a smile. With everything he'd learned, he felt like he was carrying a whole new, larger stack of books out with him. One that weighed a thousand pounds. But he didn't want Ava to see how much it had affected him. "Thanks," he said. "You were a huge help. And you're good at this stuff."

"This stuff being . . . ?" Ava asked, sitting up straighter.

"Advice. And telling people the stuff they need to know. You're good at it. A little direct, but good at it."

Her eyes narrowed, and he couldn't tell whether it was in approval or suspicion. "Thanks."

"You're welcome."

Ava reached for her novel again, eyes still on him. "If you have more questions or need more help, feel free to visit."

Peter's grin grew. "Will do. See ya later."

After weaving his way back through the maze of bookshelves, he exited the library and headed for the Jeep. He hadn't spent as much time out as he'd anticipated, but he felt he'd found a fresh task to occupy his time. He had a brand-new problem to solve. Spencer might be cruising along in DeVerre at the moment, but it had been inevitable that they would hit a bump in the road at some point.

And Peter would get ahead of that roadblock and smooth out the trouble before it even had a chance to stop them.

Pulling onto the roundabout, Peter headed back toward Occasus. He drove past the police station just as Marshal Garnier rushed out the door. Whipping his head around, Peter's eyes followed the man as he sprinted toward his patrol car. The sirens wailed to life before the marshal had even closed the door.

Peter stopped the car, waiting for the cop to pass him. Lights flashing, the marshal sped around the roundabout and followed it left down Harmony Road. He could see the patrol car as it continued past all the businesses and on toward the farming side of DeVerre.

Staring after the disappearing police car, Peter gaped out the window.

For such a small town, there sure seemed to be a high demand on their marshal. Whether their crime rate was higher than they let on or if Marshal Garnier was off to chase the seemingly uncatchable wolf, he couldn't be sure. But whatever had been going on since they'd arrived, Peter decided that he didn't care what Ava had said.

Outsider or not, if Peter was going to live in DeVerre, he wasn't about to let it fall apart just because the founding families wanted to cling to their ridiculous popularity contest and prideful agendas. If he was forced to pick between minding his own business and the success of his and Spencer's future, he'd get involved.

He'd find a way to fix it.

Resolute in his agitation, Peter took the turn back to Occasus. He had work to do. And he would make sure that nothing would threaten their future happiness and success within DeVerre.

CHAPTER NINE

Spencer

"**A**nother animal attack? Really?" Peter grumbled as he plunked down at the dining table.

Spencer finished typing out a sentence before turning to look at his brother. Once Peter had risen that morning—far later than Spencer, as usual—he'd obsessively speculated about what had sent the marshal tearing out of town. When Spencer couldn't take any more of his wild theories and complaints, he'd suggested that Peter go down to the tavern to see if Anna knew anything. Since he didn't particularly care to get invested in the crime news of DeVerre, Spencer had stayed home and worked on the novel.

Tossing the keys onto the table, Peter scoffed. "They can't expect us to believe that."

Irritated by Peter's sudden obsession with solving all DeVerre's problems, Spencer leveled an annoyed glare at his brother. "Why would it be anything else?"

"You're the one who thought Diane was murdered," Peter defended, the pitch of his voice rising. "Why is my theory any more ridiculous? In fact, I'd venture to say mine makes a million times more sense."

"How?" Spencer felt his brow pinch together. "A couple animal attacks is all it takes to convince you that the marshal is covering up a crazy person on a murder spree? We practically live in the middle of the woods. Animals pass through here all the time, I'm sure. What proof do you have that this new conspiracy of yours is any more realistic than mine?"

Peter hesitated at the challenge, his dark eyes scanning Spencer's face. It was obvious that his brother was checking to see if the idea of a serial killer on the loose had scared him. But Peter was always overly cautious with Spencer's fears. And with how annoyed Spencer was feeling at the moment, it was more than enough to overcome whatever typical anxieties might have arisen another time. He wasn't scared of a stupid theory that his brother had come up with in a moment of melodrama.

Spencer drew his shoulders back to assure Peter that he wasn't fazed. He met his brother's impassioned gaze with a calm one of his own.

"Well, none yet, but. . . ." Peter finally shrugged. "I dunno, man, it's just weird. Three deaths from wolf attacks within a month?"

"It makes more sense than wolf attacks spread out," Spencer argued. "If this wolf is rabid—which I'm assuming it is as it seems to attack at random—then of course there are going to be regular attacks reported. People are going to be in the wrong place at the wrong time, and there will be attacks until this thing is caught."

"But isn't it weird that they haven't caught it yet?"

"We're surrounded by a massive forest. It'd be easy for a single wolf to hide in all these trees."

"Yeah, but it's a wolf, right? Don't they usually live and hunt in packs?"

Spencer frowned. "Maybe the pack kicked it out when it went rabid?"

"I'm not sure that's how it works." Peter scratched his head.

"Me either."

They fell silent, both running through the little they knew about wolves. Spencer came up empty.

Peter nudged his wrist. "Hey, that reminds me actually. Ava suggested we check out the lake nearby. She said it's really cool."

"Oh, yeah?" Spencer tried to let the change in subject distract him from the idea of killer wolves hiding out in the woods around them. "Mkay, that sounds like fun. When do you wanna go?"

"How about now?"

"Now?" He looked at the clock on his laptop. Though he'd gotten most of his morning tasks done and this was his rest day from the gym, there were still several things on his to-do list. He'd nearly completed chapter one, and he wanted to attempt plotting out the rest of the novel. That's what all the articles and videos he'd studied had suggested, at least. And since they'd never tried such a detailed plotting technique in the past, Spencer figured it might be the key to helping them finish the book this time.

"Forget your freakin' schedule, dude," Peter said, as if he could read his thoughts. He reached across to shove his shoulder. "And chill for a couple hours."

Spencer sighed and reached for the keys. "Fine."

Peter slapped his hand away. "We don't need those." A grin spread across his face. "But you will need your hiking boots."

"I don't have hiking boots."

He rolled his eyes as he stood. "I meant metaphorically."

Spencer shut the laptop and rose to follow. "How far of a hike is it?"

"Not sure." Peter headed for the coat closet. "Ava said we could make it in half an hour."

"From here?"

"Yeah." He passed Spencer his demin jacket.

"Through the woods?"

"Yeah." He shrugged on his own leather one.

Spencer narrowed his eyes. "The woods where a rabid wolf is currently hiding out?"

Peter adjusted the collar as he met his brother's glare. "Yeah."

"Forget it." Spencer turned away from the door. "I'm not going."

"Come on, Spence!" Peter's hand shot out to grab his arm. "It's daylight. The wolf won't even be out."

"Wolves aren't nocturnal, idiot."

"Whatever. There's two of us and one of it. It would know better than to attack."

"Not if it's rabid and insane," he argued. "*I'm not going.*"

Without warning, a loud *thump* echoed through the house. The brothers jumped, their heads tipping back to stare at the spot on the ceiling.

Spencer's muscles tensed, eyes locked on where he estimated the sound had originated above them. "What was that?" His voice only managed to come out in a whisper. His skin prickled with goosebumps as the unmistakable feeling that they weren't alone in the house washed over him once again.

Peter gaped at the underside of the floor above them. "Prob— probably just some of the stuff we put in the attic. Must've fallen over."

"Like the stack of books in the office?"

"Yeah."

Old houses shifted. They creaked and had drafts and trapped wind in the flues of the chimneys. Spencer knew this, and he'd come to justify a lot of his irrational tendencies over the past week. But he'd had enough of the continual coincidences of Occasus.

Spencer shoved past Peter. "Let's go," he said, ready to get out of the house. It didn't matter if he had to live there. For the moment he needed to ignore the spooky reoccurring accidents and refocus his thoughts on something else.

Peter didn't hesitate to follow. He caught up with Spencer and took the lead as they crossed the yard, headed toward the back of the property, and took the curve toward the right. Anguis came running up to follow at Spencer's side as they walked.

The wrought iron and brick fence that surrounded Occasus wrapped around the property. The main gate was in the front, but there was a small, working gate near the back that Spencer had discovered on one of his walks with the dogs. While trees dotted the property making it feel a part of the forest that surrounded it, walking outside of the gate put them right into the thick of the woods.

Spencer instructed Anguis to stay behind, and the dog sat watching from the other side of the metalwork gate as they continued on their journey.

It was one of the few sunny days they'd had in DeVerre despite the remaining chill in the air. While the Washington climate was far colder than Virginia's, Spencer had already begun to grow accustomed to the permeating cold. The first few days he hadn't been able to help but shiver even while wearing his thickest shirts and socks. But now that they'd lived there a couple of weeks, he felt himself acclimating. He enjoyed the patches of sun that broke through the treetops and didn't bristle as much when the wind cut through.

Peter led the way as they talked through their ideas for the novel. He had several new suggestions, including the addition of a few characters. He suggested bringing in a love interest for Wenzel or Frankly, but Spencer shot the idea down in an instant. They didn't write romance, he insisted. Not because they didn't know how, but because it was a distraction from the main plot. They were mystery authors. Romance was an unnecessary addition.

The trees grew thicker as they wound through the rocky, wet terrain. The soles of their boots caked up with gray-brown mud. There was no specific trail to follow, so they made their own way through the undergrowth of the forest floor. Everything was so green in DeVerre. Mossy, damp, and foggy. If Spencer hadn't had the conversation to distract him from his thoughts, he would have sunk deep into imagining that the forest was alive with ghostly creatures.

He had to admit to himself that it felt almost magical, with its stillness and paradisiacal atmosphere. So untouched by the outside world. The pines grew taller and taller as they walked, the roots larger and larger. It was easy to imagine wraithlike creatures drifting amongst these trees. Floating about in the hazy fog.

Suddenly realizing that they'd been walking for far longer than half an hour, Spencer came to a stop.

Peter turned around. "What?"

Crossing his arms, Spencer glared at him. "You don't know where you're going, do you?"

He watched impatiently as his brother looked around at the trees, then back to him, shrugging. "I know it's north."

"Pete. . . ."

"We've been heading north, right?"

"I don't know!"

Peter tossed his hands out to the side. "Well, you're the one who's studied all that survival stuff for stories, right? How do you find north?"

Spencer heaved a sigh and looked to the sky. *How did you find north?* Something about the clouds came to mind, but even if he could remember the details, the trees were too thick to get a clear view of the sky. The sun hardly got through either, so they couldn't count on shadows to help. There was plenty of moss around, but it seemed to cover all the plant life and rocks rather than just one side.

"Wait," Peter exclaimed, digging his phone out of his pocket. "I've got it."

Slapping his palm to his forehead, Spencer didn't know whether to be more irritated with himself for forgetting about GPS or with Peter for not using it from the start.

"Okay, so. . . ." Peter stepped up to Spencer's side and showed him the screen. He pointed to the right. "That is north. And this. . . ." He zoomed in on the screen and pointed to a giant blob of blue. "This is the lake. So we just have to walk the rest of this path, and we'll be there, no problem."

"And where's Occasus?"

"Uh. . . ." Peter searched the forest on the screen. It was all green. "I dunno. It's not labeled."

"So how are we gonna get home?"

He shrugged. "I mean, we walk south until we run into the fence."

Spencer didn't have a kind response to his brother's casual reply, so he turned away to head north.

It took them another hour or so of traversing through the mud and trees to crest over the hill and see the water. Winded from the prolonged hike, they rested at the top as they took in the lake.

"Dude. . . ." Peter gasped around his heavy breaths.

"Yeah," Spencer agreed.

It *was* a beautiful lake. Probably the most beautiful lake Spencer had ever seen.

Tranquil and serene, the dark blue-black water looked like glass, reflecting the trees and sky in a perfect mirror image. The rocks and trees surrounded it as if they were guardians, a fortress to protect the peaceful atmosphere. Everything was so quiet, so at rest here. It felt surreal.

Spencer stepped toward the lake. He couldn't explain it, but such stillness was captivating. It was enticing. He felt as though he could sit down and watch the lake for hours without having to worry about the chaos of the world beyond this forest.

For once in his life, he wondered if he'd found a place untouched by fear.

"This is . . . freakin' cool, man," Peter said, stepping toward the lake. "It's . . . it's just . . . perfect."

Spencer nodded, smiling at the calm around him. "Yeah, it is."

This late in the season, the hibernation and migration of animals left the lake's ambiance thoroughly unhindered. Quiet and unmoving. What few ripples appeared radiated in such tiny circles that they hardly disrupted the surface.

Here the trees thinned out over the water, giving them a clear view of the rust and gold sun as it dipped below the branches. Knowing they'd been out in the forest for far longer than Peter had promised, thoughts of the trek home began to concern Spencer. There was little doubt they'd be walking through the darkness if they didn't leave immediately. But he struggled to care as he followed Peter around the edge of the massive lake.

"Who would've thought something this awesome was hiding way out here?" Peter asked in a hushed, almost reverent, tone.

"Yeah, it's. . . ." Spencer couldn't finish the sentence. He didn't know how to label the aura that lingered around the lake. There were no words to explain what it was. But it *was*. And he wanted to stick around it.

They continued through the trees and rocks. Getting closer to the water's edge, Spencer caught glimpses of fish swimming under the glassy surface. Tiny little guys that swam with sharp, jerky movements. The roots of the pines penetrated the edge of the water, curling down into the lake. Spencer wondered how deep it went. Naturally, it was too dark to see the bottom, and in the fading evening light, the water was only growing darker as the minutes passed.

Glancing up and across to the other side, Spencer did a double take.

"Pete." He gasped, grabbing onto his brother's jacket.

"What?" Peter followed his gaze.

On the far side of the lake, almost obscured by the fog and trees, they spotted the man in the dark green jacket. The same man who was always walking in the woods. The man they hadn't seen anywhere else in town.

He stood alone at the water's rocky edge. Leaning against a tree, he was facing to the side, away from the brothers. And he was talking.

Spencer searched the area, angling himself to get a better view of the stranger's companion.

But there was no one there.

"Whoa, that's. . . ." Peter whispered. "Yeah, not gonna lie, that's pretty creepy. Is he talking to himself?"

"I . . . I don't think so," Spencer replied, keeping his voice low. "I mean, I don't think he thinks so. He's waiting for responses."

"Dude, you were right." Peter slugged his arm. His voice came out in a hushed shriek. "This guy is freakin' weird!"

"Yeah."

"What do you think he's doing?"

Spencer shook his head. "I don't know, and I don't care. Let's get out of here." He turned to leave.

A resounding *snap* from the branch he'd failed to see in front of him broke under his foot.

The brothers whipped back around to find the stranger staring at them.

"Come on," Peter said, grabbing Spencer's arm and pulling him through the trees.

They hurried back around the lake in the direction they'd come. Peter pulled out his phone to follow the GPS's compass again as they picked up speed to a jog. They went back up and over the hill and out of view of the lake, Spencer glancing over his shoulder the whole time. His heart raced from more than just the physical exertion. Though there was no sign the man was following them, his optimism was at an all-time low.

Pushing through the undergrowth once more, Spencer shoved his fists into his pockets. He knew he was overreacting. This wasn't a big deal. There was a good chance the guy was talking to himself, but . . . Spencer's brain buzzed with questions. Why was the stranger out here? And why did he walk past Occasus so often? They'd lived in DeVerre for almost three weeks now, and he'd seen the man near their property almost a dozen times already. Always alone. Always headed in the same direction.

Spencer looked back over his shoulder at the sudden realization.

The man was always headed toward the lake.

"I don't like this," he muttered, picking up speed as the brothers jogged toward the south. "I don't like this one bit."

Peter kept pace with a similarly nervous gait, his jaw tense as he turned to Spencer. He attempted a smirk that fell short of lighthearted. "What's the big deal?" His voice was tighter than normal, and he cleared his throat. "So he likes to talk to the air? He's probably just—I dunno, running some lines for a play or psyching himself up to ask a girl out or something."

Spencer gave him a withering stare.

"Seriously!" Peter insisted, though he seemed to be trying to convince himself as much as Spencer. "We have no proof that he's crazy or dangerous or anything at all. There's no reason to freak out."

"I'm not freaking out," Spencer protested.

"You kind of are."

"Well, it's weird, okay?" He yanked his hands from his pockets to gesture wildly back toward the lake. "This guy is roaming the woods around our house, Pete. And now we catch him talking to no one by a giant lake in the middle of nowhere. Why?"

Peter blanched, stopping in his tracks as he stared back in the lake's direction.

"What?" Spencer asked, tension building in his chest at his brother's strange reaction.

Peter drew a hand over his mouth, then he shook his head, the same failed smirk in place. "Nothing." He turned to go.

Spencer jumped in front of him, forcing him to a halt. "What was that face?"

"I don't know what you're talking about. This is my normal face."

He shook his head. "You looked scared, Pete. Why?"

"It's nothing."

"Tell me."

"No."

"Why not?"

Peter glared at him. "'Cause you'll want to leave, and I'm not ready to give up yet!"

Eyes wide at the tension in his brother's voice and the insinuation of his words, Spencer took a step back. "Tell me, Peter."

Pushing a hand through his hair, Peter hardened his jaw. Spencer worried for a minute that he wouldn't relent. But then Peter's eyes caught his and his shoulders closed in as he sighed. "Ava said that some people in town believe the lake is haunted."

Spencer felt the blood drain from his face and his stomach drop.

"But it's not!" Peter promised quickly. "She said it's all stupid rumors."

Rumors or not, Spencer fought the urge to run all the way back to Occasus.

He wet his lips, glanced over his shoulder, and rubbed his hands along his thighs. "But you think that guy back there thinks it's true, don't you?"

"Maybe."

Spencer nodded. It made sense. If he was some crazy person into the occult or whatever, he would probably spend a ton of time communing with a presumed haunted lake. But the guy looked pretty normal. There was nothing about him that screamed insanity or obsession with dark practices.

Turning back to his brother, Spencer took in a deep breath. What did it matter? This was *one* crazy guy in the midst of three hundred other normal ones. There were people in Norfolk who could beat this man's crazy meter by a million points. What did it matter what he believed about the lake when Spencer had been there himself and seen how beautiful and peaceful it was? Why should he let this one creepy guy ruin a perfect and wonderful place?

"Okay," Spencer whispered, attempting to sound brave.

Peter's eyes went wide. "Okay?"

"Yeah. Okay."

"So. . . ." He edged closer, a hopeful expression on his face. "You're cool?"

"I'm cool."

"You're not gonna panic?"

Spencer sighed. "We live in a dead lady's creepy old house where things seem to fall at random, there's a lake nearby that's supposedly haunted, and a crazy dude who talks to ghosts takes the shortcut through our woods, but yeah . . . yeah, I'm somehow managing to stay calm."

He watched his brother's eyes narrow. "You're sure?"

"No."

Peter stared at him as if waiting for him to explode in terror any second.

"I'm fine, Pete."

"If you aren't, you know it's all right, right?"

"I know."

"I'm happy to do whatever you need," he promised. "Even if that means leaving."

"No, I'm. . . ." Spencer sucked in a deep breath. "I'm fine."

Peter didn't look convinced.

Spencer didn't feel convinced.

But what he felt didn't matter. He couldn't give up on their year in DeVerre. Not when he'd lived in the town long enough to enjoy it up until a few minutes ago. Not when it was Peter's last hope.

"Let's go home," Spencer tipped his head back toward the south.

"All right."

Peter led them back through the trees, the orange sunlight disappearing as it faded on their right. It was growing harder and harder to see the tangled roots of the trees in the encroaching shadows, and they had to slow their pace to be sure they didn't trip. The air was growing colder too. If Peter hadn't had his phone, Spencer didn't think he'd have managed to keep his rationale.

He'd thought the forest eerie in the day. Now that the sky was turning from orange to brown to purple to black, he struggled to keep his imagination from seeing ghosts and monsters in the shadow of every tree.

He felt like he could take his first real breath in hours when the dark brick fence appeared in the gaps of the trees.

Keeping his eyes open for Nex and Anguis as they stepped through the back gate, Spencer scanned the dark yard. Back out of the thick of the forest, he could look up and see the hundreds of thousands of white dots that surrounded the bright silver moon. Occasus waited in the darkness, the porch light on as well as a handful of others in the house. Spencer didn't remember leaving them on, but Peter wasn't good about turning them off when he left a room, and they were a welcome sight after their time in the woods.

Beyond the front gate, Spencer caught sight of the glow of a pair of oncoming headlights. There was no through road past Occasus, so whoever was driving down Whitehill Way was coming to see them.

"Hey." Spencer nudged his brother. "Are we expecting company?"

Peter's brow furrowed. "No."

They watched as an old red truck pulled up to the gates.

A deep, rumbling growl sounded on their left. Its low and menacing timbre causing both brothers to jump in surprise.

"Stupid dogs," Peter grumbled, turning toward the sound. "Yes, I get it. You guys don't like me."

The growl grew louder and angrier as he spoke.

"Pete," Spencer said, grabbing his brother's arm to keep him from moving. "That's not Anguis and Nex."

"What are you talking about?"

Spencer pointed, hand shaking, to the porch. The dogs stood on its edge, watching the oncoming truck several yards away from them.

The growl grew closer.

"Uh," Peter spun to face the sound, all the while edging back to stand at Spencer's side. "Okay."

Spencer watched in horror as a hulking shadow crept around the tree beside them. Neon yellow eyes glowed in the darkness as a large, black, dog-like creature revealed itself. Its head was the size of the Jeep's tires. Viscous drool dripped from its jowls, lips curling back over the sharp fangs.

"I think we've found that wolf, J.B."

"That's not a wolf," Spencer whispered, his voice strained.

The hound's growl tightened and turned into a snarl as, all at once, it reared back and charged.

Peter and Spencer bolted.

"Holy crap!"

"I know!"

Rushing toward the back of the house, the brothers tore across the yard.

"Around back!" Peter called, veering right.

"What? Why?"

"Maybe we can lose it."

The way the hound's paw slammed against the ground behind them in heavy, thumping strides made Spencer doubt that possibility.

Still, he doubled his speed and followed Peter around the back of the house. He could hear his brother letting out a long hum of panic as they ran. "This. Is. *Insane*," he muttered between rapid breaths.

They angled around the back of the house to the far side of Occasus and out of the hound's sight.

Their gamble was almost a success. With its large form, the hound skidded, unable to take the tight turn as fast as they could. The creature was massive. In the brief glimpses he'd had of it, Spencer guessed that it was as tall as he was and as broad around as two men. The animal looked canine in nature, but its abnormal and impossible build convinced him that it was no normal beast.

They sped toward the front of the house, Spencer glancing over his shoulder in hopes they were gaining some ground. But the hound learned from its mistake and made a wider turn at the corner, swiftly closing the distance between them.

It was smart. Too smart. And it was gaining.

Lungs and legs burning with the maximum effort of their sprint, Spencer rushed along the front yard. In his panicked fog, his mind vaguely registered that someone was standing on the porch by the front door, but he couldn't take in any detail as he ran for his life.

Peter dashed forward and got a fraction ahead of Spencer as they neared the vehicles. The newly arrived truck and their Jeep were parked side by side.

Chancing another glance behind him to check on the hound, Spencer's leg clipped the front bumper of the Jeep. He grunted as he lost his footing.

"Spence!" Peter called as he fell, his momentum causing him to stumble as he turned back.

Rolling on the dirt, Spencer tried to regain his footing, but it was no use.

The hound was upon him and ready to pounce.

Spencer's eyes grew wide as his body tensed, ready for impact.

The hound reared back and Spencer grimaced, paralyzed in the face of his wildest imaginations come to life.

This was it.

It would be a creature from his nightmares that killed him after all.

In a flicker of movement, a shadow fell over Spencer and blocked the hound's path.

Its massive paws sunk into the dirt as it tripped out of its primed stance.

Spencer stared in shock at the woman standing between him and the hound. She held her hands out before her, unflinching as the giant creature came within inches of her. "Stay," she ordered, her voice tilting up powerfully at the end.

The hound snarled, but listened, its head pulling away from her.

Hastily, Peter helped Spencer to stand behind the woman, hands tight on his jacket at they watched. Their breaths coiled into fog upon the cold night air.

The beast stood at level with her shoulders, its giant yellow eyes locked onto her as it licked its lips in agitation.

"That's it. Now. . . ." She adjusted her stance and started to raise her hands. "We're gonna send you back where you belong."

The hound growled in fury and lunged for her.

The woman raised her hands above her head, curling them into fists as she twisted her wrists.

At her quick motion, the hound tore apart in a burst of smoke and shadow.

Spencer and Peter both gaped at her in shock, their breathing the only sound in the newly quiet night.

"Holy crap," Peter muttered, still clutching Spencer's jacket.

The woman shifted at the sound, hands dropping to her sides. Now that they weren't running, Spencer rapidly took in her details. Black boots, black jeans, black leather jacket. Trim, but strong. About his height and around their age. Dark hair, hanging to just below the shoulders.

She turned around to look at them, a glare of disbelief on her face. "What did you two do?"

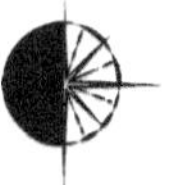

Spencer

Spencer stared at her, too dumbfounded in total shock to reply. There was something about her bearing that commanded they answer. She gave the unmistakable impression of being completely in charge of the conversation. Maybe it was the way the young woman stood, shoulders back and stance strong as she studied them the same way they studied her. There was an inherent seriousness to the structure of her face. Something that hinted of power in the intensity of her sharp cheekbones and strong, angular jawline. The all black of her outfit and the dark brown of her hair were a stark contrast against her pale, yet warm skin tone.

Peter stepped forward, positioning himself in front of Spencer like a guard. "Hi," he said, the sarcasm and irritation thick in his tone. "I'm Pete. What exactly just happened?"

The woman crossed her arms. "Hi, Pete. I just saved your life. Now," she raised her dark eyebrows. "*What did you two do?*"

"Nothing!"

She gave him a shrewd grin. "Well, you must have done *something* for someone to send a hellhound after you."

"A hellhound?" Spencer gasped.

Peter screwed up his face in confusion, turning back to look at him.

Spencer shifted from foot to foot. "Like . . . in Greek mythology?"

She eyed the two of them as if she weren't sure whether they were playing dumb or actually didn't know. "Yeah," she said. "I mean, they're from a dozen or more mythologies, but the principle is the same. And the term 'hellhound' is a misnomer anyway. They're not really from hell."

That wasn't the response Spencer had hoped for.

"Sooo. . . ." Peter rocked back on his heels, studying her with a suspicious glint in his eyes. "This . . . *hellhound.* . . . How'd it get here?"

"How should I know?" she scoffed. "I got back in town less than an hour ago. Seems like you've pissed someone off."

"We haven't done anything!" Peter insisted again, but Spencer held up his hand to silence him.

"Wait!" He eyed the woman again. "Wait."

Both she and Peter stared at him. Waiting.

"Wait." He whispered, understanding dawning.

The woman met his eyes.

"You're Cassandra Clement."

"Yeah."

Peter's jaw dropped.

"I thought you guys were expecting me," she said, taking a step back as her arms dropped to her sides.

"Well, yeah, we were, kind of." Peter gestured to her. "But we weren't expecting you to be hot."

Spencer wanted to sigh and roll his eyes, but he was as shocked by the young, attractive woman as his brother.

A soft chuckle escaped Cassandra as she smirked, eyes narrowing on Peter. "Somehow you managed to make a compliment sound like a problem."

Peter shook his head. "Nah, no, not a problem. Just weird."

"Uh," Spencer nodded toward the house. "We should probably go inside. There could be another of those . . . things out here."

She turned back to him, the amusement in her smile softening to something akin to compassion. "Actually, there can't. If there were more than one, they would have fought together."

"Still," Peter said. "Cassandra Clement or not, you've got a lot of explaining to do, and it's cold out here."

A single moment of surprise lit Cassandra's face before she nodded in understanding. Peter headed up the steps, digging the key out of his pocket while Spencer motioned for her to go next. She proceeded to the porch where the dogs still waited, wagging their tails. While Peter unlocked the door, she grabbed the strap of a large, leather messenger bag and slung it over her shoulder.

After the door swung open, the brothers allowed her and the dogs to enter first. They followed her at a halting pace, stuck in their alarmed and confused state.

"I, uh. . . ." Peter cleared his throat, but the tension remained in his tone. "I can take your jacket, if you want."

Cassandra had started making her way into the living room, but she spun around at the offer. "Oh, uh . . . sure." She unzipped the moto-style jacket and passed it to him, readjusting the bag to her shoulder. "Thanks."

"Uh-huh," he muttered, hanging it up with terse movements.

Spencer understood his brother's irritation. He was having trouble figuring out what to feel after all of that himself. There was a cord of anger running through him. They'd nearly died, and her first instinct was to blame them. But she'd saved their lives, so how could they hold onto that frustration? She'd shown up out of the blue, and that fact alone had already created a thread of intrigue within him. They might actually get some answers to all of their questions now. And yet his heart wouldn't stop racing after that chase. He kept getting images of those flashing neon eyes and sharp fangs barreling after them.

Peter elbowed Spencer's arm before he started hanging his own jacket.

Spencer stared at him, confused.

His brother pressed his lips together and tipped his head toward Cassandra, then farther back to the kitchen. "Drink?" he mouthed.

"Oh," Spencer nodded and turned back to her. "Would you like something to drink?"

Cassandra tugged on the high neck of her black sweater. "You know," she said with a sigh. "This place was practically my second home. You don't have to treat me like a guest."

"Ah, nah." Peter let out a huff, tugging on the collar of Spencer's jacket.

Spencer shoved him away, then shrugged it off and passed it over.

Peter didn't lose his stride. "We're happy to . . . host."

Biting her bottom lip around a smile, Cassandra looked at her feet.

"So. . . ." Spencer tried again. "Did you want a drink?"

"No," she said, meeting his eyes. "Thank you, though."

Nex leaned against Spencer's leg as they all stared at each other in silence.

"We can sit down," Peter offered, gesturing toward the living room.

Cassandra nodded. "That's a good idea."

As the other two moved for the couches, Spencer turned on a couple extra lamps to make it less awkward. And to make himself feel a little safer after the hellhound.

Cassandra sat on the far couch, dropping her bag down beside her, and the brothers took the seat opposite. "So," she began. "You guys have been here a couple of weeks now, right?"

Peter nodded. "Almost three."

"Nice."

"Yeah."

A beat of silence.

Nex spread out in the center of the rug between them.

Anguis sat at Cassandra's side.

Rubbing the back of his neck, Spencer tried to remember what they knew about Cassandra Clement. She lived in town, so Anna had said. And she'd been out of town for over two months because her mother had had an accident. If she was back, it likely meant that the news was positive on that front.

"How's your mom?" Spencer asked.

Cassandra took a second to respond, lips parting as she stared at him. "She's . . . she's fine. Awake, but she'll need a lot of time to recover. Lots of therapy."

"Right. Sorry about that."

"Thanks."

"But you're back?" Peter asked.

"I am."

"Like . . . for good or . . . ?"

"For good, I hope."

"That's good."

"Mm-hm."

There was another beat of silence before Peter tossed his hands in the air and shifted forward in his seat.

"I'm sorry," he said, his tone suggesting that he was anything but apologetic. "I'm not good with polite, awkward conversations. Why are you here?"

Cassandra tipped her head to the side. "Here in DeVerre or here at Occasus?"

"At Occasus. In our house."

"Right," she nodded. "Well, I'm here for a few reasons. First, because Diane was my closest friend and you two are her family. I'm honoring her memory by making an attempt to start a friendship with you two. Second, because Diane left me a letter requesting that I take care of you."

"She asked us to do the same with you," Spencer said.

Cassandra's smile turned a hint bashful at that. "Yeah, she told me that too. So—" She shrugged. "Like I said, I got back into town a little over an hour ago, and I thought I'd just . . . stop by to introduce myself."

Peter and Spencer glanced at each other.

"Glad I did," she continued. "Or we might never have met."

Spencer swallowed past the sudden constriction in his throat. "Yeah, thanks for that."

"Happy to help." She rubbed her hands together. "And I know that you sort of figured it out for yourselves out there, but . . . I meant to introduce myself formally. I'm Diane's friend, Cassandra. But you can call me Cass or Cassie or whatever. I'm not picky."

The brothers nodded but struggled to come up with any audible response.

"As per your introduction earlier," she said, smirking at Peter. "I take it that you're the older brother, Peter. Which makes you—" She turned toward him. "Spencer."

"Uh-huh," he replied lamely.

"Nice to officially meet you both," she said. "It's too bad it's under these circumstances."

"Right, yeah," Peter said. "You too."

Another awkward pause.

"I don't have to stay," Cassandra offered, taking hold of the edge of her seat as if to rise. "I know I surprised you guys."

"No, that's—that's fine," Spencer insisted, though he couldn't keep himself from wringing his hands nervously. "We don't mind. Like you said, Diane wanted us to . . . to take care of each other."

She chuckled at that. "Yeah, well that doesn't mean you have to put up with me crashing your evening."

"You didn't," Spencer replied, shrugging. "We didn't have any plans."

The humor lit up her eyes. "What? A Tuesday night and you two bachelors don't have plans in a small town like DeVerre? How lucky am I?"

"How do you know that we're single?" Peter's inflection was more suspicious than Spencer thought appropriate.

"As if it weren't obvious," he muttered.

"Hey, we could have girlfriends waiting back in Norfolk."

"I know," Cassandra interjected, "because Diane told me."

They both looked at her, surprise written across their faces.

"Diane knew stuff like that about us?" Spencer asked.

"Of course. She wanted to know everything about her family." She motioned to the two of them. "And she made sure to tell me everything she knew about both of you."

"Why?" Peter asked, incredulously.

"Because she knew one day we'd meet."

"How?"

"She was eighty-three." Cassandra's eyebrows pinched together. "She knew she wouldn't live forever."

"And she wanted to prepare you to meet us because she knew she'd leave the house to us?"

"Yeah."

The brothers shared another look of surprise.

Cassandra took the chance to scan the room. "You've redecorated."

Peter scoffed. "I mean, barely. We moved stuff around."

"And removed a few things."

He cleared his throat. "So anyways . . . that hellhound. Care to explain?"

Spencer watched a curious blend of humor and skepticism cross her face as she turned to his brother. "You're rather direct."

"Just weirded out is all."

"Hm." She sat back and rubbed her lips together as she studied them. "You don't know anything, do you?"

"Well, I wouldn't say we don't know *anything*, but—"

"No," Spencer interrupted. It was clear that she was referring to something deeper. Something neither of them had any comprehension of. "We don't know anything."

"Great," she muttered, clasping her hands together between her knees. Anguis nudged them with his nose, and she responded to the prompting absentmindedly. "Well, let's start at the beginning then."

The brothers sat forward, ready and waiting. Peter's eyes were wide; Spencer's knee began to bounce.

Cassandra took a deep breath. "I'm not sure what your personal beliefs are, but let me be plain with you before I begin. Diane and I are both firm Christians." She grimaced and frowned against her words. "Well, Diane . . . Diane *was*. But our shared faith . . . it was imperative to both of our lives. And I think you need to know that one important fact to be able to understand everything else I tell you."

That was not the start Spencer had expected, but it gave him a sense of relief as she continued.

"Okay, how do I explain this?" She stared at the floor, gathering her thoughts before she looked back at them. "This is the simplest way I can think of: there is a spiritual world out there that runs parallel to our own. One that we can reach into and harness if we want."

Spencer had heard people say things like that the past, but he wasn't sure Cassandra was getting at the same thing as they were.

"Not everyone can do it, and not everyone who *can* has the same strength, but . . . we can harness the power of that spiritual world and use it here in the physical world. I can't give you too much more explanation because . . . well, because, frankly, Diane was the knowledgeable one between the two of us. She and her husband had studied this stuff for years before I ever met her, and it was her knowledge that really gave me the ability to understand what it was that I could do.

"But. . . ." She slowed her words to get the point across. "Essentially what I'm trying to tell you is that here in DeVerre, people like me and Diane have the ability to reach between this world and the spirit world and access stuff that others can't."

Peter's eyes narrowed as Spencer cocked his head to the side. He already didn't like where this was going. The word *spirits* didn't always carry the best connotation in his mind. Everyone had a spirit. He knew that. But often the discussion of spiritual beings and worlds led to conversations that got his imagination running in directions he couldn't control. Scary directions that he'd rather not think about . . . ever.

"This is . . . freakin' weird, man. I don't even—hang on!" Peter held a finger in the air, interrupting his own words. "Liam's notes. His research. It was all on this subject. I didn't understand it because it was all in old English and, just, *really* intense stuff, but it—it all revolved around the spirit world."

Cassandra nodded. "Yeah, Liam began researching the spirit world back in the '90s. When they moved to DeVerre, Diane began to see ghosts, so he wanted to figure out what was going on."

"Wait, what?" Terror jolted Spencer upright. A tremor rippled through his body, starting in his chest and moving through his limbs. "She saw ghosts?"

"Yes. So can I."

"Oh no," Peter muttered.

Spencer pressed his hands to either side of his face. His cheeks burned like fire against his ice-cold fingertips. It wasn't possible. It *couldn't* be possible.

"What?" Cassandra watched Spencer with concern. "What's wrong?"

Peter ignored her and grabbed Spencer's arm. "Chill, dude, okay? You can't have a panic attack right now."

Spencer knocked his hand away and rose off the couch. "I'm not having a panic attack," he insisted, spinning back to face his brother. "They're real, Pete! Ghosts are—oh, God." He set a hand on the arm of the sofa and leaned against it. A chill ran down his back as he felt his head grow light. "Ghosts are real."

Peter glared at Cassandra as if to say 'look what you've done.'

"Is he okay?" she asked, worry lacing her voice.

He scowled at her. "Yeah, he's fine. He's just scared of the entire world, and now you've told him that his fears are valid. Spence," he practically shouted. "Sit down."

Cassandra looked between them. "I mean there's nothing to be afraid of. They can't hurt you."

Spencer gaped at her. "Tell that to the thing that almost killed us."

She gave him a smile that reminded him of the one his mother used to give him when he was a little boy afraid of the monster under his bed, convinced it was waiting to attack. A smile that said he was being overdramatic and silly. "That wasn't a ghost."

"Then what was it?"

"Look—" Cassandra sighed, her hand stilling its movement on Anguis's head. "There are a bunch of layers to the spirit world that even I'm not totally aware of, so bear with me. But what I *do* know is that there are two basic types of creatures within it. Ghosts and beasts. What you faced tonight was a beast. One that took the form of a hellhound, as it's most commonly known.

"But ghosts are merely souls with unfinished business who aren't willing to let go," she continued as though that information should calm him down. "They're not dangerous. They can't even interact with the tangible world around them."

"What does that mean?" Peter asked.

"They're incorporeal," she explained. "They can't touch anything, and they can only talk to people like me."

"People like you?" Spencer repeated.

She turned to him, smile gone. "I don't know what . . . we never found a name for what I can do. But . . . I know I'm different. Even different from Diane. She could see ghosts, but she couldn't talk to them. I can. And I've never met anyone else who could do that too."

Spencer pressed his lips together as he and Peter shared a look.

The man in the woods had been talking to someone. Someone that neither of the brothers had been able to see.

"Diane and I were working together to try to figure this out," Cassandra continued. "She and Liam had done research for decades. He died before I got the chance to meet him, but she and I tried to continue the same work. We wanted to know why we could see what others couldn't."

She paused, hand running along Anguis's fur again. "And I wanted to know why I can do even more than that."

Peter dropped his chin into his hand. "And you found out, what? That this . . . spirit world exists, and you have access to it? How?"

"How do we access it?"

"How did you find out about it?" he clarified. "'Cause from all I've ever heard, that concept of a spiritual dimension is a highly abstract one and not at all something you can just reach into."

Cassandra nodded. "Most people think that. That the spirit world is present but separate from us. That our only chance to ever grab hold of it is through enough prayer and faith. And they're partially right. But . . . that faith? It can grant you more access than you ever imagined.

"We learned about it from Liam's research," she continued. "Back in '93, he began to study the theology most prevalent in DeVerre. The church denomination is technically an uncommon form of Lutheranism. One that focuses heavily on the spiritual aspects of Christianity. Liam began to notice this unique emphasis in the teaching of the church, and he wanted more information on it. He was meeting with the reverend at the time, and he learned a lot about its origins. A man in Amesbury, England, by the name of John William Lawrence, published dozens of writings based on the studies of him and his mentor, Reverend Heinrich Schwarz. Their particularly brand of theology became known as Spiritualism.

"Lawrence and Schwarz believed in a literal ability to interact with the spirit world," she explained. "To reach in and utilize its power to affect change here within our own. They were predominant at the start of the studies, but Lawrence's son, Elijah, went on to publish his own, lesser-known works as well. Liam and Diane discovered that through his continued studies, Elijah Lawrence had found other people who were actually interacting with the spirit world just as Diane was. He had found people who could see ghosts. And more than that. There were people who could talk to them, connect with them, and help them.

"Then they discovered that those people could also call forth these beasts. Like the hellhound."

The air escaped Spencer's lungs in a loud *whoosh.*

"What?" Peter gasped, anger evident in his tone. "You mean . . . you created that *thing*?"

"No, no," Cassandra protested, shaking her head. "I just *can* if I want to. That's how I sent it back. I have the ability to reach into the spirit world and act as the bridge to release those beasts, but I never have. It's too dangerous."

"Dangerous for you or dangerous for others?"

"Both," she said. There was now a clear look of worry in her eyes. "I can control them once they're here, but . . . opening myself up to their spirits . . . it makes me uncomfortable."

"Why?" Spencer asked, his curiosity temporarily overcoming his fear.

"Because it's spirit-to-spirit contact. I don't know what that would do to me—coming in that close of contact with a beast."

"Are they evil?"

She hesitated. "I . . . I don't know. I don't think so. At least, not in the way we think of good and evil."

"You don't know?" Peter asked, doubtful.

"I told you. There's a lot I still don't know. Diane was helping me to figure all this out. She didn't have nearly the abilities that I do and . . . well, it was hard to find answers. Especially here in DeVerre."

"Why?"

"Because the powers that be don't want this information out there."

Peter gaped at her. "You mean they know?"

She shrugged. "Some of them do. The Chapelles have some inkling, at the least, but they don't like to talk about it. We never could figure out who it was who *actually* knew and who was only protecting the ones with all the information."

Spencer sat down on the arm of the chair, his eyes never leaving her face. "This is why Diane wanted us to take care of you, wasn't it? She wanted us to help you figure it out."

Cassandra met his eyes as she gave him a hopeful smile. "I think so."

Peter scratched the side of his nose. "Why us? If Diane couldn't figure all this out with her decades of research, what made her think we'd be of any help?"

"I don't know," Cassandra shifted in her seat. "And maybe you can't help me. But . . . I can't give up. And I'd rather not do it alone."

Spencer looked over his shoulder at Peter.

"Listen, I know it's a lot, but it's not just this that I need your help with." Cassandra crossed her arms, scooting to the edge of her seat. "I don't believe that Diane died of natural causes. She was completely healthy when I left, and it's too coincidental that I was out of town for months while all of this was going on. I think someone waited for my absence and then took the opportunity to get rid of her."

"I knew it!" Spencer jumped up and whirled around to point at Peter. "I told you! They murdered her, and now they're trying to kill us too. Holy crap!" He dropped back to the sofa and put his head in his hands. "We're gonna die."

"I'd like to say that you're wrong," Cassandra's tone was apologetic. "But after tonight, that'd be naive. Hellhounds are servants. People summon them to do a job—one that often involves violence. They don't enter the physical world without a specific task, and they're laser focused on that task until it's completed. Only then do they return home."

"We're being targeted?" Peter's voice sounded hollow.

She nodded.

"I can't believe this." Spencer pinched the bridge of his nose, trying to keep calm. "I can't believe this."

Peter ran a hand over his mouth. "So . . . so what do we do? Someone's trying to kill us, right? Why?"

"That's what I'd like to know," Cassandra said. "It could be because they're upset that you're here, but I don't see that being a strong enough motive for murder. Did you piss someone off recently?"

Pursing his lips, Peter glanced at Spencer out of the corner of his eye.

Spencer sighed. "It could be the marshal. Or maybe that Gia-woman."

"Gia Frossard?"

"Yeah."

She shook her head. "I doubt it. She's not the nicest woman in the world, but I don't see her getting off her pedestal to commit a murder anytime soon."

"So . . . the marshal then?"

"Tom?" Cassandra frowned. "He's a tough cookie, but trust me, he's no murderer. He's too much of a cop for that. He wants justice more than he wants his own way."

"Well, who then?" Peter leaned forward. Spencer could feel the blend of concern and intrigue radiating off his brother. He worried that he was enjoying the discovery of new mysteries to solve a bit too much.

Cassandra shrugged. "Whoever killed Diane."

Attempting to steady his breathing, Spencer looked at the ceiling. Someone was trying to kill them. Someone who could summon hellhounds and maybe other forms of beasts. And what could they do about it? Leave? They hadn't done anything, and yet, they were still targets. Who was to say the person wouldn't chase them down no matter where they went?

Finally regaining enough control to manage some shallow breaths, Spencer met Cassandra's eyes. "How do we find out who killed Diane?"

"I've got a couple ideas about that." She shifted on the couch. "But first, I need you to stay calm."

Spencer bristled. "Why?"

"Because if just learning about the existence of ghosts freaked you out, it's pretty evident that what I'm about to tell you is going to be a difficult pill to swallow."

Peter and Spencer both drew their shoulders back, preparing for her words.

Cassandra took a deep breath and tilted her head to the side as she kept her eyes locked on the brothers. "Gerard," she called. "It'd be nice if you'd show yourself."

If Spencer hadn't seen it with his own eyes, he wouldn't have believed it. One second the room held only the three of them and the dogs, and the next a tall man in gray trousers, black suspenders, and a vintage button-down leaned against the fireplace. His dark brown hair was slicked back, and his eyes were trained on Cassandra.

"Evening, Cassie." The stranger tipped his chin toward her in greeting. "Been a while."

"Aaahhhaahh!" Peter, sitting nearest to the sudden arrival, sprang back on the couch toward Spencer. "What the hell?"

Spencer couldn't breathe as his brother inched closer. He watched Peter's arm stretch out as if to defend him. His eyes locked on the man, too frightened to move or speak.

Cassandra didn't flinch. She smirked at the man instead. "Hi, Gerard. Sorry about the delay. Dad tried convincing me that I should stay about, mmm, twenty times a day."

"I'm surprised he thought it would work."

"I don't think he did." She gestured toward the brothers. "I've got some friends for you to meet."

The man glanced at them, a wily grin on his face. "Oh, I've met the Collins brothers. Unofficially, of course." He dipped his head in a polite nod. "Hello, boys."

Peter and Spencer stared at him. Peter looked as aghast as Spencer felt.

"Well, I'm glad you've gotten to know them for yourself, but I'm afraid they'll need an introduction of their own. Peter, Spencer," she said, turning to them. "This is Gerard Alarie. He lived in DeVerre in the '50s."

"In the '50s?" Peter almost yelled. "How's he—what *is* he?"

"He's a phantom," Cassandra clarified. "Once only a ghost with unfinished business, I tethered him to Occasus with Diane's approval so that he could help us."

Spencer looked with horror between the man and Cassandra. "You tethered him to Occasus? What does that even mean?"

"It means that he can tangibly interact with the world under my supervision. If I give him a direct command, he *has* to follow it. As I live in town with my mom's cousin, it gave Diane some company as well as providing us with some much-needed answers."

"Wait." Peter held up his hand. "So, he *lives* here? With us?"

"Yes."

"And it's been a nuisance," Gerard interjected. "I may have agreed to help Cassie and Di out, but I didn't sign up to live with you two idiots. Though it hasn't been all boring, I'll admit."

Spencer gaped at him. "It was *you*!"

"What was?" Cassandra looked between them.

"He's been messing with us!" Spencer pointed to the office. "He's been knocking stuff over to freak us out. He moved my book and messed with stuff around the house."

"That I did." Gerard raised his chin, a proud glint in his eyes. "And it was damn fun."

"Gerard," Cassandra chided.

The phantom shrugged. "What? I've had nothing to do for weeks. I couldn't show myself to them. You see how this one is," he said, motioning to Spencer. "He's like a child, jumping at shadows."

Spencer felt his face grow hot despite the accuracy of Gerard's statement.

"Yeah, but you have to live with them. And you didn't make a very good first impression."

"Wait just a darn second." Peter stood abruptly. "*He* has to live with *us*? What if we don't want him here?"

Cassandra grimaced. "Yeah . . . I can't really do anything about that."

"Why not?"

"Now that he's tethered here, there's no releasing him until he's ready to move on."

Spencer pushed his fingers through his hair. "You can't be serious."

"I mean, there's a chance I'm wrong," she offered. "I don't know everything about phantoms, but . . . I'm sorry, everything we've read so far says that until they're ready to let go, they're stuck wherever they've been tethered."

"Then why'd you tether him in the first place?" Peter asked.

"Because we needed his help." Cassandra rose to stand next to Gerard. "Listen, I know he comes across as rough, and he's not exactly made friends of you guys so far, but he's a good man. Deep down. And he's helped us out a lot."

"That's a nice endorsement there, Cassie," Gerard said, eyes on the brothers. "Thank you."

"You're welcome." She held her hands out toward the brothers. "I know this is strange and difficult to understand, but you've got to trust me. And that means trusting Gerard too. If you're worried, he can't do anything that's actually dangerous. He can only interact with inanimate objects. Nothing living. So he can't touch either of you or the dogs."

"But he could touch a knife and use it to stab us."

Gerard chuckled at Spencer's sharp tone.

"No," Cassandra promised. "He can't. That was the first rule I made for him when he became corporeal. He *cannot* harm *anyone*. If he were to try, he would revert to his ghostly form, and I wouldn't trust him ever again."

"What other rules have you given him?" Peter asked.

"Too many," Gerard muttered.

Cassandra shot him an amused grin. "There are several. First, he wasn't allowed to enter Diane's room without making himself visible. For her own privacy's sake. Which reminds me. . . ." She turned to Gerard. "I am now officially instituting the same rule with these two. You enter either of their rooms, you must make yourself visible. And no more scaring Spencer."

"Come on, Cass," the phantom complained. "You're taking all the fun out of it."

"Not at all. You can still scare Peter all you want."

"Hey!" Peter frowned.

"Relax. How often do you think it would be possible for him to scare you and not your brother?"

Gerard smiled. "I'll find ways."

Peter glared at him.

"Also," Cassandra continued, pointing at Gerard. "You must listen to them. If they tell you to leave them alone, you leave them alone. They don't have total say, but you need to respect them like you'd respect me."

"You're giving them authority over me if you say it like that." He glowered at her.

"Not complete authority, but the same authority that Diane had, yeah."

"Di was my friend."

"And they're your friends now too."

"Uh," Spencer broke in, not sure whether he felt safe removing his eyes from the phantom just yet. "May I ask something?"

"Of course."

"How does he help us find Diane's murderer?"

Cassandra sighed. "Well, he knows more about the town and its history than anyone I know. While he didn't see anything the day Diane died, he was by her side in those last moments. If anyone can help us put clues together and make connections, it's going to be Gerard."

"Because he's old?" Peter asked.

"I'm hardly older than you," Gerard snapped. "I only happened to be born far earlier."

"Because he knows things about the history of DeVerre that no one else does," Cassandra corrected. "We bring him the information we find, and he can help us analyze it to see if it lines up."

"And you're convinced she was murdered?" Peter asked, eyes narrowing.

"I am."

Spencer met his brother's eyes. It was clear that neither of them was sure about the entire situation. It was one thing to learn that ghosts were real. It was another to learn that you had to live with one.

The question in Peter's eyes was evident to Spencer. Were they willing to help Cassandra Clement find Diane Larkin's murderer or were they going to walk away?

"I just...." Spencer sighed, turning to Cassandra. "I feel like we need more time to . . . to process all of this."

"Sure," she nodded. "I get it. It's a lot."

He nodded along with her.

Cassandra pressed her lips together and took a deep breath. "How about this?" She shifted away from Gerard and toward them. "We meet for lunch tomorrow, and I'll tell you a bit more about myself? From there you can decide if you trust me and if you want to help me. If not...." She shrugged. "We can figure out what we need to do next."

Spencer glanced at Peter, who raised his brow in deference to him.

"All right, yeah," Spencer agreed. "That sounds fine."

"We'll meet at The Glass Tavern," Peter interjected.

"Okay." The young woman gave them both a smile, then reached for her bag.

"Do any other ghosts have access to our house that we should know about?" Peter crossed his arms, eyeing the phantom warily.

Cassandra chuckled. "No. It's just Gerard."

"But...." Spencer raised his chin, already nervous at the answer to his next question. "What about beasts like the hellhound? Can they get in here?"

"Technically? Yeah, I guess they could. But I don't think you'll have to worry about that."

"Why not?"

"Because whoever summoned that hellhound will assume the job has been done. Again, the hounds don't return to the spirit world until their work is complete. So whoever was after you won't try again until at least tomorrow."

Spencer didn't find that reassuring. "And what if they do try again?"

"Then I'll save your life again."

"What if you're not here?" Peter asked.

Cassandra sighed. "Look, it's not going to happen, okay? Whoever wanted to kill you doesn't know that I saved you. They're going to assume that you saved yourselves. Which means they aren't going to try to kill you when they think you can already defeat them."

The brothers shared a doubtful glance.

"I promise." She took a step closer to them. "Nothing is going to happen."

"And if it does," Gerard interjected with a sly grin. "We can all thank our lucky stars that we won't have to deal with you anymore."

Cassandra looked over her shoulder and frowned at him. "Be nice."

"Whatever you say," he replied.

She tossed him an amused grin, then looked back to the brothers. The question was clear in her eyes. Would they be all right if she left?

They were both silent.

Cassandra sighed. "Look, if you're really worried," she gestured to the office. "Diane kept a pistol in the hidden compartment of the desk."

"There's a hidden compartment in the desk?" Peter's eyes grew wide with excitement.

She smirked. "Yeah, it's pretty cool, I know. It's hidden at the back of the top left drawer. Just pull the drawer completely out and you'll find a false back with a simple latch attached to the desk. The gun and bullets should be in there."

Spencer stared at Peter. Their great-grandfather had served in the navy for his entire career. It's what had led the Collins family to Norfolk in the first place. Growing up, they'd been taught to have respect for firearms and how to use them properly. While neither of them had enough knowledge to recognize the make or caliber of a weapon at first glance, both brothers knew how to handle one.

"All right," Spencer said with a sigh. "Thanks, we'll keep that in mind."

"You're welcome." Cassandra smiled. "I guess I'll get going, if that's all?"

Peter nudged Spencer. "Her jacket. . . ." He nodded toward the door.

Spencer motioned for her to follow him. They moved into the foyer together, Peter following behind them. He leaned against the doorway as Spencer retrieved her jacket.

"Thanks." She took it from him.

"No problem." Spencer reached for the handle of the front door.

"See you both tomorrow."

"Yeah."

"Goodnight."

"Goodnight."

Cassandra stepped out into the night, and Spencer shut the door firmly behind her.

"Well," Gerard said, stepping around the corner into view. "You boys have a pleasant evening. I'll just be wandering the halls."

Peter scowled as he walked past him, but Spencer forced himself to swallow the painful lump in his throat. "We're gonna have dinner." His voice came out as empty as he felt. "If you want to join. . . ."

"I'm dead, friend," Gerard replied, disappearing up the stairs. "Eating isn't possible for me anymore."

Spencer looked to his brother, who mirrored his grimace. How was any of this possible? Somehow every fear of his was coming to life. And here he was, trying to figure out if he should walk away or face it.

"What have we gotten ourselves into, Pete?"

"I don't know," Peter replied, voice hushed. "But . . . if you want out, say the word."

Spencer glanced out the window and caught a glimpse of the taillights of Cassandra's truck through the front gate. "Believe me, I'll be keeping that in mind."

Peter

Peter rounded the corner into the office to see Spencer sitting at the desk. His brother was staring into the living room, distracted as he approached. "Hey," he said, taking a seat on the edge of the desk.

"Hey," Spencer muttered, eyes falling back to his laptop.

Looking toward the living room, Peter caught sight of Gerard. The phantom was lounging on the sofa, reading a book. "You get much work done this morning?" he asked his brother, taking a sip of his coffee.

"Eh, a bit," Spencer's gaze angled toward the ghost again. "It's just . . . hard to get anything done knowing that. . . ."

"Yeah." Peter whispered as he frowned in Gerard's direction. "It's a bit annoying, isn't it?"

Spencer pressed the heel of his hands to his forehead. "I keep thinking about everything that happened before." He kept his voice low. "The books falling, the random thumps, the coffee neither of us remembered making. Everything. I wasn't crazy. We *really* did have a ghost haunting our house."

Thinking about the coffee, Peter shrugged as he looked down at his mug. "At least he's a helpful ghost."

"He did stuff to freak us out on purpose."

"He didn't have to make us coffee."

Spencer sighed. "That doesn't make it any easier."

"Would it help if I disappeared?" Gerard called from the couch. His deep voice was gruff as he flipped a page in his book. Now that they knew the ghost's origins, it was easy to see by his outfit that he was, in fact, straight out of the 1950s. "You two can go back to pretending I'm not around."

Peter raised his brow, wondering how much the ghost had heard. Or maybe he had simply guessed that they were talking about him. "Yeah, I don't think that would help much," he replied. "We wouldn't know whether you were looking over our shoulders or listening in on our conversations then."

"Your conversations aren't that interesting. Believe me," Gerard called over his shoulder, eyes still locked on his book.

Turning back to each other, Peter and Spencer both heaved annoyed sighs. Peter wasn't sure what irritated him more, the unexpected arrival of the phantom or the fact that he'd been with them the whole time.

Spencer grabbed a folder from the desk next to him. "Here." He offered it to Peter. "I finished the first two chapters. You'll need to adjust Wenzel's stuff, but everything we talked about is in there."

"Oh, nice." Peter set his mug down to flip the folder open and take a quick look over the chapters. As he thumbed through the first couple of pages, he realized that the story was moving faster than he had anticipated. "This means it's my turn to write the next chapters, right?"

"Yeah. Also, I need the episode for the webpage so that I can edit it."

Peter furrowed his brow. "I've got another week on that."

Spencer pinched the bridge of his nose. "Pete, I need you to take this more seriously. If you wait until the last second to write your stuff, then I'm stuck waiting on *you* so that I can do anything. In fact, that's what I'm doing now. I've got nothing to work on *because* I'm waiting on you."

"All right," Peter conceded. He held up his hands—one still clutching the folder—in mock surrender. "I'll work on it."

"Thanks."

"Sure."

Tapping the folder against his open palm, Peter mentally reviewed the tasks Spencer had set on his plate. Yes, he still had to write the next episode for the serial. But now he also had to read the first two chapters of the novel, edit them with his suggestions and Wenzel's 'approved' dialogue, *and* write the following two chapters from Wenzel's perspective. All that work would take days. Maybe even weeks. And Spencer would be waiting impatiently for him the entire time.

Yet there was a more pressing matter currently on his mind.

Peter glanced across to Gerard once more. "What time were we supposed to meet Cassandra?"

His brother shrugged. "Noon, I guess. She just said lunch."

"Everyone's definition of lunch is different."

"But noon is most common."

"Is it?" Peter pursed his lips in interest. "I don't usually eat until two."

"That's because you don't get up until ten."

"What's your point?"

"My point," Spencer looked at him. "Is that you've got a little over an hour to get some writing done before we need to leave."

Peter screwed up his face, incredulous at the suggestion. "I can't get quality work done in an hour."

"Hey, you're the one who said you work best under pressure. I'm giving you the pressure of an hour to get at least one paragraph written toward your next post."

Peter pressed his lips together and heaved an exaggerated sigh. "Fine."

Bounding upstairs, Peter exchanged the folder for his notebook on the nightstand. While Spencer wrote exclusively on his laptop, Peter preferred to handwrite his work. It felt like a more *authorly* method. However, it also took way longer.

"Just a paragraph," he muttered to himself, heading back down to sit at the dining room table. He pulled the pen out of its loop and opened the notebook. "Just a paragraph."

It took him the first half hour to double-check Spencer's last episode and write four failed starts before he truly got going. But when Spencer tapped his shoulder to let him know it was time to leave for their appointment, Peter discovered that he had wound up with three and a half pages worth of solid work. Mentally patting himself on the back, he was confident he would be able get on track again later that evening with the start he'd already made.

When they arrived at The Glass Tavern, the brothers scanned the rather empty interior. Only one table held a pair of businessmen. They spotted Aaron sitting at the bar talking with Anna. As Cassandra was nowhere in sight, they headed for their friends.

On their approach, Peter pointed a finger straight at Anna with a playful rise of his brows. "I've got a bone to pick with you."

A look of mild concern crossed her face. "What's up?"

He tossed his arms wide in feigned agitation. "Why didn't you tell us that Cassandra is our age?"

All the worry in her face dissolved as she grinned. "For this exact moment. It didn't disappoint."

"That was a mean trick." He took the seat next to Aaron. "Can you believe that your sister would let me think our aunt's best friend was an old woman?"

"You thought Cassandra was old?" Aaron scoffed. "Whatever embarrassment you felt is your own fault."

"We weren't really embarrassed," Spencer said. "She doesn't know we thought she was old."

"She does now." Cassandra appeared at his side without warning. She was dressed in a similar outfit to the day before: all black, leather jacket, military style boots.

Spencer flinched, and Peter drew his head back to stare at her, surprised by her sudden arrival. He turned back to Anna. "And you didn't think to tell us she was here?"

"You didn't ask," Anna shrugged. "Would you like your drink?"

Peter shook his head as he smirked. "Nah, it's only noon. I'll stick with the boring stuff today."

"Coming right up."

Cassandra backed away from the bar, gesturing to the far side of the room. "I already set my stuff in the booth back there. If that's all right with you guys?"

The brothers exchanged a nervous glance as they slipped off the barstools.

Peter gave Aaron's arm a friendly smack and tipped his chin toward Anna. "We'll see you guys later."

Sliding across from Cassandra in the booth, the three settled into another long, awkward pause. Anna dropped off the waters, took their orders, and returned to the bar. Overhead, a trumpet accompanied a jazz piano as they stared at each other.

"We aren't good at starting conversations, are we?" Cassandra finally broke the silence.

Peter shrugged. "It's hard to know what to say."

An amused grin spread over her face as she leaned forward and rested her arms on the tabletop. "Well, here's a good talking point." Her dark eyes shifted from one of them to the other. "Why'd you assume I was old?"

Spencer scratched his jaw and looked at the tabletop.

Peter raised his brow. "I mean, Diane was in her eighties, right?"

"Right."

"It's a natural assumption that her closest friend would be at least somewhat near her age. It isn't every day that a woman is best friends with someone who could be her granddaughter."

"Diane wasn't a typical eighty-year-old," Cassandra countered. "And I'm not a typical thirty-year-old."

"You're thirty?" Spencer stared at her, an edge of shock in his tone.

"I will be in about six months."

"Oh."

Her grin turned sly as she eyed him. "Your charming surprise suggests that you do indeed think I'm old."

"No!" Spencer shook his head. "I mean, Pete's only a year younger than you."

"I know your ages."

"You do?"

"I know most things about you."

"How?" Peter asked. "We never even met Diane."

"I told you. Diane wanted to know everything about her family. Especially since you two were going to inherit everything that she and Liam built together. She made sure to keep in contact with her siblings for regular updates."

"Why didn't she ever make an effort to meet us, then?"

"She was a bit preoccupied."

"But she found out our ages and relationship status?"

Cassandra tipped her head to the side, studying him. "Mm-hm. Trust me, if there's a piece of trivia about you two, Diane knew it."

"Which means you know it too?" Spencer asked.

She shrugged. "More or less."

"And we know nothing about you yet."

Her grin spread. "Well, now you know that I'm older than both of you."

"Mm," Peter leaned back in his seat, uncomfortable with the knowing way she observed them. "It seems as if you're at an unfair advantage. Knowing so much about us when we know so little about you."

"That *is* why we're here, right? For you two to get to know me?"

Anna reappeared with three plates balanced on her arm. She passed them out and scanned the table. "Anything else I can get you?"

They all shook their heads.

"Thanks, Ann." Peter gave her a smile.

She nodded to him and retreated.

Peter turned back just as Cassandra dipped her head in a silent prayer. The brothers exchanged glances. After a moment, she picked up her utensils and began to unwrap them.

Feeling a bit shamed, Peter made sure to offer up his own thanksgiving for the meal, and Spencer followed suit, bowing his head.

"So," Cassandra began as they prepared to dig into their meals. "What would you like to know about me first?"

"That's kind of a weird way to start." Peter picked up his sandwich. "How should we know what to ask?"

Spencer nudged his side in what he knew was an urging to be more tactful, then turned back to her. "We've heard that you have family here in DeVerre. Is that true?"

Cassandra scooped some mac and cheese from her plate. "Yeah, I've got lots of family in the area. I was born in DeVerre."

"You were?"

She nodded.

"But . . . you and your family live in Spokane, right?" Peter asked.

"Technically. Yes, Spokane is still my permanent official residence. However, I moved back to DeVerre almost four years ago. My mom's cousin, Debbie Mercier, and her husband have been kind enough to let me stay with them."

Spencer leaned forward. "You said something to Gerard last night about your dad trying to get you to move back?"

"Yeah." Cassandra looked down at her plate and took a moment before giving them a look that Peter thought she intended to appear as amused indifference. But it came across as resigned disappointment. "They don't like me being here."

"Why not?" Peter asked.

"They, uh. . . ." She glanced around the restaurant, lowering her voice a fraction. "They don't like that it lets me . . . do the things I can do."

"Wait. . . ." Spencer cocked his head. "You mean you can only do those things here?"

"Yeah."

"Why?"

"I don't know." Cassandra set her fork down, abandoning her meal. She kept her voice quiet and conspiratorial. "My entire childhood here, I could see the ghosts. I remember being . . . three or four and pretending to have a tea party with them."

Peter couldn't imagine a more morbid childhood memory. "You had tea parties with ghosts?"

"Yeah, but . . . I didn't know they were ghosts. And neither did my parents. They thought I was just talking to my imaginary friends. They had no idea that I was actually talking to real people who had died."

Glancing toward his brother, Peter caught Spencer staring at the woman as if she were a terrifying anomaly.

"It wasn't until my first year at school that my parents finally realized what was going on," she continued. "My teacher heard me talking to my 'imaginary friends' and she was curious about it. When she asked my parents about it, they told her that I'd always had an overactive imagination and to humor me until I got more comfortable in school. But then she started listening and asking me questions about my friends. To her shock, she realized that one of them was her grandfather."

"That's. . . ." Peter huffed. "Bizarre."

Cassandra played with the straw in her water. "When my teacher told my parents, they freaked out. It was concerning to them that their daughter was talking to ghosts."

"I can understand why," Spencer muttered.

She narrowed her eyes at him. "Because ghosts scare you?"

He hesitated. "Yeah."

"Ghosts are nothing to fear. They can't hurt anyone. They're just people who aren't ready to die and need to set things right before they move on."

Spencer dipped his head in resignation, but Peter doubted that her argument changed his mind.

"My parents went to the reverend at the time—Samuel's father, John-Daniel—and he advised my parents to take me away from DeVerre. He warned them not to let me indulge in these dangerous fantasies. That they should help me forget that I'd ever *imagined* I could see these ghosts."

"Hold up," Peter said, raising a hand. "The pastor told your parents to *lie* to you."

Her left brow rose as she smirked. "He did."

"Wow."

"Mm." Cassandra took a deep breath and went on. "My parents took his advice. We moved to Spokane, and they tried to get me to forget all my 'imaginary friends.' I didn't forget. Even though I didn't see another ghost for the next twenty years."

She paused, taking a moment to meet their stares as if she was looking for someone to understand her. "I know it sounds strange, but . . . they were my friends, the ghosts. When I was a little girl, they were the people I knew. I talked to them about everything, and they talked to me. I guess it was amazing to them—having someone they *could* talk to. Ghosts can't even interact with one another, you see. They are wholly isolated in their incorporeal form. And that's why it's so sad. They're stuck in this . . . purgatory. Trying to right a wrong in their life. Whether a wrong done to them or one they did to someone else. And they're all alone, unable to let go.

"I remember," her eyes grew wistful. "There was one woman, Katherine. She had lied to her husband—I don't remember why—but she felt so guilty because she said that it . . . it had led to his death and . . . she felt responsible for it. She said that she wanted to correct it."

"How?" Spencer interrupted.

Cassandra turned to him and shook her head. "I'm not sure. I was . . . I don't know, probably only four at the time. But I remember that she used to come and talk to me for hours. She'd sit there and tell me everything. It felt like she was telling me a fairy tale or something. And . . . at the end of it, I would tell her that I was sorry, but I didn't think that she should blame herself.

"It didn't do anything at first," she admitted with a shrug. "She stuck around for . . . well, everything feels like an eternity when you're a kid. But it was a while longer. She kept telling me reasons she couldn't let go. Reasons she felt that she'd failed or needed to go back and . . . warn someone or do something. I don't remember. But after a while, I convinced her to let go."

Peter felt his jaw drop. He propped his chin on his hand, listening to her in fascination. "Let go how?"

She gave him an unsure grin. "I guess her soul found peace in it all. She thanked me and . . . then she disappeared, and I never saw her again."

"Whoa," Peter gasped. Spencer shifted on the booth next to him.

She nodded. "What I do remember was how the experience made me feel." Peter watched as a lightness entered Cassandra's face. It softened her whole expression. "There was this sensation of total peace and love. Like . . . everything was suddenly right in the world and I'd somehow been able to play a role in that."

A thin laugh escaped her. "That's a feeling you can never forget. No matter how far your parents take you from it."

Spencer blinked, a dazed look in his eyes. "That's why you came back?"

"Yes," she confirmed. "I spent most of my life outside of DeVerre fighting to regain that feeling with no success. I went to college and studied theology, hoping to find some answers on ghosts and their origins. But I came up empty. And everyone I talked to discouraged me from following the pursuit. Eventually I got tired of it, and I decided to come back here. I knew that if I wanted answers, I needed to go to the place it had all started. The place where I had seen the ghosts in the first place."

For once, Peter felt like he had nothing to say. He was stunned. Shaken by this woman's past.

The brothers remained silent, taking in her story as she divulged detail after detail. Her desire to reconnect with the memories from her childhood seemed like a legitimate reason to do what she'd done. If Peter had ever experienced something like that, he imagined he'd seek it out with abandon as well.

"I don't pretend to think that's quite enough to get you to trust me," Cassandra finally said. "But now you know why I'm here and what I'm searching for. Why I was working with Diane. We both wanted the answers no one else could or would give us."

There was a long pause. Peter pushed at the fries on his plate. How did you respond to a story like that? It still sounded impossible. Just because it turned out that ghosts were real and he'd seen the proof, it wasn't making it any easier for him to accept. Not after almost three decades of thinking the opposite was true.

"Why did Diane and Liam choose DeVerre to do their research in the first place?" Spencer asked. Peter noticed that his food was completely untouched on the plate before him.

Cassandra looked confused. Her lips parted in surprise. "Well, DeVerre held all the answers for her. Even if they were hard to find. And Liam was happy to support her in her search."

"So she'd always been able to see ghosts like you?"

"No, that didn't happen until she got to DeVerre."

Spencer drew back, his eyes going wide. "So DeVerre *is* known for ghosts?"

She shook her head. "Not to the general populace."

"Why'd she pick it, then?" Peter pressed. His confusion matched his brothers.

Cassandra dropped her hands into her lap. She sat up straighter as she stared at them. Her brow pulled together. "You don't know?"

"No."

Her mouth opened, and she let out an amazed chuckle. "I assumed your family told you."

"Told us what?" Spencer asked.

"Didn't you wonder why she left Occasus to the two of you?"

"Well, yeah," Peter replied. "We've been asking that question since we got here, but nobody has known the answer."

"Of course they wouldn't. She didn't make it known here, but. . . ." Cassandra paused and shook her head. "None of your aunts or uncles ever said anything?"

"About what?" Spencer demanded.

Cassandra twisted the silver ring on her right hand. "Wow, okay." The huff she expelled prepared Peter to feel as overwhelmed by the impending explanation as she appeared to be. "Well, Diane always knew that she wanted the two of you to inherit the House of Occasus. She told me that she'd leave it to me if you didn't want it, but she wanted it to go to her family if possible."

"But why only the two of us?" Peter asked, leaning forward. "We have ten second cousins that are just as related to her as us. Why not include any of them?"

"Because they're not related to her."

At her calmly spoken words, Peter jerked so abruptly that his arm slipped off the table. Spencer just stared at her, dumbfounded.

"Diane and Phillip—your grandfather—were not Collinses. And neither are you."

They stared at her without reply.

She shrugged. "At least, not biologically."

"I'm sorry." Peter waved a hand in the air, trying to comprehend what she was telling them. "What–wha . . . what are you talking about?"

"Diane and Phillip were adopted by Ronald and Helen Collins in December of 1940. She was almost three, and he was only a few months old. Phillip knew nothing of their previous life. But Diane did. She remembered her mother, and she knew that she never would have given them up willingly."

"She was two." He scoffed. "She could remember that much detail?"

Spencer's shoulders drooped, and he leaned heavily against the tabletop. "If we aren't Collinses, who are we?"

"I don't know." Cassandra's tone was apologetic. "Diane came here with the hope of figuring it out, but . . . the people of DeVerre haven't been forthcoming, and it was a closed adoption. She only found out that DeVerre was her birthplace by accident.

"Helen died a while before Ronald, but after his death, the family was sorting through their things. They gave Diane a box they'd found that was filled with her belongings from before the adoption. The box held a crocheted blanket, a stuffed rabbit, a small gold bracelet, and a picture of her and Phillip labeled as their adoption day with an unknown man in the corner of the picture. Diane had never seen any of those things. Presumably because the Collinses wished to honor the closed adoption policy and made sure that she and Phillip felt like they were fully their own children.

"But Diane never felt like she truly belonged to the family, and she wanted to know what her lingering memory of her real mother meant. The picture was her first clue," Cassandra explained. "On the back of the photo, Helen had inscribed: 'Meeting Diane and Phillip with Mr. F.'"

"Who?"

"An anonymous man who she didn't remember. But. . . ." Cassandra grinned. "She talked with your Great-Uncle Mark, who had been six at the time of their adoption. He *did* remember the man, but he struggled to remember the name at first. All he could come up with was that the man had had a unique accent, that his name sounded something like Fosse or Frost, and that he was from Washington state. It took them three years to research all the last names in the state that started with the letter F. When they finally came across the last name *Frossard*, he made the connection in an instant."

"Frossard?" Peter gasped. "Like . . . Dr. Frossard?"

"Exactly like that. They researched the name immediately, and finally in 1983, they visited DeVerre and Diane saw ghosts for the first time in her life. She knew immediately this was her birthplace and that she was meant to be here. They moved to DeVerre the following year, bought the decrepit Varon estate a few years later, and fixed it up. She named it the House of Occasus as an homage to the sun setting on her questions."

"So. . . ." Spencer leaned farther toward her. His entranced expression indicated that this mystery had engaged his imagination. "She found her mother?"

"No," Cassandra replied, the single word landing on Peter with immediate disappointment. "Like I said, the people of DeVerre have no interest in sharing their secrets. They saw Diane as an outsider from the moment she arrived, and she knew it would do her no good to claim her heritage openly here. There had to be a reason for all the secrecy around her parentage. She guessed that it was likely due to her ability to see ghosts and that perhaps it was a family trait. And as I experienced similar treatment as a child, it seems that asking for straight answers is more likely to get you run out of town rather than the truth."

Peter ran a hand over his face. "It's a conspiracy."

"What?" Spencer asked.

"Ava told me that the Frossards, Garniers, Chapelles, and Guillaumes run this town. What they want, goes. The Varons were once part of it, but . . . the son went crazy."

"Diane questioned that," Cassandra inserted. "She believed that Michael Varon was against the corruption of the rest of the town and wanted to end it. She theorized that the Frossards forged documents to state he was a schizophrenic. She thought they either had the family wiped out or did it themselves with the help of the other founding families."

"Why would they do that?" Spencer asked.

"If he threatened their ability to control this town and whatever it is it can access, why wouldn't they?"

Peter shook his head. "But it was the Varons who were in charge. They controlled the whole governmental system of DeVerre."

"So maybe some of the townspeople wanted to change who was in control?" Spencer suggested.

Pinching the bridge of his nose, Peter closed his eyes. The whole thing was getting way too complicated. Ghosts and phantoms were one thing. Suddenly losing his family name and finding out that they were somehow tied up in the whole mess of DeVerre's secrets was way too much.

"This is why you believe Diane was murdered?" Spencer continued. "She was threatening their hold on the town?"

Cassandra shrugged. "It's the best theory I have. All her research in the past forty years has been focused on understanding the foundation of DeVerre and what's happened here. How are ghosts in the area? Why can only some people see them? Whose lineage does she belong to? But with no one here willing to help and no opportunity to be honest with anyone, she had to do everything in the dark. It's impossible to uncover information when there is seemingly no information to find."

"So what do you want us to do?" Spencer asked. "If there's nothing left to find, how do we prove . . . whatever it is we're trying to prove?"

In agreement with his brother, Peter drew his shoulders back and stared at Cassandra. "What *are* you asking us to help you with?"

"I'm asking. . . ." Desperation glinted in her eyes as she met each of theirs in turn. "That you help me finish what Diane and Liam started. Help me find the answers."

"Why?" Peter pressed. "You already said that someone sent that hellhound after us, intending to kill us. Why are these answers worth risking our lives?"

Cassandra's face fell as though she hadn't expected him to ask such a problematic question. She bit the corner of her lip, glancing at Spencer before responding. "Don't you want to know who killed Diane? Don't you want to know who you are?" Her voice hushed. "Why your grandfather and Diane were sent away from their mother? How this all connects? Aren't you curious?"

Peter *was* curious. The whole mystery intrigued him more than he could say. He wanted the answers to all these strange, life-altering questions that had sprung themselves upon him.

But he also wanted to write novels with his brother. He wanted to build a life for himself. He wanted to stop living like a college kid still waiting for his big break when he should be an adult with a serious life. He wanted to grow up and start living like a successful man, with a family and a career and a house. And dropping everything to pursue some crazy small-town conspiracy didn't fit that vision.

But as he studied Cassandra Clement, Peter knew that helping them find the answers wasn't a wholly selfless endeavor on her part. She wanted answers for herself too. She wanted to know why she was different. Why she could see things and do things that no one else could. Why the people of DeVerre were opposed to those with her abilities. He and his brother might have an unexpected and unexplained ancestry, but Cassandra was as unsure of her identity as they were.

Pressing his lips together, Peter grabbed Spencer's arm. "Give us a minute, would you?" He yanked his brother out of the booth behind him and dragged him to the far side of the room.

From the corner of his eye, he could see Anna and Aaron watching curiously from the bar. The businessmen at lunch had left a while back so the brothers had the space to themselves.

"So," Spencer whispered, looking over his shoulder at Cassandra, "what do we do?"

"I don't know, man." Peter sighed, pushing his fingers through his hair. "This is pretty screwed up."

"Yeah."

"But I sort of want to help her."

Spencer eyed him. "Because she's attractive?"

"What?" he scoffed. "No. Wait . . . do you find her attractive?"

"What? No."

Peter smirked at the amusing idea of his brother dating a woman who spoke to ghosts. "Dude, she's weird, but I'm for it. You could use someone pushing you out of your comfort zone."

"Shut up." Spencer crossed his arms. "Why do you want to help her?"

"I mean her life is sort of tragic, isn't it?" He nodded back toward her. "Her mom was just in a coma, *and* she lost her best friend. Granted her best friend was an old woman, but still. Her family sounds like they aren't super supportive, and she's alone now. It sucks."

"Yeah," Spencer muttered. "Yeah, it does."

They both looked toward the young woman. She sat in the booth, playing with her ring as she stared at her plate. In her all-black ensemble, she looked like a shadow hovering at the back of the room.

"But also," Spencer continued in a whisper. "She's creepy."

"And attractive," Peter teased.

Spencer glared at him. "She summons ghosts, Pete."

"Sounds like that's the least weird thing she can do. Dude, I don't know what you want me to say. I think we should help her. Yeah, it's freakin' weird. But . . . she's alone and she needs help. And clearly, Diane trusted her."

"Diane was crazy too, remember?"

"Only if you don't believe what she believed. But as we've got a ghost living in our house, it's pretty obvious that she was right. There *are* ghosts. There *is* some spirit world at work here. And if she was right about all that and everything weird going on in this town, we'd be jerks to ignore the problem."

Spencer pressed a fist to the bridge of his nose.

"What's the hold up?"

His brother tossed his hands in the air, then let them slap against his legs. "*Everything*," he hissed. "This isn't what I signed up for, Pete. This isn't what I agreed to when you wanted to move out here. You said we'd write. That we'd get to live our dream. Well, this isn't my dream. This is literally every nightmare I've ever had.

"This is everything that I've been afraid of since I can remember," he continued. "Ghosts and spirits? People out to kill us? A freaking conspiracy? A town where everyone is fighting to control their secrets? It's a recipe for disaster."

"And what about her?" Peter asked, gesturing toward the woman in the booth. "This is your nightmare, but this is her life."

Spencer sighed and stared at the floor.

"And apparently," Peter shrugged. "It's our life too, now. Whatever that means. Whoever the heck we even are."

"I hate this."

"I know."

Spencer shoved his hands into the pockets of his denim jacket but stayed silent.

"What do you want to do?" Peter asked, keeping his voice calm and patient. He wouldn't push Spencer this time. He had promised to leave if he wanted. He'd promised to let it all go and move back home. If it meant losing their dreams, so be it. He wouldn't lose his brother in the process.

Glancing once more at Cassandra, Spencer grimaced and nodded. "You're right," he whispered. "Ignoring the truth won't stop it from being true. And who's to say that leaving will end it? These people may be crazy enough to chase us down just because they suspect we're onto them."

"So . . . you're on board with helping?"

"Yeah, I'm on board."

Peter couldn't help the grin that came to his face. Hope bubbled up in his chest even in the face of all the questions that remained. He clasped Spencer's shoulders and gave him a shake. "We're gonna solve a mystery, Sherlock. A real one this time."

Spencer

"All right," Cassandra said, dropping her leather messenger bag on the desk in the office with a *thump*. "Here's everything Diane left to me. Her notes, her book draft, her laptop. I picked it all up from Nicole when I got back into town."

After their lunch the previous day, they'd agreed to meet up at Occasus to work out just how the brothers might help her find Diane's murderer and figure out what exactly was going on in DeVerre. Spencer chewed on the inside of his cheek as he watched her pull out the binder, folders, notebooks, tablet, and computer. He'd already tried to clear the desk to create room, but somehow things were still overlapped and in the way.

"You guys are just like her," she chuckled, sorting through the items. "She couldn't keep her desk straight either."

"Sorry," Spencer muttered.

Cassandra shook her head and reached over to give his arm a pat. "I like it. It makes me think of her."

Not sure that he liked reminding her of her dead best friend who also happened to be a woman in her eighties, Spencer scratched the back of his head. He was trying not to let Cassandra's presence bother him. Peter was right. She was alone and needed help. And Diane had requested that they help her. But it didn't change the fact that she was everything he wished she wasn't. She hung out with ghosts, pursued more knowledge of the spiritual world that said ghosts came from, treated his fears like they were silly misunderstandings, and didn't seem to comprehend the danger she was putting the three of them in.

Worse, Peter's early assessment of her had been correct. Cassandra *was* hot. And Spencer found it unnerving.

"So what do we do with all this?" Peter asked, lifting a notebook from the pile. "Just start reading?"

Cassandra smirked, a strange hollow forming on the right side of her mouth. It wasn't quite a dimple, but against her pronounced cheekbones, it created a sort of divot that certainly resembled one. Spencer was disappointed in himself for noticing. "Well, I've already read it all," she said. "So I can tell you more or less what it says, but yes, I would recommend that you two read it. You might catch something I didn't."

Gerard hovered in the corner, watching their progress. "It's a difficult read," he spoke suddenly, voice graveled and taut. "I've tried my hand at it a time or two."

"You have?" Spencer asked, eyes darting toward him. He let his eyes rest on the ghost's form briefly. He had yet to gather the courage to settle on him fully for any length of time.

"I have," Gerard confirmed. "It gets pretty boring being dead. But I wouldn't recommend you take it up as one of your nighttime reads, my friend. You're bound to find yourself with some particularly troublesome dreams that way."

Spencer frowned, drawing back from the desk. He massaged the palm of his hand with his thumb. He already was having troublesome dreams. Ones that involved ghosts, hellhounds, and other creatures that lurked in the shadows and chased him in the woods of DeVerre.

"Don't listen to him," Cassandra interjected, breaking into his troubling thoughts. She stepped between him and the phantom and nudged his hand before motioning back to the desk. "Come on. I'll show you what Diane and I learned."

She took the next fifteen or so minutes to walk them through the basic premise of Diane's work. With a working title of *Secrets of the Lake*, the book had never been intended for publishing, she explained. It was, instead, an excuse for Diane to do her research and pursue more information under the guise of writing a book.

There were three major parts to the incomplete draft: the history of DeVerre, a detailed list on the ghosts within the town, and everything Diane had learned about the spirit world.

They overviewed the history first as it was rather thin. Cassandra explained that historical information was hard to come by in DeVerre since the residents were so secretive about everything. There were the basic dates and facts that one might find on a website somewhere, but nothing that could give them any real understanding of how the missing pieces fit together.

The list of ghosts was longer than Spencer liked. Though, to be fair, even one name was too many in his mind. But the way Cassandra spoke about each one that she'd talked with and had asked for help from bothered him even more. Nearly as much as the way Gerard occasionally chimed in to say he'd known the person she mentioned.

"So you asked others to help you besides Gerard?" Peter asked, far more intrigued than Spencer.

"Of course," she said. "I talked with several others before I met him. And while Gerard has been helpful, I've asked others since then as he can't give us all the information we need."

Gerard drew his hand along his beard. "I do apologize for that," he said. Spencer heard a blend of indifference and sincerity in his tone.

"Though we Alaries have been around since the beginning, we weren't exactly in the 'inner circle.'"

"I know," she gave him an understanding smile. "And while it would be nice if you knew more, you *were* the only one good enough to agree to help at all."

He shrugged, staring out the window as the dogs ran across the yard. "It wasn't for free."

"And I'm doing what I can," Cassandra promised, turning back to the book without further explanation. Spencer narrowed his eyes in the phantom's direction, wondering at their cryptic back and forth, but she pushed on. "So the final bit of the book dealt heavily with Diane and Liam's research on the Lawrences and their writing. Back in '97, they visited Bushmills, Ireland, to get a better look at Elijah Lawrence's writing. Though the Lawrence family originated in Amesbury, UK, Elijah moved his family to Ireland in 1624 to become a reverend at a church there. As he was lesser known than his father, and both of them had been heavily ridiculed for their beliefs, most of his writings were hard to come by. However, his church has a collection of all his original work, so they decided to visit.

"The reverend there gave them copies of the writings, and they brought it back with them to study further." Spencer watched quietly as Cassandra paused and pressed her lips together as if in thought. "Diane told the reverend about her ability to see ghosts, hopeful to find someone who could tell her more."

The brothers stared at her, waiting for her to continue.

Cassandra flipped a page in the binder. "He told her that . . . she wasn't alone. There are others out there with abilities like hers, and some have even greater ones beyond just seeing ghosts." Her tone became weighty and almost reverent. "That . . . that there is a whole other world that we can access if we have the faith for it. But he also warned her that she shouldn't try to pursue it."

"Why?" Peter asked, his mouth dropping ajar.

"He told her," she explained, meeting Peter's eyes first, then shifting to Spencer, "that this world—the spirit world—was a great temptation and danger. That it could be a blessing, but it could also be a curse. And to seek it out was not for the faint of heart."

Spencer resumed rubbing his hands together. "And she still sought it out?"

Cassandra grinned at him. "Does it scare you? This idea of danger that you can't understand? This world of ghosts and spirits?"

An amused grunt came from Peter, a smirk tugging up the corner of his mouth as he watched the two of them.

Fighting his urge to avoid her gaze, Spencer met her intense stare with one of his own. "Yes," he admitted. "I don't understand why someone would run headlong into something they know could kill them."

"Death isn't the worst thing that could happen, kid," Gerard said, leaning against the bookshelf at the back of the room. "Trust me."

An unexpected boldness filled Spencer as he turned to glare at the phantom. "You're dead," he reminded him, then gestured to Cassandra. "And it's only by some miracle that she found you and gave you the chance to connect with people again. You want to tell me that death isn't that bad? You were *alone* before she came along. How could it get any worse?"

"Not everyone becomes a ghost, Spencer," Cassandra reminded him, drawing his gaze back to her. "Only those who can't let go."

"How can anyone let go?"

"By knowing that what's coming is far greater than anything we leave behind." Her brows dropped low over her eyes. "As a Christian, you should know this."

Spencer did know it. In theory. But it wasn't enough to know. He knew a lot of things. And yet he still found himself scared of everything. He knew that you only had a one-in-a-million chance of getting injured on a roller coaster. He knew that there was a .0003% chance of dying from a skydiving accident. The odds of something bad happening were slim, but he refused to risk either of them. Because *what if?*

What if it was the one time? What if he was the one death? What if someone made a mistake and he suffered the consequence because of it? What if he did something stupid and got himself injured? *What if?*

Spencer wasn't as scared of dying as he was of the question: *What if?* He believed in God. He believed in Heaven. He prayed the prayers, lived the life, walked the walk, and talked the talk every Christian should. But *what if?*

The pain of that question was far worse than losing his life.

"So, uh," Peter interrupted, eyeing Spencer nervously. "Do we want to get back to the book?"

Spencer felt Cassandra's eyes on him a second longer. Then she turned away. "Yeah." She flipped to another page. "Anyway, when they got back from Ireland, Diane and Liam continued to research as much as they could. They . . . they started. . . ." She paused, turning the page back, then skipping a few ahead. Her brow furrowed. "They started to, uh . . . read Elijah's . . . uh. . . . Gerard?"

"Yes, Cass?"

She turned around to look at him against the bookshelf. "Has anyone touched this book since Diane's death besides Nicole?"

He narrowed his dark eyes. "Not that I know of. Why?"

"There are pages missing."

Spencer felt his heart drop into his stomach. Peter stood up straight.

"Are you sure?" Gerard asked.

Cassandra nodded. "I'm positive."

"You think someone took them?"

"I don't know." She thumbed through the pages as if they might reappear. "Nicole . . . she said she had it in her safe the whole time."

Peter pursed his lips, scanning her face. "Could she have taken them?"

"Nicole is the lawyer lady, right?" Gerard asked.

"Yeah."

He scoffed. "She didn't seem the type to care about this sort of business."

Cassandra tucked some hair behind her ear nervously. "I can't imagine it was Nicole. But . . . you're sure no one else touched it?"

"Of course I'm not sure." Gerard tugged loose the dark red tie around his neck. "I didn't spend every second babysitting the thing."

"These missing pages," Spencer interjected, bringing them back to the topic at hand. "What were they about?"

Playing with the signet ring on her pinky finger, Cassandra turned to him. "Well. . . ." Her voice was thinner than usual. "It contained most of Elijah's writings. She stored all her copies in the binder because . . . well, because it just made sense. There was no reason for her to have multiple copies when she had no reason to suspect that anyone would want to take them. But now I wish she would have at least kept a spare."

"Why would someone want his writings?" Peter asked.

Two lines creased together over the bridge of her nose. "I don't know." She shook her head. "Diane . . . she was convinced that Elijah's writings held the key to—well, to whatever answers we needed because it was—it was really confusing. He kept referring to things—strange things that we couldn't understand."

A tightness formed in Spencer's throat, and he pressed his fingers harder against his palm.

"What kinds of things?" Peter prompted.

"Well, he regularly talked about a fight between two . . . *somethings*. Groups, peoples, entities—we didn't know what they were exactly. The 'Immortal Deceivers' and the 'Divine Prophets' were what he called them."

Spencer's skin crawled at the sinister and ominous sounding names.

Peter's mouth fell ajar. "What does *that* mean?"

"We couldn't figure it out," Cassandra said with a shrug. "Everything is in old English. Which is difficult enough on its own, but he also referred to things that we had no way of cross referencing. He discussed the 'Spirit Seekers' who denied life, and the 'Protectors' who worked to end those Seekers' heretical beliefs. He also mentioned an event called 'The Release of the Great Wolf in Amesbury.' That these Seekers had found a way to unchain him. We assume he's referring to some prisoner with extraordinary powers. Later he mentioned an Irishman . . . 'the one who betrayed our trust' . . . and his grandson, Saulf. As 'Saulf' is Irish for 'sea wolf,' we assumed he was the Great Wolf referenced."

Peter glanced at Spencer. "What does that have to do with anything in DeVerre?"

Cassandra tossed her hands to the side. "I have no idea."

Fighting through the tension building within him, Spencer managed to clear his throat. "Why did Diane think that was so important?" he asked.

"She, uh. . . ." Cassandra took in a deep breath, then heaved a sigh. "It wasn't so much the Great Wolf or the Spirit Seekers or any of that. It was about the fact that there were people out there with powers like ours that were even more developed. Elijah talked about the ways that people could summon forth the spirit world to assist and defend them. 'Like a shield of light,' he wrote. His work is also how we first discovered the way to tether a ghost and turn them into a phantom."

"So it's essentially a how-to book?" Peter concluded.

Cassandra let out a scoffing chuckle. "Something like that." Spencer watched as her frown pulled down her whole face. "But Diane must have been right. Elijah's writings had to be important, or someone wouldn't have stolen them."

Tugging on his fingers in his unease, Spencer stared at the binder. "But we don't know that the pages were actually stolen," he said. "You were gone for, what, a week before Diane's death?"

"A little over."

"Maybe she removed them herself," he suggested. "She could have been studying them and taken them to her room. Or they could be in the attic with the other stuff we moved up there."

It took a second, but finally Cassandra nodded, a glimmer of hope coming to her eyes. "Maybe."

"But if that's not the case," Peter added. "If someone really did take them, we will know for sure that Diane was right and they were important. And we'll have evidence to be on the lookout for."

"Okay," she sighed. "So we search the house then?"

"Yeah," Peter nodded, glancing at Spencer. "I think that's the best way to start. We search the house. Would it work for you to come back after church on Sunday?"

Cassandra hesitated, her lips parting in surprise. Her hand came to rest on Diane's draft as she leaned forward. "Wait, why wouldn't we start searching for them now?"

Peter crossed his arms. "Because as much as I'd love to drop everything to solve this mystery for you, we've got work to do."

Spencer felt some of the tension in his chest release at his brother's firm statement. They couldn't ignore their writing. If they wanted to remain in DeVerre—which was an increasingly diminishing desire for him—they had to write their novel to earn an income. And even if they didn't decide to stay, writing the book was still their best chance to get their careers moving forward. They could return to Norfolk and go back to their old life with a book published and the promise of the future ahead of them. But it would only happen if they stayed the course and kept pursuing their work.

"You can't be serious?" A disbelieving snarl crossed the woman's lips. "We can't lose time on this. If we don't figure out who killed Diane, it won't matter if you write your little stories or not."

"*Little* stories?" Peter huffed. Spencer shifted uncomfortably, unsure whether to feel bad for Cassandra with his brother's oncoming anger or if he should be just as offended. "Wow! Okay, cool. Sure, we'll help you out, and you'll insult our writing."

She rolled her eyes at his dramatics. "I didn't mean it as an insult."

"Oh, all right. All's forgiven, then."

"Look, I think you two are perfectly good writers, but I've already been gone too long. We don't have any more time to waste."

"You're pressing your luck, Cass," Gerard warned.

Peter tossed a hand in the ghost's direction. "Yes, listen to him!"

"They're both too stubborn to realize they've chosen a stupid career."

"Hey!"

Quickly, Spencer set a hand on Peter's arm to calm him down. Then he turned to Cassandra to meet her incredulous glare with a sympathetic one of his own. While he understood her sense of urgency, Peter was right. They needed to pace themselves for what would inevitably be a long investigation.

"We're going to help you," he promised. "But we're also going to write. And you're right, we don't have a lot of time. Every day we wait is a day that whoever's behind all this can clean up after themselves. But we still have to live our lives. And we aren't going to solve this in one day. You have your goals and we have ours. We can work together to make sure *everyone* gets what they want."

Cassandra studied him, arms crossed and head tilted to the side. The late afternoon light beamed through the windows, turning her eyes a fascinating blend of jade and copper. Holding her intent gaze like that made his throat dry up. He didn't know if it was her looks or her confidence that made his whole body forget how to function whenever she turned that intense stare his way.

Finally, she broke the charged silence. "All right. I get it."

Spencer returned her nod. "Thanks."

"And I meant it," she added in an obvious attempt to smooth over her previous words. "You two are good writers."

"You've read our stuff?"

She smiled. "Of course I have. Diane and I read every post together."

Spencer scratched the back of his head, a slow grin spreading across his face. "And you liked it?"

"Yeah," she replied. "I like it a lot actually. Wenzel and Frankly are a fun team. And though I'm sort of surprised *you* write about monsters, you do quite a good job. Even Gerard likes it."

Peter hopped up to sit on the desk. "Really?"

Gerard let out a grunt from the other side of the room. "It's passable for entertainment."

"Who's your favorite character?" Peter prodded her. "Wenzel or Frankly?"

Cassandra laughed. "Oh, no." She shook her head. "I'm not playing that game."

"What?" Peter reached over to nudge her arm. "We won't care."

"Not a chance." Cassandra gave his hand a playful shove. "I'm not stupid enough to say which of you I like better."

"Which of *us*?" Peter raised his brow.

Spencer let out an exasperated sigh.

"Mm-hm. It's obvious. You're Wenzel, and Spence is Frankly. If I tell you that I like either of the characters better, you're going to know which one of you I like better. And I'm not ready to reveal all my secrets yet."

A sly grin spread over Peter's mouth. He glanced at Spencer. "So you *do* like one of us better?"

She cocked her right eyebrow. "Maybe."

"It's Spencer, isn't it?" His brother pointed toward him. "It's those baby blue eyes. Gets 'em every time."

Pressing his lips together, Spencer glared at Peter, silently warning him to stop. He hated it when his brother did this to him. He'd never understood why Peter was so obsessed with finding him a girlfriend in the first place. But he had absolutely no interest in getting involved with any woman in DeVerre, let alone the frustratingly beautiful ghost whisperer standing on the other side of the desk.

"If it's any consolation," Gerard called as he left the room, "I don't like either of you."

Cassandra chuckled and started to repack her bag. "I'll just let you keep guessing," she teased. "And in the meantime, I'll eagerly await your next post. Is it Wenzel or Frankly this time?"

"Wenzel," Spencer said. He hoped that Gerard's interruption and his encouragement would successfully move them away from the previous topic.

But Cassandra eyed him mischievously as she slipped the bag's strap onto her shoulder. "Hm, that's too bad."

Peter laughed as Spencer gaped at her joke. At least he hoped it was a joke. Not that it wouldn't be nice to know she liked him—Frankly, he sternly corrected his own thoughts. It would be nice to know that she liked *Frankly*. Because anytime someone complimented his character, it was a compliment to his writing.

"I'd leave some of Diane's stuff behind, but I don't want any more of it going missing," Cassandra said, her smile still a hint sly. "I'll make some copies over the next few days and look through her digital docs to see if there's anything in there. I'll bring it with me Sunday. See you boys then."

"See you Sunday," Peter confirmed.

She gave Peter a nod and patted Spencer's arm as she walked past him. "Have fun writing."

The smirk on Peter's face lingered even as the brothers listened to the front door click shut behind her.

"Oh, shut up," Spencer muttered in his direction as he plunked in the desk chair and opened the laptop.

"What?" Peter replied innocently. "I didn't say anything."

~

For the next several days, the brothers worked on the novel and posted the next episode of the serial on their blog. Spencer was as grateful as he was surprised to discover that his brother matched his own dedication to the tasks on their list. It wasn't often that Peter dropped everything to write. He was generally too focused on the world around him and the random ideas he'd come up with to actually sit down to finish his writing tasks.

But Peter's focus seemed unwavering over the following days, and they managed to get far more work done than Spencer expected.

Spencer knew that his brother's sudden diligence was for his sake. He could tell by the way Peter kept deferring to him on everything. Any idea he came up with, Peter would double check to be sure Spencer thought it made sense. After each completed task, he'd immediately ask what was next. For the first time ever, Spencer felt like they were really collaborating. Not because they had never wanted to, but because they'd never had this freedom of time.

Spencer was proud of them for how much they got done. Especially considering how distracting it was to have Gerard literally haunting the halls now. Despite Cassandra's rule against scaring Spencer, the phantom found ways around the restriction. He'd peer over their shoulders as they were working, so silent in his arrival that they'd jump when he finally spoke up to offer a piece of unsolicited advice. And it was obvious that he enjoyed appearing out of thin air at the most unexpected times.

However, Spencer soon discovered that the extent of the phantom's torments were relegated to the occasional biting remark. Gerard tended to hang around like an irritating shadow, the bulk of his time spent reading through the entirety of Diane's massive collection of books. Spencer couldn't deny that it was still weird though, having the phantom pop in and out whenever he felt like it. Gerard was so unlike his expectations of ghosts. He walked, moved, and talked like a normal human. There was nothing translucent or otherworldly about his appearance beyond the muted, almost technicolor quality to his whole person.

But to Spencer's relief, the phantom's presence stopped being quite so unnerving after the first couple days.

Spencer was proud of himself for that too. Not only had he gotten comfortable living with a ghost—or phantom, whatever the difference was—but so far, he hadn't allowed himself to dwell on the fact that their lives were in danger either.

After finding the small, black handgun in the hidden compartment of the desk, both of the brothers had begun to feel much more confident in their circumstances. Peter was better with guns. Spencer always felt a bit nervous that he'd inadvertently mishandle them, so they agreed that Peter would hold onto it.

"I don't think I should carry it though," Peter said, taking the gun and extra ammo from the desktop. "I'm not really sure what the laws are here."

When the gun was safely stashed in Peter's nightstand, they both felt much more confident that, should there be another attack, they could defend themselves. Though Spencer had to wonder to himself what good a bullet would do against a beast of the spirit world. But he had pushed that thought out of his mind the second it entered.

Late on Saturday, they went to The Glass Tavern to hang out with Anna, Aaron, and Haley. Anna was on duty, and they all decided to keep her company during her shift. So they sat at the bar as some of the only patrons for the evening. Haley and Peter kept most of the conversation going, Anna jumping in whenever she didn't have to serve her other customers. It was nice, Spencer decided, seeing his brother making friends with such ease.

Spencer mused over his brother's persona as he sat quietly nursing his drink, watching the others banter back and forth. He knew that Peter came across as confident and sure of himself to people. His easygoing nature and overly enthusiastic disposition made him appear uninhibited by social interaction to those around him. But Spencer knew the truth: his brother's insecurities ran deeper than anyone would expect. Possibly even deeper than Spencer's own fears.

By presenting a gregarious and open demeanor, Peter was protecting himself. He tried too hard. And when he ended up scaring people off with how honest and caring he was, he inevitably blamed them for it. He would shrug off the rejection, and the cycle would continue with the next person.

No one but Spencer saw the way those failed relationships actually affected his brother. No one else saw how each friendship ending or premature breakup caused his brother to block off another part of himself.

Peter gave people every piece of who he was, and then he gave up on them when they pushed him away. It was all or nothing. And it wasn't working.

But strangely enough, here in DeVerre, it seemed that Peter's all-or-nothing style of friendship was appreciated. At least by the Lambert family.

Perhaps it was because Anna and Aaron were used to Ava's intense and direct manner. While Peter didn't have her abrasive edge, Spencer could see that there was a similarity in how the two of them approached life. That take it or leave it mentality that either drew people in or pushed them away.

Spencer glanced at Aaron in thought. Of the group, he felt like Aaron's personality resembled his own the most. He kept quiet, didn't care to be a part of the social scene, and lived his life however he thought best. Yet his girlfriend was far more like Peter, constantly in conversation and always with a friendly word for those around them. It made sense that he too wouldn't be put off by Peter's more polarizing personality.

While the three more talkative members of their party focused on one another, Spencer decided to get up and shift to Aaron's other side.

Pushing his glasses farther up his nose, Aaron tipped his chin toward Spencer. "How's the Jeep running?"

"Still great," Spencer said, setting his pint glass down on the bar top. "Better than ever actually."

Aaron grinned. "Glad to hear it. It's a beautiful Jeep. Still in great condition for being over twenty years old. Where'd you get it?"

Spencer adjusted the collar of his denim jacket. "Uh, it was our dad's," he explained. "He always kept it clean and detailed. Though I don't remember it ever running this well."

"Your dad knows how to take care of cars," Aaron said. "Seems like he taught you well."

"Yeah," Spencer nodded, not interested in correcting the tense of Aaron's assumption of his dad's whereabouts. "Yeah, he did."

While Peter, Anna, and Haley discussed the recurring wolf attacks and failed hunting parties, Spencer and Aaron kept up their own conversation. Spencer was happy to get to know the Lambert brother better. Since Aaron was the middle sibling, it turned out that the two of them were the same age. The conversation remained on vehicles for a while as they discussed the Jeep and Aaron's motorcycle, but it soon shifted to other sorts of entertainment. Though Aaron wasn't much of a reader, he and Spencer shared a similar taste in movies.

When the evening drew to a close, Aaron invited both Spencer and Peter to join him and his brother-in-law Owen the next time they hung out. "Ava kicks him out of the house so she can have a girls' night with Anna," he explained. "So I always have him over, and we play video games or watch movies or whatever."

"Sure, that'd be great," Spencer agreed, wondering when he'd last made a new friend. He'd always gotten along with his coworkers and extended family, but he had never really considered them friends. Not the sort that he'd actually go out of his way to spend time with, at least.

Glancing over at Peter, Spencer couldn't help but smile. They were doing it. Despite the strangeness of DeVerre, the dangers they had and would face, and the fact that there was a spirit world encroaching on their lives, he was beginning to feel a connection to the place.

And that they just might be able to make DeVerre their home.

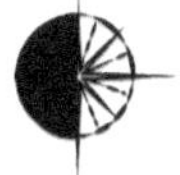

Spencer

The service on Sunday was another morning filled with subdued chatter and tense conversation. It was like a black cloud had settled onto DeVerre after the third animal attack. And if it wasn't enough that they still hadn't found the wolf, this time it was a kid who had died.

Reverend Chapelle gave a particularly poignant eulogy for seventeen-year-old Brendan Descoteaux. Though the majority of the congregation bore long faces and hunched shoulders as they listened in sorrow, the reverend looked particularly downcast. His ruddy complexion was paler than usual. Dark circles lingered under his eyes as he wrung his hands behind the pulpit. He applauded Brendan as one of the best young men in town. A few people within earshot began to whisper, and Spencer overheard them discussing the notable absence of the reverend's daughter.

Spencer and Peter shared a glance. They didn't have any knowledge of the ins and outs of the town's romantic gossip, but it seemed like a safe assumption that Brendan and the reverend's daughter had had more than a passing acquaintance, if the way the busybodies were muttering was any indication.

Even after the sermon that the reverend struggled through, the congregation moved at a slow, lethargic pace. No one spoke with any sense of animation as they milled around Peter and Spencer, casting suspicious glares their way whenever they could.

Feeling the muscles tighten in his neck as they worked their way to the back of the church, Spencer shoved his fists into his pockets. How could these people be suspicious of them? It was a wolf that was killing their family and friends, right? Why did it feel as if they were turning their blame on them?

Before he could slip out into the bright morning, Peter grabbed Spencer's arm and pulled him to the side at the back of the church. "Hang on," he muttered. "Cass is coming."

Turning around, Spencer and Peter watched as Cassandra approached from the front, a middle-aged man and woman trailing behind her. She smiled as she pushed through the crowd to get to them. "Hey," she said, her messenger bag hanging at her side. "You guys ready to go?"

"Yep," Peter said, then glanced at the couple behind her. "How's it going?"

"Oh," Cassandra looked over her shoulder as if just realizing the couple was still standing there. "Uh, Peter, Spencer, this is the family I'm staying with. Debbie, Mike, these are Diane's nephews."

Despite Cassandra's cheery introduction, the couple eyed the pair of them with obvious distaste.

"Nice to meet you." Peter's unwavering friendliness never failed to impress Spencer. And faced with the middle-aged couple's glares, it was even more amazing.

Resting her hand on Cassandra's shoulder, Debbie frowned. "Are you sure you don't want to have lunch with us, Cassie?"

The woman had the same sharply arched brows as Cassandra, but the rest of her appearance made her seem far too normal to be the younger woman's family member. Debbie's light brown hair, rounded features, and floral print dress stood in high contrast to Cassandra's dark and striking exterior. Even the overly sweet tone of the older woman's voice set them apart.

"Thanks, Deb, but I promised I'd help them organize some of Diane's stuff," Cassandra replied, pulling out of the woman's grip. "I'll try to be home for dinner though."

Despite her excessively agreeable tone, Debbie and Mike gave the brothers a withering glare and followed the rest of the congregation out of the chapel.

"You've got a real nice family there, Cass," Peter said with a smirk. "Absolute sweethearts."

Casandra scoffed. "I told you," she said, pulling her keys from her bag. "None of my family wants me here. The only reason Deb lets me live with them is because she and my mom were best friends growing up. It's my mom's way of keeping an eye on me while Deb not-so-subtly suggests that I should return home whenever she gets a chance."

As the church cleared, they made their way back to Occasus. Cassandra followed them in her vintage red truck. It was a cool truck, Spencer had to admit to himself. Not as cool as the Jeep, of course, but the glossy finish of the paint and shining rims showed the great care that had been taken over the years.

When they arrived home, Peter forced them to sit down and have some lunch. "I'm not much of a chef," he told Cassandra. "But I can make a mean sandwich."

Meal done, the three of them headed to the library in case they'd overlooked anything in the original files. Once assured that they wouldn't find anything there, they moved to Diane's room. Spencer had hesitated at the threshold but forced himself forward after the other two.

It felt wrong to go through Diane's room. The brothers agreed that they weren't comfortable searching her dresser or closet, so Cassandra volunteered to handle those areas while they searched the nightstand, sitting area, and the short bookshelves on the far side of the room.

"Still nothing," Cassandra said, stepping back in from the bathroom.

"Guess we should check the attic?" Peter suggested.

"What about that locked room?" Spencer reminded his brother, tipping his chin toward the ceiling. He looked at Cassandra. "Do you know where she kept the key?"

Cassandra bit her bottom lip around a smile. "Oh, yeah, uh," she reached beneath the collar of her high neck sweater and drew out a silver chain. A small skeleton key dangled on the end of it. "Diane had a secret pocket sewn into her briefcase, and I knew she always kept the key there. When I checked, sure enough, I found it."

"You could have told us," Peter said, crossing his arms.

"Yeah, I just . . . I wanted to be there when you opened it."

"Why?" Spencer asked.

"Because I've never actually seen it. It's where Diane kept all her research about her family. It's fairly empty from what she said, but she didn't want people accidentally discovering her real reason for coming to DeVerre."

"And you want to see it because . . . ?"

"Because Diane never talked to me about her genealogical research. She would only ever say that she'd hit a dead end and that she didn't know how to proceed."

"Well, let's go check it out then." Peter shoved Spencer toward the door.

The stairs creaked under their weight as they headed for the third floor. Since moving into the house, Spencer had strictly avoided this staircase. He knew that it was another of his irrational fears, but he didn't like the idea that there was a locked room and attic above his head. Daily, his mind tried to convince him that the rooms housed evil shadow creatures. And with the increasing frequency that those same kinds of creatures were showing up in his dreams, he'd done his best to pretend the staircase didn't exist at all.

Reaching the small landing between the attic and the locked room, Peter pressed himself to the back wall to make way for Cassandra. Her shoulder brushed Spencer's as she slipped the key from her neck and went to unlock the door. Holding his breath as the door swung open, Spencer braced himself for what awaited them on the other side.

His breath puffed out when it proved to be exactly what Cassandra had said. Dust danced in the beams of sunlight from the three large windows as they peered into the small room. Short stacks of boxes rested against the rounded wall on their right. A few more sat next to a simple oak desk against the left. Hanging over the desk was a cork board with dozens of pictures, news articles, and sticky notes marking Diane's research. On the desk, there were notebooks and a jar of pens, a spool of black thread and push pins, a file box, and loose papers. But other than the chair pushed in place, the room was as empty as expected.

No monsters, ghouls, or ghosts in sight.

A surge of irritation sparked through Spencer at his irrational imagination.

Cassandra stepped in first, making a beeline to the cork board.

The brothers followed. They flanked her, staring at the various things Diane had collected, marked up, and connected with that black thread from the desk. In the very center of the board was a pinned picture of a baby and a toddler. The children were held in the arms of a young couple. Spencer recognized them immediately as their great-grandparents, Helen and Ronald. But his eyes quickly veered to the corner of the photo. Off in the corner was the focus of Diane's work.

A sticky note labeled the stranger as 'Mr. F' and a string connected him to a list of names and dates. Spencer scanned the list.

Leon Frossard, 1871-1953

Lloyd Frossard, 1895-1978

Lee Frossard, 1899-1968

Wallace Frossard, 1928-1966

Bill Frossard, 1935-1965

"Wow." Peter gasped as he lightly touched some of the notes and pictures scattered across the board. "She was . . . kind of off her rocker, wasn't she?"

Cassandra frowned at him. "She wanted to know who her family was."

"Yeah, well, I'm interested too. But I'm not creating some sort of serial killer's murder board now, am I?"

Ignoring their chatter, Spencer narrowed his eyes on the picture. Though the man was out of frame, it was evident that he looked a lot like the present Dr. Frossard. He checked the dates again. Diane had crossed the names of the oldest and two youngest men off the list. It seemed that she had decided that their ages absolved them of being the man in the picture.

"Do you know if Diane ever asked the Frossards about this?" Spencer asked, still studying the board.

"Are you kidding?" Cassandra scoffed. "Even if Alexander Frossard knew the truth, he wouldn't tell *us*."

"Do you think he'd tell Anna?" Peter asked.

"Anna Lambert?"

"Yeah."

Cassandra pursed her lips and considered it before shrugging. "I doubt it. The Frossards like Anna, but . . . let's just say they have a very specific set of requirements for their inner circle. And I don't see a descendent of the Raynes being on that list of people. No matter how much their son likes her."

"Anna's mentioned the Rayne name before," Spencer recalled, angling to look at her. "Were they a major part of DeVerre's history like the Frossards and Chapelles?"

"Oh, yeah! The Varons, Chapelles, and Garniers may have been best friends, but Yvan Rayne was Matthias's right-hand man. He maintained the town records and practically kept the place running."

Peter's mouth dropped open in understanding. "Which is why they're in charge of the library."

"Exactly."

"Well great!" Spencer said, motioning to the board. "We can take all this stuff and talk to Ava about it. If the Rayne family held all the records of DeVerre, surely she can research it for us."

Cassandra's brow pulled down as she backed up toward the boxes. "You *could* try, but it isn't likely to help."

"Why not?"

"Because Diane already tried getting information out of the Raynes." Cassandra sifted through the boxes. "Their mother, Aimee, was the librarian before Ava, and Diane went to talk with her several times. Aimee was helpful, but she didn't know much."

"You sure?" Peter asked, leaning against the desk. "Ava told me that every one of the founding families of DeVerre has had the same job since the start. If the Raynes were the ones keeping the records, surely they have the genealogies as well."

Cassandra threw him a snide smirk. "Have you forgotten how secretive DeVerre is? Aimee didn't give Diane any information, which means one of two things: She was being honest and really couldn't help. Or, more likely, she was lying because she didn't want to give away town secrets to a stranger."

"Even if that stranger was a DeVerrean themselves?"

"What proof does Diane have that she's from DeVerre beyond that photo?" Cassandra asked, tossing her hand toward the board. "It's obvious that's a Frossard to me, but how is anyone going to prove that makes her from DeVerre? When the Collinses adopted Diane and Phillip, they registered delayed birth certificates. Certificates now stating that their births happened in Virginia."

"How'd they do that?"

Cassandra shook her head. "I suppose they forged the appropriate documents with the help of our mystery Frossard. But that's the thing—

the Frossards and the Raynes have ties back to the start of DeVerre. Why would a Rayne give up their fellow founding family members to a stranger who *claims* to be a long-lost child of a past resident?"

Scanning the board again, Spencer supposed she was right. It seemed that this town was nothing but a tangle of lies, deceit, and duplicity of all forms. The reason why was still unclear, but he no longer doubted that most of the people in DeVerre were hiding something.

"I trust Anna," Peter protested, interrupting his thoughts. "And Ava."

"You can't trust anyone in DeVerre," Cassandra countered. "Not when you're an outsider."

"Can we trust you?" He challenged.

A slow smile spread over her face. "Do you think you can trust me?"

"I don't know."

She turned to Spencer.

Realizing that she was waiting for his own answer, Spencer raised his brow in surprise. "Uh. . . ." He ran a hand over his mouth, stalling to figure out the answer. Did he trust her? Did he trust Anna and Ava? Did he trust anyone but Peter?

Cassandra's lips twisted into a wry and disappointed smirk as his hesitation lasted too long. "That's answer enough." She turned back to the boxes.

Peter and Spencer shared an uncomfortable look. Why should they trust her? Because Diane trusted her? They'd known her for less than a week. That wasn't enough time to test her loyalties and motives.

Yet Spencer felt guilt churn in his stomach as he watched Cassandra hunch over the boxes on the far side of the room.

Deciding he should join her in the search so they could get out of the secret office space, Spencer sorted through the papers on the desk. There were lists of more names and dates; some crossed out, some circled and then crossed out, some with question marks or arrows beside them. His eyes zeroed in a line with a familiar name.

"Uh, Cass," Spencer called, lifting the paper. "Why is Gerard's name on here?"

She looked up from the box, brushing some of the hair hanging in her face out of the way. "Huh?" She narrowed her eyes on the page. "Oh, I think that's just Diane's list of residents."

"Just that, eh?" Peter asked, taking the page from Spencer. "Hm, yeah, that actually does look like all it is. Where'd Diane get this information?"

"From me," Gerard said, appearing at the door.

"Gah!" Peter jumped. "Warn a guy, would you?"

"No," he replied, then waved his hand at the paper. "Diane sat down with me on a regular basis to talk about that list. We developed it shortly after Cassie tethered me here. Its intent was to help her figure out her parentage and to help me figure out the answer to my own problem."

Peter's brow rose. "Which is?"

"None of your business."

Spencer ignored the questions Gerard's unfinished business raised in his own mind and pointed to his name on the sheet. "Why'd she put four question marks next to your name?"

Cassandra and Peter both turned to Gerard with equal interest.

The phantom appeared unfazed. "Because I was alive during her lifetime, and she was curious if I might know her parents. She kept cross-referencing people that I knew and the relationships my family had formed to see if there was any connection. She never could find one. It would have been convenient though. I'll tell you that."

"Parents. . . ." Peter muttered, then pointed to Cassandra. "You said she remembered her mom, but . . . not her dad?"

"Yeah," she confirmed. "Diane remembered her mom talking about her father, but she didn't remember anything about him or even ever seeing him. She always assumed that meant that she and Phillip had been illegitimate. Possibly the result of a love affair gone wrong. She thought that could be the reason they were taken from their mother in the first place. Maybe their father had wanted to get rid of any evidence that he'd done anything wrong."

"Oh!" Spencer gasped as an idea sparked in his head, and he pointed back to the photo. "That's her dad!"

Cassandra shrugged as if that were old news. "She did consider that."

"But it isn't true," Gerard said. "That man was either Lloyd or Lee Frossard. Leon was too old at the time, but the other two were in their forties. And though technically either of them could have fathered her, the Frossards aren't known for illicit behavior. They have a specific way they do things. Family is first, and if you mess with their family, they'll come for you. Lloyd and Lee were far too dedicated to their wives and children to carry on an affair long enough to father two children."

Peter crossed his arms. "That's heavy speculation you're offering."

"So is your brother's theory," Gerard countered, tone cool as ever. "I *knew* the Frossards. You've got nothing but a picture as your proof."

"But then why would one of them escort the kids all the way to Virginia for their adoption?" Spencer asked. "If these weren't his children, what stake did he have in it?"

"The Frossards are doctors," he reminded them. "Granted, Lee was a veterinarian, but he still studied medicine of some sort. I'll concede that Diane and Phillip were probably the children of some prominent member of the town. Garnering an escort of the Frossard notoriety almost guarantees that. However, I'd imagine it's because of the importance of keeping their existence quiet rather than their relation that provided such special treatment."

"What's your theory, then?" Peter asked, crossing his arms. "Who do you think was their dad?"

Gerard took a few seconds to think about it, his dark eyes drifting to the dusty floorboards. "I'm not sure," he muttered. "I've had a few thoughts in the past, but none of them make much sense. I was only a teen at the time of Diane's birth. The politics of the town didn't mean much to me then."

Spencer scanned him. "But you remember them? Diane and our grandfather?"

He shook his head, then slicked his dark hair back. "Sorry, can't say I do."

Peter grumbled and tossed the paper back on the desk with the others. "You finding anything over there, Cass?"

"No," she sighed. "It's just more books and photos."

"Photos? Of what?"

"The Collins family."

Gerard disappeared in disinterest as Peter and Spencer hurried to join Cassandra. Sure enough, there were three shoeboxes full of their own family's photos. Most of them were of their great-aunts and uncles, and several others of their aunts and uncles. But there were a handful of them and their distant cousins. Spencer found one of their dad and mom at their wedding. He grinned and showed it to Peter.

"Whoa," he chuckled, taking the picture. "Dang, it's been a while since I've seen this."

Cassandra looked over their shoulder. "Ah, that's awesome." She set a hand on Peter's arm as she leaned in. "You guys look just like your dad. He's really handsome."

"Yeah," Peter smirked, and Spencer caught the nostalgic look that gleamed in his dark eyes. "He was a stud."

She laughed and pointed to their mom. "But she was a knockout. He was a lucky man."

Spencer felt his chest constrict. He tried to take a deep breath around it, but only managed a shallow intake of air. "Yeah, he was," he muttered.

A beat of tense silence passed as Peter dipped his head.

He could feel Cassandra's eyes on each of them as she studied their reaction. Her initial confusion seemed to melt quickly into compassion.

She edged away from Peter and dusted her hands off. "Should we check out the attic now?"

The pressure inside his chest building, Spencer could only manage a nod. Peter watched him closely.

"You good?" he whispered as Cassandra walked around them.

"Mm. . . ." was all he could manage. He looked across the room, trying to regain some sense of place. He wasn't a kid mourning the loss of his dad anymore. He was an adult living in Washington State, chasing his dreams with his brother. And fighting off hellhounds in the process.

Staring at the streams of sunlight that glowed against the wall next to the desk, Spencer blinked away the emotions rising within him. The golden beams of light made the dark wood slats glitter almost unnaturally. He reached up to rub away any tears he hadn't realized had risen but discovered his eyes were dry.

Peter slapped his shoulder, distracting him with an encouraging grin. "C'mon. Let's find those pages."

But they didn't find them. They sorted through the entirety of the boxes they'd brought up to the attic and found nothing. Not even after Cassandra had checked everything twice.

Letting the last box drop back to the ground beside her, she blew out a sigh that ruffled the edges of her hair. "Someone took them."

Spencer pressed his lips together, sharing in her disappointment. His hopes that this had all been a misunderstanding were gone for good.

"Seems like it," Peter said, giving the box at his side a shove. "What now?"

Cassandra shrugged, hands falling back to her lap as she sat crisscross on the attic floor. "I mean, we need to find out who took them. Whoever has them clearly had something to do with her murder. But if we can find them, we can make a huge step toward figuring all this out."

"But how are we going to find them?" Spencer asked. "It isn't like we can run around town asking everyone if they or anyone they knew stole some papers from Diane's draft."

"No," she frowned. "I know."

"Well, if we can't find who took the pages right off the bat," Peter said from his seat a few feet away. "We can try to figure out what the pages were about."

Cassandra scrunched her nose at the idea, then sneezed from the dust surrounding them.

"Bless you," Spencer muttered.

"Thank you." She turned back to Peter. "I don't think I can remember them that well. Like I said, they were really complex writings. Diane understood far more because she could read Latin and knew the roots of the Old English alphabet. But I'm not a scholar like her or Liam. Even if we found the pages, I couldn't be much help with them anyway."

"Spence could." Peter nodded toward him.

"You could?" The surprise in her voice was obvious.

Spencer hesitated, massaging the palm of his hand. He couldn't decide whether he should feel proud that he could help or annoyed that his brother had volunteered him for such grueling work. "Yeah, technically. I studied linguistics in college and picked up the basics of Latin. I'm not great at it though."

"You'd be better than me," she said with a laugh.

He shrugged. "I could give it a try."

"Mkay, well, maybe that would be helpful," she concluded. "But I'm not sure how we'd find them. Diane and Liam had to go to Ireland to get those copies."

"Yeah, but that was in the '90s," Peter said. "We're in the twenty-first century now. We've got the internet."

"So you're going to scour the internet for Elijah Lawrence's texts?"

"Sure."

Cassandra tilted her head to the side with a shrug. "It's not a bad idea."

"Thanks." Peter turned back to Spencer. "I still think we should talk with Ava though. She knows everything about DeVerre. There's a good chance she knows about the connection to his writings too."

Spencer opened his mouth to agree, but Cassandra interrupted.

"Uh. . . ." She grimaced. "I wouldn't recommend that."

They both looked at her, brows furrowed.

"She, uh . . . she doesn't like me much."

"What?" Spencer asked. "Why not?"

Cassandra sucked in her bottom lip as she stared at the floor. "She doesn't approve of my. . . ." She wiggled her fingers in the air.

"Your hands?" Peter asked with a smirk.

Cassandra threw him an annoyed glare. "My abilities. She's against communicating with spirits."

The brothers sat upright in shock.

"Wait," Peter stared at her. "She knows about all this?"

"Yeah. All the Raynes know."

"She told me that ghosts weren't real!"

"Again, she's against it all." Cassandra tugged on her collar as she shifted on the floor. "She probably didn't want you getting involved."

"Yeah. And I had just told her that Spence is a scaredy cat."

Spencer glowered at him, even though it was true.

"Hang on, though. Does that mean Anna knows?"

Cassandra hesitated as she considered it. "I'm not sure, actually. We've never talked about it."

"And you have talked with Ava about it?" Spencer pressed, not ready to completely discount the woman based on Cassandra's words alone. There was a chance she was right; Ava might have been lying to them. But he needed to make sure.

"Not . . . not technically," Cassandra admitted. "She's made comments though, and she refused to help Diane after she took charge of the library on the grounds that she didn't want to assist in pursuing 'dangerous and unnatural things.'"

"But her mom helped Diane?"

"Yeah, though they never openly discussed the subject."

Spencer dropped his gaze in thought. Perhaps Ava was hiding things.

But if her mother was willing to help Diane, then there was no reason to lose total faith in her. "Maybe Ava *is* the person to talk to."

"How could she be?"

"If she's against accessing the spirit world, she wouldn't have an interest in using it, right? So she wouldn't be the one who sent the hellhound after us. And if our goal is to find the person who *did* send it, then surely she'd want them caught too?"

"True," Cassandra acquiesced. "But I don't think she'd like that you're working with me."

"Even if you have a common enemy?"

She smirked. "You clearly don't know Ava well."

Peter let out a huff. "I feel like we don't know anyone anymore. Who else knows about all this?"

Brow rising in doubt, Cassandra shook her head. "Not many people. As far as I know, I'm the only one here who can do what I can do. And I've never heard people talk about it. My guess? The Chapelles and the Raynes know for sure. Other than that . . . there's a chance the rest of the founding families know—or knew once—but it wouldn't surprise me to find that none of them know now. Again, Diane and I couldn't find *any* information on it, and something like this is hard to hide."

"Hm." Peter pursed his lips. "Okay, so how about this? We don't ask Ava about it if that will put us on her bad side. But Spence and I *do* go to see if we can find any books on either of the Lawrence guys and the history of DeVerre and the surrounding areas. Maybe we can find something? And maybe we could cross reference Diane's list to an updated genealogy of the town."

"Maybe." There was a thread of reluctance in her tone.

Spencer shifted onto his knees, ready to be off the floor. "I've got a better idea," he said.

"Oh, yeah?" Peter asked, grinning. "Whatcha got, Matlock?"

"You go by yourself," he said, standing the rest of the way up. "If I'm there, Ava may take it more seriously. If you go on your own, she won't think twice about you asking a million questions or looking for random books."

Peter nodded in acceptance. "True. I've already done that once. A second time won't be weird."

"All right." Cassandra sighed. "As long as you don't mention me or ghosts or the spirit world. I don't need her or this town any more against me than they already are."

~

"Nothing," Peter said, dropping the final book down on the coffee table. "Absolutely *nothing*."

Spencer looked up from his laptop and toward the living room. Peter lounged on one couch while Gerard sat on the other.

Resting his head against the arm of the couch, Peter stared at the ceiling. "How is it possible to read as much boring history as we have in the past week, scour the internet for *anything* about the Lawrences, read all Diane's stuff, and still not find a *single* clue?"

Determining that this was as good a time as any to take a break from editing the minimal writing Peter had managed over the last few days, Spencer shut his laptop and rose from the desk. Nex hopped up to follow. After their talks of Diane's penchant for Latin, he'd decided to look up the dogs' names. He'd immediately regretted it.

It wasn't so much Anguis's name that bothered him. His simply meant 'snake' or 'dragon.' A weird name for a dog, but nothing too sinister.

However, Nex's name was another story. He'd come to see the dog as his shadow, following him around the house and sticking closest to his side on their walks. But after learning the meaning of his name, he had to question if he liked having a dog named 'violent death' as his faithful friend. But, like everything else in this strange town, Spencer resolved to ignore its eerie connotations to focus on the task at hand.

Spencer leaned against the living room door frame as Nex settled at his side. "I'll admit, I'm surprised too," he said. "I thought we would have found something of use."

"You're looking in the wrong places." Gerard flicked to the next page of his novel.

Peter raised his head. "It would have been nice to know that before we wasted the last four days."

"It wouldn't have made any difference."

"Why not?"

"Because I don't have a better suggestion. And you would have found some way to avoid writing either way."

Spencer couldn't help laughing as Peter snarled at the ghost.

"I'm not avoiding writing," he argued. "I'm just trying to give Cassandra as much consideration as she's giving us."

"That's a pleasant lie to tell yourself."

"Hey," Peter sat up, hands gripping the cushions on either side of him. "You don't know us, bud. You may have watched us for three weeks like some creepy freak, but that doesn't mean you know who we are. And until I hear some actual, *helpful* advice, I don't see any reason that we should listen to you."

"I've helped both Di and Cassie plenty. It's not part of my deal to help you two."

Spencer moved farther into the room. "What is your deal anyway? What do you get out of all this?"

Gerard turned his sharp, dark eyes on him. The phantom's glare was weighty and challenging, like he expected Spencer to wilt under it. But after living in the same house as a ghost, Spencer realized that Cassandra was right—ghosts couldn't hurt him. It was the matter of his nightmares that were causing his real problems these days. Gerard didn't pose any threat. There was no *what if* left with him.

Seeing that Spencer wouldn't back down from the question, Gerard closed the paperback and tossed it on the table. It landed with a light *thump* next to the library books. "I promised to help Cass in whatever way I could in exchange for her help finding someone."

"Who?"

"It doesn't pertain to you." His voice was a low growl. "What I'll tell you is what I told Di a million times. Stop trying to find the answers."

Peter gave him an annoyed frown. "Some help you are."

"It *is* helpful," Gerard insisted. "DeVerre is a town of secrets. It always has been. And when you're looking to find answers, all you're going to find are more secrets. If you want to know what's going on, stop looking for answers and start pursuing those secrets."

"Huh?" Peter's brow quirked up in confusion.

Spencer scratched his jaw, reminding himself that he should probably shave soon. "How would that help?"

"Because the only way to find the truth is to become part of this town. And the only way to be part of this town is to become part of its secrets."

Peter shook his head. "I don't get it."

"I do," Spencer said, then hesitated. "Or I think I do. You're saying that we should try to blend in? Become like the others so they stop thinking of us as outsiders?"

Gerard shrugged. "Essentially."

Spencer took a deep breath as he tried to understand. "So . . . we need to, what? Hang out with the people who have the most secrets?"

"Yes."

"And then what?" Peter asked. "Wait for years until they finally let us in on their freaky cult of a town?"

Gerard grunted out a laugh. "It is a bit of a cult, now that you mention it."

Spencer met Peter's eyes in panicked surprise. "Like, literally?" he asked, nervous of the answer.

"Depends on who you ask." The phantom brushed some of his long dark hair back. "Technically, no, it's not a cult. But some of the people in DeVerre were into weird shit."

"Like summoning ghosts?" Peter asked.

"Yes."

"So, Cass would've been part of this little club you're calling a cult?"

"Probably. Listen, I wasn't exactly the most . . . connected DeVerrean in my day. My grandfather was an original town member, but he signed up to help start the lumber camp. And despite the fact that he married a Frossard girl, the Alaries have never been successful or popular. No one liked us much. We were laborers and outsiders. That is, until my brother decided he wanted to try to get a name for us.

"He did all right, but it cost him the rest of his family," Gerard continued. "While he went off to become a teacher and socialize with the 'elite' of the town, the rest of us remained undesirable. We weren't on the inside with the Varons, Chapelles, and Garniers, and our connection with the Frossards was tenuous.

"Because of this unfortunate status of mine, I don't have much information to offer on the inner workings of the town." He twisted the gold band on his left ring finger. "But I did hear enough in my day to know that the town is full of narcissists, liars, and devious bastards. On the surface, they act like they all get along and want the best for one another, but they don't. They're fighting each other for control and they just aren't willing to do it like men. They hide behind their social games and veiled words and attempt to cut each other out at every opportunity.

"What I *can* tell you, and *have* told Cass, is that there was once a secret group of people like her. People who could do things that no one could explain. Or would explain." He tipped his chin toward the books on the table. "No amount of reading will tell you any of this because none of these books were written to tell you the truth. They were written to conceal it. If you want to know the truth, you need to know the secrets."

A muscle in Spencer's bicep spasmed and he realized that he was holding his arm in a white-knuckled death grip. He flexed his fingers and dropped his hands to his sides.

It all kept getting worse. More and more convoluted. More and more confusing.

"If there was a group of people like Cass in the '50s," Peter muttered, chin resting in his hand as he stared at Gerard, "shouldn't we be looking for them?"

"No."

"Why not?"

Gerard raised his thick brows. "Despite the fact that I was tied to the lake for seventy years, fewer and fewer people noticed me as I haunted this town. Trust me: whoever was in that group is long dead. Cass is the only one left."

Peter narrowed his eyes. "You sure about that?"

"As sure as I can be," the phantom said with a shrug. "Which, admittedly, isn't as sure as I'd like to think. But if I'm being honest with you two, I doubt the ruling class of DeVerre would let people like that live."

Spencer sucked in a shallow breath. "Why?"

"Like I said—" Gerard cast him a morbid grin. "They want control of the town. And what's a bigger threat than someone who can control the dead?"

Nex pressed against Spencer's leg, staring up at him while he stared at Gerard.

It *really* did keep getting worse. Every bit of it. Ghosts and phantoms. Murder and theft. Secrets and lies.

When Cassandra had first explained everything to them, Spencer couldn't figure out how Diane and Liam had gone almost thirty years without finding the answers they sought. But the more he learned, the more clear it became that Gerard was right. Any time they looked for answers, they only found more secrets blocking their path. They didn't even know who they were anymore, for goodness' sake. No longer Collinses, but . . . who? Another secret with no answer. Another lie protected by the people of DeVerre. Another dead end with no more clues.

This wasn't a mystery they'd be able to solve with detective work. It would take patience and relationships. Things that required time. More time than he thought he was willing to give.

Peter tapped his thumb against the side of his leg. "Does . . . do people know? About Cass?"

Spencer glanced up and caught the slow, resigned look as it crossed Gerard's face. One that suggested he felt a great deal of regret. "I don't know."

Spencer's lips parted in concern. "But if they do, then she's in danger?"

"Yes."

"They'll try to kill her?"

"Same way they tried to kill you."

Peter lifted his head. "Why *did* they try to kill us? We didn't know about any of this before . . . well, we didn't know until she got back."

"Look," the phantom said, a rough edge to his voice. "I can only speculate as much as you. There is no way for me to know the truth behind *why*. But I'll give you my *guess* if you'd like it."

"Guess away, Casper."

Gerard narrowed his eyes, but otherwise ignored the nickname. "You've disrupted the flow of DeVerre with your very presence. You are Diane's family. You present a threat to the way they live their lives. To the discovery of their secrets.

"Whoever killed Diane," he continued, "was clearly hoping to remove the obstacle in their path. When the house fell to the two of you, I'm sure that put a damper on their plans. Getting rid of you would clear it right back up."

"And what about Cass?" Peter asked. "Have there been any attempts on her life yet?"

"Not that I'm aware of."

"Why not?"

"I wouldn't know."

Spencer chewed on the inside of his cheek. Staying in DeVerre was becoming less and less appealing. His gut reaction was to tell Peter that he'd had enough and to get the hell out of Dodge. They could take Nex and Anguis and even Cassandra with them. Run from all those who were trying to kill them for whatever petty reasons they had.

But he knew it wouldn't work.

Cassandra wouldn't go. Not when it meant abandoning the answers to Diane's murder and all that they'd worked on together. But that didn't have to stop him and Peter, did it?

Sighing, Spencer shook his head. "We've got to figure this out." He looked at Gerard, feeling his desperation mounting. "One way or another. We've tried Diane's way. Research didn't work. Now we may as well try yours."

The phantom grinned. "You gonna infiltrate the enemy camp, kid?"

"Not me," Spencer said.

Both men turned to Peter.

His hand dropped away from his mouth. "Me?" he scoffed. "How?"

CHAPTER FOURTEEN

Peter

Peter didn't like it. He didn't like it one bit. But he also couldn't refute a good plan. And he *had* been wanting an excuse to spend more time with Anna anyway. Not that using her to further their investigation was his ideal method of building a friendship. But it would have to do for now.

So the next day Peter went down to The Glass Tavern, pulled up a seat at the bar, and kept her company during her lunch shift. He'd done his best for the past week not to bring up anything they'd been working on around her. He knew he wasn't good at keeping his mouth shut when he had burning questions on his mind. But he also knew it wasn't smart to bring up the whole ghost thing yet. Not when he was still trying to earn his new friend's trust.

But keeping their project a secret was getting more and more difficult. Especially when she started off their conversation by asking about their relationship with Cassandra.

"You seem to be spending a lot of time together," she said, tucking a few wisps of hair behind her ear. "Does that mean you're friends now?"

Peter tried not to read too much into the question. He'd come to the realization that he'd worked up a bit of an infatuation with Anna. After all, she was sweet and pretty and friendly. Drifting closer and closer to thirty, it was weird to admit it, but he definitely had a crush.

However, he had no interest in ruining their perfectly good, budding friendship when he knew she already had a boyfriend—even if their status wasn't official.

"Uh, yeah, I guess so," he replied, working hard to appear nonchalant.

"That's good," Anna said, rearranging some cups behind the bar. "I've always thought she seemed cool. It's nice that you're all getting along well."

Peter chuckled. "Yeah, well, I'm beginning to suspect that she and Spence might get along a little more than 'well.'"

Her eyes grew wide as she smiled. "Really?"

"Oh, yeah," he said, then hesitated. "Mm, well to be honest, I'm not sure. Neither of them has really shown an interest in each other so far. But I know he thinks she's attractive. And you've seen him. Few girls don't wind up with a crush on him."

"That's cocky of you."

He huffed. "How?"

"You look exactly like him."

"No, I don't," Peter insisted. "I'm two inches taller *and* he's got blue eyes, in case you haven't noticed."

"Mm, you're right," she teased. "That's *totally* different."

Peter shook his head. "It'd be like me saying that you and Ava look the same. Sure, you have a lot of common features, and you're both beautiful, but it's in totally different ways. She's got her whole hip librarian thing going on, and you've got that sophisticated girl-next-door vibe. And, as a resident expert on the curse of being the older sibling, I promise you that *you're* the one with the whole town in love with you. Just like Spence."

Anna stared at him for a few extra seconds, a sly grin tugging at her lips. "You think the whole town is in love with Spencer?"

"Aren't they?"

"No."

"Really?" He asked, skeptical.

She shrugged. "It's a dead heat. Trust me, I know every girl in DeVerre, and in the competition between the cute new Collins brothers, it's fifty-fifty."

Peter scoffed and reached across to pat her hand. "It's nice of you to lie, but I don't need my ego stroked."

"Believe whatever you want, but I'm not lying."

Torn between asking her opinion on the matter and wanting to move on, Peter slid his empty glass back and forth in his hands. He needed to be careful. He was edging perilously close to saying something he'd regret. "Anyway," he replied, "Cass is nice. And I wouldn't be totally against it if they *did* wind up together. Though it's a bit soon for all that, I suppose. I'll give 'em another couple of weeks to get it figured out."

"You're quite the matchmaker," Anna teased, grabbing his cup mid-slide. She refilled the water, her hesitation obvious before she spoke again. "We should . . . I mean, if you guys wanted, we could do another game night. I'm sure Aaron and Haley would be up for it too. It'd be nice to get to know her better. Especially if she's gonna hang around you guys from now on."

Peter furrowed his brow, confused by her halted speech. It wasn't like Anna to act nervous about spending time with them. They'd hung out over a dozen times over the past several weeks, whether at the tavern or an outside event. It wasn't until the last week with Cassandra around that they'd been too busy to see her.

Understanding dawned on Peter. "Hey," he gave her hand a tap as she set the glass back down in front of him. "She's not gonna replace you, you know? You're the first friend we made here."

"Oh, yeah, no, I mean. . . ." She bit her lip, shaking her head as she grimaced. "Is it ridiculous of me? Like, I don't mean to be—weird about it or whatever. It's just—I mean, she got back in town, and I haven't really seen you guys much since. So I—I don't want to be that weird girl who thinks she's everyone's best friend, but—"

"Ann—" Peter cut her off. "It isn't weird. It's great."

"Are you sure?"

"Heck yeah!" He leaned against the counter. "I can't tell you how many people are the worst about this sort of thing. I don't care how long I've known someone. If they're my friend, they're my friend. It's nice to know you care."

"But—" she interrupted herself with a sigh. "Ugh, this is all so stupid."

"What about it's stupid?"

Anna played with her necklace, her head falling back in exasperation. "Ah, I don't know, I just. . . ." She pressed her lips together and met his gaze. "If I tell you the truth, are you gonna laugh at me?"

"Maybe."

Her eyes narrowed.

"No."

"All right." She glanced around the bar and then shifted closer to him. "It's not only that I'm . . . oh, God, this is so dumb. Look, I'm not just jealous because you guys are suddenly best friends with Cassandra. But also because you guys actually get to be best friends with *her*."

"What?"

"She's *freaking cool*, Pete. And she's super intimidating! I've always wanted to be her friend, but how's someone supposed to talk to someone like that?"

Peter tried not to laugh. He *really* did. But he couldn't help it.

Anna reached across and slapped his arm.

"I'm sorry!" he promised. "I'm sorry! I get it, she is pretty cool. I just didn't expect anyone to intimidate the most popular girl in DeVerre."

She rolled her eyes. "I'm not the—look, she's just got this vibe about her, and I've admired it ever since she moved to town. She's so confident and pulled together. I wish I could be like that. And it'd be neat to be her friend."

"So you don't miss us," he teased. "You want to use us to become friends with her?"

Anna smirked and reached over to playfully shove his shoulder again just as the bell chimed at the front door. Her laughter stopped short, and she froze as though momentarily paralyzed. Her whole face lit up in an instant. "Hey!" she called, voice light and excited.

Whirling in his seat, Peter turned to see who'd caused this sudden, strange change in his friend. He found himself staring at a young man who he could only describe as a golden god parading through DeVerre as a suburban king. As if Zeus had stepped down from Olympus to head to the country club. The young man's hair was sleek and perfectly trimmed and so blond that it looked like sunlight. His square jaw looked to be molded from marble, strong and smooth as it was. And his outfit—well, that added insult to injury. He'd tucked his crisp blue button up into his slacks like some sort of refined businessman. If he didn't own a yacht, he was missing his calling.

Peter felt like a schlump in his flannel and jeans.

The guy's blindingly white smile flashed in the dim lighting of the tavern. He only had eyes for Anna, ignoring Peter as he approached the bar. "Hey." He reached across the bar to give her arm an affectionate pat. "I hoped you'd be here."

If it were possible for a person to melt, Anna would have turned into a puddle on the floor as she gazed up at the guy. "You always did have the best luck."

Peter smashed his lips together and turned back to his drink. So *this* was the competition, huh? All-American-meets-Greek-god. *No problem.*

"Who's your friend?" The young man turned to Peter.

"Oh, uh. . . ." Anna gasped as though she'd forgotten he sat there. "Connor, this is Peter. Pete, this is Connor."

"Sup?" Peter said, tipping his chin up toward the guy in greeting.

"Nice to meet you, man," Connor said, holding out his hand. His shake was firm and respectful. This close, Peter could see the toned muscles as they flexed in his forearms.

Yeah, no problem at all.

"I didn't know you were coming back to town," Anna said, attention locked on the dreamboat again.

Connor gave her a penitent smile. "Yeah, it was sort of a surprise. You know how Mom is about the party this weekend. So I decided I'd come home. I left as soon as classes ended this morning. This is my first stop, actually."

"Really?" Her girlish gasp made it sound as though it was an honor to be first on his list.

"Yeah, I mean, once I get to the house, I'll be stuck there with family for the rest of the weekend. And I had to be sure I saw my best friend before I lost my chance."

Anna's smile was sickening.

'Best friend' like hell, Peter thought, taking a sip of his water.

"Don't you worry," Anna nudged Connor's arm where it rested against the counter. He had to arch his back quite a bit to manage it, since he had the height of a giant. "I'm helping your mom pull it all together. You'll see me more than you'd ever want all day tomorrow."

"Well, that's a relief!" Connor grinned. "We never get to see enough of each other these days."

"And who's fault is that?"

"I blame medical school."

She laughed as though it were the cleverest thing a man could say. "Right, and who applied to medical school?"

Connor nodded in admission. "Yeah, okay, it was me. But one more semester and I'm back, all right. So don't be pissed at me forever."

"No promises," she teased.

He chuckled as he drew back from the counter. "All right, well, I can't stay, but, like I said, I wanted to be sure I saw you. We'll hang out tomorrow." He drew his eyes away from Anna and gave Peter's shoulder a friendly whack. "Good to meet you, man. You coming to the party tomorrow?"

"The party?" Peter asked, trying not to glare at him too harshly.

"The Halloween party," Anna reminded him. "I told you about it a couple weeks ago."

"Oh, yeah," he shrugged. "Didn't know I was invited."

Connor grinned at him. "The whole town's invited. It'd be a shame not to have you there too. Any friend of Anna's is a friend of mine."

"Right," Peter cleared his throat. "Cool, yeah, sure, I'll come. Is it a costume party or is there a dress code or something?"

"Nah, I mean, most people dress up, but it's not required."

"Cool." Peter tried to keep his smile cool and disinterested. "I'll come as me."

Connor's laughter was immediate and polite. "Sounds good." He turned back to Anna. "I'd better get a move on. Lily's waiting in the car, so. . . ."

"Oh. . . ." Anna's smile faltered, and she let out a nervous laugh. "I didn't realize she was with you. Yeah, for sure, go take care of her. I'll see you tomorrow."

"Great, yeah." Connor reached over the bar and squeezed her arm. "See you tomorrow, Banana. See ya, Pete."

With that, Connor Frossard turned and disappeared as quickly as he'd arrived.

Narrowing his eyes, Peter turned back to Anna. "First of all," he said. '*Banana*?'"

Anna gave him an annoyed glare. "It's been his nickname for me since we were five."

"You've been best friends since you were five?"

"Yeah."

"Wow." Peter pulled in a deep breath and continued. "Second and more important question: Who the heck is Lily?"

Anna averted her gaze, adjusting some bottles. "His girlfriend."

A disbelieving scoff escaped Peter. "I'm sorry, what?"

She shrugged. "They met at the college."

Attempting to reconcile everything he'd witnessed moments before with this new information, Peter felt as though he were solving the world's most complicated math equation. "Hold on," he said, raising a finger into the air. "You're telling me that all *that* was just two best friends saying hi to one another?"

"Yeah."

"Do you think I'm stupid?"

Anna scowled at him. "What are you talking about?"

"Come on, Annie," he laughed. "You can't pretend that I didn't see all that."

"See what?"

"You like him." He huffed. "No, forget that. You're head over heels for the guy. It's gross."

"I am not!"

Peter smirked. He had to admit, he was disappointed. Meeting Connor had certainly crushed the little hope he'd carried to pursue Anna himself. But the chemistry between the two 'friends' was palpable. If that medical beefcake was stupid enough to not notice Anna and get himself another girlfriend, he didn't deserve her in the first place.

Setting her hands on her hips, Anna glared at him. "*I am not!* Connor and I are *friends*. That's it."

"His loss."

Her jaw dropped.

Peter grinned at her. "To be honest," he said, raising his glass for a sip, "I thought you were secretly dating before he mentioned that chick."

Anna grimaced, eyes falling to the counter as she wrapped her arms around her waist. "No."

Seeing beyond the simple word, Peter nodded. "But you want to be?"

Her gaze didn't budge. "Yeah."

"Does he know that?"

"Kind of," she whispered.

Peter's brow drew together. "*Kind of?*"

"I. . . ." She took a deep breath and shrugged. "I mentioned it once . . . in the past, but . . . he was about to go to college and. . . ."

"And he's an idiot."

"What?" Her eyes flew up to his face. "No, Connor is the best, sweetest, and most intelligent guy I know."

"But he doesn't return your feelings?"

Her shoulders drooped. "I mean . . . he never said *that*."

"What did he say?" Peter pressed.

Anna's usual confidence—or perhaps it was her gumption—seemed to return as she glared at him. "I really don't want to talk about this, Pete," she said, tone firm. "Connor is my best friend, and, yeah sure, it would be *amazing* to be his gir—but I'm not. And he's got a lot going for him, and I don't blame him for recognizing that he doesn't need to settle for just any girl who shows an interest."

Peter frowned. "Any man who thought being with you meant *settling*, Anna, would be an absolute ass."

Silence fell between them, gazes locked.

Finally, her lips pressed together around a grin that seemed both appreciative and embarrassed. "Thanks."

"Anytime." Peter downed the rest of his water. "Now, where would a guy go in a town like this to get a Halloween costume?"

A thin laugh escaped her. "I thought you were going as yourself?"

"Yeah, well now I gotta show up Country Club Ken, thanks to you." He tipped his chin toward her. "What are you going as?"

"Oh, uh. . . ." She played with the edge of the counter and shrugged. "Connor and I have always done this thing where we dressed up as what we wanted to be when we grew up, so . . . he'll be a doctor, and I'll be an artist."

Peter raised his brow. "Ann, that's not a costume. That's what you guys *are*. That'd be like Spence or me dressing up as writers."

She laughed. "No, I mean, we choose famous doctors or artists to dress up as."

"That sounds complicated."

Her right shoulder lifted in a shrug. "It's fun."

"All right, fine. So where do I get a costume?"

~

"You look real dumb, you know that, right?" The glow of Spencer's laptop lit up his face in the fading evening light.

Peter held his hands out to the side, the houndstooth cape rolling off his arms in the process. "It's all I could find." He adjusted the deerstalker. "Come on, I look kinda cool, right? The coolest Sherlock you'll ever find."

Gerard walked past them in the hall, raised his brow at the outfit, grinned smugly, and kept on going without a word.

"Yeah, sure," Spencer said, returning his focus to his work. "You look awesome. You should totally win an award for most realistic costume."

"I know you're mocking me." Peter crossed his arms. "But I don't care. I'm gonna go to this party and have fun and you can sit here alone in the dark with our irritating ghostly roommate."

"I can't be alone if someone else is here."

"Gerard is hardly someone."

"I heard that," the phantom called from the kitchen.

Peter grimaced.

Spencer continued typing on the laptop.

Pursing his lips, Peter eyed him. "You can still come," he said. "Not everyone is dressing up."

"No thanks," Spencer muttered.

He smirked. "Anna said that Cassandra will be there."

His teasing tone got Spencer to look up from his writing, but it was only to glare at him. "Why would that change anything?"

Peter sighed. "You're really boring sometimes, you know? Have fun being a hermit."

"Thanks" Spencer muttered, the clacking of his keyboard continuing without pause.

Seeing no hope for his brother, Peter tossed his hands into the air and headed for the party.

Haven Boulevard was the nicest neighborhood in DeVerre, lined with large, modern mansions. As he walked down the street, he estimated that they all had a similar square footage to Occasus, though none of them were nearly as tall. And none were as unique. The houses on Haven Boulevard all bore an identical boring architecture. White brick and columned façades, black shutters and doors, green pines and bushes. Everything was pristine and polished. He guessed that this was where the elites of the town—the founding families—must have lived.

Dozens of vehicles lined both sides of Trinity Lane, leaving the boulevard clear for people to roam. Parking was already a nightmare when he pulled up in the Jeep. But the sight of hundreds of people milling around drew him to join the party as quickly as he could.

Children ran up to the little booths that stood in each of the massive front yards. Though most of the people wore costumes, there were a few here and there who didn't quite match the spirit of the day. But the same couldn't be said for the décor of the neighborhood. It was elaborate. Fake webs wrapped around every streetlight, paper bats hung on the trees, waist high ghosts haunted the yards. Every booth had a different theme. Nothing too spectacularly spooky. It was all rather cute if Peter was being honest. Like the planning committee hadn't wanted this to be a scary event, though no less festive.

Peter walked along the sidewalk, scanning the yards for anyone he knew. He could still sense a thin atmosphere of negligible tension running through the air. Though almost two full weeks had passed since the last wolf attack, the citizens walked around the gathering with alert gazes and rigid shoulders. He caught a glimpse of the marshal and deputy in uniform, chatting as they watched some kids chase each other around the yard.

But all in all, the partygoers seemed to be enjoying themselves. They laughed and engaged with those around them. He recognized dozens of people from the softball games and church, even if he didn't know their names. He spotted Haley with a large group of friends on the far side of the street, but Aaron appeared to be missing from their numbers.

When he passed the second house on the left side of the street, he heard a voice call his name. Turning toward the sound, he spotted Cassandra waving to him from the booth, a middle-aged woman whom he recognized standing next to her.

He waved back.

The woman—Debbie, he remembered—paused her task of helping a couple of kids fill their bags with candy as Cassandra excused herself. She looked between her young cousin and Peter, brow pulling together in a displeased frown. Then one of the kids tugged on the wings of her bumblebee costume, and she turned back to attend to them.

"Hey," Cassandra said, meeting him at the edge of the yard. "Nice costume. Where's your Watson?"

Peter grinned. "He's being antisocial tonight."

"I thought we decided that wasn't the right method of investigation," she said, brow arching up in amusement.

"Yeah, well, we've got some deadlines coming up for the serial, so he's been freaking out the past couple days. By the way. . . ." He motioned to her outfit. "That's a nice look for you, too. Glad to see you're not abandoning your sense of style."

Cassandra laughed, reaching up to brush the straps that affixed the bat wings to her shoulders over her otherwise normal all-black ensemble. "I'm not much of a costume person," she admitted. "So you're lucky I dressed up at all."

"Really? I had you pegged as a Halloween girl."

"Why? Because of my *hobbies*?"

"Pretty much."

She nodded, smile wide. "No, I don't particularly care for the holiday. I don't see any point in trying to scare yourself with things that should be mundane. It's stuff like this that gives ghosts a bad name," she concluded with a wink.

Peter nodded. "Fair point." He turned toward the rest of the neighborhood. "Hey, do you know where I might find Anna?"

"Mm, yeah." Cassandra stepped forward and pointed toward the end of the boulevard. "She's Gia's right hand tonight, so you'll find her down at the Frossards'."

Pursing his lips, Peter considered asking her if she knew anything about the strange relationship between Anna and the Frossard family. But due to her friendship with Diane, he figured that would have precluded her from knowing much more than he did. "Cool, thanks." He gestured at Debbie and their booth. "You tied up here for the evening?"

"Just the next hour or so."

"All right. Well, when you get done, you should come find us. I think you'd like Anna."

Cassandra nodded, beginning to edge back toward the booth. "Sounds good. I'll see you later."

Peter waved and headed on his way. It got busier the deeper into Haven Boulevard he went. The crowds grew and their ages rose with them. There were far more teens around the middle houses while the adults had congregated in the cul-de-sac. Most of the enthusiasm died down as the age increased as well. When he reached the end of the street, the vibe was far more subdued as people conversed and snacked, the booths turning from games and candy to fancy drink stations and hors d'oeuvres.

Stopping by one of the bars, Peter settled for a beer, sure that he shouldn't explain his cocktail to the frazzled soccer mom. He continued, catching a glimpse of Connor talking with a large group of people. He'd dressed up as an old timey doctor, his arm draped around a fairy-like girl— the infamous Lily, he assumed. She was cute, he supposed, with her light brown curls, warm tan, and dainty figure. Her costume was flashy and boring. She had dressed as Dorothy from *The Wizard of Oz*. Her red shoes looked like they were exact replicas.

Connor laughed at something that was said, the sound only half-hearted. Peter watched him glance over his shoulder and followed the direction of his gaze. Several feet up the road, Anna was busily restocking the finger foods. Her costume was more elaborate than Lily's, but it was far less assuming. She wore a long dark blue coat with a yellow silk scarf tied into a bow. In typical fashion, her dark curls were attempting to escape the vintage hat she'd tied on with a matching silk tie.

Peter smiled, watching her brush some of those curly wisps from her eyes before returning to her work. He crossed the street and headed straight for her. He glanced back over at Connor just as the doc pressed his lips together and began to turn back to his friends. Then he caught sight of Peter.

The golden doc raised a hand in greeting. Peter gave him a tip of his hat. Without pausing his stride, he went straight to Anna, hoping the doctor was watching.

"Well, evening there, ma'am," Peter spoke, putting on his best, still awful, British accent.

Anna looked up and smiled at the sight of him.

Heartened by the sight of her pretty, welcoming smile, Peter carried on. "I'm in the midst of a very important case," he continued in his miserable accent. "Could you perhaps help me out?"

"Of course, Mr. Holmes, it'd be an honor." She tugged on the white gloves she wore. "How can I be of service?"

"I'm trying to deduce who you happen to be?"

Anna laughed. "What, it's not obvious?"

Tired of carrying on the accent, Peter slipped back to his natural speech. "I'm a writer, Annie. I can't name famous painters to save my life."

"I'm Mary Cassatt."

"Great, yeah, I totally see it now."

She gave his arm a playful shove. "She was an impressionist in the late 1800s. She's one of the most famous female painters of all time."

"Right. Don't know how I didn't guess that right away."

Anna shook her head as she finished refilling the platters. "When'd you get here?"

"Just a bit ago." He nodded to the trays. "You busy all night? Or does your taskmaster give you breaks sometimes?"

"I'm actually about to finish up," she replied. "I told Gia I'd help for as long as she needed, but she said she'd take care of the rest of it. She wanted me to have a good time too, so I'm free here in a minute."

"Can I help so you get done sooner?"

She grinned. "Yeah, that'd be great, actually."

They worked on stocking the last of the booths for a short fifteen minutes before they left to join the party. Haley's group found them along the way, and Cassandra eventually made her way to them as well. The evening was more fun than Peter had expected. He didn't spend time away from Spencer often, and when he did, it always made him feel off balance. There were few people in the world who he could rely on besides his brother. Anytime he started getting too enthusiastic or chatty in public, Spencer would tap his elbow or cut him off or otherwise keep him from making a total fool of himself.

It was a weird dynamic, he knew. Most older brothers were the ones who had to keep their siblings in check. But between the two of them, Peter was the one who needed help in keeping his cool.

Yet in the midst of these new friends, Peter felt as though he was getting the hang of life here in DeVerre.

While the group talked in an animated circle near the Frossards' house, Peter glanced over Anna's shoulder. He did a double take and narrowed his gaze.

In the shadow of their home, Peter caught sight of Connor and his father, Alex. The two men were in the midst of what appeared to be a heated argument. One that included a lot of wide gestures and leaning in to get their point across.

Peter drew his shoulders back, distracted from the conversation around him. He locked in on the exchange. They were far enough away that even if there hadn't been so much noise and activity on the street, he doubted he'd be able to hear what they were saying. But it didn't look pleasant.

As he watched, Connor shook his head and Alex shoved a finger into his son's chest in response.

Connor pushed it away and motioned wildly toward Peter's group.

Eyes going wide, Peter nearly looked away, not wanting to get caught if the men looked in his direction. But he had no need to worry. The father and son were absorbed in their argument.

With a level of aggression that made Peter flinch, Alex grabbed his son's collar and pointed to the side.

Peter followed the direction of his finger to where Lily and Gia stood among a few other DeVerrean women. He turned back just in time to see Connor whack his father's hand, freeing his collar. The young doctor's face twisted into a snarl. He shoved a finger at his own chest, his mouth moving rapidly in the midst of a long diatribe.

Without warning, Alex cut off his son's rant, grabbing two fists full of his costume lab coat and pulling him closer.

Connor grimaced and looked at the ground, hands curled tight at his sides as his father berated him for several long seconds.

As his father's words trailed off, silence fell between the two men.

Connor gave a sharp, curt nod.

Alex returned the nod, then shoved Connor back before walking away.

Taking a sip of his beer, Peter watched as Connor remained in the shadows of the house, chin tucked to his chest. Whatever that was about, Peter didn't like it. They'd pointed in his direction. Why? What could he possibly have to do with them?

"Pete," Cassandra whispered, sharp elbow digging into his side.

"Huh?" Startled, he turned to her, rubbing his side. "What?"

She nodded toward the others, and he tuned in to hear Haley's hushed tones.

"It's weird though, isn't it?" She was speaking directly to Anna. "You would think that the marshal would have said something."

Peter perked up, the argument between the Frossards forgotten at the mention of the marshal.

"I don't know," Anna said. Her voice was even lower than Haley's. "I can understand why Sam wouldn't want that getting out. And he's been best friends with Tom for years."

"Want what getting out?" Peter jumped into the conversation. Cassandra elbowed him again, harder this time. "Ow," he grumbled.

"Uh. . . ." Anna glanced between the two of them. "Well, Haley was just saying that—I mean, it's a rumor so you can't put much stock in it. But some people are saying that Sam's daughter was with Brendan when he died."

Peter furrowed his brow. "Sam? You mean the reverend?"

"Yeah," Haley confirmed. "His daughter, Juliet, was dating Brendan. They'd been together for a couple years, and everyone expected they'd get married once they were old enough."

"Seriously?" Peter gaped at them. "They were only in high school, right?"

Cassandra smirked at him. "They say when you know, you know."

"Yeah, well *they* say a lot of things." He turned back to Haley and Anna. "But she was with him? When the wolf attacked?"

"That's what *they* are saying," Anna said, a teasing grin pulling at the side of her mouth, lightening the growing intensity of the moment.

"Actually—" Haley jumped in again. "That's the most interesting part."

The three of them turned to her.

"Apparently Juliet is claiming that it wasn't a wolf."

"What?" Cassandra glanced at Peter.

His stomach dropped. "What did she say it was then?"

"I'm not sure," Haley said, the farmer's overalls of her costume slipping from her shoulder as she shrugged. "Again, nothing is really confirmed. People are just talking. And I've already heard several people say different things."

"Like what?" Cassandra asked, leaning toward her. Peter wondered if she was making her interest a little too obvious.

Haley's freckled nose wrinkled in confusion. "I mean, it's all just weird stuff. That it was a monster or a massive shadow or a bear. Someone even said she thought it was a werewolf."

"She must have been so scared," Anna said, worry forming a crease in the middle of her forehead. "I can't imagine going through something like that."

"I know!" Haley gasped, setting a hand on Anna's arm. "The poor girl. They were the cutest couple too. Young and adorable. I can't blame her for being so freaked out that she's refused to leave the house."

Cassandra inched closer to Peter. Her chin angled back to whisper to him. "Is this as suspicious to you as it to me?"

Peter opened his mouth to respond, but a loud commotion broke out amongst the crowd on the far side of the road. A surge of shock rumbled through the air as the chatter rose. The group whipped around at the sound. Expecting to see another hellhound, Peter's heart leaped into his throat as he scanned the area. But instead of running in fear, cheers erupted from the crowd. Trying to see what caused the disturbance, the four of them peered around the crowd just as it parted.

A thin gasp escaped Anna at Peter's side as they both saw what the fuss was about.

Connor Frossard was down on one knee in front of Lily, a small box clutched in his hand as she smiled and nodded. He leaped up to hug and kiss his new fiancée and slipped the ring on her finger.

Mouth ajar, Peter shook his head. The dude was an idiot for sure.

The news began to travel through the crowd as people applauded and called out their congratulations.

Without a word, Anna turned and walked away.

"Uh," Peter kept an eye on her as he patted Cassandra's arm. "I gotta— I'll see ya."

Anna was moving with purpose, working through the crowd at top speed as she removed her hat and cut across one of the lawns. Peter tried to push through the hundreds of people at the party, but it took him longer than he hoped. He finally caught up to her as she neared the end of the boulevard.

"Hey," he called.

She glanced over her shoulder, tears glinting in the streetlights.

Peter clamped his jaw tight, irritated with the jerk who considered himself her best friend. "Hey, hey." He took her arm with a gentle grip and walked on with her to the end of the road. "C'mon, let me drive you home, okay?"

Anna shook her head, face dry despite her brimming eyes. "No—no, it's—I'm fine."

"Don't do that," he insisted. "I'm your friend, I want to help."

"Pete, I don't—"

"Anna. . . ." He pulled her to a stop. "Let me help you."

She stared up at him, her deep brown eyes wide.

"Please."

A sad smile crossed her face. "It isn't—it isn't that I don't want help, Pete," she whispered.

"What is it, then?"

She motioned down the road toward Hope Court. "I live right there," she explained, brushing the dampness away from her lower lashes. "It'll take less time to walk there than it will for you to find your car and get out of here."

"Oh." He scanned the street to realize that she was right. There was no doubt that the innumerable cars parked along the street had blocked in the Jeep.

Anna pulled away. "Thank you, though. I . . . it really does mean a lot."

Peter nodded, feeling awkward. He reached up to remove his deerstalker and ran his fingers through his hair. "Could I, uh . . . could I, at least, walk you home or something? Just to be sure you're . . . okay, I guess."

She pressed her lips together, took a few breaths, then nodded. "That'd be nice. Thanks."

"Mm-hm."

Peter stepped back and let her lead the way. They skirted around the cars to the main road and headed onto Hope Court. The houses along the new street were far less elegant and resembled much more of the style he expected from a small town. Quaint and cozy-looking with front porches, wind-chimes, and screen doors.

"Thanks," Anna said again as they walked. "I know—the average friend wouldn't do this, I mean."

Peter grinned. "I like to think I'm an above average friend."

"That's a good friend to have."

He bit his tongue. He wanted to say that it was better than a friend who got engaged to someone else in front of you when they knew you were in love with them. But he kept that tidbit to himself.

"Connor kind of sucks, doesn't he?" She said with a scoff.

The chuckle that escaped him was both nervous and relieved that she'd said it first. "Yeah, he does."

"I've been in love with him ever since I can remember," she muttered.

Peter didn't have a response for that.

"I told him that before he went to college."

He waited, but she didn't continue. "What'd he say to that?"

"He kissed me."

"What?"

"Then he told me that we weren't right for each other."

"*What?*" Peter shook his head. "He's a douchebag, Anna. You're better off without him."

"Maybe," she whispered.

"Definitely! Look. . . ." He grabbed her arm just long enough to bring her to a stop and face him. "Any guy—literally *any* guy who cares about a girl should never—and I mean *never*—do that to her. It doesn't matter what his reasons were. What he did was a shitty move."

She ran her fingers over the band of her hat. "I don't think he meant it that way."

"What other way could he have meant it?"

"I—I don't know, I just—Connor's not like that. I know it sounds weird, but—I know him, okay? And I just don't think he meant to hurt me."

"It doesn't matter if he meant it," Peter protested. "He hurt you, plain and simple. And then he asked you to stick around and . . . be his best friend while he went on to date Thumbelina?"

A depressed laugh eked out of her. "She is pretty adorable, isn't she?"

"She's the worst."

She tipped her head to the side. "Did you even meet her?"

"I didn't have to. And I don't have to have twenty-some-odd years of friendship with you to know that you don't deserve to be treated that way."

"It's been nineteen years," Anna corrected in a whisper, staring at the hat in her hands.

Scanning her, Peter questioned his motives in walking her home. This was always what happened to him. He was quick to form an attachment and then ended up pushing the relationship too far, too fast. It didn't matter if he and Anna weren't meant to be. Or that he wasn't even sure about the idea of pursuing something romantic with her in the first place. He was on the verge of doing something dumb, and he knew it.

In the lingering silence, Peter felt his heart drop. He'd stepped in to protect her too quickly. He couldn't blame her if she looked up at him and told him to back off. That he'd stepped over a line by daring to tell her how to manage her friendships and love life. That he'd assumed too much by telling her that he knew her worth.

But when Anna looked at him again, she was smiling. "Do you want to come in for a minute?"

"Huh?" Peter's mouth dropped open.

"That's my house," she said, pointing to the small, quaint building to her left. "Or, rather, it's Ava and Owen's. I just live with them."

"Oh, yeah, cool. I'd love to!"

Stepping onto the porch, Peter followed her past the wicker furniture and dozens of potted plants, into the house. The living space was small, set up in a typical fashion. A couch stood on one side; a TV hung on the far wall. Books lay scattered everywhere, along with more plants on every surface. It was the exact style of house he would have expected from Ava. Eclectic and vintage. A dark gray cat slept curled up on a mustard yellow chair.

"Hey," Anna called, striding into the living room. "I brought a friend."

Sitting on the couch, Ava looked over. Her sharp brow rose at the sight of him. "Peter."

"Ava." He mimicked her serious tone with his reply.

"You enjoying those books?"

"Uh, no, not really. They're kind of boring."

She smirked at that. "I know."

Anna shut the front door behind him. "Where's Owen?"

"I'm here," a voice called from deeper in the house. "Just waiting on the popcorn."

"Don't burn it this time," Ava called, an unusual smile crossing her lips. Peter recognized the gentle, wry tilt as flirtatious in nature. A strange thought in reference to the librarian.

"That's why I'm still in here, Socrates."

Anna headed away from the living room, and Peter followed. "It's movie night," she explained. "It's a Saturday night tradition in my family."

"And you almost missed out on it," Owen said as they turned the corner. "Your friend planning to stay?"

Peter stopped in his tracks. His heart stalled in fear.

It was him.

The man from the woods.

Tunnel vision caught hold of him as he desperately took in everything about the man. He had to memorize every detail to relay it to Spencer. Blond hair, blue eyes, lightly tanned, and tall with a trim, narrow frame. His long, oval face had a serious, yet peaceful quality to it. And even making popcorn for movie night, the guy wore a nice sweater and slacks.

Though Peter had hesitated at the sight of him, the man didn't. He held out his hand and smiled. "How's it going? I'm Owen." His voice was warm and smooth.

Forcing himself to move, Peter accepted the handshake. "Uh, hey, I'm Peter."

"Nice to meet you, Peter," Owen said, holding his gaze. There was no look of recognition in his eyes and no sign that he knew who he was. But this was the guy. The same stranger who had been talking to the air by the lake.

And he was Ava's husband.

"You're welcome to stay for the movie," Owen offered, nodding toward the living room as he stopped the microwave. The room filled with the smell of butter and salt as Peter watched him work. "We're watching *The Last Crusade* tonight."

Peter tried to get his brain to function at a normal level again. "Sure." Instantly, he regretted his hasty acceptance. "That sounds like fun."

"Great," he replied, passing the bag of popcorn to Anna. "I'd better make another of those, then."

"Can I get you something to drink?" Anna asked.

Fighting the urge to run out the door, drive straight home, and tell Spencer the news, Peter sucked in a short breath and resigned himself to the mess he'd gotten himself into. "Yeah, that sounds great. Thanks."

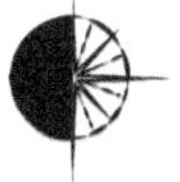

Spencer

"So, you ended up staying the whole time?" Cassandra asked, leaning forward in the back seat. She rested a hand on the side of the driver's seat, her knuckles grazing Spencer's shoulder.

From the second Peter had walked downstairs that morning, he'd seemed on edge. It had been clear that he'd dressed in a rush, and his fingers were either drumming against his thigh or mussing up his hair as he waited for Spencer to finish his breakfast. When Spencer asked him what was going on, Peter's cryptic reply had been, "It's big," before practically dragging Spencer out the door to church.

That caused a cascade of a million questions from Spencer, but Peter wouldn't relent until they reached Cassandra. The moment the service ended, Peter rushed forward to abduct Cassandra from her family. Then he hurried them back to the Jeep and on to Occasus.

Peter huffed at her question, turning around to look at her. "Of course, I stayed! What was I gonna do? Tell Anna, 'Sorry that your best friend turned out to be a douchebag, but your brother-in-law weirds me out, so

I gotta go'?" He shook his head. "No thanks."

Spencer tapped the steering wheel with the butt of his hand before taking the turn onto Whitehill. "You're sure it was the same guy?"

"Positive, Spence," Peter promised. "I even saw that freakin' green jacket of his hanging by the door."

Cassandra rested against Spencer's seat and pursed her lips. After everything that had happened over the last week, they'd not thought to mention anything about the stranger walking through the woods. But once Peter revealed his discovery, they'd explained everything to her. "And he was definitely talking to a ghost when you saw him by the lake?" She asked.

Though Peter's nod was immediate, Spencer cocked his head to the side in doubt. "I mean, it isn't like we *saw* a ghost," he explained. "But he was definitely having a conversation with *someone*. Even if it was just the voices in his head. Which, as a writer, let me tell you, isn't that strange."

Peter sat back, hand pressed to his mouth. "That's a good point," he muttered. "We do talk to ourselves all the time."

"Less to ourselves and more to our characters," Spencer clarified, glancing at Cassandra in the rearview mirror. "And if he's Ava's husband . . . I mean, I like Ava, but she *is* kind of. . . ."

"Crazy?" Cassandra offered.

"Intense?" Peter suggested.

"I was gonna say eccentric." Spencer shrugged. "But, yeah, she's not exactly the typical girl, is she? Why would her husband be any more *normal* than she is?"

Cassandra's brow drew together in thought, but Peter shook his head. "Think about it, man. . . ." He gave Spencer's arm a shove, then pointed toward the woods as they neared Occasus. "It wasn't a coincidence, was it? We catch him at the lake being all weird and sneaky, and then we're attacked by a freakin' hellhound."

"I thought you said everything's a coincidence?" Spencer challenged, throwing him a patronizing glare.

Peter narrowed his eyes. "Shut up," he said, slapping Spencer's cheek. "Dude, I'm driving!"

"Then don't sass me." Peter motioned to the gates ahead of them with a dramatic raise of his brows. "You can't tell me you don't see it. That this isn't strange timing. We've caught our killer, man!"

"Even if you're right," Spencer glanced over at him. "We haven't caught him yet. And we have no proof."

"Uh, guys. . . ." Cassandra patted Spencer's arm and pointed straight ahead. "I think you have a visitor."

Spencer and Peter followed the direction of her finger toward the porch of Occasus.

Relaxing in a chair, Owen watched their approach. He wore the same green jacket as he had during their previous encounters. He still wore his Sunday best from church: a cream button up under that jacket with gray slacks and nice dress shoes. During the service, Peter had pointed him out to Spencer—though he'd refused to say anything more than that he was Ava's husband at the time. The reason for their failure to see him in the past became obvious as they craned their necks back to catch a glimpse of him. He sat in the production booth, hidden from the congregation, as he ran the projector and soundboard. Due to the dark and tucked away nature of the little room, he was easy to overlook.

Spencer's chest tightened as the man watched them approach. It was evident that he'd walked to the house. There was no car in the driveway. But it wasn't surprising that he'd beat them here. Peter had mentioned when he'd left the church before the service ended.

"Ehhhhh. . . ." Peter gritted his teeth as Owen stood, watching their arrival. "He's come for us."

Spencer caught the way Cassandra rolled her eyes in the mirror. "First of all—" she gave his arm a firm punch. "Stop being so dramatic. Second, we don't even know that he knows anything."

"Then why is he here?" Spencer muttered as he pulled the Jeep next to the house.

None of them had an answer to the question.

They climbed out of the Jeep while Owen stepped to the edge of the porch.

"Morning," Peter said, his tone betraying his nervousness as he shoved his hands into his pockets.

Spencer walked around the hood to stand by his brother. Cassandra waited on his other side. Anguis and Nex padded past Owen and down the porch to greet the trio.

"Morning," Owen said, a calm, almost monotone quality in his voice. "I think we've got some things to talk about."

"What kind of things?" Cassandra challenged, crossing her arms.

Scanning her, he raised his chin. The trim shadow of his beard was as sharp and well-kept as his short blond hair. "First, as I've only technically met one of you, let me introduce myself." He stepped down the stairs and held out his hand to her. "I'm Owen Bernard. And I'm a Wielder like you."

Cassandra drew back, eyeing both him and his hand. "A what?"

His small, round eyes narrowed on her in confusion as he dropped his hand. "A Wielder," he repeated. "You don't know the term?"

"No."

"But . . . you *do* wield the spirit world?"

The three of them gaped at him.

"Yes," Cassandra whispered. A strange glint of fear and hope began to grow in her eyes.

Spencer took a step forward, Nex faithfully at his side. "Why are you here?"

Owen turned to him. "Because I was suspicious of Diane and Cassandra's research, and last night Ava confirmed it for me."

"She did?" Peter asked.

He nodded. "After you left, she waited for Anna to disappear and then freaked out."

"Why?"

"Because she doesn't like how close you're getting to her sister."

Peter blinked and scratched his head. "Ahhhh, okay. . . ."

"It's not so much about you as it is about her," he said, pointing to Cassandra.

She sighed. "I told you guys she doesn't like me."

"No, she doesn't," Owen confirmed. "And that's why I'm here. Like I said, I've had my suspicions, but last night, in her exasperation, she told me flat out that Cassandra is a Wielder. Though she didn't use that exact term."

"Wait. . . ." Spencer held up his hand. "If she doesn't like Cass because of her abilities, then why doesn't she have a problem with you?"

A look of shame crossed Owen's face. He swallowed. "She doesn't know."

"Dude," Peter muttered. "This place is messed up."

"She doesn't know?" Spencer demanded. "You're lying to your wife?"

Owen met his accusing glare. "Yes," he admitted. "And, trust me, I don't like it. But I don't have a choice."

"You chose to marry her without telling her the truth," Spencer argued. "Sounds like a pretty important deal breaker to me."

Cassandra chewed on her bottom lip. "It isn't that easy," she countered. "The more people you tell, the more likely you are to get a reputation for being insane. And that often ends up leaving you alone in your insanity."

"I didn't mean to lie to her," Owen explained, his low voice serious. "I was going to tell her if things went well, but she's not exactly subtle with her thoughts and feelings."

"You can say that again," Peter mumbled.

"When we met," he continued, "it took her two days to tell me that she wanted to marry me. Ridiculous, I know, but I found it refreshing. Most women aren't bold enough to be that obvious. I found her honesty amusing and, frankly, I appreciated it. Though I suggested we get to know one another better first. We dated for about a month before she told me about DeVerre. At that point . . . well, I almost broke it off, but. . . ."

Spencer frowned. "You fell in love with her in a month?"

Owen shrugged. "She's not the sort of person you break up with. If she loves you, you'd be a fool not to spend eternity with her."

"But she doesn't even know who you are," Cassandra said. "And she hates who you are on a fundamental level. How can you be okay with that?"

"She doesn't understand it," he defended. "It scares her, the idea that there's something so powerful and dangerous out there. I've been waiting for the right time to explain it to her, but time doesn't seem to be making her fears any better. Especially not now that people have started dying."

Spencer could understand that. The potential of what was happening alone terrified him. And they didn't even know that much about how this all worked yet. Someone who could summon ghosts and beasts couldn't be good. But Owen's last words hit him deeper than the others. "The deaths have a connection to the spirit world?"

"Everything in DeVerre has a connection to the spirit world," he said as though it should be obvious. "Look, I can't stick around long. Ava knows I took a walk, but I'm supposed to be back for lunch, so we gotta make this quick.

"I want to help you guys," he continued. "That's why I'm here in DeVerre."

Peter cocked his brow. "Not because you're married to Ava?"

"I was coming here either way."

The three of them exchanged surprised and worried looks.

"I'm originally from Harmony, Saskatchewan," he said, tipping his head down to emphasize the point. Knowing his home seemed to emphasize the way his vowel sounds lengthened. "The hometown of Matthias Varon, Frederic Chapelle, and all the others who founded DeVerre. Those of us in Harmony have helped DeVerre since its founding. But after all the Varons died, our connection with DeVerre began to wear thin. As time went on, we grew concerned. All contact with DeVerre was lost over the years. Our only source of information was what we could find through research and news articles. Which were few and far between. The number of questions we developed about DeVerre had become far greater than the number of answers we had.

"So a little less than fifteen years ago, I volunteered to come here," Owen continued. "I headed to Spokane to get my degree in teaching so that I could come here and work in the school. That's where I met Ava. I didn't know she was from DeVerre and didn't have any clue of her knowledge of Wielders until I already wanted to marry her. At that point, I didn't feel it would benefit either of us for me to break it off when I was going to move here anyway."

"And you don't think that'll be a problem if she ever finds out?" Peter asked.

"I know it will," he admitted. "But if I can prove to her that the spirit world isn't as evil as she thinks, then it won't be nearly as bad."

"Can you teach me about it?" Cassandra interrupted, a look of wonder in her eyes as she stared up at him. "The spirit world? Our abilities?"

Owen scanned her, then nodded. "Yeah, that's why I came here today," he said. "I want to help in whatever way I can."

"Why?" Spencer asked, not convinced by the offer. If he was shady enough to lie to his wife, why wouldn't he lie to them too? "If you didn't help Diane and Cassandra before, why help now?"

He frowned, turning back to him. "I didn't know before," he explained. "And, like Cassandra said, it isn't the best idea to go around talking about it. But when Ava confirmed my suspicions last night, I knew I had to come here. I had to help you."

"Help us how?"

Owen pondered the question, then turned to Cassandra. "How much do you know?"

"About the spirit world?" she asked.

He nodded.

Cassandra's shoulders nearly met her ears as she shrugged. "Not much. I can talk to ghosts, control beasts, and tether phantoms, but . . . I don't know much more than that. I read once that it's possible to . . . 'harness' the power of it somehow, but I don't know what that means."

Owen's brow furrowed as he studied her. "Do you know about the lake?"

"The lake?" Peter gasped. "It *is* haunted?"

Spencer ran a hand over his face, feeling more and more overwhelmed by the second.

"Not exactly," Owen said. He waited a beat, then continued when Cassandra showed no indication that she knew what he was referring to. "All right, it seems that there's more to teach you than I thought. I've got to get home now, but . . . if it's okay, I can come back tomorrow?"

Spencer looked to Peter and Cassandra.

This was getting far too complicated.

Gerard was right. There were secrets upon secrets upon secrets in DeVerre. And when you uncovered one, you found ten more to go with it.

He wondered if the inheritance was worth it for the hundredth time. If they should just pack up and get Cassandra out of there. Nothing Owen said tomorrow could make their situation better. Nothing would simplify this bizarre town and its connection to the spirit world.

But the small smile that crept onto Cassandra's face at the prospect of gaining an understanding of her abilities was enough to tell him that leaving wasn't an option. And, as Peter had said before, to abandon her now that they knew the truth was the most cowardly thing they could do.

Spencer's jaw tensed as he resigned himself to their fate. He hated the idea that they were dealing with things they didn't understand. Things that could get them killed. But he already knew that he wouldn't leave Cassandra to face this alone.

"Yeah," Spencer said, turning back to Owen. "Tomorrow sounds good."

"Great." Owen gave them all a small, closed-mouthed smile. "Does nine work for you?"

Peter raised his brow. "Nine? As in nine in the morning?"

"Yes."

He sighed. "That's fine."

Owen nodded and stepped around them. "I'll see you tomorrow," he said, an amused grin spreading across his face. "Try not to get yourselves killed before then."

Spencer frowned at Peter, wondering if that was an actual possibility.

CHAPTER SIXTEEN

Peter

At least a minute passed while Owen and Gerard stared at each other without a single word. They had come face-to-face in the halls of Occasus when Owen arrived and immediately started sizing each other up.

It was a funny sight to see. Despite the weekday, Owen was still dressed in slacks and a button up while Gerard remained forever frozen in his '50s trousers and suspenders. There wasn't much in common between the two men despite their similar height and narrow frames.

Peter wondered which of them would win the staring contest. They both had a quiet energy that seemed stubborn enough to wait out the other person. But Gerard struck him as being of a prouder disposition than Owen; the phantom far more unwilling to back down. Owen's demeanor was calm and suggested that he put less stock in other people's opinions.

"You did this?" Owen asked, gesturing to the phantom.

Cassandra nodded. "Yeah."

"How'd you figure it out?"

"Diane found some of Elijah Lawrence's writing."

Owen tipped his chin up in understanding. "He always was more interested in ghosts than anything else." He looked back to Gerard. "You're not helping her selflessly, I take it?"

"Not exactly." Gerard said, his voice low and harsh. It was a noticeable contrast to Owen's smoother inflection.

"All right." He gave him a suspicious once over. "Just know that I can put an end to it if you become a problem."

Gerard's eyes narrowed, and Cassandra's jaw dropped.

"You can end it?" Spencer asked, a thread of expectation in his tone. "Like, remove the tether?"

Owen nodded. "Yeah."

"I thought that could only happen if he found peace." Cassandra crossed her arms. There was a nervous glint in her eyes as she stared at Owen. As though she weren't sure if she should welcome the news or if she should worry that he'd remove her phantom against her will.

"No, if the Wielder is strong enough, they can sever the tie," he explained. "Takes a strong connection to the spirit world, though. Which is why it's not the best idea to tether them in the first place. Especially not close to a Veil."

Peter shook his head to clear his thoughts. Owen's words were already loaded with unintelligible information. "Mkay," he said, holding out his hands to halt the conversation. "Before we get any farther, why don't we sit down? I don't care to have hours' worth of conversation in the entryway."

They moved into the living room, causing a few seconds of awkward back and forth as they chose their seats. Gerard went to the office to sit at the desk while Owen took the far couch. Peter and Spencer flanked Cassandra on the other.

Resting his forearms on his legs, Owen leaned forward and met each of their gazes. "Unless you have specific questions you'd like the answers to," he said, "I'd prefer to start with a basic overview. There's a lot you need to know, and it's not likely to make sense if I don't start at the beginning."

"I doubt it'll make much sense even then," Peter countered.

Owen gave him a small grin. It seemed he tempered all his emotions like that. As though he didn't have the need for wide smiles or enthusiastic responses to convey his feelings. "There's a chance you're right."

"Go on," Cassandra said, imitating Owen by leaning forward. She clasped her hands together, eyes wide in anticipation.

"It's a lot."

"Then you may as well get started," Spencer suggested.

Owen took a deep breath and straightened his shoulders. "The spirit world is accessible to everyone," he began. "For people like you and me, Cassandra, it comes more easily than for others. Sometimes people need to be around it to discover it. Other times they're just given the ability. Compare it to the servants with the talents in the Bible. Their master went away, charging them with differing levels of responsibility. That's what it's like for us.

"Everyone *can* become a Wielder," he continued. "But not everyone will reach the same level of power."

"Elijah said it was according to their faith," Cassandra offered, watching him intently.

"Exactly," Owen nodded. "We are all granted different levels of faith by God. The amount isn't up to us, but the job is always the same: take care of what God has given you."

"So He gave you guys the faith required to be Wielders?" Peter asked.

"Being a Wielder isn't a measure of faith," he corrected. "We can *all* become Wielders with whatever level of faith we have. But our abilities will vary based off our individual level of faith."

Cassandra's brow dropped low over her eyes. "Is that why I can't see ghosts outside of DeVerre? Is my faith too small?"

Owen tipped his head to the side in thought. "Sometimes it takes a while for our full measure of faith to reveal itself. It's like any other gift from God; it's there, but if you don't take hold of it, it remains unused. Same reason most people, Christians or not, miss out on the spirit world. They're not even aware it exists. Or, at least, that it exists like this."

"So, I *could* see them in other places then?"

"The fact that you have the ability to tether a phantom without any real knowledge tells me that it's likely."

Cassandra rubbed her hands together as she nodded.

Though her potential level of power interested him, Peter was more intrigued by the prior suggestion Owen had made. "You're saying that Spence and I could become Wielders too?"

"Yes. It's probably inevitable for you two at this point."

Peter's eyes grew wide at the idea.

Spencer frowned. "You mean, we're going to start seeing ghosts everywhere?"

Laughing, Cassandra patted his knee. "Don't worry. You get used to it."

"I don't think I want to," he muttered.

"It's more than just seeing ghosts," Owen said, a look of concern drawing his eyebrows together. "You do know that, right?"

"Well, yeah," Cassandra said, shrugging. "But, I mean . . .I don't know *what* else it is exactly."

He sighed. "Being a Wielder is about touching the spirit," he explained. "Seeing past the natural world and bringing Heaven to Earth."

Accustomed to church rhetoric, Peter could relate to some of the terms Owen was using. But turning around and applying them to something tangible and supernatural was more difficult than he had anticipated.

Owen continued without pause. "As Wielders, yes, we have the ability to see and connect with ghosts, but that's the most basic level of our powers. Ideally there wouldn't be any ghosts at all."

"Excuse me?" Gerard grumbled from his seat in the office.

Owen looked over his shoulder. "No offense, friend, but if you had a softer heart, you wouldn't be here. You're too attached to this life, and you won't be happy until you let it go."

"I'll be happy when I get justice," Gerard argued.

"You don't get to choose what justice looks like."

"Watch me."

Owen looked ready to argue, but instead he ran a hand over his mouth and turned back to the three of them. "Point being," he resumed, "it's the hardness of our hearts that makes us become ghosts."

"Which is why they need help finding closure," Cassandra concluded.

"No," he corrected. "They need help finding God."

Spencer wrung his hands. "Do we all have the potential to become ghosts?"

"Technically, yes. But a person must have some level of contact with the spirit world themselves before their spirit can attach to it."

"What does that mean?" Peter asked.

"It means they have to have some level of proficiency as a Wielder."

"Hang on," Cassandra stopped him, staring over his shoulder to Gerard in the office. "You were like us? A Wielder?"

Gerard didn't appear surprised or interested in the topic. "I wasn't."

"You had to be," Owen contradicted.

"Well, I don't know what to tell you," the phantom said. "I wasn't like you people. I didn't see ghosts, and I didn't care to."

"But you knew about it?" Spencer asked.

He slicked back the hair on the right side of his head. "I had an inkling."

Peter thought it sounded more like he had had knowledge and simply refused to participate. "You knew. The secret group in the '50s, they were Wielders."

"I didn't know what they were called, but I already told you, they had abilities like Cassie."

"They wanted you to join them, didn't they?"

He glowered at them. It was confirmation enough.

"Who were these people?" Owen asked, curiosity turning him around to face the phantom.

Gerard narrowed his eyes. "A lot of people you wouldn't know."

"I'd know their last names."

"As all the last names in DeVerre tend to repeat themselves, I bet you would." He crossed his arms. "But it won't do you much good. It was the usual suspects and others you've never heard of."

"The Frossards?"

A nod.

"The Chapelles?"

Another nod.

"The Varons?"

A half-nod that turned into a tilt. "Actually," Gerard replied, brow rising, "they were dead by then. Michael had already killed himself. Right here in this room actually."

Spencer blanched, and Peter pinched the bridge of his nose, knowing his brother was likely regretting how much time he'd spent in that office.

"How much do you know about the Varon deaths?" Owen prodded.

Gerard pursed his lips. "Not much. I was twelve when it happened. My mom didn't care to share the gory details with us kids."

"Hm." Owen dropped his gaze to the red cushions of the couch.

Seeing that he wanted to ask more questions, Peter edged forward. "Does that have something to do with Wielders?"

Owen pulled in a deep breath and let out a cynical chuckle. "Yeah." He shifted back to face them again. "And it sort of brings me to the next point: DeVerre's original purpose."

Peter, Spencer, and Cassandra leaned in, ready for whatever he would say next.

"Like I said, the founding families of DeVerre came from Harmony," he explained, a subtle Canadian accent slipping through as he talked about his home. "And while my family isn't native to Harmony itself, I am a third-generation citizen. We grew rather fast in the social ranks there due to our adept abilities as Wielders. This provided me with a good amount of knowledge on the foundation of both towns.

"Matthias Varon was the three times great-grandson of Philippe Varon, founder of Harmony. The Varons originated in France, and they immigrated to Canada back in the late 1600s. Back in Nova Scotia, one of the Varon daughters married a man with the surname Chapelle. This started the everlasting bond between the families. It took them years to spread across the continent and make it this far west. The Varons left France to pursue a . . . prophecy, essentially. They had information that suggested they needed to come out west. They didn't know why, but they trusted the source. So they came.

"In 1883, Matthias Varon received more information," Owen continued. "An answer to why they'd come. They needed to build DeVerre."

"Why?" Peter asked.

"Because of the Veil."

"What veil?"

"The lake."

Peter sucked in a deep breath and he caught the way Spencer's jaw tighten in his periphery.

"Veils are pockets of space where the distance between the natural world and the spirit world is thin," he explained. "They function like a curtain where there is normally a wall. You don't have to break down a wall to get to the spirit world; you only have to lift the curtain back. The Varons and Chapelles moved here to protect it. To make sure the Veil didn't fall into the wrong hands."

The three on the couch opposite exchanged worried glances.

"That's the thing about being a Wielder." Owen's dark blue eyes grew intense. "You can become so enamored by your own abilities that you forget where they came from in the first place. Because, yes, a Wielder can see ghosts and tether them into corporeal phantoms. But they can also summon beasts and charge them to do their bidding. They can reach into the spirit world and create an army if they have the strength for it. And, as you alluded to earlier, Cassandra, they can harness the power of the spirit world and bring it fully into our own reality. In bursts of energy—light or shadow.”

Peter’s jaw dropped. “What does that mean?”

Owen eyed him. “I’d demonstrate, but I try not to access it unless I have to.”

“Then how do we know you can do it?” He challenged more out of fun than real doubt.

“It isn’t a game.”

“I know,” he shrugged. “But it’d be nice to see what’s possible.”

Owen rubbed the thumb of one hand along his fingertips, then nodded. “Something small.”

Peter nodded, excited that something impossible was about to happen in front of him.

It took a moment as Owen’s eyes roved around the room as if to make sure he understood his surroundings before disrupting them. He shook out his hands, straightened his collar, and sat forward, holding both fists out in front of him.

A two second delay ticked on the clock in the corner.

Owen opened his hands.

A rift of amber-like energy tore through the air above his palms, a thin halo of pure white surrounding the edge. It rippled and pulled itself apart like an arc of electricity or wisps of smoke.

Then it blinked and disappeared.

Cassandra’s breathing had grown rapid, her eyes locked on the spot.

“Whoa,” Peter muttered, gaze flickering over to check on Spencer.

His brother had thrown a hand over his mouth, sinking back into the couch cushions. His shock was evident, but otherwise he appeared calm in his contemplation of what they’d just witnessed.

“That’s not something everyone can do,” Owen told them. “But it’s more possible than you’d think.”

Hesitant, Cassandra met his eyes. “Could I do that?”

“I’d assume so.”

An amazed chuckle escaped her.

"But you get it, don't you?" His words were weighty. "What I just did is dangerous."

"What *did* you just do?" Peter asked, still in awe.

"I pulled back the curtain and brought the essence of the spirit world into the natural."

"And . . . that's dangerous because . . . ?"

"Because it bypasses the physical and meets the spiritual. If I were to use it as a weapon, for example, it wouldn't hit like a blade or a bullet or a fist. There would be no sign of physical damage. But it would hit the spirit. It could tear a soul to pieces and damage the innermost parts of a person's mind, will, and emotions. You can never kill a spirit, but you can corrupt it enough to kill the soul and completely destroy the physical form."

Spencer's hand rose to cover his forehead as he slumped deeper into the cushions.

"You can use its essence in other ways," Owen continued. "To open a portal for beasts to walk through. To bend reality and overcome the limitations of what's natural. But the most obvious use for it is to defend oneself."

"And you can do this because of the Veil?" Peter asked, beginning to see the danger.

"I can do it *more easily* because of the Veil," he said. "But I can do it whenever and wherever I like. There may be a wall between me and the spirit world outside of the radius of a Veil, but that doesn't stop me from breaking down that wall."

Spencer's hand dropped into his lap, a defeated expression on his face. "So the Varons," he muttered. "They came here to protect the Veil?"

"Yes."

"That's why the house is here? To be close to the lake?"

"Presumably."

"Did anyone ever consider that's why one of them went crazy?" Spencer asked, looking at each of them. "Maybe the Veil corrupted him with its power, and he went insane from it."

Owen took a second before giving a firm shake of his head. "I've never heard of a Veil driving someone mad."

"So he was just a psychopath then?"

"Maybe."

"Great."

Wanting to direct the conversation away from the violent past of their home, Peter grasped at the first straw he could find. "Why the Varons? You said the Chapelles were with them from the beginning. Why was it the Varons who were protecting the Veil and not the Chapelles? They're the pastors here. Why not have the most spiritual people protect the spirit world?"

Owen drew back in his seat. "I can't tell you what happened once they got here, but I can tell you what we know in Harmony," he replied. "The Varons are some of the strongest Wielders alive. It's been a lineage of powerful people since the start. Coming here, the Varons were in charge because they had the strongest hold on the Veil. The Chapelles, having ancestral Varon blood themselves, come in a close second. But no one is as strong as a Varon."

"Why?"

He shrugged. "Why was Paul one of the most prolific and profound writers of the Bible despite being a murderer earlier in his life? Who knows why God chooses His strongest hands? It's why they're still in charge of Harmony."

"You still have Varons in Harmony?" Gerard asked, startling Peter as he'd forgotten the phantom was listening.

"Yeah," Owen called over his shoulder. "There are Varons scattered all over North America. Their line only ended here."

Gerard turned away, apparently no longer interested.

Owen met Cassandra's stare. "The point of me giving you all this information is so you can understand why I didn't say anything before," he explained. "Harmony was a parent town to DeVerre. We sent them out here with the intention of keeping an eye on them and supporting their protection of the Veil. When we lost contact with them, we knew something was wrong.

"That's why I came here," he concluded. "To figure out what's happened, and to try to stand in the way if anyone makes a play for control of the Veil."

"By yourself?" Peter asked.

Owen shrugged. "We have no real reason to suspect that I'll face much opposition. No one knows I'm a Wielder but you four, and I'm far more powerful than the average person with our abilities. I could hold my own long enough to get away and warn the others."

"Warn them of what exactly?" Spencer asked. "All of this is esoteric information. The very information Diane was searching for over the last thirty years. And she found nothing. Not even with the writings of the Lawrences in hand. So why would you suspect that someone is after the Veil? Why would you think that DeVerre is in danger?"

"Because we're not alone," Owen said, a tension in his words. "My people—the people of Harmony and of old DeVerre—they weren't the only ones who were looking for Veils."

Cassandra lifted her head, lips parting. "The missing pages," she whispered.

As one, the men looked at her, waiting expectantly.

"Elijah referenced them," she said, motioning to Owen. "To his people and to the others. The Divine Prophets and the Immortal Deceivers."

Owen furrowed his brow.

"The Protectors and Spirit Seekers."

He scratched his beard. "Well, I've never heard them called that, but I think you're right. My people, the Warden, are working to protect the Veils from the ancient Druids who are seeking to control them and release the spirit world on the Earth."

Peter felt his blood running cold. "Why?"

"Because they believe that we're divine beings now locked in mortal forms. They think that if they can unlock the spirit world, they can free their immortal forms and become their once-divine selves."

Cassandra worked her jaw back and forth as she studied him. "And you think there are Druids here in DeVerre who are trying to get control of the Veil?"

"I don't know," he said with a shrug. "I hope not, but I can't fathom who else would be looking to get control of a tiny town like this. Whatever happened after the Varons died, whatever caused all the secrets in this town, it all makes sense if there are Druids involved."

"What if it's all a misunderstanding?" Cassandra asked. "What if it's as simple as people who've become obsessed with the idea of power and only want to control the town, not the Veil?"

He shook his head. "I can't believe that these people are as innocent as that. Whatever the current state of DeVerre, these families got their start in Harmony. Their ancestors knew what I know. A century didn't wipe away all their knowledge. Not when only seventy years ago there was a secret band of them trying to recruit your phantom. Not when Ava still knows about the ghosts and Wielders, even if she doesn't understand the truth behind any of it."

The weight of all these secrets were compounding in Peter's head. It was so much knowledge. There were so many layers of half-truths and complex facts. It was hard to keep them straight.

But Owen was right. This town couldn't be as innocent as they liked to pretend. Whoever did or didn't know about the Veil, one thing was clear: there were people working to conceal the truth. It could be any of the founding families in pursuit of power. And if Owen were any indication of a how easily a Wielder could hide in plain sight, their enemy could be any regular citizen as well. Anyone could be working to cover up their actions. Anyone could be the one summoning hellhounds to do their bidding.

"Wait," Peter exclaimed, the dots lining up in his head. "The animal attacks."

"What about them?" Spencer asked, a thread of irritation in his tone.

"They were real."

"Yeah. . . ."

"No." Peter shook his head. "I mean, they weren't actually animal attacks. They were hellhound attacks."

Owen sat up straighter. "What makes you say that?"

"Because we were freakin' attacked by a hellhound a week ago!"

Cassandra nodded, looking to Peter. "And Juliet Chapelle has been claiming that her boyfriend was killed by a werewolf."

Owen sighed, setting a hand over his lips.

"Someone is using hellhounds to murder people," Peter concluded.

"Why?" Spencer asked.

"It's a Druid," Owen said. "It has to be."

"How can you be sure?" Cassandra asked.

"Only a Wielder can summon a hound," he said. "Do you believe that someone like you or me would do that?"

"But why would they suddenly start murdering people?" She asked. "Wouldn't it draw unnecessary attention to them? If they're trying to stay a secret, they wouldn't risk that sort of thing."

"They would if they were getting desperate."

"Desperate how?"

"I don't know," Owen admitted. "But the Druids have plans for the Veils. What those plans are exactly, we haven't gotten the answers to yet. But whatever the case, they believe the celestial patterns are the key to strong power. Full moons, equinoxes, eclipses. If they're looking to make their move, they'd do it when a major event is about to happen."

Spencer raised his head. "Wait, when does winter start this year?"

"December sometime," Peter offered.

"I knew *that*. I meant what exact day?"

"I dunno."

Spencer rolled his eyes and sat up. "What if they're preparing for it? We're only a month and a half or so away. They could be getting ready."

"What about a full moon?" Peter offered.

They were all quiet.

"Wow, guys." He gave them a sarcastic smile. "We all really know our celestial calendars. So what do we think is happening here? They're killing people because . . . they're preparing for something? Why now? And why kill them? Are they sacrifices?"

"No, that's far too archaic for even them." Owen replied. "Human death has little bearing on the spirit world beyond creating ghosts who can't affect the natural world anyway."

"Unless they're made into phantoms," Cassandra offered.

"But they'd have to be Wielders to become ghosts, right?" Peter reminded them. "Or at least be aware of the spirit world. And if no one in DeVerre is willing to talk about this stuff, then how sure are we that it's common knowledge?"

"It's not," Owen confirmed. "From the past decade that I've lived here and with Ava's knowledge, it seems that there's a handful who know about the spirit world at most. And even the people who do know, don't necessarily know everything or know who else knows too. Every conversation is like walking on eggshells with these people. Trust me. Ava gets pissed about it daily."

"So why the murders?"

Owen sat forward. "There have been three animal attacks in the last month, all resulting in death. First was one of the farmers, Taylor Ozanne. He was thirty-eight, single, and rather reclusive. Second was Jessica Calderon, a distant relative of Tom Garnier. She was thirty, married with two little girls, worked at the Foxglove as a waitress on weekends, and was one of the sweetest people in town. Finally, Brendan Descoteaux died this past week. He was seventeen and about to finish high school. His mother was a Guillaume *and* he was dating the reverend's daughter, which put him on the inside of the social scene."

"What do they have in common?" Peter asked.

They were all quiet for a moment.

Owen shrugged. "Aside from being from DeVerre, nothing obvious that I know of."

"So why kill them?"

"A better question," Spencer said. "Why kill them and try to kill us too?"

"Maybe you annoyed them," Gerard offered. "As far as the first question goes, I might be able to answer that."

"You can?" Peter asked as they all turned to him.

"Potentially."

"By all means, Gerry, go for it!"

Gerard narrowed his eyes at Peter but continued. "Jerome Ozanne was a rather zealous member of that little group I told you about back in the '50s. If my memory serves me, he was Taylor's grandfather. As far as the other two go, it's a bit more of a long shot. But since one was a descendant of a Garnier and the other a Guillaume, odds are that they had ancestors in that little band as well."

"The Garniers and Guillaumes are Wielders?" Cassandra asked.

"I don't know if they are anymore, but they were once upon a time."

Peter sighed, dropping his gaze to the navy and brown rug under his feet. "So they're killing Wielders then?"

"We don't know that," Owen said. "I knew Jessica, and she showed no signs of utilizing the spirit world. I also taught Brendan at the school. He was as normal a kid as they come."

"Then why kill them?" Spencer pressed.

"They had the lineage," Cassandra suggested. "Maybe they weren't Wielders in an official capacity, but they had a better chance of becoming one than others, didn't they?"

Owen ran his thumb over his lips in thought.

"As someone who has lived in DeVerre longer than any of you," Gerard said, coming to stand in the doorway, "allow me to enlighten you. Whatever your personal beliefs or agendas, whatever groups you align yourselves with, get this straight: DeVerreans don't care. They're looking out for their own interests. Druid, Warden, Wielder, phantom, doesn't matter. If you're right and some family here has formed some allegiance to these Druids, they will do whatever it takes to see their plans come to fruition. Killing someone who *might* get in their way is perfectly within those bounds."

They all stared at him.

"And if you don't think someone could be that cruel—" He smirked. "You never met my brother."

The tension was taut like a rubber band that had been stretched too far. It was bound to snap if someone didn't let go.

Peter cleared his throat.

"So we're fighting Druids now?" he asked, attempting to keep his tone light. "Cool. How do we find them?"

Owen pulled his intense glare away from Gerard. "Well, I suppose I should ask some of the ghosts if they have any answers for me. Most of them refuse to have anything to do with me, but there are a few who will talk. And I could see if Ava suspects any others with powers in the town. She's got a keen eye for that sort of thing."

"Yet she hasn't noticed you." Cassandra's brow was raised.

"People overlook a lot when they don't want to see the truth."

"What can we do?" Peter asked.

Owen thought about it. "Keep connecting with people. One of my limitations here stems from being married to Ava. Though everyone likes me well enough, she can be a bit abrasive. And when she believes in something, she can become obsessive. People steer clear of Ava, which means they steer clear of me.

"But you two are making friends and getting on people's good sides for the most part." He nodded. "Keep it up. And maybe avoid the marshal for a while longer, Peter. He's not your biggest fan."

Spencer grinned while Peter frowned.

"And me?" Cassandra asked.

Owen eyed her. "Stay out of trouble. People are suspicious of you because of your connection to Diane. But try to join the guys when you can. Making friends, especially with people our age, will go a long way to giving you an access into people's lives. And that's how you're going to get the answers we're looking for.

"Listen and watch carefully," he charged, a tone of finality in his words. "Everything people do in DeVerre can be a potential clue. Interpersonal secrets will inevitably get revealed if you are patient and attentive. No one can hide what's really in their heart. Good or bad."

Peter looked over each person in the room. Gerard leaned against the doorframe, still glaring at Owen who in turn was watching the three of them intently. Spencer had gone back to wringing his hands, eyes on the ground. And Cassandra stared over at Gerard, hand partially covering the frown across her lips.

So this was it, Peter realized. They were now an undercover band of secret agents trying to infiltrate the inner workings of DeVerre. The moment didn't feel like he would have thought. He wasn't excited, and he didn't feel very special.

But without doubt he knew this was important. They were on the precipice of something huge. Something that would change everything. This wasn't just their careers as authors or their lifestyle on the line. This was their whole future.

Looking past them all, Peter grinned at Spencer. "Well, Frankly," he said. "Looks like we're about to be investigators after all."

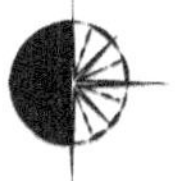

Spencer

Spencer scratched behind Nex's ear as the group watched Owen walk through the gates of Occasus and back toward town. His chest felt like a tangle of cables twisted into impossible knots that would never release. This wasn't what he wanted. Any of it. They'd moved to DeVerre to let go of all their problems. To leave behind their worries. To write and escape from the chaos of reality.

But now life had become more complicated than ever.

Anguis padded up next to Spencer and nudged his other hand, jealous for attention.

Spencer gave the dog a half-hearted grin and crouched down to pet both of them. They pressed closer to him. He accepted the minimal comfort offered by their closeness.

"I guess I should go too," Cassandra said, an unusual sense of distance in her voice.

Scanning her, Spencer wondered swhat had caused the sudden change. It had begun while Owen talked with them, he knew. He'd seen how her shoulders began to droop during the conversation. But what had Owen said that could have shaken the confidence he'd come to expect from Cassandra Clement? Normally, her crossed arms were a sign of her surety and strength. But as they stood on the porch, they looked like a wall defending her, a barrier to keep her safe. Her chin was tilted downward. And instead of the unnerving eye contact he was accustomed to from her, her hazel eyes shifted as if they couldn't settle on anything for long.

"Cool," Peter muttered, pushing away from the porch railing. "Guess we'll . . . I dunno. What do we do now? Try to behave normally?"

Cassandra let out a cynical, breathy laugh. "If that's possible."

"Hey, it'll be okay," Peter promised, giving her shoulder a nudge. "We'll get this figured out."

Spencer met Nex's warm brown eyes and wondered if that was true. How could they figure out something so convoluted and beyond belief?

The unamused grin on Cassandra's lips suggested that she felt the same.

"You're like the freakin' Raven. Don't be so gloomy, all right?" Peter patted her arm, moving for the door.

Her smile turned more genuine at that. "Bye, Pete." The door clicked shut behind him and Cassandra moved toward the steps. "See ya, Spence."

Spencer opened his mouth to say goodbye but found other words tumbling out instead. "Can I ask you a question?"

Cassandra halted on the top step. She turned back toward him, hand on the railing. "Yeah, of course."

Giving each dog one last pat, Spencer stood. Now that they were out here alone and she was meeting his gaze again, he didn't know if he actually wanted to ask what was on his mind. He slipped his hands into the pockets of his denim jacket and forced the question out anyway. "Are you okay?"

Her face went blank for a second, as though unsure of what he was asking. Then the hollow in her right cheek made its appearance with the smile that blossomed across her face. "Yeah, Spencer, I'm fine." She drew her keys from her pocket.

"You sure?"

"I'm positive," she assured him, taking a backwards step down the stairs.

Spencer didn't respond but simply watched as she took another step. She froze, eyes locked on him as his were on her.

"You don't believe me, do you?"

Spencer shook his head.

Her smile turned to a knowing smirk as Cassandra headed back up the steps, keys jingling at her side. She leaned against the rail, arms crossed in their usual proud manner. "All right, so I'm not totally fine. But it's no big deal." Her shoulder lifted in a shrug. "It's . . . it's just odd, you know? All this time, I've thought I was the only one. I thought I was alone. Sure, Diane could see ghosts, but that was it. And now. . . ."

He waited for her to conclude her thoughts.

"Now there's not only Owen, but there's also these . . . Druids, or whatever, out there that may want to kill me. It's kind of overwhelming," she admitted. "But I'm all right. I promise."

Spencer studied her, trying to find any lie in her words. Yet her posture suggested total openness and honesty. She rested against the railing, head tipped to the side in an air of lazy patience.

Shaking his head in awe, Spencer huffed. "Doesn't it scare you?"

Cassandra's chin dipped down as her grin turned playful. "I've seen ghosts since I was a kid," she reminded him. "Little scares me anymore."

"Ghosts are different from people," he replied. "You taught me that there's nothing to fear from them because they can't touch you or hurt you. But these are *real* people, Cass."

"So . . . what? I'm supposed to be afraid of them because they can hurt me?"

"Yeah!"

She chuckled, shaking her head at him. "Spencer, why would I be afraid of getting hurt?"

He felt his face grow tense with confusion.

"Every day we face pain," she continued. "Whether physical or mental or emotional, it doesn't really matter. Every moment we make choices based off what hurts. It's part of what makes us alive. So why would I be afraid of pain? It's only temporary, and it only tells me that I'm living."

Spencer couldn't understand her words. Sure, he got the concept and he appreciated the sentiment, but it was so far beyond what he could imagine for himself. He ran from pain every chance he got. The pain was what he feared most. The *what if* came down to the pain he might experience *if* the *what* happened.

Stretching her foot out to cross the distance, Cassandra tapped the toe of her boot on his. "The only thing to fear is fear itself, Spencer."

Letting out a tense laugh at the cliché, Spencer stared at the weathered porch planks. "Yeah, well I've got a lot of that."

"Mm, so I've learned. You should try to be more like me. I don't have any."

He lifted a single brow. "Well, you're some kind of magic, if that's true."

She rolled her eyes at him, smile growing brighter. "No, I've just learned the difference between what's actually dangerous and what's not."

"Everything's dangerous."

Her laugh was short but warm and heartening. "We're gonna have to work on your sense of danger if you plan to stick around DeVerre."

Spencer swallowed past the tension in his throat. "And what if I don't?"

Cassandra's smile slipped, and her dark eyebrows lowered. "Then I hope you change your mind." She straightened. The keys rattled in her right hand as she set the other on his arm and stepped closer. Her fingers squeezed his bicep. "You're braver than you think, Spencer. And I'd be sad to see you go before you figured that out for yourself."

The tangle in Spencer's chest coiled tighter at her proximity. Her hand was warm through his jacket and her smile encouraging. He wasn't sure if he should say something in reply or not. He doubted he could get words out through the constriction in his throat.

Her thumb gave a final quick rub as she squeezed again. "I'll see you later, Spence."

Managing to find his voice, he nodded. "Thanks, Cass."

"Anytime."

She turned and took the stairs with a light-footed gait, almost bouncing down the steps. The door of the truck creaked open, then banged shut as the engine rumbled to life. She lifted her hand in a wave before putting the truck in gear and driving away from Occasus.

Spencer watched her go. Nex lay at his feet while Anguis sat leaning against his leg. He wished he could be as fearless as Cassandra. That he could carry that much conviction and confidence. But he couldn't help doubting that she felt it herself. How could she? How could anyone?

Fear was inevitable. Fear taught you not to touch a hot stove or to step out onto the road without looking both ways. Fear kept you from getting hurt. It saved you from trouble. It was your friend.

So then why did he wish that he could be as fearless as her?

~

Hopping out of the Jeep, Peter tossed a hundredth knowing look at Spencer. He'd been smirking and chuckling under his breath all that next morning.

Annoyed, Spencer grabbed the books from the backseat. "Would you stop it?" he demanded. "Nothing happened."

"I'm sure it didn't." Peter waited on the sidewalk, rolling back and forth from heels to toes.

Spencer made sure to time it right and shoved his shoulder into his brother's as he walked past.

Peter stumbled but kept his footing. "You spent like thirty minutes out there talking," he teased. "What was I supposed to think?"

"Would you let it go?"

"Nevermore."

"Oh, shut up."

"You've always thought ravens were cool."

Spencer shook his head, stopped at the library door, and turned back to block his brother's path. "Listen, I have no interest in getting involved with anyone, least of all someone who deals with—" He glanced around the empty square but lowered his voice anyway. "With ghosts and wants to continue pursuing those abilities. I like Cassandra—"

Peter nodded.

"As a *friend*, and I'm happy to help her. But anything more is not something I'm interested in."

"Of course."

"I'm serious."

"Yeah, man, I know."

"Stop smirking."

Peter brushed a hand through the air to dismiss the issue. "I'm just happy to visit Ava, dude. It's got nothing to do with your crush on Cassie."

"I will find a way to kill off Wenzel if you don't let it go," Spencer threatened.

Brow pulling down, Peter's grin fell away. "You can't."

"I'm the one who edits everything, remember?"

His eyes narrowed. "You wouldn't dare. He's a titular character."

"I can always change the title."

They stared each other down for a long time. Peter's eyes squinted. Spencer's gaze relaxed. They both knew who held the power when it came to their writing.

"Fine."

"Fine."

Peter sulked as Spencer pushed into the library.

Neither of them wasted time at the front, weaving through the shelves to the back. A gentle concerto played while the fresh smell of black tea wafted through the room.

"Hey, Ava," Peter called as they rounded the corner. "We've brought your books back."

Standing in the corner rather than at her usual seat at the desk, Ava finished pouring her tea. She didn't even look up at them as she motioned to the table. "Just put 'em down," she said, disinterested. "I'll get to them later."

They did as ordered.

Ava carried her large green mug to the table, took a seat, and picked up her novel without a word.

Spencer turned to Peter.

Peter frowned at Spencer.

"Did you need something else?" Ava asked.

"Uh," Peter shrugged. "I guess not."

"Cool."

Spencer sighed, understanding her indifferent response. Owen had said she didn't like how much time they were spending with Cassandra. That she didn't want Anna hanging out with them for fear that their new friend would become part of her life too.

But what did Ava expect them to do? She knew that Diane had been close to Cassandra. She'd even suggested they talk with her when she got back into town. It was inevitable that they'd become friends with her, wasn't it?

Owen's defense of his wife came back to Spencer. She was afraid, just like him. She feared the spirit world and what it could do to the people she loved. She wanted to protect her home and her family, and the recent deaths had intensified her fears.

Taking a step back, Spencer grabbed Peter's arm and began to pull him away. "Thanks for everything, Ava," he said, keeping his voice calm and sympathetic.

Her eyes flickered from her book for a second as they started to walk away.

Spencer gave her a nod and began to turn.

"I remember her, you know?" she called, halting his progress. "Cassandra. We started school together here in DeVerre."

The brothers turned to meet her serious stare.

"And I remember how she used to talk to ghosts like it was normal. I didn't understand it at first," she said. "Why she was talking to thin air like someone was there. But my mother explained it all to me. About the spirit world and the ghosts."

Spencer and Peter exchanged a nervous look.

"I know she's talked to you about it." She dropped the book on the table and crossed her arms. "She and Diane were constantly trying to find more information to prove their theories. And those books you checked out—Diane and Liam checked them out years ago. I doubt you found any more answers in them than they did."

Spencer dipped his chin down. "You're right."

She nodded, pulling in a deep breath. "Why are you helping her?"

"Why wouldn't we?" Peter challenged.

"Because she's dangerous."

The brothers shared a look. The fact that her husband was far more powerful than Cassandra made him a far greater danger by her own standards.

Ava shifted forward in her seat, braids cascading over her shoulders. "I would be very careful trusting her." The early afternoon sunlight turned her brown skin almost golden. "The Varon estate is more than a landmark."

The warning hit Spencer like a punch to the gut. "What does that mean?"

"Where do you think all that dangerous information was kept safe in this town?" Ava asked, her tone suggesting they'd missed the obvious. "Why do you think everyone was so pissed when Diane bought the house and began renovating? She may not have known it, but she was threatening to uncover everything. That house holds the key to every secret in DeVerre, and when Michael Varon killed himself, that key went with him."

"Wait, wait, wait." Peter held up his hands, head shaking in disbelief. "Are you telling me that *Occasus* holds all the information we've been looking for this whole time?"

"And more."

In shock, the brothers' jaws dropped as they turned to each other.

"But no one knows how to get to it," Ava explained.

"What?" Peter gasped, his interest drawing him forward a step.

Ava huffed, setting a hand to her forehead. "I shouldn't even be telling you this," she muttered before her eyes snapped back up to them. "The town deemed the loss of the vault acceptable because no one in their right mind would seek to deal in such dark matters. We accepted that this information was lost. We were fine with that. But then Diane started poking around and disrupting it."

Spencer thought back to the board in Diane's secret office. The one that had tried to connect the dots of her ancestry. He wondered if she had known that her search was kicking up the dust of long hidden secrets.

"Thankfully," Ava continued, "it seems that Diane never figured it out. But if you're looking for some reason to question Cassandra Clement's motives, ask yourself: Why did a woman our age befriend an old eccentric in the first place?"

Seeing no reason to lie, Spencer shrugged. "Because Diane could see ghosts too."

That didn't surprise Ava. She tipped her head to glare at them with a condescending glint in her eyes. "So what? Why did Cassandra come back here in the first place? Why seek to expand her knowledge of the supernatural?"

"She wanted to understand it."

"To what end?"

Spencer blinked, dropping his eyes to the dark green rug beneath his feet. He couldn't answer that question. Cassandra had never told them what she wanted out of her powers. Just that she wanted to know what they were. It was an excellent question: What was the point of it all? Why did she care?

"Didn't you two find it suspicious," Ava asked, eyes flickering between the two of them, "the way she wormed her way into Diane's will? Who is she to Diane? Why would *she* ever deserve that sort of treatment?"

"We'd never met Diane," Peter reminded her. "It was weird enough that she left it to us."

"You're still family," she countered. "Also writers, like her. Even if she was a crazy old woman with strange notions, why would she leave her enormous fortune and estate to a young woman she only met four years ago? Why would she trust her more than anyone else?"

"Because they both saw ghosts?" Spencer offered.

"Right, they did." Ava nodded. "And Cassandra showed up six months after Diane lost her husband. When she was more alone than she'd been in decades."

A sudden emptiness formed a hole in Spencer's stomach. He didn't like the suspicious thoughts Ava's suggestions were triggering. He didn't like how she was making him question the faith they'd placed in Cassandra. How it felt like she was shining a light on the gaps in the young woman's story that they'd ignored.

"You think she's after Occasus?" Peter asked, his voice as hollow sounding as Spencer felt. "And what's hidden inside."

"I do."

"Why didn't you tell us before?"

She raised her brow. "I didn't know you'd fall for her lies as easily as Diane did."

Spencer placed a hand over his mouth, attempting to calm the threatening doom that awoke panic within him. Why had they trusted

Cassandra in the first place? She'd shown up right as they were being attacked by a hellhound that she'd admitted she could have summoned herself. Saving their life could have been a play to 'prove' herself to them. In every story she'd told them, there'd always been something missing. Something that was unexplainable. Some information she didn't possess that she needed them to find for her.

Or did she?

Was that part of the game too? Was she lying to them to lull them into a false sense of security while she searched their house? Was she using Gerard to spy on them? Was the phantom as harmless as she claimed?

"Do you really believe this?" Peter asked, an edge of anger in his words. "Or is it all based off your own bias toward her?"

The question didn't appear to offend Ava. "Of course I'm biased. But that doesn't mean I'm blind."

"Do you. . . ." Spencer cleared his throat and tried again to ask the question that he'd been wondering the whole conversation. "Do you believe that Diane died of natural causes?"

Ava met his gaze. "No."

He closed his eyes and took a deep breath.

"And yes," she said, answering the unspoken follow up. "I'm of the persuasion that it was Cassandra who did it."

"She was out of town," Peter reminded them both.

"Was she?"

"Yes."

Ava shrugged. "I wasn't with her the whole time, were you?"

They clearly weren't.

"Maybe it wasn't her," she said. "But who else would want Diane dead? DeVerre long ago accepted the loss of the hidden vault in Occasus. We can't get in, but that means no one else can either. We were happy to forget it."

"If it's a vault, why don't you just tear the house down and destroy it?" Peter asked.

She shook her head. "Do you think it's unprotected? That it's some normal basement they just turned into a giant safe? The Varons were whatever Cassandra is. My mom told me the stories. Of how they could do things that no one ever should. That vault is locked in some unnatural way. Not just anyone can get to it."

"But Cassandra could," Spencer surmised.

"I believe she could," she affirmed. "With enough time and practice."

The vacancy echoing in his gut made Spencer want to drop to the floor. What had they gotten themselves into? And what could they do about it? If Cassandra was after this vault and the information inside—if she'd killed Diane to get to it— how could they walk away? They couldn't let her get to it. But how could they really stop her?

"And now that you're the only thing that stands between her and Occasus," Ava said, her sharp words cutting through Spencer's worries to start the slow bleed of panic, "do you really think that she won't take it from you by any means necessary?"

CHAPTER EIGHTEEN

Peter

Stepping back outside, Peter tried to comprehend everything Ava had just shared. He didn't want to believe it could be true. He didn't want to doubt Cassandra's intentions. But the way Ava had laid it all out for them . . . how could they argue against it?

Clouds drifted overhead, threatening the warm glow of the afternoon.

Peter ran his fingers through his hair, trying to regain some semblance of order to his thoughts. They'd learned so much over the past week and even more in the last two days. First, the full presence of the spirit world. Then, the existence of Wielders and Druids. Now, a magical vault hiding within in their own home. What was next?

Spencer walked like a zombie all the way to the Jeep, stepped up into the driver's seat, and shut the door. He stared straight through the windshield, a dull look in his eyes.

This was the end, Peter realized. The true end to their time here.

He couldn't ask Spencer to stay anymore. Not when a madwoman was attempting to get their house from them. Better to let her take it and leave with their lives.

Would she let them leave though, he wondered, now that they knew what they knew? Would she try to kill them anyway?

Hands shaking at the thought, Peter climbed into the Jeep and sat next to Spencer. Was this his fault? He'd been the one to insist they come here after all. Any time resistance had come up, he'd made sure they pushed past it without regard for the possibility of danger. He'd asked Spencer to ignore all his concerns, and in the end, each one had been well-founded.

"Oh, God," Peter dropped his head into his hands. "I've really screwed this up."

Spencer didn't reply, eyes locked onto nothing.

Could they drive away now? Turn on the Jeep and leave everything behind? She wouldn't follow them, would she? Not if they gave her everything she wanted.

"Do you believe her?" Spencer whispered.

Peter looked up. "Which one?"

A beat of silence passed.

"Ava."

Frowning, Peter nodded. "Yeah, I mean. . . ." He sighed. "I definitely believe *she* believes it."

"But do you believe what she believes?"

He gulped down the guilt in his thoughts. "That Cassandra's after the house?"

"Yeah."

"I guess."

Spencer's eyebrows drew together, and he turned to him. "You *guess*?"

Peter shrugged. "I mean, why wouldn't I? It makes sense."

"Yeah." Spencer turned away again. "It does."

Another beat of silence.

"What do we do?"

Letting out a huff, Peter passed his brother a half-hearted smirk. "Run for our lives?"

Spencer scowled.

"Ask for help?"

That seemed to spark an idea in Spencer. "We could go to Owen."

"We've known him for two days, dude," he reminded him. "Do we *really* trust a guy who lies to his wife more than we trust Cass?"

"This isn't about trust, Peter," Spencer said, glaring back at him. The clouds angled over the sun, casting a shadow on half of his face. The effect made him look more like his age, possibly for the first time ever. "I don't trust either of them. I don't trust Ava. I don't trust anyone in this town but you. But if we're gonna do the right thing here, I think we need to *try* and find someone who can stop Cassandra from finding this vault. Because we sure can't do it on our own."

Peter stared at his brother, surprised at this unexpected resolve. "All right," he agreed, nodding. "All right yeah, I think you're right. Is Owen the guy we want to go to for help though?"

"Who else do we ask?"

That was a fair point. They didn't know anyone else in the town well enough to know if there actually were any other Wielders within its borders. And while there was still the lingering suggestion that more people knew of the spirit world than they let on, there was great doubt that they held any more power than Peter or Spencer.

"Let's go, then," Peter said.

Spencer didn't hesitate.

It took them less than five minutes to round the square, go up the lane, and turn onto Hope. The irony of the court's name wasn't lost on Peter as they pulled up to the Bernard house. The brothers jumped out and hurried up to the door.

Peter worried that Owen wouldn't be home. Just because they didn't have jobs didn't mean no one else did. He tried not to knock in too noticeable of a panic.

It took about thirty seconds for the door to open.

"Oh." Anna smiled at the sight of them. "Hey, what's up?"

"Ah, Anna." Peter grinned, trying to overcome his nerves. "Yeah, yeah, uh, we're actually here to see Owen."

"You are?" Her nose scrunched up in surprise. He hoped that meant he wasn't gone. She moved to the side to let them in. "All right, yeah, he's in his office."

"His office, yeah." Peter nodded as he stepped into the house. "Great."

"It's just straight back." She pointed past the kitchen.

"Cool, thanks."

"Uh-huh."

Peter hurried on as Spencer followed, muttering a hello to her. They moved through the small house, past the kitchen and circular dining table, and stopped at the door to the office. Feeling sure they should appear confident about their meeting, he gave a quick knock before cracking the door open.

"Just a sec," Owen said, sitting in the corner at a small desk as he typed. It wasn't exactly what Peter would call an office so much as a closed in porch that had been converted to a workspace. There were windows on all sides, short bookshelves filled to the brim, and a love seat on the far side of the room where the cat slept.

Owen hit a couple final keys before turning around to see them, the sudden confusion clear in his furrowed brow. "Oh, it's, uh. . . ." He stood up and shook off his surprise, then gave them a polite smile. "I wasn't expecting you two. What's up? You look shaken."

Moving far enough into the room so that Spencer could shut the door, Peter nodded. He could feel that the motion was more frantic than it should be. "Yeah, that's one way to describe it," he said, diving right in. "So there's no reason to waste your time—we just got done dropping some books back off at the library—"

"Ah," Owen tipped his chin up as if he knew what was coming.

"Yeah, so Ava kind of went off about Cass."

"Yeah."

"So you know her theory?"

Owen looked between the two of them, lips parting in hesitation. "Which one?"

"Which one?" Spencer repeated.

"She has a lot."

"The one regarding Cass," Peter clarified.

Owen nodded. "Which one?"

"The one where Cassandra killed Diane and wants to kill us to take the house and find the vault," Spencer said, words rushing out in a panic.

Dark blue eyes narrowing, Owen took a step forward. "Excuse me?"

"Oh." Peter raised his brow. "So, you don't know *that* theory?"

"No," Owen said, head cocked to the side. "What vault?"

"You don't know?"

"No."

"Oh, cool, ummmm. . . ." Peter took a deep breath. "So apparently there's this vault, uh, in Occasus that . . . holds all the information about, pfft, uh—the Wielders and stuff? I dunno, she wasn't really specific, but basically every secret of DeVerre is locked up in this vault in Occasus and only the Varons knew how to get into it. But Ava's pretty dang convinced that Cassandra is trying to get to this vault and open it so that she can unlock her powers or whatever and . . . take over DeVerre?"

Owen stared at them in silence. He straightened his shoulders and ran a hand along his jaw. "All right," he whispered. "All right."

"Do you believe her?" Spencer asked.

Owen sighed. "You mean, do I believe that my wife is correct in accusing someone she fears of murder when she doesn't have any proof?"

Peter pressed his lips together at the way that sounded.

"I don't know," Owen admitted. "I know that Ava has a serious prejudice against Wielders whether she has all the information about them or not, but . . . that's not enough reason to totally discount her opinions. She's got knowledge of this town that no one else does. And . . . this vault . . . it more than explains why someone might have murdered Diane. It could explain the hellhound attacks too. The growing silence between DeVerre and Harmony. Why I've been here for ten years and can't find the answers I'm searching for. It could even explain why the Varons died."

He was right. This could be the final clue for solving every mystery in DeVerre. If the Druids were after the Veil so that they could put into motion whatever they were plotting, the vault could hold the information they needed. The animal attacks had started a few weeks after Diane's death. Perhaps they believed that her death would free them up to access the vault and finally take hold of the Veil?

But then the brothers had shown up and gotten in their way.

"Do you believe that Cassandra has played a role in it?" Spencer asked, drawing them back to the original fear.

Owen continued to run his fingers along his jaw in thought. "I don't know."

"We need a better answer than that," Spencer demanded.

"I don't have a better answer," he said, calm and composed. "Like I said, Ava has no proof that Cassandra did this. She's basing it off her personal prejudice and the circumstantial information she has about the town. She doesn't even understand the Druid/Warden component.

"Now if you're asking if I believe that it is *possible* that Cassandra is working with the Druids, then yes," he clarified. "I do. But do I believe in that strongly enough to make a judgment on it? No, I don't. And I won't until I see firm evidence that shows me that Cassandra Clement is in fact against us."

Peter drew his head back, eyeing Owen. "You want us to find evidence?"

"That would be preferable to defaming the woman you claimed as a friend just yesterday and then finding out that you're wrong."

"Right, right." Peter nodded, looking through the windows toward Haven Boulevard far across the way. He could see the backyards of a couple of the massive white homes. "We can get evidence. In defense of her or against."

"How?" Spencer asked, watching Peter carefully.

"I know where Cass lives," he said. "We can get in and go through her things."

Spencer glared at him. "Be serious, would you? We're not breaking into someone's house."

"We wouldn't *break* anything," Peter defended. "We'd just sneak in, search her room, and sneak right back out with whatever evidence we found."

Owen held up a hand to stop the idea. "First of all, you'd get caught and, second, it's a felony."

"How else do you want us to get evidence?" Peter asked, tossing his hands out to the side. "We can't exactly go down to the marshal and say, 'Hey, so you know that Cassandra chick? We think she's trying to kill us and take our house so that she can rule this place with her spirit powers.' We'd sound insane! And what if she *is* innocent?"

Owen and Spencer both gave him unamused glares.

"We can't do this through the proper channels, guys," he insisted. "This place is full of people who are lying and covering up the truth. Even people like you, Owen, have something to hide. It doesn't matter what their reasons. If we want to stop whatever is happening, we have to know if Cassandra's a part of it. If she's not, then great! We've cleared her off the list of suspects. But right now, she's looking pretty dang guilty. So we need to find out the truth. And as we can't straight up ask her about it, we're gonna have to go behind her back."

There was a long pause as the other two men considered it. The sun had almost faded from view, only thin pockets of light breaking through the gray clouds.

"Do you two have plans with Cassandra tonight?" Owen asked.

"No," Spencer replied.

"The softball tournament ends this Friday," he said, staring out across the lawn. "It's the Angels against the Ravens."

The brothers waited to find out what this information had to do with the problem at hand.

Owen turned back to them. "Mike Mercier plays for the Angels," he explained. "He and Debbie will be at the final practice tonight with the rest of the team."

Peter nodded in understanding as Spencer dipped his head.

"If you two want to do this," Owen said, words slow and serious, "I can take care of Cassandra for you. I'll invite her to come with me to the lake to try to talk with some of the past Wielders in DeVerre. Practice is from six to seven thirty, but the team always goes to the tavern afterward. You should have until almost nine o'clock to search her room. But you'd better be sure you want to risk it. Because if you get caught, no one in DeVerre will trust you and we'll lose whatever upper hand we might have had on Cassandra."

Peter shrugged. "It was my plan to begin with, so I'm good with it."

They both turned to Spencer.

His eyes shifted between the two of them over and over, then he scowled and pressed his hands to his face. "Oh, God, I don't want to do this," he muttered. He took a deep breath, dropped his hands, stared at the ceiling, and let the air out of his lungs. "All right. Fine."

Peter reached over. "Hey," he gave his brother's shoulder a squeeze. "If you want to call it off, call it off."

"No," Spencer said, shaking his head. "We don't have much of a choice. If we're wrong, it's not that big a deal, but if we're right . . . there's no getting out of this. Even if we left, we'd be leaving a mess behind us. We'd be putting Owen and Ava and Anna and everyone else in this town in danger. We'd be handing over the key to . . . whatever it is that the Druids want from the Veil. How can we walk away in good conscience? How can we leave knowing that by saving ourselves we may cause the deaths of three hundred others?"

Shifting his hand to give a playful slap to Spencer's cheek, Peter grinned. "All right," he said. "I'm proud of you."

Spencer smirked but drew away. "Thanks."

Owen nodded to each of them. "I'll call Cassandra." He picked up his cell phone. It rang for a few seconds before she answered, and he invited her to the lake. "Ava and Anna are having a girl's night, so I'm supposed to clear out. I was going to talk with some of the ghosts there. Would you have any interest in joining?" A pause, then he chuckled. "Yeah, no, I didn't think Spencer would enjoy it either." A shorter pause. "Great. How does six o'clock sound? All right, I'll meet you at the park." Another pause. "Of course, glad to have you join. See you in a couple of hours."

He hung up, set the phone back on the desk, and sighed. "We're ready."

Peter felt his hands starting to shake. "Great, great. What, uh—what do we do for the next couple hours?"

Owen sat back down in his chair. "Go home, lay low, and head to the Merciers' through the woods around five. Watch them leave, wait fifteen minutes, then go in through the back."

"Right."

"Now you should go," he said. "I'd rather Anna not have reasons to ask questions about this."

They both nodded and headed for the door.

"Good luck," Owen said.

"Thanks, man." Peter replied with a two-fingered salute. "You too."

They walked back through the house and Anna rose from the couch on their reappearance. She smiled, dropping a sketch pad to the side. "You, uh . . . figure out what you needed?"

"Yeah," Peter said, motioning back toward the office. "Just, uh . . . we got talking the other day and asked him if he'd read some of our stuff. You know, kind of like a first reader situation."

"Oh, yeah?" Anna raised her brow. "Owen's a good person for that. He loves books and analysis and all that stuff. One of the reasons he and Ava are so perfect for each other."

"Yeah." Peter nodded.

She opened the door for them and followed them onto the porch.

"Well," he tipped his chin toward her. "We'll see—"

"Hey," she interrupted as they started down the stairs. She hesitated when Spencer turned back to look at her too. "Could, uh . . . could I talk with you for a second?"

Peter gaped at her and pointed a finger to his chest.

"Yeah."

Spencer looked between them and took another step away. "I'll be in the Jeep. See ya, Anna."

"Bye, Spencer."

They both watched as he hopped into the driver's seat and shut the door.

Peter turned back to her, unsure if this was going to be a good kind of talk or a bad one. He'd experienced this kind of thing in the past. Far too often, in fact. Usually, these talks ended with a girl telling him that she liked him a whole lot, but they just weren't compatible or something of the sort.

Anna gave him a nervous smile that matched his own, her curly hair loose and framing her face. She took a deep breath and held her hands out as if offering him some silly notion. "Hey, so I know . . . well, it's been a couple days, but I just thought I should thank you."

"Thank me?" Peter chuckled, trying to relax the tension in his shoulders. "For what?"

Her expression softened. "For being there," she explained. "Not many people would step up like you did the other night, even if they'd known the person for years. And you've only known me for . . . what, a month?"

"A month and a day, actually."

She laughed. "You are so weird remembering that, you know?" She shook her head and grinned up at him. "But I appreciate it. You're a good friend."

So that *was* what this conversation was.

Peter had received the friend zone speech so often that he knew he should have expected it. Particularly after everything with that Frossard jerk. It was the same old story. Whether or not he'd meant to, he'd wound up giving Anna the impression that he was looking for more from their relationship than he'd intended, and now she was letting him down easy.

But Peter was pleasantly surprised to find that this one didn't hurt as much as some of the other speeches he'd been given. Anna was cute and nice, but since he'd already thought she had a secret boyfriend for the majority of their friendship, he'd been smart enough to keep himself from getting too attached. Which made the moment far less devastating than it might have been otherwise.

However, accepting her premature rejection made it no less awkward.

Scratching the back of his head, Peter smirked. "Wow, yeah. That's pretty effective." He kept his tone light to let her know there were no hard feelings.

"What?" Her smile dropped a fraction.

"I don't mind," he promised, hoping she would hear the sincerity. "I mean, I get it. I'm a decent amount older than you, and I'm nothing like Doctor Muscles. Don't worry. I already assumed I was in the friend zone."

Anna stared at him, her smile gone.

Peter blinked.

So that *wasn't* what this conversation was.

"Uh-oh," he whispered. "I read that wrong, didn't I?"

Anna nodded. "Yeah."

"You were just being nice and—yeah, mkay, uh, cool. Soooooo. . . ." Peter snapped out finger guns, further adding to his embarrassment. He backed away. "I'm gonna go and, uh, crawl under a rock for a little while and—well, I didn't mean anything by all that, but I appreciate what, uh, you were—ah, you know and—kay, bye."

Whipping around, Peter rushed down the stairs, mortified by his own presumption. It was bad enough getting put in the friend zone. But telling the other person you had assumed you were already there meant that you had, at one point, hoped to not be in that zone. If Anna hadn't realized that he'd had an interest in her before, she definitely did now.

Peter refused to look back as he yanked open the door and leaped in the Jeep. "Let's get out of here," he told Spencer.

"Everything okay?"

"Yeah, let's go."

"You sure?"

"Yeah, dude," he insisted. "I just freakin' embarrassed myself, but I'm totally good."

Spencer hesitated, an amused grin on his face. "What?"

"Seriously?" Peter glared at him. "Drive away!"

"What'd you do?"

Peter punched his arm. "I am gonna murder you if you don't drive away right now."

"Anna's staring at us."

Grumbling, Peter put on his seat belt and refused to look at the porch.

Spencer chuckled. "You told her that you liked her, didn't you?"

"Kind of," he spat.

"You're an idiot."

"I know."

Peter

"This is so stupid," Spencer whispered in Peter's ear as they hid in the woods about a hundred yards away from the Merciers' a few hours later. "We're gonna to get caught."

Pushing his brother back, Peter glared over his shoulder. "Chill out, man. If we lose our cool we *will* get caught. Now, watch the house."

They had done exactly as Owen suggested the minute they'd left Anna standing on the porch. Peter felt awful about the way he'd handled the situation. And it didn't help that Spencer had laughed at him the whole way home. But rather than worry about the awkward mess he'd made, the events of the evening were taking the brunt of his anxiety for now.

When they'd returned to Occasus, they both had changed into their darkest clothing. They did their best to avoid Gerard to keep from explaining their evening plans to him. Spencer took the easy way out and left on a walk with the dogs. Peter had to putter around the house trying to appear as though he weren't constantly wondering where the vault could be hidden.

At exactly five o'clock, they headed into the woods. It took them almost forty minutes to get to their hiding spot. Only a sliver of the sun remained, casting a deep brown shade over the houses along the street. They sat in the impending darkness as they kept watch. Cassandra's red truck left first. The Merciers' silver SUV soon followed. They waited for the sky to turn completely black and the streetlights to flicker on before they emerged.

"Come on," Peter said, pulling Spencer up.

"This is too dangerous, Pete," he argued, clinging to the woods. "They have a light right next to the door. We're gonna get spotted."

Sighing, Peter turned back and motioned to the houses. "Look, everyone in this neighborhood is on the same team. If the Merciers are gone, everyone else is too. We don't have to worry about some stupid light because no one else is home to see us."

Spencer narrowed his eyes as though about to challenge Peter's knowledge.

Not willing to take the risk of having his assumptions proved false, Peter grabbed hold of his brother's jacket. "Hurry up," he said, yanking him along. "The sooner we get in there, the sooner we get done."

They crouched low and darted across the grass. Though open, the land rolled with small mounds of earth. They rushed across, keeping close to the terrain in hopes that it would adequately hide them from anyone on the street. However, Peter knew that if he was wrong and someone looked down from the second story of the surrounding houses, they'd get spotted.

Doubling his speed, he dashed to the back door. "All right," he said, still crouched low as he pulled out the bobby pins he'd found in Diane's bathroom. "Let's give this a shot."

Spencer grabbed his arm. "Are you crazy?"

"What?"

"Look for a spare first."

Peter frowned, but lifted the mat, checked the pots, and felt along the door frame. "Nothing."

"Try it."

He prepped the hair pins.

"No, you idiot," Spencer hissed. "Try the door."

"You think they left it unlocked?"

He shrugged. "It's a small town."

Peter narrowed his eyes in doubt but tried the knob.

The door opened.

Spencer raised his brow in an 'I told you so' fashion.

Peter shoved him into the house and shut the door silently behind them.

They stood in a huge living room. Fancy, modern furniture filled out the space—couches, side tables, chairs, rugs, coffee table, and excessive décor. It wasn't opulent by any stretch of the imagination, but it was far more luxurious than anything their family had back in Norfolk.

"Wow," Peter whispered, though he supposed he needn't have bothered. "This is nice."

The lights were on, prepared for the late return of the owners, but the curtains and blinds were all closed. They'd have to try to stay out of the lamplight so that they didn't cast shadows. To their right was the kitchen—equally as fancy as the living room—and straight ahead a hall led to the front door. To the left there was another hall and a staircase. At the top of the stairs, they could see an open hall and several doors. One was ajar; the rest were closed.

Concerned that their shoes would make too much noise on the wood floors should anyone happen to walk by the house, Peter knelt down and untied his boots. Spencer followed his lead.

Once they were both in their socks, Peter took the lead, knowing that Spencer wouldn't. They checked the front entry first and found the dining room.

They checked the far hall, which led to the master and an office.

Making their way to the stairs, Peter tested the first to be sure it didn't creak.

Nothing.

He put his full weight on it.

Silence met him.

They took the stairs at a slow pace anyway, testing each step as they went.

Why they were so hesitant to move around freely, Peter wasn't sure. No one was home. But his lungs were tight against his ribcage, and he could feel his palms sweating as they inched through the house. The idea of walking around like they owned the place didn't fit the nerves eating away at his gut.

Figuring it would be more convenient to check the room with the door ajar first, Peter headed straight for it. His heart pounded rapid-fire beats as they inched their way toward the room. He hoped it was Cassandra's and there would be immediate, obvious evidence to clear her. He didn't like thinking that she could murder anyone. He especially didn't like the thought that she wanted to murder them.

As they neared the door, Peter could see through thanks to the dim light of one lamp. He caught a glimpse of a closet door and a hamper with some black clothing hanging over the side. A bed came into view, books sitting on the nightstand next to it.

Peter pushed the door the rest of the way open and grimaced as it gave a faint whine of noise. A drawer slammed shut to their right, causing both of the brothers to jump.

Whirling toward the sound, Peter and Spencer found themselves standing face to face with Debbie Mercier. She stood next to a desk against the far wall, her hand poised mid-air. Three of the five drawers were still open as she stared back at them.

"Oh." The older woman gasped, tucking some light brown hair behind her ear. A nervous chuckle escaped her. "Hello, boys. I thought Cassandra was meeting you at your place?"

"Uh. . . ." Peter gaped at her, trying to comprehend what they'd walked in on and come up with a response at the same time. "Yeah."

Her brown eyes narrowed.

"Yeah," he repeated, his tone more confident. He tried to smile. "She was, but we changed plans."

"Did you?"

"Mm-hm."

Spencer peered around him. "What are you doing in here?"

Crossing her arms, Debbie glared at him. Peter caught the family resemblance by the way her dark brows pulled together. "I'm cleaning up for Cassandra," she said, the words an evident lie. "What are *you* doing here?"

"Like I said," Peter shrugged. "We're supposed to meet Cass."

"She left thirty minutes ago."

Peter knew that. They'd watched her go.

"What are you looking for?" Spencer asked, taking another step into the room. His unusual level of bravery surprised Peter.

"Nothing," Debbie insisted. "I'm cleaning up. And you are very clearly not supposed to be here."

"Neither are you," Peter countered.

She snarled at him.

The dots connected and a thin gasp of disbelief escaped Peter. "You're a Druid, aren't you?"

Her eyes grew wide. "What?" It wasn't confusion but shock that made her voice tremble over that single word.

"Is Cass one too?"

The element of surprise disappeared and Debbie's whole demeanor shifted. She raised her chin, closed her gaping mouth, and grinned. A glimmer of irritation lit up her eyes. "Get out of my house."

"All right," Peter said, holding up a hand. "But first, I have an offer for you."

She granted him the gift of a pause.

"Tell me what you're looking for, and I bet that we can get it for you."

She laughed. "I doubt that, sweetheart."

"You shouldn't," he told her. "You're looking at the two people in this town who could make it happen, I promise."

"And what makes you think that Cassandra trusts you more than she trusts me?"

"Oh, no." Peter smirked and set a hand to his chest. "It isn't *me*. It's him." He gestured to Spencer, who did a terrible job of looking confident. "And it has nothing to do with trust."

Debbie took a step toward the two of them, her demeanor confident, as though she weren't outnumbered. "What is it, then?"

Peter shrugged, attempting to remain calm despite the warning alarms that were blaring in his head. "They've got the hots for each other."

Spencer pressed his lips together and closed his eyes in embarrassment as Debbie laughed.

"Really?"

"Yeah," he assured her. "They can't stop flirting with one another. Believe me, it's awkward to watch, but, you know, who can blame her? My brother's cute as a button, right?"

She took another step, unimpressed by his fabrications.

"But the point is. . . ." Peter added in a rush, holding his hand higher. "Is that he can distract her with . . . you know, romantic stuff or whatever, and I can search her bag."

"You're a terrible liar," Debbie said.

"Yeah," Peter admitted, taking a step back. He wished he'd been smart enough to bring the gun with him. "But the thing is, there's two of us and one of you. If you're lucky, you may be able to kill one of us, but do you really think you're fast enough to get us both?"

"Oh, *I'm* not going to kill you, sweetie." The woman's voice was eerily soft. Her right hand drifted to hover at her side. As she spoke, the shadows at the corner of the room deepened from a soft black to the color of obsidian. "My friends will do it for me."

Spencer's breathing grew ragged at Peter's side as they watched dark figures begin to emerge from the blackness. Small, writhing creatures that bubbled up, then burst outwards with tentacle-like limbs. They crawled from every shadow, all around the room. Under the bed, by the nightstand, around the curtains, behind the door.

"Pete," Spencer whispered.

"Huh?"

"I don't like this."

"Me either."

Debbie watched them as the beasts seeped from the darkness and into the room, bringing even more shadows in their wake. "Before I let them devour you," she said. "I need to know something."

Peter held out his arm as though it would somehow protect his brother. "What's that?"

"Has she found the vault?"

His first thought was that Cassandra *was* working with the Druids, but then he realized that scenario wouldn't make sense. If she was helping them, she would have already told them that she'd found it.

"Yes." He chanced the lie.

"I knew it," Debbie said, shaking her head in frustration. "Diane always was a shrewd one. They were all *so sure* she had no clue, but I knew—she'd discovered it ages ago."

Spencer glanced at him. "What are you doing?" he whispered.

"Getting us out alive," Peter whispered back.

"Oh, you're both going to die," she assured them. "We need that house, and you're standing in the way. Unfortunately for Cassandra, now that she knows about the vault, she'll have to go too."

"You won't get in if you kill us," Spencer said, playing his own bluff. "Diane may have learned about it, but it was Pete and I who found it."

Her eyes narrowed.

"You want to get in that vault?" His voice was still shaky. "You'll need us."

Though Debbie hesitated, the creatures she'd summoned kept crawling from the shadows, covering the walls and ceiling. It was as if a million black tendrils had been hung in the room, dangling and coiling as they waited for their charge. Their writhing gave off a sucking *slurp* as they tangled together and pulled apart.

They were getting bigger, Peter thought. Growing in size every second that they waited for her command. Each tentacle was now twice the size it had been when they had first crept into existence. The only reason they hadn't yet attacked was the woman who held them at bay as she searched for answers of her own.

"How did you find it?" she challenged.

Spencer hesitated, and Peter had no answer.

Debbie chuckled, a condescending tilt to the sound. "That's what I thought."

The creatures pressed closer, reaching out from all sides to grab at them.

"Wait," Peter called, holding up his hand. "Wait, wait, wait! Wait!"

"Don't waste my time with any more of your stupidity," she spat. The beasts coiled to box them in.

Peter knew they should run out the door while they had the chance, but he had to ask. "Is Cassandra a Druid?"

The look of dumbfounded shock that crossed her face told Peter all that he needed to know.

Their friend was innocent.

"Cool." He grabbed Spencer's arm with a death grip and barreled for the door.

CHAPTER TWENTY

Spencer

S pencer's brain stopped working.

There was no logic filtering his thoughts anymore. If Peter hadn't been there to pull him along at his side, Spencer wasn't sure that he could have told his feet to run. But now only the instinct for flight remained as they bolted out of the room—narrowly escaping the clutches of the bulbous, tentacled creatures—and into the hall.

His every worst fear had come to light in that room.

Or to darkness, in this case.

The beasts creeping out of the shadows were nothing new to Spencer. His imagination concocted horrors like that daily. The same sorts of terrors that haunted him in both his waking and his sleeping. Monstrous, vicious creatures made of fiendish, grotesque forms. Things that kept him lying awake at night. The same fears that told him that should he look at the wrong moment, the ceiling might open to reveal a supernatural alien waiting to dive down and tear him to shreds.

To see the darkness that clung to the shadows finally reveal such horrifying beasts was paralyzing.

But Peter yanked on Spencer's arm and flung him toward the stairs ahead of him. "Go," he yelled, pushing on his back. "Go, go, go!"

Spencer grabbed the stair rail, socks sliding against the hardwood as he turned the corner to start down the stairs. It was a mistake to look up and see Debbie stepping out of the bedroom as the beasts followed. They were much larger now, coiling limbs pulling them together to create new, slow building bodies that rose to her hips.

Shocked at the sight, Spencer slipped and dropped down the first few steps. His hand on the rail saved him from tumbling to the bottom of the stairs, but he rolled his ankle in the process.

Peter grabbed hold of him once more. "You okay?"

"Yeah." Spencer grimaced as he put weight on the sore ankle, sending tense shots of pain up his leg.

The room grew darker.

"You know," Debbie said, starting down the stairs behind them. Her pace was leisurely. She was in no hurry. "You're making this harder than it needs to be."

Shadows climbed the walls of the house, turning into more tentacled beasts as they ran through the living room and toward the back door. Peter jumped over the couch as Spencer limped around it.

"If you would cooperate, I could make your deaths rather painless."

Peter got to the door first.

He twisted the knob and flung it open.

The brothers froze.

A hulking hellhound waited on the concrete patio. The light by the door was now far dimmer than when they'd arrived. Though this hound was smaller than the one that had chased them through the grounds of Occasus, it was no less terrifying.

The low growl of the hound pushed Peter back a few steps.

"That's better," Debbie said as the hound corralled the brothers into the house.

Spencer grabbed onto his brother's arm, staring around the ever-darkening room. It wasn't just the growing shadows that caused the eerie gloom; it was the encroaching beasts on every side. They peeled out from the walls and furniture, surrounding them. This close, Spencer could see their neon yellow eyes cutting through the black of their forms. The round orbs of the hound and the slitted eyes of the others locked onto them with a furious hunger. The hellhound's growl rumbled on as the sickening *slurp* caused his skin to crawl.

The two of them couldn't fight these things. Not by any physical means. And what else did they have?

There was a wild resolve in Peter's brown eyes when he turned to look at Spencer. One that declared this danger wasn't going to faze him. That he refused to let shadows and spirits take him down. That he was going to do something stupid.

Hands held to her sides to keep the creatures at bay, Debbie walked around the couch. "Now which would you boys prefer," she asked, the tentacled beasts as tall as her shoulders now. Their coiled limbs reached toward them as though desperate to attack. "Death by hellhound or by scylla? I will warn you, neither is awfully pleasant."

Spencer let go of Peter, straightening his back. This wasn't the time for him to be afraid of the darkness pressing in around him. The *what if* no longer mattered. The worst *what if* was here.

They were going to die.

So he might as well try something to stop it.

"Pete," he muttered.

"Yeah?"

"What do you think?" He kept watch on the hound as it inched a step closer to them.

Peter shrugged, an angry smirk on his lips. "You always were the dog person."

"Fine," Spencer curled his hands into fists.

"Move!"

Knowing it was the dumbest thing he'd ever done in his life, Spencer dropped down to sweep the front legs out from under the hound as Peter sprinted for Debbie. He had no clue if it would work. He doubted he'd be able to touch a creature made of shadow. But it was the only thing he could think of that was worth trying.

From all his years of karate competitions, Spencer knew the feeling of landing blows. It hurt, striking muscle and bone. But you learned to overcome the pain and toughen up.

This strike felt like hitting wood and metal.

Spencer grunted from the hit, convinced it had done nothing at all.

Though the hellhound didn't fall, it did stumble from the surprise of the impact.

Taking advantage of its distraction, Spencer leaped up from the ground, careful of his ankle, and leaned all his weight into its side. He wrapped his arm around its thick neck. The hound's growl vibrated through its throat, causing his body to shake, but the deadweight Spencer forced against its side pushed the beast's already teetering form to the ground. The heft of the creature's body landed on Spencer's arm, but he refused to let it loose even as tingles shot into his shoulder and fingers.

He caught a glimpse of Peter struggling against the scylla as Debbie rose from the ground where he'd knocked her down. The tentacles twisted around Peter's arms and legs, pulling him in opposite directions toward the creatures as more slunk toward them.

Spencer's eyes darted around the room as the hellhound bucked and kicked under him. It was useless. Their attempt was foolish. It didn't matter what they tried, there were too many creatures coming for them.

A scylla flung its inky arm and narrowly missed Spencer's leg as he quickly pulled back.

The hellhound snarled and lurched, causing his arm to slip.

It didn't matter, he realized, if he held onto the beast or not.

Spencer watched in horror as the scylla's tentacles coiled around Peter's limbs, working their way over his body. Like boa constrictors, they were working to slowly subdue their prey.

"Stupid boy," Debbie spat, standing over Peter as his knees buckled under the pressure. "What was the point of that? You don't have what it takes to fight a Druid. You and your brother are powerless here."

"Maybe they are," Cassandra called. The front door flung against the wall with a *bang*. The group's eyes shot straight to her. "But I'm not."

Lifting her hands as she marched into the house, an ash-tinged rift opened up before Cassandra, a halo of dull alabaster shimmering around its edge.

"No," Debbie gasped, a furious scowl on her lips. She thrust one hand toward Peter and the other at Cassandra.

A surge of scylla made a rush at Cassandra while two more latched onto Peter. They whipped their tentacles around his neck and torso. He coughed, unable to fight against them.

Spencer wanted to rush to his brother and help, but the hellhound threw him off with one final buck, and he slammed into the couch.

Footing regained, the hellhound reared and lunged for Spencer. Its fangs were bared, ready to tear into him. He tensed in anticipation of impact.

A deep gray arc slammed into its side, and it howled in agony, evaporating into smoke inches from Spencer's face.

Spencer struggled to find air for his lungs as he caught Cassandra shift her hand back toward Debbie, commanding the ashen rift in front of her.

The scylla made a rush for Cassandra, but they did nothing to stop the gray, rippling mass that flew like an arc toward Debbie. It smacked into her chest. The woman's shoulders slumped forward as she recoiled in shock.

Hand to her chest, Debbie lifted her dark eyes to Cassandra. "Look at you," she sneered, a demeaning edge to her voice. "You've finally figured it out, haven't you, Cassie? Our power is far more than just ghosts, isn't it?"

"Don't make me do this, Deb," Cassandra said, the rift still billowing in the air before her hands like a plume of smoke. "Please."

"You can't do anything to me, Cassie." She scoffed. "You can't kill someone. It's not in you."

"Don't make me."

Peter's face turned red. He gasped for air as Spencer managed to scramble to his feet. His body ached and the scylla were coming for him, but he couldn't wait any longer. Not when his brother was dying.

Steeling himself, Spencer burst forward.

Debbie turned and raised a hand. A black energy shot forth, a direct arc aimed straight at Spencer.

"Spencer!" Cassandra yelled, but it was too late.

The force of the impact knocked Spencer clear off his feet. He landed on his back, gasping in pain.

Pain was pain, he thought, but this was different. It was unlike anything he'd ever experienced. The sensation tore through him. His muscles spasmed and tensed in agony. His brain refused to function. His lungs forgot how to breathe. His heart skipped a million beats.

And when the pain finally subsided, he felt more hollow and alone than he ever had in his life.

Spencer couldn't move even as the scylla crept closer, their slimy tentacles slipping around his arms and legs. He couldn't fight back or attempt to rise as he watched more gray and black arcs sail through the air between Cassandra and Debbie.

It was as though he were lifeless, staring up at the ceiling as the shadows created more beasts around him.

"Give it up, Cassandra," Debbie called. "I'm far stronger than you."

Thought resumed like a slow ticking clock in Spencer's mind as he realized that the woman was right. Cassandra's arcs didn't have half the impact that Debbie's had had on him. Which either meant that she could withstand greater pain or Cassandra's didn't hit hard enough. Possibly both.

They wouldn't make it out of here. Not even with Cassandra's help.

The lamp on Spencer's right flickered. His eyes shifted to it. The light was getting dimmer by the second as more shadows encroached on the room. A scylla tentacle squeezed tighter on his chest as his heart kicked to life again. His body began to shake, but he still had no control of his muscles.

One of Cassandra's soft gray and ivory arcs hit the lamp. It flashed with a sudden jolt of energy.

The scylla recoiled around him in response to burst of light. Their hold on him loosened.

Spencer's diaphragm contracted, and he managed to suck air into his lungs. Control of his body flooded back to him. His fingers flexed, his eyes went wide, and his back arched as he figured out how to move again.

The light next to him pulsated—on and off, on and off—giving him the chance to shake free of the agitated scylla. He clambered to his feet just as Debbie grabbed hold of Cassandra's arm, twisted it around, and shoved her against the wall.

"I told you, girl," she snarled. "You can't do anything."

Through the flickering light, Spencer could see his brother across the room. Still wrapped in the scylla's tentacles, they towered over him now. Peter's head lulled to the side.

Heart leaping to his throat, Spencer sucked in a breath. This wasn't how it was allowed to end.

But what could he do? How could he stop what was happening?

The scylla around him slunk back as the light grew brighter, then surged forward as it dimmed again.

"Light," Spencer muttered.

That was the answer.

But Debbie was keeping it dark. All through the house the light had been dimmed to almost nothing.

Except this one light that Cassandra's arc had hit.

It flared once more, a whine emitting from its glass casing.

Spencer huffed at the stupid thought that popped into his head, but he took the risk anyway.

Grabbing the lamp, Spencer twisted the topper off the shade. "C'mon," he muttered. "C'mon."

Debbie drew back her hand, another black rift forming around it. "I hate to do this to you, Cassie," she said. "I really do. But you should have listened to your mother."

Tossing the lampshade to the side, Spencer waited for the bulb to flare again.

"You could have lived if you had just stayed home."

The bulb went black, then burst into light.

Spencer threw the lamp down with all the force he could muster.

The glass shattered and the electric current snapped, catching both women's attention.

For a second, that's all Spencer thought it would do. But then a glitter of sparks leaped through the air, landing on a handful of scylla, the side of the couch, and the rug. The scylla ignited. The furniture followed.

Spencer gaped at his success.

Exploiting Debbie's distraction, Cassandra pushed against the wall with her free arm and shoved the woman away from her. She whipped around and threw out an arc of ivory-lined charcoal.

Debbie dropped with the impact and rolled across the ground, clutching her heart.

The fire began to spread around Spencer.

"Oh, shit," he muttered, realizing the flaw in his plan.

Flames licked up the side of the couch as they surged across the rug. The scylla's slurping sounds grew enraged and pained as they crawled away from the fire. But it caught on the creatures better than he'd anticipated, and they were now carrying the flames away with them.

Seeing the fire catch on everything the creatures touched, Spencer bolted for Peter. The scylla around him were already beginning to retreat as well. He dropped next to his brother and pulled him close. He pressed his fingers to the side of Peter's neck and waited one . . . two . . . three . . . four . . . five . . . six . . . there. A soft, slow, but present, beat.

Debbie struggled to her feet, and Cassandra ducked away from the black arc that missed her by an inch. She crouched near him and Peter.

"Cass," Spencer called.

She chanced a glance his way.

"We have to leave."

"I know," she said, facing Debbie as the woman approached again.

"That won't be possible, I'm afraid," Debbie said, raising her hands. A rift of dark shadows tore open a hole in the wall as two more hellhounds stepped out of the spirit world. Beyond the portal, Spencer caught a single glimpse of what looked like water and trees.

The fire caught on the curtains and lit up the room around them. It cast a sinister, inhuman glow on Debbie as she stepped closer. "As I won't let you go as long as I'm breathing and neither of you have the guts to kill me, it seems you lose."

Cassandra inched away from the brothers, hands held out to her sides as the gray rift drifted back around her fingers. "If it's between you and them, I know my choice."

Debbie laughed, the firelight glowing in her eyes. "Oh, sweetie." She shook her head. "I don't think so."

"Spence?"

Knowing what she was asking, Spencer hesitated. Was it right? Killing someone to save your own life? To save the lives of others? There was no doubt this woman was a murderer. And that she intended to kill them too. But did that make them the judge?

The hellhounds at her side moved in, their growls cutting through the crackling of growing flames.

Spencer pulled his brother closer to him and grit his teeth. "Do it."

Cassandra sprang to her feet, hand extended.

The hounds lunged and turned to smoke before her.

She reached out with her other hand, but Debbie sneered at her and mirrored her action.

Cassandra gasped as her cousin's fingers curled around her throat.

But her hand—still alight with the rift—rose to slam against the Druid's chest.

A tremor shook Debbie's body. Her fingers loosened as she stumbled back. Hands falling limp at her sides, her eyes were vacant. She crumbled to the ground as her knees gave way underneath her.

Cassandra and Spencer stared as the shadows immediately dissipated around them. The lights in the room flickered back to life.

It felt wrong, being in such brightness again.

The fire roiled faster around them, and Spencer had to pull Peter away from the center of the room to keep clear of the flames. "Is she dead?"

Cassandra stood there without response, her eyes locked on the woman.

Knowing they didn't have time to linger, Spencer rested Peter on the ground and rushed to her side. "Cass," he said, grabbing her shoulders.

Her dark eyes met his.

"Is she dead?"

"I don't know," she muttered. "I don't think so."

Spencer looked between Debbie and Peter, then back to Cassandra. "Keep Pete safe," he ordered, setting her on the path toward his brother before turning to check on the Druid.

She was breathing, though her eyes stared into nothingness. It was clear that while her physical form might be functioning, she was far from alive. A flash of memory brought Owen's voice to the back of his mind reminding him that the essence of the spirit world could shatter a soul when used as a weapon. He had no doubt this was what he had meant.

Guilt roiled in his stomach. Was it right, what they'd done to her? Had there been any other choice?

Pushing himself away, Spencer hurried as the fire sparked higher. He knelt next to Cassandra and set a hand on her arm. "Do you have everything?"

"What?" she yelled over the building blaze, brows pulled together in shock and confusion as she glanced beyond him toward Debbie.

Spencer leaned in to block her view of the body. "Do you have everything you need out of your room?"

She stared into his eyes, lips parted as her breathing shook along with her shoulders.

"Cass," he whispered, reaching up to cup her cheek. "Stay with me, okay?"

She nodded.

"You have everything?"

"Everything that matters."

Spencer swallowed past the smoke in the air. "All right." He pulled back and took hold of Peter. "Let's get out of here."

Hefting his brother up, Spencer dragged him through the back door as Cassandra grabbed their shoes. The fire burned brighter, and glass began to shatter inside as they inched their way across the lawn.

"My truck," Cassandra said, nodding to the street. "It's parked out front."

Spencer frowned. They couldn't leave it. What if someone saw it there? But someone would have already seen it, wouldn't they?

"Is everyone gone? To the practice?"

"I think so."

"Go get it," he ordered. "And meet me on the road to Occasus."

"What?"

"We can't leave it, Cass. They'll think you killed her."

She blinked. "I did."

"No," he corrected. "She was alive."

"She was alive?" She gasped, turning back to the house. "We have to save her."

Spencer had to drop Peter to grab her arm and stop her. "No," he insisted. "No, she wasn't there, Cass. She was alive, but . . . Debbie is gone."

Cassandra shook her head, not comprehending.

"Her *soul* is gone."

She gaped at him in horror. "I did that?"

He felt his chest tighten, but he fought off the panic. "She was going to kill us."

"But. . . ."

There was no 'but.'

It was clear. Debbie Mercier had intended to kill them, and there was no way around it.

"You have to move your truck," he reminded her. "Now."

Cassandra nodded and backed away.

"Meet me on the road," he called after her.

She nodded again, then turned and bolted for the street.

He watched until he saw the red truck pull up the road before reaching down to lift Peter again. It would be an arduous trek back to her. He hoped she didn't get antsy waiting.

Spencer had slipped his arms under Peter's and around his chest when his brother began to moan. "Whhhaaatt. . . ."

Dragging him away, Spencer shushed him. "We're getting out of here."

Peter grunted.

By the time Spencer had pulled him through the tree line, Peter began to attempt to take on his own weight. "Wh—what. . . ." He coughed. "What're you doin'?"

"I'm saving your life."

"Mm, cool," he mumbled. "Thanks."

"You're welcome." Spencer dragged him into the brush, his ankle sending sharp bursts of pain into his calf with each step. "Can you walk?"

Peter snorted. "I basically died, dude." His voice was scratchy, and his words less emphatic than usual. "What *can't* I do?"

"All right." Spencer let him stand, then draped his arm over his shoulders. Despite his bravado, Peter was like a deadweight, leaning against him. "C'mon."

They walked back through the woods, slow but safe as the fire lit their path home.

It took them far longer than it should have to reach the road. Spencer's ankle burned from the sprain as the siren of the town fire truck reached their ears. He worried that there would be a homicide investigation to face tomorrow.

"What happened?" Peter asked as they stumbled through the trees.

"I'll tell you later."

When they broke onto the road, Cassandra was there, leaning against her truck and chewing on her lip. She turned to them instantly and rushed over to wrap her arms around both of them.

"Whoa." Peter gasped. "Kinda still recovering."

"Sorry," she said as she pulled back. Her eyes were wide as she took them both in. "Are you okay?"

Peter lifted his hand and gave her the 'okay' sign. "Peachy keen."

A thin chuckle escaped her, and a small smile came to her lips despite her furrowed brow. Turning back toward town, she stared at the smoke in the distance. The occasional burst of flame broke over the trees, but the black cloud hovered like an omen.

Spencer helped Peter step onto the road as they all watched.

"So," Peter said, still resting heavily against Spencer. "That's your family's house, right?"

Cassandra nodded. "Yeah."

There was a pause of silence.

Spencer sighed. "I'm sorry."

She looked at him with a sad smile. "Me too."

"Hmph," Peter pressed his lips together, lifting his left shoulder in a shrug. "Guess you'll have to stay with us then."

Cassandra's mouth dropped open. "What?"

"Well, we can't exactly let you be homeless," he said. "Not when Diane specifically asked us to take care of you."

Spencer smirked at his brother's gut reactions. "Besides," he added, "we have an extra room."

"An extra *two* rooms," Peter corrected.

Cassandra's smile fell away, and she turned back to the smoke.

"Hey." Spencer reached over and nudged her elbow. "Stop it. It wasn't your fault."

"Wasn't it?"

"No."

She turned back to them. "You're sure?"

Peter raised his brow. "That it wasn't your fault that your mom's crazy cousin turned out to be a Druid intent on murdering us and taking over this town?" His head cocked to the side. "Or that we want you to live with us?"

"Either way," Spencer said, "the answer's the same."

It took a second, but a slow, appreciative smile spread over Cassandra's face. "It'll be dangerous," she warned. "Not only is there the possibility that they'll try us as murderers, but the Druids will know that we're against them now. They'll see this as an attack. As a start to something."

Spencer felt his gut drop. She was right. This was only the beginning. If they stuck around, they'd have far worse troubles to face.

But between running away and doing the right thing, Spencer knew what choice he'd make.

"Hang on," Peter said, frowning at the two of them. "Why would we be tried as murderers?"

Spencer sighed and nodded to the truck. "Let's go home," he said. "We've got a lot to talk about."

Also Available from V. K. Dixon

ARCHIVES OF THE WARDEN
Vault of Stone (Coming 2023)
Book Three (Coming 2024)

Other Works
AN INTRODUCTION: a book of poetry

Want to be the first to know about updates?
Sign up for V.K. Dixon's author newsletter:

And for more follow her on social media:
Instagram: @v.k.dixon

Glossary of Terms & Names

Aaron Lambert — *[Lam—bert]* — Middle of the three Lambert children; boyfriend of Haley Roux; mechanic

Aimee Lambert — Mother of Ava, Aaron, and Anna; previous town librarian

Anguis — *[An—gwis]* — German Wirehaired Pointer; one of Diane Larkin's two dogs

Alexander Frossard — *[Fros—sard]* — *aka 'Alex'* — Doctor in DeVerre; husband of Giana Frossard; father of Connor Frossard

Anna Lambert — Youngest of the three Lambert children; descended from the Rayne family; bartender/waitress and artist

Arthur Wenzel — *[Wen—zuhl]* — Private investigator of the online serial *Wenzel & Frankly* written by Peter and Spencer Collins

Ava Bernard — Oldest of the three Lambert children; married to Owen Bernard; town librarian

beast — A creature summoned from the spirit world to work on behalf of a Wielder

Brendan Descoteaux — *[Des—co—toe]* — High school student; boyfriend of Juliet Chapelle; third victim of the attacks

Cassandra Clement — *[Kuh—san—druh Klem—ent]* — *aka 'Cass' or 'Cassie'* — Best friend of Diane Larkin; Wielder

Charles Frankly — Ex-doctor and private investigator of the online serial *Wenzel & Frankly* written by Peter and Spencer Collins

Connor Frossard — Best friends with Anna Lambert; medical student

Cory Durand — Member of Anna Lambert's Bible study; husband of Reagan Durand; mechanic

Danielle MacDonald — Member of Anna Lambert's Bible study; waitress at diner

Debra Mercier — *[Mercy—ay]* — *aka 'Debbie'* — First cousin of

Cassandra Clement's mother

Descoteaux, Durand, and Descoteaux —Joint law firm, realty office, and brokerage firm in DeVerre, WA

DeVerre, WA — *[Deh—Vair]* — Small town in northeastern Washington State

Diane Larkin — Great-aunt of Peter and Spencer Collins; left the brothers her estate upon her death

Druids — *aka 'Immortal Deceivers' and 'Spirit Seekers'* — A cult of Wielders who want to release the spirit world upon the physical world

Elijah Lawrence — Son of John William Lawrence; reverend and theologian from Bushmills, Ireland, in the early 1600s

Eloise Chastain — *[Shas(rhymes with sass)—tane]* — Co-owner of Goldfinch Books, the bookshop in DeVerre

Frank Chastain — Co-owner of Goldfinch Books, the bookshop in DeVerre

Fred Guillaume — *[Ghee—uh—may]* — Current mayor of DeVerre

Frederic Chapelle — *[Sha—pell]* — Original reverend of DeVerre; cousin of Matthias Varon

Gerard Alarie — *[Uh—lar—e]* — Phantom from 1950s

ghost — The lingering spirit of a dead Wielder with unfinished business in the physical world

Giana Frossard — *[Gee—ah—nah]* — *aka 'Gia'* — Friend of Anna Lambert; wife of Alexander Frossard; mother of Connor Frossard

'The Release of the Great Wolf in Amesbury' — An event chronicled in Elijah Lawrence's essay

Haley Roux — *[Rue]* — Girlfriend of Aaron Lambert; friend and co-worker of Anna Lambert

Harmony, Saskatchewan — *[Suh—ska—chew—on]* — Original hometown of the founders of DeVerre, WA

Heinrich Schwarz — *[Sh—warts]* — Mentor of John William Lawrence; co-founder of the Spiritualists

hellhound — Hound-like beast from the spirit world

Horace Garnier — *[Gar—knee—ay]* — Original marshal of DeVerre; best friend of Matthias Varon and Frederic Chapelle

House of Occasus — *[Oh—kay—sus]* — Diane Larkin's home, left to the Collins brothers; previously built and owned by the Varon family

Jessica Calderon — *[Call—der—on]* — *aka 'Jess'* — Wife, mother, and part-time waitress; distant relative of Thomas Garnier; second victim of the attacks

Jill Descoteaux — Niece of Nicole; receptionist for Descoteaux, Durand, and Descoteaux

Joel Dumont — *[Dew—mont]* — Co-owner of Coffee & Croissants, the coffee shop and bakery in DeVerre

John William Lawrence — Theologian, co-founder of the Spiritualists, and founder of the Warden

Juliet Chapelle — High school student; daughter of Samuel Chapelle; girlfriend of Brendan Descoteaux

Leopold Frossard — Original doctor of DeVerre

Matthias Varon — *[Vair—en]* — Founder of DeVerre

Michael Mercier — *aka 'Mike'* — Husband of Debbie Mercier

Nex — German Wirehaired Pointer; one of Diane Larkin's two dogs

Nicole Descoteaux — Estate lawyer for Diane Larkin

Owen Bernard — Husband of Ava Bernard; substitute teacher for DeVerre School; freelance article writer for online publications; originally from Harmony, Saskatchewan; Wielder

Peter Collins — *aka 'Pete'* — Older of the two Collins brothers (twenty-eight); writer; former bartender

phantom — A ghost that has been tethered to a specific location in the natural world

Phillipe Varon — Founder of Harmony, Saskatchewan; Matthias Varon's 3x great grandfather

Reagan Durand — Member of Anna Lambert's Bible study; wife of

Cory Durand; co-worker of Anna Lambert's

Samuel Chapelle — *aka 'Sam'* — Current reverend in DeVerre

scylla — *[sky—luh]* — Tentacled beast from the spirit world

Spencer Collins — *aka 'Spence'* — Younger of the two Collins brothers (twenty-six); writer; former barista and freelancer

spirit world — A parallel world that exists alongside the physical world

Taylor Ozanne — *[Oh—zawn]* — Farmer; first victim of the attacks

Thomas Garnier — *aka 'Tom'* — Current marshal in DeVerre

Veil — Specific locations around the world where the boundary between the spirit world and the physical world is thin

The Warden — *aka 'Divine Prophets' and 'Protectors'* — An organization of Wielders dedicated to protecting the spirit world from the control of the Druids

Wenzel & Frankly — Serial historical-fantasy blog written by Peter and Spencer Collins

Wielder — A human with the ability to wield the spirit world

William Larkin — *aka 'Liam'* — Late husband of Diane Larkin; writer; researcher of history and theology

Yvan Rayne — *[Ee-vahn Rain]* — Original record keeper in DeVerre; the Lambert siblings' ancestor

Acknowledgements

First, I have to thank my husband. Josh, you are the true champion for hearing my daily ramblings, random sparks of excitement and doubt, listening to every question, and being patient as I desperately try to figure out what I'm doing. You are my first reader, always. You get the roughest version of my drafts, and you are still my biggest fan. Your encouragement and love has been more than I could have asked for. Thank you for being amazing! (And for being my social interactions manager, advising every email, text, and DM when I was too nervous to send it on my own!)

Next, I want to thank my family and friends. Without your patience and kind support, this book wouldn't be here. Not only were you understanding with my antisocial self, you cheered me on as I pursued my passion. I couldn't be more grateful for you!

A special shout-out to my wonderful friend, Rachel, for being the best and listening to me talk about my 'kids' for hours when she hadn't even met them yet. I couldn't ask for a better friend, dear!

Thank you to my editor, Brittany. You are more than just an editor; you are a friend, a mentor, a marketing advisor, a cheerleader, and a truly wonderful woman of God! Thank you for all your encouragement on this project and all the future ones to come. I'm so blessed to have you in my life!

A special thank you to my proofreader, Katie. I'm so glad I got the opportunity to have you as a part of this project.

And to my illustrators, Hannah and Celia. You two brought my visions to life, and I couldn't be more thrilled. Thank you!

Thank you to my beta readers: Julie, Alexandra, Shelley, Serenity, Noah, and Emily. All your notes and feedback were so helpful and encouraging! I'm so grateful to you for the time and effort you gave my story.

Thank you to my writing community that has helped my launch this book via sharing my Instagram posts and cover reveal and for giving me hope that I may just have a future in this book universe of ours.

And thank you to you! A book without readers is like a house without residents. Without someone to love and care for it, there can be no true joy within. I'm so glad that you've come along on this journey with Peter and Spencer—and me!

Finally, I want to thank God. Lots of people start with this acknowledgement, but I wanted to save the best for last. I am so thankful to You, Father, for giving me this story to write. From the moment of Peter and Spencer stepping into my brain to the details that You helped me refine to the complexity of the world that You helped me design. My imagination is from You and for You.

About the Author

V. K. Dixon started writing at the early age of seven when spelling was just a jumble of letters to her. Over the years, her skills improved along with her understanding of story. It took her twenty years to write a novel worth publishing, but her passion has always been to tell stories of connection, family, and adventure.

V. K. writes fantasy and romance novels filled with found family, lasting love, and unique magic. She believes that the extraordinary gives us a deeper desire for the things beyond us; for the things of God. Faith, art, and community are her guiding values as she pursues the vision on her heart.

Currently, V. K. and her husband, Josh, live the life of the nomads as they each build their careers and seek out their long-term home. They dream of living by the sea with two dogs, at least one cat, several kids, and a table large enough to host uproarious dinner parties.

www.ingramcontent.com/pod-product-compliance
Lightning Source LLC
Chambersburg PA
CBHW021212310726
48971CB00006B/1538